COPPERS

The Good and the Bad

ALAN DUFFIN

Published in Australia by Silverbird Publishing.

First published in Australia 2025
This edition published 2025
Copyright © Alan Duffin 2025
Cover design, typesetting: WorkingType (www.workingtype.com.au)

The right of Alan Duffin to be identified as the
Author of the Work has been asserted in accordance with the
Copyright, Designs and Patents Act 1988.

ISBN: 978-1-7641905-0-3

About the Author

Following a get-together over a few beers, Alan and a couple of friends in Devon England, made a decision to see the world.

They arrived in Melbourne in 1967, and Australia became home. Arthur and Jim stayed in Melbourne and raised their families. Alan decided to see more of Australia and travelled north, finding work in a sugar mill. On returning to Melbourne, he met and married his much-loved Margaretha, and raised a wonderful daughter, Tracey.

However, after seven years in Victoria, it was time to move on. Following three and a half years running a PO general store in NSW, they settled on the Gold Coast.

Since semi-retiring some twenty years ago, Alan and Margaretha have travelled around the entire coast of Australia towing a caravan and also ventured into the incredible outback.

These days, Alan and Margaretha are enjoying life in a lifestyle village at Beachmere, north of Brisbane.

Note from the Author

I appreciate that some of my stories do not exactly portray Police in the best light. I firmly state that they are all fiction. My father was a Police officer in Devon, England for some thirty years. A school friend and a cousin also served in the London Metropolitan force. I also had a friendly officer and family living next door when I lived in Melbourne. Accordingly, I have a great deal of respect for all members of the Police Force as I am fully aware of just how stressful the job is.

Content Warning:

This book contains themes and scenes that may disturb some readers. Reader discretion is advised.

- Torture and mutilation (on and off page)
- Rape (off page)
- Suicide (on and off page)
- Drugs/Drug use (on and off page)
- Murder (on page)

Acknowledgements

I thank my wonderful wife, Margaretha, for putting up with me over so many years, and for her suggestions after first reading my stories. I also thank friends who have read my stories and expressed enthusiasm regarding publication.

There is no doubt that the places I have been, where I have lived and worked and the people met along the way, have all helped to bring a story to life.

My thanks also to Kerry Collins at Sid Harta Publishing, to Luke Harris at Working Type Studios, and especially my editor, Jenn Zabinskas of Redink Creative, for her suggestions, advice and amendments that have been so greatly appreciated. Their suggestions, skill and assistance are so very much appreciated.

Jordan

BOOK 1: A COPPER'S LIFE

Prologue

Constable Steve Carmichael picked up the two glasses of beer he had ordered from the bar, thanked the barman and steadily made his way to a corner table.

'Didn't spill a drop, sir,' he remarked as he placed the glasses down.

Senior Sergeant Winston Bailey picked up his glass and downed half the beer in one go. 'Thanks, Steve, I'll get the next.'

'No worries, sir,' replied Carmichael. He took a quick sip of his beer. 'Sir, can I ask you about Harris as he's never told me anything about his background? I know you've known each other for many years, but when did you first meet and what's his record?'

'How much time have you got?'

'I'm in no rush, sir,' said Carmichael with a shrug of his shoulders.

Bailey took a sip of his beer and leant back in his chair. At fifty-five, he still looked fit and healthy. However, his once thick head of dark hair had reduced to a thin covering of grey that was closely shaved. The slight bags under his eyes and lines on his face were an indication of the stress of thirty years of policing. He shook his head as a faint smile crossed his face.

'You want to know his history, eh?'

Carmichael, in his early twenties and physically fit from time spent in the gym, nodded. 'Yeah, that'd be great, sir.'

Bailey took a deep breath. 'There's a lot to tell, Steve, as we first crossed paths thirty years ago and the first couple of years shaped how the next years would progress.'

PART 1:
RETRIBUTION

Chapter 1

The study bore all the hallmarks of a successful businessman. The timber walls adorned with framed documents and letters of appreciation from various notables and government departments. One wall was fully occupied by shelves of books and binders. At the desk, sat in a high-backed leather chair, was Alistair Jordan. With his gold-rimmed spectacles, grey, neatly combed hair, dark business suit and club tie, even at this early hour, he was the polished professional.

His son, Harris Jordan, twenty-four, tall and lean, wearing jeans and open-neck shirt, stood uncomfortably facing the large desk where his father was studying paperwork from one of the companies on which he sat as a board member.

'Bloody waste,' said Alistair Jordan gruffly. 'Law and economics degrees and you want to be a policeman.'

'Yes, Dad,' replied Harris Jordan.

'Madness,' continued Alistair.

'Yes, Dad.'

Alistair waved a hand in dismissal without looking up from his paperwork. Harris grimaced and half-heartedly put out his arm to shake his father's hand. No hand was proffered so he withdrew his and resignedly walked out of the study. Alistair glanced up at his son's retreating back and shook his head.

Alistair Jordan had come to Australia as an immigrant in the early fifties, and had made his money by buying rundown property and then on-selling to developers when the need for housing arose due to the increase in population. He had subsequently become friends with many of the more "well-to-do" members of the city. On meeting and falling in love with the head of the city's Chamber of Commerce's daughter, his business contacts multiplied, and accordingly opportunities for making more money increased dramatically.

Harris Jordan had benefited from his father's fortune by being sent to Melbourne's best private school, and thereafter to university.

On the steps of the large, sprawling, Georgian style mansion in one of Melbourne's trendiest suburbs that Jordan called home, his mother, Veronica Jordan, gave Harris a warm hug. 'Give him time, Harris, you know he expected you to go into business.'

'This is something I really want to do, Mum,' said Harris. He gave her a quick kiss on the cheek. 'I promise I'll keep in touch.'

He ran down the steps, which were flanked by tall Corinthian columns, to a flashy sports car that had a smiling young woman, his nineteen-year-old sister Fiona, behind the wheel. He threw a large holdall into the back seat and jumped in beside her. 'Let's go, sis.'

Harris turned and waved to his mother as the sports car, with a spray of gravel, headed down the long driveway, past manicured lawns and gardens, out onto the main road.

Chapter 2

In the Police Academy gymnasium, self-defence instructor Sergeant Ray Hermans was addressing the recruits. Hermans was in his late forties, heavily built, with close-cut, greying hair and dressed in blue singlet and track pants.

Hermans was an arrogant bully, and during each intake he singled out one recruit for "special treatment". During the current intake, he had singled out Jordan, who had managed to keep his feelings to himself despite repeated bullying.

The recruits dressed in white shorts and T-shirts stood to attention as Hermans paced up and down in front of them.

'This is our last get-together, boys, and I have to admit that most of you have done great. However, there's always one who's only good for school crossing duty.' He stopped pacing in front of Jordan. 'And I guess this time it's you, Jordan, but seeing as how I'm such a softie, I'll give you one last chance to prove yourself.'

He moved in close to Jordan, virtually nose to nose. 'Fancy a last go at your friendly old Sergeant, arsehole, or don't you have the guts?'

Jordan suddenly snapped. 'You're a prick, Hermans; a bloody disgrace to the force. Why you weren't chucked out years ago is beyond me.'

'I guess that means no, eh arsehole?' growled Hermans.

He turned to the other recruits. 'Seems like our "mummy's boy" with the private school education just can't take it.'

He looked back at Jordan. 'Why don't you go back to your fancy estate, or whatever the fuck it is, where Mummy and Daddy can look after you, and leave the real men to look after the real world.'

Jordan stepped back and stared at Hermans. 'Okay, you prick … let's do it!'

Hermans grinned and walked over to a table from which he picked up a knife and tossed it to Jordan.

Jordan caught it, expecting it to be a rubber imitation. His jaw dropped. 'This is real, Hermans.'

Hermans laughed. 'Really! Look at me, I'm shakin'.'

Jordan stood transfixed, staring at the knife in his hand. Hermans stepped forward and slapped Jordan across the face. 'Come on, gutless … use it.'

Jordan dropped the knife on the floor. 'You're crazy, Hermans.'

Hermans bent down and picked the knife up. 'Well, if you don't want it.'

Jordan backed away as Hermans waved the knife around in front of him.

Another recruit, Winston Bailey, came forward and stood between them. 'Sarge, this is stupid, pack it in.'

Hermans pushed Bailey aside, stepped up to Jordan and slapped him in the face again.

'Come on, arsehole, do something.'

Jordan reacted instantly and instinctively to the provocation. He grabbed Hermans's knife arm, twisted and pushed.

Hermans stepped back and looked down in disbelief at the knife that was now embedded in his chest with him holding the handle. His jaw trembled, his mouth slowly opened, he coughed as blood dribbled down his chin. He slowly sank to his knees then tumbled sideways onto the floor.

Jordan looked at Bailey and then at the other recruits who stood still … frozen … silent.

Chapter 3

Two days later, Jordan, dressed in full police uniform, stood at attention before a desk behind which sat a Chief Inspector. Behind him stood three more senior officers. The Chief Inspector looked up from the papers in front of him.

'We have heard from all those present at the time of this, ahem, unfortunate occurrence.' He shook his head. 'Most regrettable, most regrettable. Sergeant Hermans was a long-serving officer whose ability will be sadly missed.'

He paused and re-inspected the papers before continuing. 'In view of the evidence before us, we do not hold you to blame for the incident and accordingly no charges will be laid.'

Jordan smiled with relief. 'Thank you, sir,' he said.

During the involved selection process, he had passed all requirements with flying colours and was now looking forward to actually getting on with the job.

'Sergeant Hermans will be laid to rest with full police honours,' said the Chief Inspector.

The officers behind him shuffled uneasily. 'However, unfortunately, we cannot allow you to continue your career in the police force.' He took a deep breath and swallowed. 'Please hand in your uniform and equipment before you leave,' he said quickly.

Without another word, the Chief Inspector stood and walked out of the room closely followed by the other three officers. One of the officers stopped at the door, turned to Jordan, shook his head and shrugged apologetically before leaving.

Jordan stood there alone, unable to fully comprehend what had just taken place. He stared at the door through which the officers had departed as it swung shut with a bang.

Chapter 4

n the busy Melbourne suburb of Carlton, a tram rumbled to a stop. An elderly lady carefully stepped down from the tram and immediately adjusted her coat against the cold June wind. Jerkily, she walked along the pavement, glancing into the shop windows. She turned her nose up on passing a dark and depressing alleyway. The alleyway was strewn with litter: crumpled drink cans, a KFC packet with discarded chips, a couple of hypodermic needles. The first two doors in the alley had real estate for lease signs attached. The third had a paper sign stuck on the glass panel that read "HARRIS JORDAN: INVESTIGATOR".

The office was small and sparsely furnished with a desk, three chairs and a well-worn couch. A single light bulb hung from the ceiling, and the door to a small bathroom was ajar.

Jordan lay sprawled asleep on the couch snoring loudly, an empty whiskey bottle lay on the floor beside him. His hair lank and matted, his face unshaven. Dressed in jeans and grubby T-shirt desperately in need of a good clean, he was far from the picture of health and enthusiasm the day he left home for the Police Academy some four years previously.

Insistent knocking at his door at last aroused him. He struggled from the couch, wobbled unsteadily to the office door and opened it.

He squinted and looked out. 'Oh ... it's you.'

Shakily he returned to the couch and flopped back down as Detective Winston Bailey entered the office and closed the door behind him. Bailey had remained a friend of Jordan's since their time at the Academy and had on occasion managed to send the odd job Jordan's way that the police felt disinclined to pursue.

Bailey looked around the office with distaste. 'Yeah, it's me, and ain't you lucky? If I was the health department you'd be condemned. Do you ever clean this place up? You really could use some fresh air in here.'

Jordan belched. 'If you've anything to tell me, get on with it then piss off.' He curled up on the couch. 'I need a couple more hours sleep.'

Bailey picked up the whiskey bottle from the floor, opened a desk drawer and dropped it in. 'I'm here to tell you you'll be getting visitors in a short while, Mr and Mrs Ackland, I'm trying to do you a favour, though God knows why.'

Bailey was startled by another knock at the door. 'Shit! They're here already. Come on, Harris, shake yourself.'

Jordan slipped off the couch and blinked as his eyes slowly focused. He ambled into the bathroom and closed the door behind him.

Bailey went to the office door. 'Aah, Mr and Mrs Ackland, won't you please come in?'

He stood to the side as Mr and Mrs Ackland, both in their early fifties, surveyed the office as they entered. Neither seemed impressed, particularly Mr Ackland, who gave Bailey a severe look and rolled his eyes.

The door to the bathroom opened and Jordan came out. He had managed to find a clean T-shirt, comb his hair and even given himself a quick spray with deodorant.

'This is Harris Jordan, the man I told you about,' said Bailey. 'He's an experienced investigator and I'm sure he will be able to help you.'

A brief moment of silence followed as the Acklands looked over Jordan.

'Well, I have to be off, so I'll leave you both in Mr Jordan's capable hands,' said Bailey as he walked towards the door.

Jordan managed a smile at the Acklands before he addressed Bailey. 'Thank you, Winston.'

'Winston?' said Mrs Ackland inquiringly.

Bailey stopped and grimaced. 'My father wanted a PM, but got a cop.' He gave Jordan an icy stare before leaving.

'Winston!' repeated Mrs Ackland. 'As in Churchill?'

'Yeah, that's right,' replied Jordan with a grin. 'He's a little touchy about it.'

'No need to be,' said Mrs Ackland seriously. 'It's a strong name.'

Jordan quickly wiped the grin off his face. 'So true,' he said.

He made his way to the back of his desk and sat down while pointing at the other chairs. 'Please, take a seat and tell me what's up.'

Jordan saw that the Acklands were reluctant to move. 'Please forgive my dishevelled appearance,' he said. 'But when you have to deal with the unsavoury characters that I meet in my line of work, it's important to at least try to fit in and not to look like a policeman in a suit and tie.'

The Acklands glanced at each other, shrugged, then came forward and sat down.

'It's our son Phillip, he's not come home,' said Mrs Ackland.

'How old is Phillip?' asked Jordan while taking a notepad and biro out of the desk's top drawer.

'He'll be twenty-eight next birthday.'

Jordan looked up at the Acklands. 'Twenty-eight you say.' *At that age it's time he got away from his parents,* he thought.

'And since when has he gone missing?' he said without enthusiasm.

'Two years last Thursday. Phillip rang me from Townsville for my birthday and told me he had a job in the Victoria Sugar Mill.' Mrs Ackland managed a smile. 'Phillip's always been thoughtful like that. Birthdays, Christmas and in between. Phillip's a good boy, Mr Jordan, never in any trouble ...'

Mrs Ackland took a handkerchief out of her handbag and screwed it around nervously while Mr Ackland stared at the ceiling in apparent disinterest.

Jordan leant back in his chair, stretched and scratched his face. 'Two years is a long time ago to trace anyone from, and since Detective Bailey sent you here, then it would appear the police have put it in the too hard basket.' He shrugged and spread his hands. 'Look, maybe he just doesn't want to be found.'

'No!' said Mrs Ackland passionately. 'Phillip's always kept in touch; there's no reason for him to ...'

Jordan interrupted. 'There is the possibility that he's ... ah ... you know ... ah died.'

Jordan glanced at Mr Ackland who turned away with a slight nod of his head. Mrs Ackland straightened up in her chair and stared defiantly at Jordan. 'If that's what's happened then I want to know.'

Jordan felt the determination and need for answers coming from Mrs Ackland. A moment's silence ensued as he considered the situation. 'Okay, here's what I'll do. Ten days, I'll give it ten days and if nothing turns up, we call it quits and you get on with your lives.'

Mrs Ackland fumbled in her handbag. 'We have five thousand dollars. I know it's not a lot but ...'

Jordan raised his hands in surprise at the amount offered. 'No, not that much, not now ... look ... it'll be a hundred and fifty a day plus expenses. I reckon five hundred up front will be fine.'

Mrs Ackland leant forward, grabbed Jordan's arm and pushed a bundle of cash into his hand. 'He's our only child, Mr Jordan.'

Jordan counted the cash. 'There's a couple of thousand here, I said five hundred—'

'Take it,' interrupted Mrs Ackland with a smile.

Jordan smiled back, pulled open a desk drawer, put the cash in and picked up his biro.

'Okay, let's get some background. Can you give me Phillip's full name, his weight and height, any distinguishing features, colour of hair and eyes, and do you have a reasonably recent photo?'

Mrs Ackland took a small notebook from her handbag and

passed it to Jordan. 'I'd written it all down to give to the police, but if you need anything else our phone number is in there as well.'

Jordan flicked through the notebook's pages. 'This looks fine.'

'We did meet a friend of Phillip's once; we haven't seen him since either.'

'Maybe they went off together,' said Jordan as he continued looking at the notes.

'What was his name again?' pondered Mrs Ackland. She turned to her husband. 'Can you remember, John?'

Mr Ackland shook his head. 'Oh, it's on the tip of my tongue,' continued Mrs Ackland. 'Ha ... something, Harold, no ... Happy ... yes, that's it, Happy.'

Jordan was suddenly attentive. Images of a dead girl, his sister Fiona, and a grinning man who Jordan believed responsible for supplying the drugs that killed her flashed through his mind. He shook his head to clear it.

'Phillip had a friend called Happy?' asked Jordan urgently.

'Yes, that's right, Happy,' replied Mrs Ackland.

'And you met him?'

'Yes, just the once.'

'Did you mention this to Detective Bailey?'

'Well, no,' said Mrs Ackland with a shake of her head. 'Never had a chance to really. Is it important?'

'Possibly. I'll look into it.' Jordan rose from his chair and extended his hand. 'I'll keep in touch.'

'Thank you, Mr Jordan.' Mrs Ackland stood and accepted Jordan's hand. She glanced at the framed photo on the desk. 'Your wife?'

'My sister, Fiona.'

'She's very pretty.'

'Yes, she was.'

'Was?' said Mrs Ackland.

'She died a while back.'

'Oh, I'm so sorry,' said Mrs Ackland as she put a hand to her face in embarrassment.

Mr Ackland stood by the opened office door. 'Come on, Marj.'

Jordan gave Mrs Ackland another smile when she raised her eyebrows upon hearing the first words her husband had uttered. He escorted her to the door and gave her a brief wave as they departed down the alley. He returned to his desk and sat back down, picked up the notebook and looked again at Phillip Ackland's photo.

'A good boy, very thoughtful, never in any trouble, that'll be a first, and low and behold, knew Happy Hapsfield,' he murmured.

Images of the pale, dead face of his sister, and the grinning face of Hapsfield flashed through his mind again. He picked up the phone and dialled.

'Detective Winston Bailey please ... ah Winston, the Acklands have just left my office; you guys still busy taking care of Mr and Mrs Public, eh?' He grinned at the response. 'Yeah, sure, you were only thinking of my wellbeing. Look ... meet me at the usual spot at one and I'll bring lunch. Okay, see you!' He replaced the receiver, looked at the photo on the desk and gently rubbed a finger along the top of the frame.

Written across the photo were the words: TO MY FAVE BRO. LUV FIONA XXX

Jordan's mind drifted back to a warm summer's evening in an apartment filled with young people drinking and dancing to loud music. He was there at the request of his sister Fiona.

She had invited him to meet some new friends she had made since renting her own place in St Kilda after securing a job with the Commonwealth Bank in the city. Initially, she had stayed with Jordan in his flat in Carlton that he had acquired with financial assistance from his mother after his non-admittance into the police force. His father had hoped that, following his inability to pursue his aim of joining the police, he would obtain a sensible job with a lawyer he knew. But Harris was determined to prove that his dismissal was a big loss to the force by becoming a private investigator. Needless to say, this prompted his father to once again wash his hands of him.

'Hi, Harris, this is my friend Bernie Hapsfield,' said Fiona. She grabbed hold of Hapsfield's hand and laughed. 'We just call him Happy.'

Hapsfield grinned and shrugged. 'No point in being miserable, eh pal.' He gave Jordan a knowing wink.

Before Jordan could reply, Fiona pulled Hapsfield back into the crowd. 'Come on, Happy, let's dance.' She smiled at Jordan, 'Enjoy yourself, Harris, see you later.'

Jordan gave a small wave and smiled back as they disappeared into the crowd.

Two days later in the city morgue, Jordan and Bailey looked down at Fiona's body on the slab.

Bailey put a hand on Jordan's shoulder. 'Sorry, Harris, Doc says overdose—heroin.'

Jordan grimaced. 'I never knew she was using. She seemed okay at the party couple of nights back. She was with a bloke called Happy.'

Bailey took a step back, startled. 'Bernie "Happy" Hapsfield?'

'Yeah, that's him ... why?'

'He's a known ...dealer and we've been watching him for some time on and off but can't pin him.'

'The bastard,' said Jordan through gritted teeth, 'he must have got to Fiona.'

'Could be, but we've no proof, Harris,' said Bailey apologetically.

Jordan snarled. 'I'll get the bastard.'

His demeanour turned to sadness as he reached out and touched Fiona's face.

Jordan sighed as his fingers gently caressed the photo frame. He picked up his coat from the floor behind the desk, put it on and left the office he now called home.

Chapter 5

The weather hadn't improved any by the time Jordan arrived at the Carlton Gardens. He found a bench under a tree that offered a little protection from the biting wind. He turned up his coat collar as he noticed Bailey come sauntering along the pathway.

'Jesus, it's cold!' said Bailey as he slumped onto the bench beside him.

'Ah, Detective Winston,' said Jordan. He handed him a McDonalds hamburger and a bottle of cola. 'Hate to ruin your diet.'

Bailey accepted the offerings and immediately took a great bite out of the hamburger. 'Yeah right ... how's business?' he managed to say between mouthfuls.

'Run off my feet; it's hard trying to fit it all in.'

'That bad huh?' said Bailey after a swig of cola.

'Oh, I found Lady McCulloch's lost poodle last week, and I'm still waiting to be paid for the rather interesting photos I took of Councillor Dorphman's wife being very creative with her pool cleaner. Oh yeah, I'm on a roll, pal.'

Bailey took another drink of cola and burped. 'Look, Harris, you know I help when I can, but shit, you haven't a lot of friends up top and I'm taking a risk just talking to you.'

'Really!' said Jordan, feigning surprise. 'I'd have thought sticking a knife in that bullying bastard Hermans's guts would endear me to all.'

'We know he was a right bastard, Harris, and so do others, but the Academy rated him tops.'

'Hah, ain't that the truth?' said Jordan angrily. 'I get the arse and good old Hermans gets a full police send off.'

'It's all political, Harris, you know that. A commended sergeant with twenty years up, versus a rookie "would-be" cop, easy choice for the brass, pal. Jeez, Harris, we've been over this a hundred times,' said Bailey, showing his frustration.

'Yeah, I know, it just pisses me off,' said Jordan.

'Called your folks lately?' asked Bailey in attempt to change the subject.

'What's the point?' said Jordan with a shrug.

'It's been two years, Harris,' said Bailey quietly.

'You don't know my father, Winston. If I hadn't asked Fiona to come visit me in the city she wouldn't have got involved in drugs ... it's all my fault.'

'Like I said, it's been two years, Harris.'

'Drop it, Winston,' said Jordan.

He threw the remains of his hamburger to the pigeons that had gathered around. 'Okay, the Acklands. Why me?'

'The father doesn't want us involved, would prefer to forget the whole thing,' said Bailey. 'Reckons the kid was into drugs and doesn't want his wife to know, but she's pushing it. Thinks the kid was all sweetness and light, and is flat out determined to find him.'

He finished the remains of his cola. 'If we do it, we can't hide things as well as you could. Thought maybe you could poke around for a bit. Tell her you can't trace him and then hopefully she'll quit pushing and get on with her life. Oh, and the bonus is, you collect a few dollars in the process.'

'So, what do you think has happened to the kid?' asked Jordan.

'Either stoned out of his mind and doesn't know who, or where he is ... or possibly dead ... hell, kids are disappearing and dying every day, you know that.' Bailey's face dropped upon realisation of what he'd just said. 'Oh shit! Sorry, Harris, I forgot about Fiona.'

Jordan shrugged. 'That's okay mate, but Fiona wasn't a junkie.'

He felt anger building. 'That bastard Hapsfield was responsible, I'm sure of it and one of these days I'll ... I'll.'

'Let it go, Harris,' said Bailey quietly. 'We'll get him, nothing surer, but you stay away from him, okay?'

Jordan took a few deep breaths and sighed. 'Well, last the mother heard, the kid had a job in Victoria Sugar Mill up north near Townsville, so guess I'll shoot up there.'

Bailey nodded in agreement. 'Sounds good.' He stood up and shuddered at the cold. 'Get some of that Queensland sunshine into you. Oh, there's an old cop in Townsville CIB named Stan Morton. He's a great guy and must be close to retirement. If you need any help, call him and mention my name.'

'Thanks, Winston,' said Jordan. 'And by the way, Mrs Ackland happened to mention that young Phillip had a friend called Happy.'

'Happy!?' exclaimed Bailey.

'Kind of makes things interesting, don't you reckon?' said Jordan off-handedly.

'Ackland knew Hapsfield!?'

'Apparently.'

'Shit!'

'Exactly,' said Jordan with a smile.

Bailey began to pace up and down. 'So, young Ackland was tied up with Hapsfield. He goes to Townsville and disappears, meanwhile Hapsfield gets heavier into dealing.'

He stopped pacing in front of Jordan. 'And since you know that Hapsfield spends most of his time in Surfers these days, don't get any clever ideas about paying him a social call while you're up that way.'

'Winston, it never crossed my mind,' said Jordan, his face a mask of innocence.

'Hah, sure, and stuff you too,' said Bailey. He glanced at his watch. 'I'd better be going; at least you don't have to clock on and off.'

Jordan nodded. 'How very true.'

'You take care, mate,' said Bailey seriously and with a short wave of his hand, strolled away.

Jordan watched Bailey's departing back, then stood, rubbed his hands together and thrust them into his coat pockets. 'Sunshine, here I come,' he murmured.

Chapter 6

t was a windy, cold and drizzly morning when Jordan left Melbourne and headed north along the Princes Freeway. Even inside the station wagon he was wearing jeans, jumper and a coat in an effort to stay warm. Late that evening, he arrived at the outskirts of Sydney and pulled into the parking area of a service station where he spent the night in the back of the wagon as a cost-saving measure.

Woken early in the morning by the sound of a semi-trailer pulling in beside him, he continued on. Now the coastal road had become the Pacific Highway bound for Queensland. Arriving at the Gold Coast, he found a parking spot near the beach with an amenities block close by. After watching a few surfers enjoying the waves, he once again settled down for the night in the back of the wagon.

The next day, the sun arose in a clear blue sky and Jordan changed into shorts and T-shirt before travelling on north on what was now named the Bruce Highway.

Two days later, he arrived at Townsville and spent the night in a layby with a group of grey nomads pulling caravans.

The following morning, the one hundred kilometre drive to Ingham took only a little over an hour and, shortly after 9 am, he pulled up in the car park outside the Victoria Sugar Mill.

Two tall chimneys spewed grey smoke into the sky, and the heady smell of molasses filled the air. Jordan walked into the complex and entered a door above which a sign indicated Site Office.

The office was small; its walls plastered with posters stating safety regulations, a graph indicating tonnage of cane harvested, pictures of the mill and harvesting activities, and information on mill tours.

Behind a paper-strewn desk sat a man reading a newspaper. Everything was covered with a fine layer of dust.

Jordan approached the desk. 'Hi, I'm looking for work … any chance?'

The man, overweight and unshaven, looked up at Jordan and sniffed. Reluctantly, he folded his newspaper. 'Any experience?'

'Not in a mill, no, but I'm willing to do anything. I've done some labouring for a builder,' he added, hoping to impress.

'Umm,' said the man as he studied Jordan. 'Could be your lucky day. Our rigger needs another offsider for general yard work—scaffolding, wire cables and the like—reckon you could handle it?'

'Sure!' replied Jordan enthusiastically.

The man extracted a form from the filing cabinet behind him and handed it to Jordan. 'Here, fill this out.'

Jordan accepted the form and picked up a pen lying on the desk. He quickly filled in the form and handed it back.

The man gave the form a momentary glance. 'I suppose you'll need a place to camp.' He picked up a book and turned over a couple of pages.

'That'd be great,' said Jordan.

'Looks like barrack room fifteen is free, so you can have that one, okay? Go to supplies where you'll get a mattress you can take to the barracks.' He pulled out a drawer and fumbled around inside. 'Here's the key.'

Jordan reached out and accepted the key. 'Thanks.'

'Then go see the rigger, he's probably in his shed just behind us here.'

Jordan extended his hand to shake and thank the man, but he had quickly renewed his interest in the newspaper.

Ignored, Jordan turned and walked out.

Chapter 7

After locating the supplies shed, Jordan carried the mattress he had been given back to his wagon and drove around to the back of the mill complex where the barracks were sited. The barracks consisted of five long wooden sheds built on stilts with each one split up into five separate rooms. A further shed housed toilets and showers. Jordan found number fifteen, parked his wagon in front, walked up the steps, unlocked the door and entered. The room was completely bare except for a metal bed and a wooden cupboard against one wall that had seen better days. He brought the mattress in from his wagon and threw it on the metal bed.

The Ritz it certainly ain't! he thought.

After locking his door, he made his way back into the mill and, after asking for directions, finally found his way to the riggers' shed.

The rigger was working on a thick piece of a cable held in a vice. He was an ex-merchant seaman in his early fifties. A life at sea, a liking for rum and being only 154 cms tall gave him the appearance of a wizened pixie. He was wearing his usual olive green "uniform" of long-sleeved shirt and long trousers with a well-worn soft hat on his head.

'Hi, I'm Jordan. I was told you needed another offsider.' He strolled over and extended his hand.

The rigger accepted Jordan's hand and gave it a firm shake. 'I'm Jack, done any of this before?' He gestured to the cable in the vice.

'Some,' replied Jordan.

'Okay, finish the splice off,' said Jack as he stepped back.

Jordan picked up a metal spike from the bench and went to work.

'Not bad, Jordan, where did you learn?' asked Jack.

'My uncle had a boat so I've spliced a few ropes before but never wire. Seems the principle's the same but a bit harder on the hands though.'

'Yeah, it is that … I guess you'll do … come on we'll take a walk around.'

Jordan placed the splicing spike back down on the bench, rubbed his hands, and followed Jack out of the shed.

The noise from the sugar cane crushers, heavy machinery and escaping steam was almost deafening. Jack stopped occasionally and explained the workings of the mill by shouting into Jordan's ear.

Back at the riggers' shed, Jack pointed to Jordan's footwear. 'Those soft runners will be no good. You'll need a pair of metal-toed safety boots, go pick them up from supplies along with a hard hat and gloves. The mill shuts down in the morning for maintenance over the weekend so we'll probably be busy. See you back here at the shed seven-thirty in the morning, okay?

'No worries. Thanks Jack. See you in the morning.'

Chapter 8

The first night in the barracks was something Jordan would never forget. The continuous cacophony of the working mill, interspersed with the rattle of cane trains passing close by could not be drowned out by placing a pillow over his head. Adding to that, when he lay on the bed, the wire mesh proved unable to bear his weight and sagged to the floor. The only way to attain a flat surface was to place the mattress on the floor.

After a sleepless night, Jordan had no trouble getting to the riggers' shed by seven-thirty the following morning.

Jack pointed to a wire sling. 'Take that to the train track running away from the weighing station towards the crushers. I'll be along in a minute.'

With the wire sling over his shoulder, Jordan set off along the train track. On the way, he passed a short and stocky workman with long hair falling out from under his hard hat.

'Hi! How ya doin'?' said Jordan in attempt at conversation.

The man glanced at Jordan and turned away. Not to be so easily put off, Jordan tried again. 'I'm new here, name's Jordan ... you worked here long?'

'Long enough,' the man answered abruptly.

'Oh, had a few seasons here eh, are you full-time?'

The man looked Jordan up and down. 'What you want, pal?'

Jordan shrugged. 'Making conversation that's all. Like I said, I'm new here and just trying to get to know you guys.' He smiled. 'You know!'

The man stared back at Jordan, his face blank. 'No, I don't know

… go chat up somebody else.' He turned and walked away.

That went well, thought Jordan. He adjusted the wire sling on his shoulder and continued along the train track to where a young man in his late teens—thin, acne, unruly fair hair—was stood beside a few cane bins pulling at a broken towing cable.

Jordan dropped the wire sling on the ground. 'Would you be Jack's offsider?'

The young man looked at Harris and nodded.

Jordan smiled. 'I'm Jordan, I'm Jack's other offsider, starting today. What do I call you?'

'I'm Coop, short for Cooper.' The young man sniffed and ran the back of his hand under his nose. His pallid complexion and sunken eyes had the look of a user.

'Nice to meet you, Coop,' said Jordan. 'Since I'm new here, what do you do round here apart from get pissed?' He gave Cooper a gentle punch. 'Anything else you do for a bit of excitement?'

Cooper shook his head. 'Nothin' much.'

Jordan gave him another gentle punch. 'Oh come on, surely there's something … how do you get your kicks?'

Cooper gave Jordan a serious stare. 'What do you mean … kicks?'

'You know … kicks!' Jordan gave Cooper a knowing wink. 'Something to help relax the mind and soothe the troubled soul.'

Cooper shook his head. 'Sorry mate, I dunno what you're talking about.'

'Oh well, never mind,' said Jordan. 'Guess something'll turn up.'

A loud shout from Jack brought an end to their conversation. 'Come on, lads, fingers out … Jordan, pull that end of cable past the bins and Coop, give me a hand over here.'

Jordan grabbed the cable and dragged it past the line of bins as Jack had requested. 'Here do?'

Jack raised his hand. 'Yeah, fine.'

With only a short break for smoko, Jack, Cooper and Jordan managed to remove and replace nearly all the broken cable by midday when Jack called a halt. 'Lunchtime lads … see you back here after.'

Before Jordan had a chance to say anything, Cooper walked away in the direction of the barracks canteen and Jack headed back to his shed. Jordan watched them go.

'Okay, I'll just make my way on my own, and thanks for allowing me to accompany you back to the barracks, Coop, and for the friendly conversation,' he muttered.

On the way to the canteen, Jordan noticed the man he had spoken to earlier standing beside the cane crushers. They stared at each other for a moment before the man turned away.

Chapter 9

n the canteen, Jordan endeavoured to make conversation with the person sitting at the table beside him. 'Hi, name's Jordan, how ya goin'?'

The man grunted and continued stuffing sausages into his mouth.

'What do you guys do for excitement round here?' continued Jordan in the hope that he could obtain an insight into the local drug scene. His attempt to obtain information from Cooper had proven entirely unsuccessful.

The man swallowed and turned to face Jordan. 'Excitement?' he said.

'Yeah, you know ... something to give the mind a little pick-me-up.'

The man rose from the table, picked up his plate and looked down at Jordan. 'Sorry, pal, can't help you.'

The man walked away to another table where Cooper and the man he had met in the morning were sat. Jordan watched as they exchanged a few words. The three of them gave Jordan a brief stare before turning away.

Jordan looked down at his plate of curried sausages and then put down his knife and fork with distaste. 'Delicious! Hope the pub makes a decent sandwich.'

Chapter 10

Jordan's afternoon in the mill had gone by quickly, although most of his conversation had been with Jack as Cooper tended to completely ignore him.

Now at the bar of the Royal Hotel in the centre of town, Jordan finished eating a thick ham and tomato sandwich. He leant back on his stool, sighed with pleasure, reached for the glass of beer on the bar in front of him and finished it off.

He managed to catch the bartender's eye. 'Could I have another beer, please?'

The bartender refilled and returned his glass.

Jordan looked around the room. The pub was empty except for only two other men sat on the other side of the bar.

'Bit quiet tonight,' said Jordan as he offered the money for the beer.

'Yeah,' she replied abruptly as she accepted the cash and turned away to put it in the till, before going over to the other two men and refilling their glasses.

Jordan finished his beer and again caught the bartender's eye. 'Same again, please.' He placed his money on the bar, and as the bartender went to pick it up, he extended his hand and smiled. 'I'm Jordan, nice to meet you.'

The bartender—blonde hair tied back in a ponytail, tanned complexion and nineteen-years-old—looked at the offered hand, then into Jordan's face. She waited a moment as if considering before returning his smile and taking his hand. 'Hi, I'm Linda.'

'I'm very pleased to meet you, Linda,' said Jordan while he

continued to hold her hand. 'Tell me, please, what's there to do around here at night, apart from drink that is?'

Linda extracted her hand. 'Nothing really.' She leant forward on the bar. 'Jordan, eh, never met a Jordan before. Is that your first name?'

'No, first name is Harris.'

'That's not a first name; that's another last name ... what are you, two people?' she said teasingly.

Jordan grinned. 'Just the one, just the one of everything.'

Linda raised her eyebrows as Jordan shrugged his shoulders and raised his hands as if in surrender.

'Reckon you could be a bit of a worry, Harris Jordan,' said Linda.

Jordan inclined his head across the bar. 'What's with the two guys over there? They keep laughing and pointing at the stool in the corner.'

'That's old Reggie's stool; he was a regular and always sat there.' Linda shook her head sadly. 'Then it happened.'

'*It* happened?' asked Jordan. 'What *it*?'

'Okay, here's the story,' said Linda. 'Reggie's nickname was Flag because every payday, after having a few beers, would buy a flagon of sherry, stroll up to the park, sit under the mango tree and polish the lot off before going home. His wife used to go spare when he got home and would beat the hell out of him. Anyway, last payday same routine but passed out under the mango tree. When he came to, he realised that someone had gone through his pockets and stolen his pay.'

'Poor devil,' said Jordan.

'Yeah, well,' continued Linda. 'Flag must have reckoned if he went home and told the wife she would have got stuck into him even harder than usual so he decided to end it all. He went to the mill, got a length of rope and then on to the bridge over the train track. Tied one end to the railing, the other end round his neck and jumped off.'

Jordan grimaced at the image.

'The first train in the morning found him,' said Linda.

'Not good,' said Jordan seriously. 'So, what do those two find so funny about that?'

'Well, Flag was pretty pissed and his calculation of distance wasn't quite up to speed, so when he jumped, instead of the rope stretching his neck, it allowed him to hit the ground. He's now in hospital with two broken ankles, the silly old bugger.'

Linda grinned. Jordan laughed and glanced at the two men across the bar and at the vacant stool in the corner.

'Great story,' said Jordan. 'Look, Linda, I'm new in town and know nothing about the place. I've just landed a job in the mill and, well, I was wondering if you could show me around, what do you reckon?'

He put his hands together and managed to put on a begging expression. 'I'd really appreciate it, Linda.'

Linda looked straight into Jordan's eyes, leant forward and smiled. 'I was right, you are a worry; you working tomorrow?'

'Should be finished by midday, so I've been told.'

'Okay, Harris Jordan, I finish 2 o'clock, be here.'

Two more customers walked into the bar and Linda turned away to serve them. Jordan drained his glass of beer and left the bar.

Chapter 11

The following afternoon at 2 pm, Jordan glanced at his watch as he was about to enter the Royal Hotel when Linda walked out and bumped into him.

'On time, eh, that's a good start.' She looked around. 'Where's your car?'

Linda had on a loose-fitting summer dress and her hair hung free. Jordan took her arm. 'This way.'

As they reached Jordan's station wagon, Linda put her hand over her eyes to shield them from the sun. 'It's too nice a day to spend driving round town, let's head for the coast. I'll show you the jetty and sugar terminal, okay?'

'Sure, suits me,' said Jordan as he opened the passenger door for her.

Linda smiled. 'Very chivalrous.'

The drive to the coast took them through the small town of Halifax, past another mill at Macknade, and took just under half an hour. At Lucinda, Jordan parked the wagon and they walked out along the old timber wharf from which several people were fishing.

Linda pointed out to sea. 'That's Hinchinbrook Island out there; it's beautiful place with lovely walks in the rainforest. This here is the old wharf and that'—she pointed again—'is the new one that goes out for six kilometres. If you fancy yourself as a fisherman, you can be assured of hooking on to something off here, but be careful, there's all sorts in there, including sharks.'

'I'm no fisherman, Linda. I prefer mine supplied with batter and chips.'

Linda laughed and took hold of Jordan's hand. 'It's a beautiful day, let's stroll on the beach.'

'Great idea!' said Jordan. 'I have to say, the temp's a damn sight better than when I left Victoria.'

Except for Linda and Jordan, the beach was deserted; their only company a few seagulls and two albatrosses that completely ignored them as they slowly walked along. The sea was perfectly calm with tiny waves gently lapping against the shore.

'Thank you for showing me this, Linda,' said Jordan. He pulled her gently towards him and kissed her on the cheek. 'It's been nice.'

Linda leant forward and kissed him back. For a moment they stood looking at each other, before Jordan stepped back and coughed, seemingly embarrassed.

'Getting on,' said Jordan with a glance at his watch. 'We'd better start heading back.'

Holding hands, they slowly walked back along the beach.

On the way back to Ingham, Jordan drove slowly, in no great rush to end the afternoon with Linda. He turned to look at her beside him on the front bench seat. She appeared to be studying him with a half-smile on her face.

'What … what is it?' he asked.

Linda leant towards him and placed a hand on his thigh. 'I think I like you, Harris Jordan.'

Jordan took a deep breath while keeping his eyes on the road. 'Thanks, I like you too.'

Linda moved her hand to between Jordan's legs. He took another quick intake of breath.

Linda smiled. 'Sorry, Harris Jordan, am I hurting you?' she asked quietly.

'No … no … no pain at all,' said Jordan.

Linda unzipped his shorts and released him. He gasped, his eyes on the road and his hands grasped firmly on the steering wheel.

'Still no pain, Harris?' asked Linda. Jordan groaned, with his eyes half-closed, he lost concentration. The wagon wandered to the side of the road and gently ploughed into a stand of sugar cane as Jordan pushed his foot down on the brake.

'Jesus, Linda!' he said with a sigh. 'You sure know how to not hurt a fella.'

Chapter 12

By the time they arrived back in Ingham it was starting to get dark. Linda had directed him to her home in a housing estate on the outskirts. The house was a small weatherboard on stilts with peeling paintwork.

'Come on in, I'll make you a coffee,' said Linda.

'Okay, thanks,' said Jordan and followed her up the steps to the front verandah.

Linda opened the front door that was unlocked and entered. 'I'll put the kettle on. Please make yourself at home and put the tellie on if you like, or the radio.'

Jordan followed Linda inside. The living area with timber floors was sparse but clean. A well-worn couch faced a TV in the corner. A small table with a three-in-one sound system was against one wall. Linda had tried to brighten up the room with a coloured scatter rug on the floor in front of the couch, and a vase of flowers on a coffee table.

Jordan turned on the radio and sat on the couch as Linda arrived with two mugs of coffee. She handed one to Jordan and sat beside him.

'Not much but it's home for a while.'

Jordan sipped his coffee. 'Been here long?'

''Bout eighteen months, I might head south after the crushing season. What about you, going to leave in December?'

'Maybe, see how things work out.'

Linda put her coffee mug on the table, leant towards Jordan and nibbled his ear. 'Well, in case you intend leaving sooner, we'd better make the most of it, Harris Jordan.'

Jordan sighed. 'Not more pain.'

Linda giggled, stood up and held out her hand. 'Come on, let me show you another part of the house.'

Later that evening, with Linda lying quietly in his arms, Jordan pushed her hair away from her face and tucked it behind her ear. 'How long you been using?' he asked gently.

Linda's face dropped and she turned away.

'I noticed ... how long?' said Jordan as he held her arm and turned it over. They both looked at the small bruises.

'A month.'

'Why?'

Linda shrugged. 'Had a few too many drinks one night and got offered, thought what the hell, see what all the fuss is about.'

'And then?'

'And then I wanted more.' She sat up and pulled the sheet up around her. 'Look, I thought we were getting on great, but if you want to go, well go!' she said indignantly.

'Linda, this can kill you,' said Jordan.

'Yeah, well, my life, not yours.'

'You got a local supplier?'

Linda stared at him. 'Why do you want to know?'

Jordan sat up. 'Might be a help.'

Linda raised her voice, confused. 'Help ... help you for what!?'

'I mean you no harm, Linda,' said Jordan calmly. 'I'd really like to help you quit this.'

'Why? We've only just met so why the hell do you want to help me?' she demanded.

Jordan remained quiet for a moment as he considered what to say. 'My sister died of an overdose,' he said almost inaudibly.

Linda slumped back down onto her pillow and her eyes moistened as she took in Jordan's remark. 'Oh Christ, Harris ... I'm so sorry.'

Jordan reached over, put his arms around her and pulled her close as tears ran down her cheeks. 'Do you want to stop, Linda?'

'Yes, yes of course,' she whispered.

'Then you go see a doctor and tell him all about it, okay?'

Linda snuggled up against him. 'Okay, Harris.'

'That's good, so tell me, who's your supplier?'

'Doug Foster ... works in the mill.'

'What does he look like?'

'Bit shorter than you, fairly stocky though with long, black hair.'

Jordan thought back to the man he had passed and tried without success to talk to when on the way to fix the cane truck cables, and later in the canteen with Cooper. 'Umm, may have seen him ... not a very friendly type.'

'Not unless it suits him,' said Linda.

'Okay, now let's keep this to ourselves, right?' Jordan said in a brighter tone of voice. He pulled Linda closer to him and stroked her hair. 'And you will go see the doc, promise?'

She sighed and pressed her face against his chest. 'Yes, Harris.'

'Good!'

As they lay together quietly, Jordan stared up at the ceiling. Images flashed before him of Hapsfield winking and grinning, and Fiona's body on the morgue slab. He rubbed a hand over his eyes and silently mouthed *bastard*.

Chapter 13

The following morning, on his way to the riggers' shed while walking past the cane bin tipping area, he stopped to look down at the cane moving along the conveyor belt towards the crushers. He felt a push in the back and, unbalanced, he toppled forward onto the conveyor.

Frantically, he tried to climb up and out, but the sheer sides presented no handholds.

He yelled for help and, just a metre short of the crushers, the conveyor came to a stop. A heavy rope landed beside him. He grabbed it and hauled himself up and out. He slumped to the ground, gasping for breath. He looked up at the man who had thrown him the rope and recognised him as the unfriendly one who had sat beside him eating sausages in the canteen.

'Lucky I heard you, mate,' he said with a grin. 'You were as close as dammit to getting juiced. You better watch your step, mate, lots of heavy machinery in this place.'

The man turned away, pressed a button and the conveyor restarted. Jordan looked down at the crushers and wiped the sweat from his face and out of his eyes. He stood up and unsteadily walked away.

Just before he reached the riggers' shed, Cooper came to meet him. 'You alright, mate? Look a bit pale.' He walked on past Jordan and beckoned him. 'Come on, we have to go to the fires, there's a bit of a problem.'

'What's up?' asked Jordan.

'Had to shut down number three fire. Chief wants us to clean it out so they can get a good look at it.'

On the mezzanine platform that gave access to the fires, the heat was intense. The workers who attended the fires were all wearing heavy woollen clothing as protection. Jordan and Cooper wearing just shorts and T-shirts cringed at the heat. Cooper pointed at a small open door and a couple of rakes that were leaning against the platform railing.

'When I'm in, pass in those rakes, then you come in.'

Jordan stared at Cooper. 'You must be joking ... there's a bloody furnace in there.'

Cooper grinned. 'No, it's all good. This fire was turned off just before midnight, it's had ages to cool off.' He eased himself inside the small doorway.

Jordan passed in the two rakes then climbed in himself. The fire chamber was about three metres square and four metres high. Cooper had already started raking the still smouldering bagasse to the rear of the chamber. The floor was a conveyor belt of metal links and the heat overpowering. Jordan picked up the other rake and started to help, believing the sooner he got the job over and done with the sooner they could get out.

Cooper stopped and wiped the sweat from his face. 'Reckon there's an easier way. I'll go grab the fire hose and we should be able to flush most of this shit away,' he said as he climbed out.

Jordan leant on his rake. He looked behind him as the door slammed shut. He waited a moment, expecting it to re-open, but it stayed shut. The embers still in the bagasse lit the inside of the fire with a faint pink glow. With sweat pouring down his face, he dropped his rake. Went to the door and tried to push it open without success. He kicked at it in panic.

The door opened and he scrambled out. Gasping for air, he collapsed on the platform.

Cooper stood there with a hose in his hand. 'Sorry, pal,' he said with a shrug. 'Door must have swung shut.'

He leant inside the door with the hose. 'Turn it on, mate.'

Jordan staggered to the tap, turned it on and leant against the railings. He glanced to the end of the platform and saw Foster. They stared at each other for a moment, before Foster turned and walked away.

Jordan watched him go. *Something tells me I'm starting to stand on somebody's toes,* he thought.

Chapter 14

erched on a bar stool in the Royal Hotel, Jordan had just finished explaining to Linda the day's events.

'Quite a day, eh Linda!'

Linda leant forward, concern written on her face. 'Be careful, Harris, Foster has a rep ...'

She stopped in mid-sentence and looked behind Jordan. Jordan felt a hand on his shoulder. He turned to see Foster with a slight smile on his face.

'Had an exciting day so I hear. Still, you look none the worse for it.' He looked at Linda. 'Hi, Linda, how you doin'?'

'Fine thanks, Dougie, wanna beer?' asked Linda.

'Thanks,' said Foster.

Jordan raised his hand. 'Let me get it. Two glasses please, Linda.'

Linda pulled the beers, set them down on the bar in front of Jordan and Foster, then turned away to serve other customers.

Foster raised his glass. 'Here's to ya!' He gulped down half the glass and smacked his lips. 'So, where ya from?'

'Melbourne,' said Jordan.

'Umm, that is a long way from home.'

'Yeah, well, needed a break.'

'Woman trouble?'

'No, not really.'

'Not running from the law are ya, pal?' said Foster, seemingly aghast at the prospect.

Jordan picked up his glass and finished the contents. He gave Foster what he hoped was a look he would interpret as ... *maybe you got it right.*

'Another beer, Doug?'

'Why not?'

It was 8 o'clock and the bar had filled up considerably. Jordan managed to catch Linda's eye. 'Couple more please, Linda.'

'And a couple of rum chasers,' added Foster.

Two hours later the bar was packed with noisy drinkers and the air thick with cigarette smoke. Linda and another bartender were kept busy. Jordan and Foster had been drinking shout for shout.

Foster, sitting on a barstool beside Jordan, waved his arms and shouted across the bar to a tall, gangly man well over two metres tall. 'Hey, Billy, how is it?' He belched. 'I need to piss.'

He slid off the bar stool and tried to stand, but his legs buckled. Jordan reached out, grabbed him and held him up.

Billy suddenly arrived and helped prevent Jordan and Foster falling to the floor. 'You two had a party, eh?'

Jordan burped. 'He must have hollow legs.'

'Yeah, he can put it away but can't handle it,' said Billy, 'Got my ute out front; give me a hand, eh and I'll take him home.'

'No worries,' said Jordan.

With Billy on one side and Jordan on the other, they part carried, part dragged Foster towards the pub door. On the way, Jordan managed to catch Linda's eye and mouthed, 'See you.'

Linda gave a small smile and nodded.

Jordan helped Billy ease Foster into the passenger seat of the ute. 'I'll come along if you like, Billy ... give you a hand.'

Billy shook his head. 'Thanks, mate, but I'll be alright; done this many times before.'

He got in the ute and drove off.

Jordan took a few deep breaths, had a stretch, straightened his back and walked away.

The next morning in the riggers' shed, Jordan was splicing a cable while Jack and Cooper were inspecting scaffold joins when Foster put his head in the door.

'How'd ya pull up, pal?'

Jack and Cooper stopped working and looked across at Jordan.

'Not too bad thanks, you?'

Foster grinned. 'Fit as a fiddle. Billy told me you saved me from falling on my face last night, so thanks for that.'

'No worries.' said Jordan.

'Party at my place Saturday night, bring Linda if you like … she knows where,' said Foster. He gave a small wave and walked off.

Jordan looked at Jack and Cooper, gave a wry smile and raised his eyebrows. Cooper stared at Jordan, mouth open with a stunned expression, and Jack went back to inspecting the scaffold joints. Jordan, whistling quietly, continued splicing.

Chapter 15

nside Foster's house a lot of young people were talking and dancing to loud music. Foster spotted Jordan and Linda as they pushed their way through the crowd.

'Glad you could make it,' said Foster, virtually shouting in order to make himself heard. 'Booze is in the kitchen, go help yourself; you know your way around, eh Linda?' He turned away to talk to another couple.

'So, Linda, been here before eh?' said Jordan inquiringly.

'Yeah, come on, we'll get a drink.' She grabbed Jordan's hand and guided him to the kitchen.

The kitchen bench was covered with assorted bottles of spirits and glasses. Jordan looked around. 'Any beer?'

Linda went to the fridge, took out a couple of stubbies and handed one to Jordan.

'Thanks,' said Jordan as he accepted the beer. He looked back through the kitchen door and watched Foster move through the crowd. He would greet some with a hug and some with a whisper in their ear. His hands continually travelled in and out of his pockets.

Jordan was fully aware of what was going on. 'He's dealing, isn't he, Linda? Is this where you got started?'

'Yes,' replied Linda sorrowfully.

Jordan was about to speak again, but stopped abruptly as Foster came towards them.

'Linda, give me a minute with Jordan will ya?' He jerked his head sideways.

'Sure, Dougie.' She gave Jordan a sad smile before turning away and leaving the kitchen.

Foster moved in close to Jordan. 'Back at the mill you were asking around about a little bit of after work excitement. I might be able to help you there.'

Jordan feigned incomprehension 'Yeah, how's that?'

Foster scowled. 'Don't stuff me round, pal, I'm not stupid, deaf or blind.' He poked Jordan in the chest. 'You've been askin' silly questions and you were watching me in there.' He jerked a thumb to behind him.

Jordan held Foster's stare for a moment before replying. 'In Melbourne I had a bit of ah ... you know ... business going and had to leave in a hurry cause of too much interest from unwanted persons.'

'Ah!' said Foster in apparent understanding.

'Yeah, well, thought that since I'm here, might as well check out the business opportunities.'

'You've contacts down south?' asked Foster becoming interested.

Jordan nodded. 'Some.'

'Umm, maybe we can help each other.'

'If, *if* I go into business,' said Jordan seriously, 'I'd want it to be worthwhile.'

Foster suddenly changed the conversation. 'Ever been pig hunting?'

'No, why?' asked Jordan, confused and caught completely by surprise.

'Be here midday tomorrow,' said Foster as he left the kitchen and walked back into the crowd.

Linda returned to the kitchen. 'Had a friendly chat?'

Jordan scratched his head. 'Yeah, asked me to go pig hunting tomorrow.'

Linda took the beer bottle from Jordan's hand and placed it and hers on the kitchen bench. She pulled at his arm. 'Take me home please, Harris.'

Together they pushed their way through the crowd to outside the house and into Jordan's wagon.

As they drove away from Foster's house, Linda kept glancing at Jordan who had gone strangely quiet. 'What did you two talk about?' she asked.

Jordan had been turning over in his mind what took place at Foster's party, and in particular why he had been invited to go pig shooting. 'Oh, this and that,' he answered.

Linda became irate. 'Look, Harris, Foster is bad news. People who mess with him get hurt, even disappear.'

'Disappear?' said Jordan.

Linda was frustrated. 'Disappear, vanish. What, are you stupid?'

Jordan was taken aback by Linda's outburst. 'Easy, Linda, do you know of anyone who has disappeared?"

'Well, not personally, no.' She became calmer. 'But people talk, especially in a bar. You overhear lots you're probably not meant to.'

Jordan was intrigued. 'Go on.'

'Well, there was this young guy who'd been pretty friendly with Foster, but apparently owed him for supplies. He was laughing about it in the bar one night and then, just gone.'

'Remember his name?'

Linda thought for a moment. 'I think it was Phil something.'

Jordan stopped the wagon and looked at Linda. 'Ackland?' he said.

'Yes, I think so, Phil Ackland, yes.' Linda was astonished. 'Christ, did you know him?'

Jordan started driving again and let the information sink in. 'Could be. Look, Linda, don't tell anyone we've talked about this okay?'

'Okay, okay!' said Linda sounding slightly annoyed. 'What is this, Harris, what's going on?'

Jordan brought the wagon to a halt outside Linda's house and considered an answer. 'Sorry, Linda, but I think it best you don't know. Like I asked, say nothing, okay?' He leant to Linda and held her face in his hands. 'Please!' He kissed her gently.

'You want to come in?' she asked quietly.

'Very much,' he replied.

Lying together in bed Linda nibbled Jordan's ear. 'I really like you, Harris Jordan,' she whispered.

Jordan smiled and held her closer. 'And I really like you, Linda.' He paused. 'Oh, good grief, I don't know your surname.'

'It's Stelling, you idiot!' She gave Jordan a gentle punch. 'You will be careful, with Dougie I mean?'

'I'll be careful, Linda Stelling.' He gave her a smile.

Linda looked into his eyes. 'I'd hate it if something happened to you.'

'Don't worry, I'll be fine.' He lifted Linda's arm and looked at the bruises. 'Did you go see the doc?'

'I've got an appointment tomorrow arvo.'

'Good, you have to stop you know, I'd hate to lose you too.'

'I'm not your sister, Harris.'

'Yeah, even so ...' His voice trailed off.

Realising the relevance of the remark she had made, she sat up, leant over Jordan and kissed him. 'I'm so sorry, Harris.'

Jordan smiled. 'It's okay.'

Linda straddled him, her hands on his chest, and slowly began to move against him. He closed his eyes and moaned. 'Oh, the pain ... the pain!'

Chapter 16

Sunday morning, as arranged, Jordan stopped his wagon at midday outside Foster's house. As he got out of his wagon, a ute pulled up beside him with three dogs in the back. Jordan realised it was Billy, the man he had helped with Foster in the Royal Hotel.

Foster came out of the house and walked towards them. 'This is Billy, Jordan.' He laughed. 'Oh, I forgot, you've already met.'

Jordan and Billy nodded at each other.

'Okay, let's climb aboard and get on with it,' said Foster. He held the passenger side door open and signalled Jordan to get in.

'Billy's heard of a family of pigs near here,' said Foster as they turned onto a dusty track. 'Thought we might grab a couple of suckers, eh Billy?'

Billy nodded and continued driving along the track deeper into the scrub.

'Not a great talker is Billy,' continued Foster, 'but not a bloke you'd wanna upset, are you, Billy?' He elbowed Jordan in the ribs and laughed. 'Worth remembering that is, eh!'

Billy stopped the ute near dense scrub and they got out. Billy gave a whistle and the three dogs jumped out and started sniffing around.

'Great dogs,' said Foster. 'Billy's trained 'em well, they'll do whatever he says. He's gonna set 'em loose and we'll come behind.'

Foster went to the ute, reached into the back and lifted out a hessian bag from which he removed a shotgun. 'All we want is the suckers, but sometimes Mum gets cranky.' He patted the gun. 'This'll take care of her if we have to.'

He saw Jordan nervously eye the shotgun and grinned. 'Don't look so worried, pal, I'll look after you ... come on, Billy, let's at 'em.'

Billy started encouraging the dogs and they sniffed around without any enthusiasm. Foster walked around, studying the ground and scrub.

'Try over there through the scrub, Billy, go along the creek bed and we'll follow you on the other side.'

Billy set off with the dogs at his heels and disappeared into the scrub. Jordan followed Foster who was keeping to the more open spaces. Suddenly, the dogs started yelping and barking.

'Over here!' shouted Billy. 'We've got a couple.'

Jordan and Foster pushed through the scrub out into a small clearing and came across Billy and the dogs. One sucker had a dog hanging onto its snout and another onto its tail.

Billy was holding the hind leg of another sucker with the third dog holding onto its snout.

The suckers were squealing, the dogs snarling and Billy was yelling as they all rolled around together.

Foster took a knife from his belt and cut the throat of the sucker that Billy was hanging onto. As he turned to get at the other one held by the dogs, he was thrown sideways by the charge of a large sow exploding out of the bush. The shotgun flew from his grasp and landed at Jordan's feet. Without thinking, he picked up the gun, pointed it at the sow that had turned around and was heading back towards Foster, and fired.

The sow rushed forward to Foster who was sat in the dirt wide-eyed as the sow came at him. Suddenly it stopped, its face inches from Foster's face and collapsed down onto his legs. The sound of the gun made the dogs release their hold on the other piglet and it ran squealing off into the scrub.

There was silence as the dogs sat looking at Billy, who was still holding the sucker, looking from Foster, to Jordan, to the dead sow, his mouth open and a stunned expression on his face.

Foster broke the silence with a loud yell. 'Shit ... shit ... shit!!' He grabbed at his face and hair, shook his head and slapped his chest. 'Bloody bull ants!'

Billy dropped the sucker. Jordan dropped the shotgun and together they pulled the sow off Foster's legs. Foster jumped to his feet and, frantically slapping himself, charged through the scrub back to the ute still shouting. 'Ouch ... shit ... shit ... ouch, you bastards!'

Jordan and Billy watched Foster disappear, then with the dogs behind followed him out.

Beside the ute, Foster had ripped off his shirt and shorts and was jumping around still trying to remove the bull ants. Jordan and Billy wandered up to him. The dogs sat quietly beside Billy.

Billy turned to Jordan with a slight smile creeping at the corner of his mouth. 'Must be one of those new-fangled dances. I didn't know Dougie was such a mover.'

Jordan grinned back at Billy as Foster continued scratching. He took a small tube from his pocket and handed it to Foster. 'Here, Dougie, try this. I brought it along just in case of mozzies, but your need seems greater than mine.'

Foster took the ointment and rubbed it all over himself. Jordan glanced at Billy and saw they were both finding it hard not to laugh.

Foster stopped rubbing on the ointment. He sighed, took a few deep breaths and stared at Jordan and Billy. 'Christ Almighty, that was fun!'

They looked from one to the other, and then simultaneously burst out laughing.

'Your mouth was so wide open, Billy, I thought the sow was gonna jump in,' said Foster.

'It was nice of you to line her up for me, Dougie,' said Jordan.

'Good job you know how to handle a shotgun, Jordan, or Dougie would have been chewed up,' said Billy.

'Never held one before,' said Jordan still laughing.

The laughing stopped as Foster and Billy looked at each other. Jordan smiled and shook his head.

'You're joking!' said Foster.

'Nope!'

'Christ!' said Billy.

'Shit!' said Foster.

'That'd be right,' said Jordan.

Billy shook his head in disbelief. 'I need a drink,' he said and went to the ute. He lifted an eskie out from the tray, took out three cans and brought them back; he handed one to Jordan and Foster.

'Never shot before?' said Billy.

'Nope!' said Jordan after taking a long swallow from his can.

'Shit!' said Billy. He went to the eskie for another three beers and handed them out.

They sat in silence, drinking, their eyes moving from one to the other, their expressions changing as they absorbed what had just taken place.

'Lucky shot?' said Foster.

Jordan nodded. 'Lucky shot.'

'Shit!' repeated Billy. He drained his beer. 'I'll go back and fetch the sucker; leave the sow, she'll be too tough.'

Billy wandered off with the dogs trotting along behind him. Foster looked at Jordan again and shook his head. He picked up his shirt and shorts, dusted them off—making sure no ants remained—and put them back on. Jordan watched with a slight smile turning up the corners of his mouth.

Two hours later, they were sat around with the remains of the sucker on a spit over a fire. Billy had done the job of skinning and gutting it, while Foster and Jordan had collected the timber for the fire.

Foster picked at his teeth with a twig and squinted at Jordan. 'Never shot before?'

Jordan shook his head. 'Nope.'

Billy stared at the fire shaking his head in a continued state of disbelief at the pure luck that must have been involved in Jordan's shot connecting with the sow in a place that stopped it in its tracks.

Foster started scratching his face, neck and head and looked at Jordan. 'That business we mentioned.'

'Yeah?' said Jordan.

'I'm expecting some stock.' He spread his hands in a way of indicating size. 'In a coupla days, probably be late … we'll talk some more after, okay?'

Jordan nodded. 'Fine.'

Foster started scratching again. 'I reckon that stuff's wearing off. Come on, I need to get back.'

They all stood up and kicked dirt over the remains of the fire before making their way to the ute. Billy whistled to the dogs and they jumped onto the tray.

Foster was still scratching himself by the time they arrived back at his house. Foster and Jordan got out of the ute and Billy drove off with the dogs.

Jordan gave Foster the remains of the tube of lotion. 'Interesting day.'

'Yeah, bloody hilarious!' said Foster as he hurriedly made his way into the house, still scratching, and slammed the door shut behind him.

Jordan grinned and walked over to his wagon. He drove a short distance that put him out of sight of the house, pulled over and took his mobile phone out of the glove box. He scrolled down through the contacts to the name Dan Morton that Winston Bailey had given him.

'Hi, is that Detective Morton?'

In the Townsville CIB, Morton answered. 'Yeah, who's calling?'

'Harris Jordan, Winston Bailey gave me your name and number.'

'Jordan eh, heard of you.'

'Yeah well, life's a bitch, Dan.'

'Word is you were hard done by. Served the prick Hermans right by what I've heard. Anyway what's up?'

'I'm in Ingham. Came here chasing a lost kid and think I've stumbled onto an H delivery.'

Morton sat up in his chair where he had been lazing with his feet up on his desk and put down the cup of coffee he'd been sipping. He was a large man in his late fifties; his shirt sleeves were rolled up and his tie undone.

His casual manner changed as he reached for a pen and paper. 'How much?'

'I got the impression a fair lump,' said Jordan.

'When?'

'Couple of days, probably Tuesday night.'

'Got a name?'

'Guy called Doug Foster … works at the mill.'

Morton busily scribbled notes. 'Okay, I'll meet you at the 60K sign south of town, 6 pm Tuesday. If it looks like going down earlier, give me a bell.'

'No worries, I'll see you then,' said Jordan.

Chapter 17

Jordan glanced at his watch as two cars pulled up beside him. Detective Morton got out of one of the cars, strode over to Jordan and shook his hand.

'How ya doin'?'

'Good thanks ... nice to meet you, Detective.'

'Call me Dan ... what's on?'

'All I know is Foster's collecting something tonight.'

'We'll get close to his place where we can keep an eye on him.' Morton pointed at Jordan's wagon. 'Guess he knows your wagon, so park it out of sight and hop in with me, okay?'

Jordan nodded. 'Right, I'll park outside the Royal Hotel and you can pick me up there.'

Half an hour later, Jordan and Morton had parked nearby Foster's house, with another car containing two more officers parked a short distance away.

'Did a check on Foster,' said Morton. 'Couple of convictions for assault in Townsville a few years back but nothing since. Local boys reckon he considers himself a bit of a hardarse and maybe dealing ... small time but nothing solid. Maybe he's stepped up.'

'Well, the implication was a big shipment,' said Jordan. 'And yes, he is dealing, I've seen him at it.'

A utility pulled up outside Foster's house and sounded its horn.

'That's Billy,' said Jordan. 'He's a mate of Foster.'

Foster came out of the house and got into the utility.

Morton picked up his two-way. 'Our man's on the move Bob; we'll stick with him and you hang back.'

'Where do you reckon they're headed?' asked Morton as they left the outskirts of Ingham.

'We're on the road to Lucinda, which tends to make sense,' said Jordan. 'That's the sugar terminal where the bulk carriers come in.'

Morton picked up his two-way. 'Bob, we're headed for Lucinda wharf.'

The utility stopped in front of the sugar terminal entrance and Morton pulled up a couple of hundred yards back. He extracted binoculars from the glove box and watched as Foster got out of the ute. A man carrying two medium sized suitcases walked from the entrance to meet him.

Morton whistled. 'If those cases are full of what we reckon then it's a bundle!'

They continued to watch as Foster took the cases to the ute and put them in the front seat before getting in. Wasting no time, the car quickly drove away.

Morton tossed the binoculars into the back seat and picked up the two-way. 'Did you see that, Bob?'

The two-way crackled. 'Yeah, Dan, want us to pick up the bag man?'

'Right,' said Morton. 'Take him to Ingham nick and keep him quiet till we find out what Foster's up to.'

He started the car. 'Let's see where Foster is off to now.'

The ute stopped outside the bus booking office and Morton brought his car to a stop on the opposite side of the road.

Jordan was incredulous. 'Don't tell me he's going to get on a bus?'

The front of the booking office was all glass so they could see Foster clearly as he walked inside to the office counter and obtained some papers. He sat down with the two cases beside him, picked up a pen and wrote on the papers. After just a few minutes, an interstate bus arrived and the driver got out and entered the office. Foster stood up, greeted the driver and handed him the papers he had completed. The driver took a moment to study the papers then shook Foster's hand and picked up the two cases. The driver walked outside and placed the cases into the bus's side storage compartment. Foster went to Billy's ute, got in and they drove off. There were no passengers for the bus and no further baggage, so the driver got back in and drove away.

Morton and Jordan got out of their car, quickly walked across the road and entered the office.

Morton showed his badge to the young girl behind the counter. 'Detective Morton, Townsville CIB,' he said brusquely. 'A man put two cases on the bus that just left, where's it headed?'

The girl looked down at the paperwork in front of her after staring at Morton's badge. 'Ah yes, two cases for delivery to Surfers Paradise.'

'Thanks,' said Morton. He went outside to where Jordan had waited.

'I'll pick up a warrant to search Foster's place and make arrangements to follow the cases to Surfers.'

'Surfers eh?' said Jordan with a knowing smile. 'Reckon I'll shoot down there, Dan. I got a good idea where the stuff is headed and I'd like to follow it through. Can you get in touch with Bailey and fill him in?'

'Okay, call me in a couple of hours.'

'Thanks, Dan, I appreciate. I'd better be off. Can you drop me off back where I left my wagon there's someone I gotta see before I go.'

Morton grinned. 'Female?'

Jordan grinned back. 'Isn't it always?'

In the Royal Hotel, Jordan leant on the bar and talked quietly to Linda.

'It should be all sorted out in a week at the most, then I'll call you, okay?'

Linda looked at Jordan with concern written on her face. 'Take care, Harris, I'll miss you.'

Jordan reached out and placed his hand over Linda's. 'Me too, and look after yourself, Linda … you know what I mean.'

Linda nodded. 'Sure, Harris!'

Silently, they gazed into each other's eyes for a few moments.

Jordan released Linda's hand. 'Better be going.' He backed away, then turned and left the bar.

Linda stared sadly at the empty space.

Chapter 18

n the Ingham Police Station, Foster was sitting in front of a desk that was bare except for two packets of white powder.

Detective Dan Morton sat across the desk, facing him. He bent forward and gestured at the packets. 'And these which we found at your place you say are not yours but in fact belong to Billy … that right?'

Foster leant back in his chair with a smug look on his face. He raised his eyebrows and shrugged. 'You got it, pal.'

Morton stared at Foster. 'Billy, eh?' He turned around to another officer who was standing at the door watching proceedings. 'Watch him, I'll be back.' Morton left his seat and walked out of the room.

Foster chuckled. 'Don't hurry back on my account, pal.'

Morton entered another room where Billy was sitting at a desk staring wide-eyed at another two packets of white powder in front of him. Another officer stood by the door.

Morton sat down behind the desk and, as with Foster, gestured to the two packets. 'So, Billy, what can you tell me about this stuff?'

Billy looked up at Morton shaking his head. 'Nothing, nothing honest!'

Morton straightened and took a deep breath. 'Well now, Billy,' he said quietly. 'That presents me with a problem.

'How's that?' said Billy, not understanding.

'Well, you see, Billy, your mate Foster has just told me it's yours.'

Billy shook his head. 'No way, it's not mine and Dougie would never say so.'

Morton reached inside his jacket pocket and took out a small recorder. He put it on the desk and pressed the play button.

"And these which we found at your place you say are not yours but in fact belong to Billy that right? You got it, pal."

Billy's eyes widened even farther, his mouth sagged open, unable to believe what he had heard. 'No ... no!'

'Want to hear it again?' said Morton as he rewound the tape and pushed play.

"And these which we found at your place you say are not yours but in fact belong to Billy that right? You got it, pal."

Billy put his hands over his ears and lowered his head; his shoulders slumped. Morton got up, walked around the desk and put a hand on Billy's shoulder.

'Unless you tell us all about this powder, you will be in a lot of trouble and probably go to jail for a long time. Is that what you want?'

'But Dougie is me mate,' mumbled Billy.

'Not anymore, Billy. Do you want me to play the tape again?' He reached his hand out towards the recorder.

Billy's hand shot out and stopped Morton's hand. He sighed. 'The powder is Dougie's.'

Morton stole a quick glance to the other officer at the door and winked before returning to his chair. He activated the recorder. 'Okay, Billy; tell me how Dougie came by the powder.'

Billy squirmed nervously. 'Dougie got a phone call ... told him when to meet the guy at the wharf.'

'Call from who?' said Morton.

Billy shook his head. 'Dunno, never said.'

'Okay, then what about this?' Morton pointed at the packets.

'Dougie opened the cases on the way back and took out four. He said it was his pay, then he put the cases on the bus.'

'What happens to the stuff he keeps?'

'Puts it in smaller packets and sells it off.' Billy hunched over. 'I knew what he did to that Ackland kid would bring bad luck.'

Morton leant forward. 'Tell me about Ackland, Billy,' he asked in a quiet, friendly voice.

'Wouldn't pay Dougie for the stuff. He was shooting his mouth off about how he'd got it for free. Dougie fronted him up one night in the car park behind the Royal.'

'That's good, Billy … then what?'

'Ackland was drunk and had no idea how much he was pissing Dougie off. Dougie told him he wanted the money he owed him bloody fast, but Ackland just laughed at him. Patted Dougie on the head. He should never have done that; Dougie don't like being laughed at.'

Billy slumped even further forward onto the desk.

'Would you like a drink of water?' asked Morton.

'Please,' said Billy.

Morton gestured to the officer at the door who went out and quickly returned with a glass of water and handed it to Billy.

Morton waited for Billy to finish drinking before speaking. 'So, you said Dougie didn't like Ackland laughing at him … what next, Billy?'

Billy swallowed hard and coughed. 'Dougie grabbed the kid; slammed him up against the wall and threw him to the ground. Told him he was a piece of shit and if he didn't pay in two days he'd break his legs. The kid got up and should have just pissed off but no, he laughed at Dougie again and gave him the finger. Dougie went bananas, took out a knife and stabbed him, not just once but several times.'

Billy covered his face with his hands. 'I can still see it … the blood, the kid was covered in it. Dougie kept kicking at him telling him he was a stupid shithead.'

Morton reached out and put his hand on Billy's shoulder. 'So, what did you do with Ackland, Billy?'

'Put him in the back of my ute.'

'Where did you take him, Billy?'

Beads of sweat were falling from Billy's face. 'Drove to Dougie's place, picked up a couple of shovels then drove out to the scrub.'

'So, you dug a hole and buried the kid?'

'Yeah, we found a soft, sandy place ... dug a hole and dropped the kid in.'

'And that was it?'

'I was looking at the place and Dougie asked if I wanted to say a few words but I couldn't, so he said "So long, arsehole!" and then we left.'

'Could you take us to the place, Billy?' asked Morton.

Billy sighed. 'Sure.'

Morton turned off the recorder. 'It's going to be okay, Billy, you've done real good. I have to go away for a minute or two, meantime ...' He opened a desk drawer and took out a pen and notebook which he placed in front of Billy.

'The other officer is going to help you write down all you've just told me; then as soon as we've checked it all out you can go home, okay?'

Billy nodded, close to tears.

Morton gestured to the other officer to come forward. 'I'll get his ute brought in and you can check it out for bloodstains. When you've got his statement sorted, we'll drive out to where he reckons the Ackland kid is buried. I'll go have a quick word with Foster, give him something to think about.'

Morton entered the other interview room to find Foster leaning back in his chair with his feet on the desk.

Foster grinned. 'No chance of a beer I suppose.'

Morton smiled back. ''Fraid not Dougie. I just popped in to let you know I'm going for a little drive into the scrub to see what I can dig up.' He gave a brief wave, turned and left.

Foster's expression changed to one of anger as realisation hit him. He took his feet off the desk and slammed his fist down. 'Billy, you bastard!' he shouted.

Two hours later, Morton was back in the police station after taking Billy into the scrub. He picked up the phone and rang Jordan who had pulled into a service station.

'Found a kilo at Foster's place. He tried to hang it all on Billy but Billy gave him up. He even mentioned helping Foster dispose of a body in the scrub, a kid named Ackland.'

'That'll be my missing lad,' said Jordan

'I reckon,' said Morton. 'I talked to Winston Bailey and he gave me the background.'

'I'll go see his parents when I get back,' said Jordan.

'By the way Jordan, Bailey seems a bit concerned you might do something stupid in Surfers ... the name Hapsfield was mentioned.'

Jordan gave a brief laugh. 'Winston is a born worrier, Dan.'

'Right, so call him and put his mind at rest ... I guess you got his number.'

'Will do, and thanks again, Dan. I'll keep in touch.'

Morton replaced the phone, stared at it and smiled. From what he'd learnt about Jordan, the idea of him not chasing up Hapsfield just didn't fit.

Jordan folded his mobile and put it on the seat beside him. 'Do something stupid ... ha!' he mumbled as he restarted the wagon and drove off.

Chapter 19

n a coffee shop across the road from the bus depot in Surfers Paradise, Jordan and Bailey were sitting at a table with empty cups in front of them.

Jordan looked at his watch. 'Should be here shortly.'

No sooner had he finished talking than a bus arrived.

'This is it,' said Bailey. 'Now remember, Harris, you're here under sufferance and I had to do a lot of explaining to allow you in on this.'

Jordan was irate. 'Bullshit, Winston! I turned up the shipment and the connection to Hapsfield. I've a right to be here.'

'You seem to forget you're not in the job and you have no rights,' said Bailey angrily. 'So, once again, it's my arse on the line.'

'Jesus, you're an old woman!' retorted Jordan.

Bailey widened his eyes and shook his head in desperation. They watched as passengers disembarked the bus and the driver opened the storage compartment and removed the luggage.

'That's the cases,' said Jordan as the driver carried the cases into the bus depot.

Bailey and Jordan watched as other passengers boarded the bus. Shortly after, the driver got back in and the bus departed.

In the coffee shop, Jordan was frustrated by the lack of action. 'An hour, it's been a bloody hour!'

'Patience has never been a virtue of yours, has it, Harris?' said Bailey.

'Yeah, yeah! Those cases should have been picked up by now.'

'Relax, for Christ's sake,' said Bailey. 'I'll get us another cup of coffee.' He got up from the table and went to the counter.

Jordan got up and held his stomach. 'Okay, but I need to pee … be right back.' He sauntered off to the toilets.

Jordan took a look across the road and saw a man leave the bus depot carrying the cases and immediately forgot about the toilet. He tried to catch Bailey's eye at the counter, but a number of other customers blocked his view. As the man disappeared among holidaymakers, Jordan hurried out of the coffee shop and across the road. He pushed his way through the holiday makers in an effort to catch up with the man with the cases while occasionally glancing behind to see if Bailey was following.

Jordan watched the man enter the Surf City high rise building. *I bloody knew it, that's Hapsfield's building.*

He waited a moment before going in. He looked at the lift floor indication sign and saw that the lift had gone all the way up to the penthouse unit. He pressed the button to bring the lift back down, got in and pressed the penthouse floor button.

On arrival at the penthouse floor, he cautiously looked out. Seeing no one, he went to the unit door from which muffled voices could be heard. To try to hear better, he pressed his ear to the door.

A slight click from behind made him turn his head.

A man had a gun pointed at him. 'Can I help you, pal?' he said with a smile.

Jordan stammered. 'I … I … think I'm on the wrong floor … sorry.'

'Really?' said the man as he knocked on the door.

Jordan started to back away. 'I'll be off then.'

The man raised a hand and shook his head as the door opened. 'This bloke reckons he's lost,' he said to the person who had opened the door. He gave Jordan a push and ushered him inside.

Inside the unit, Hapsfield and two more men stood by a table with the two opened cases on it revealing bags of white powder. One of the men shook a glass vial, studied it and nodded at Hapsfield.

Hapsfield looked at the approaching Jordan and smiled. 'Well, well. This is an unexpected pleasure.'

'Reckons he was lost, Happy,' said the man with the gun.

'Oh, this guy's not lost,' said Hapsfield. 'Though it may be a good idea to help him do just that.'

Jordan pointed at the cases. 'Nice little haul you got there, Hapsfield, should be enough to ruin a lot of lives.'

'What's your friggin' beef, Jordan?' said Hapsfield angrily. 'All I'm doin' is meeting a demand and what people do with it is their problem not mine.'

'Yeah, you're a real helper. Just like you helped my sister and your mate Ackland.'

Hapsfield was startled by the name Ackland and he stared at Jordan for a moment. 'Umm ... you have been busy,' he said quietly. 'Well now, young Phil was just plain stupid. He developed too much of a liking for what he was selling and then got smart with Dougie Foster; a big mistake that was.'

He sighed and smiled. 'And Fiona, aah! ... poor Fiona, now that was a real pity. She had a great body and was really great in ...'

Before he could speak further, Jordan, with hate and anguish welling up inside, launched himself at Hapsfield, but a couple of men grabbed him before he could get near.

'This is quality, Happy,' said the man who had been studying the vial.

'Good!' said Hapsfield sharply. 'Bag it and get out.'

'I'll get you, Hapsfield,' said Jordan as he struggled to free himself.

'Oh, shut it!' said Hapsfield with disdain. He studied Jordan and smiled. 'Reckon you should try this new batch out for us. Put him in the chair, boys.'

Jordan continued to struggle as he was forced into a chair. Hapsfield picked up a syringe and filled it from the vial.

Jordan grimaced. 'I'll get you, Hapsfield ... so help me, I'll get you.'

Hapsfield finished filling the syringe. 'Yeah, yeah, after a taste of this you'll be past caring. Oh dear! I think I've put a little too much in here!' he said with feigned concern. 'Never mind, it seems like overdosing runs in the family.' He laughed and grabbed Jordan's arm.

'You'll never get away with it, you bastard, the Feds are right behind me,' said Jordan through gritted teeth.

'You watch too much tellie, pal,' said one of the men holding on to Jordan.

Hapsfield laughed and the men all joined in.

A crash made Hapsfield stop in his tracks and turn to look towards the unit's door as Bailey and three Federal Police rushed forward with guns drawn.

'Federal Police, no one move!' shouted Bailey.

Hapsfield and his men froze, still and silent.

'You took your time,' said a much relieved Jordan.

'Shut up, Harris!' said Bailey angrily as he kept his eyes on the others. 'Okay you lot, hands up, all where I can see 'em.'

Slowly, Hapsfield and his men raised their hands. One of the men packing the powder suddenly flung his hand sideways and the room was filled with a white cloud. A gunshot followed and one of the officers yelled.

More gunshots echoed in the room as men dived for cover. The powder settled and visibility returned. The room was a mess. Windows had been shattered, the table upturned and the cases on the floor. Everything was covered with a fine layer of white powder.

Two of Hapsfield's men lay on the floor, unmoving, with blood spreading around them.

Another stood still with his hands in the air. An officer groaned and sat up, holding his shoulder.

Jordan poked his head around from behind a couch as Bailey and the other two officers stood from their crouching positions.

'Shit!' said Jordan as he looked around.

'Messy, eh?' said Bailey.

Jordan surveyed the room. 'Where's Hapsfield?' He looked up at the sound of an engine gathering revs. 'The roof!' he shouted.

Bailey pointed to a door at the back of the room. 'Over there!'

Jordan raced to the doorway and up a flight of steps and out to the roof where a small two-seater helicopter was standing.

'Of all the!' said Jordan as Bailey rushed out and bumped into him.

The helicopter started to take off with Hapsfield grinning and waving.

Jordan snarled and ran towards the helicopter.

'Harris, no!' shouted Bailey, as with the helicopter a metre off the roof Jordan leapt out and grabbed the side as it swung away.

Bailey watched, angry and exasperated, as Jordan pulled himself into the helicopter.

Inside the confined space of the helicopter, Jordan grappled with Hapsfield. Arms and legs continually collided with the pilot as he concentrated on maintaining the 'copter on an even course, but he was having little luck in doing so as it lurched from side to side.

The pilot let out a strangled yell that momentarily stopped the struggle between Jordan and Hapsfield. They both looked out and realised that the 'copter was about to plunge into the sea.

From the roof top of the Surf City high rise, Bailey watched the helicopter go down, then turned away and ran to the rooftop exit door.

Chapter 20

On the Surfers Paradise shoreline, beachgoers gathered at the water's edge as lifeguards dragged two "rubber ducks" into the sea and headed out to the helicopter.

The first lifeguards to arrive at the scene pulled the pilot, who was holding on to the side of the helicopter, into their rubber duck.

Jordan however, was doing his best to push Hapsfield's head under water, and the lifeguards in the other rubber duck had a struggle on their hands to wrench them apart.

At last, Jordan and a spluttering Hapsfield were separated, pulled into the duck, and taken to the beach just as two police cars with sirens blaring arrived.

Bailey and two officers ran down the beach. 'Take them in, boys,' said Bailey as he pointed at the pilot and Hapsfield.

As the officers neared the duck, Jordan grabbed an oar from the side of the duck and swung it at Hapsfield. Luckily for Hapsfield, he saw it coming and rolled sideways. The oar smashed into the duck's outboard motor and splintered the end. Holding it like a spear, Jordan pushed the now jagged, pointed end at Hapsfeild's throat. Hapsfield cowered on the duck's floor, sucking in air.

Bailey shouted urgently, 'Harris, don't!'

Beachgoers, lifeguards and the officers fell silent ... expectant.

Jordan stared fiercely down at Hapsfield, his breath coming in short gasps. Images of Fiona in the morgue flashed through his mind. 'Because of you Fiona and Ackland are both dead. You're a killer, Hapsfield.' He pushed the splintered end of the oar harder against Hapsfield's throat.

Hapsfield sneered. 'Go ahead! Then what'll *you* be?'

Jordan paused, his mind in turmoil. Slowly, he backed off and threw the oar onto the sand.

The watching crowd uttered a combined gasp of relieved tension.

Bailey walked up to the duck and looked down at Hapsfield. 'On your feet.'

Hapsfield stood, coughed and spat.

'Nasty cough you have, Happy,' said Bailey.

Hapsfield coughed again. 'Get fucked!'

Jordan suddenly swivelled around and threw a punch that caught Hapsfield square in the face and catapulted him back over the side of the duck. The crowd broke into applause. The officers lifted Hapsfield from the sand and placed handcuffs on him. With blood pouring from his flattened nose, he was taken away.

'Feel better now?' said Bailey.

Jordan rubbed his knuckles. 'Somewhat. I should have stuck it in him when I had the chance.'

Bailey shook his head. 'Then I would have to put both of you away, and if you ever stuff me around like this again I bloody well will.'

'May have been worth it,' said Jordan.

Bailey placed a hand on Jordan's shoulder. 'Hapsfield will be a grey old man by the time he gets out, and you, you silly bastard, I should arrest you for endangering lives including your own. I mean jumping onto that 'copter, of all the dumbarse ...!'

Jordan managed a grin. 'Yeah, I know, sorry mate, it just seemed a good idea at the time.'

'Come on, let's get out of here,' said Bailey. He slapped Jordan on the shoulder. 'I just can't wait for us to get started on the paperwork.'

'Paperwork, us?' said Jordan

'Yeah, paperwork, you and me!'

'Now?' said Jordan without enthusiasm.

'No time like the present, Harris,' said Bailey cheerfully as he slapped Jordan on the shoulder again.

Chapter 21

n a Melbourne suburb, Jordan pulled his wagon to a stop outside a neat weatherboard. The garden was well kept with flowers starting to bloom on a fine, clear spring morning.

Clean-shaven and hair neatly styled, wearing well-pressed slacks, jacket and tie, he looked a vastly different person from the man who left Melbourne a couple of months previous.

He walked up the pathway to the front door and knocked.

Mrs Ackland opened the door and smiled. 'Oh, Mr Jordan, please come in.'

She ushered Jordan into her bright lounge room.

'Thank you, Mrs Ackland,' said Jordan. He stood still in the room and looked around.

Mrs Ackland gestured to a chair. 'Please sit down, my husband John is out playing bowls ... Would you like a cup of tea?'

'No, thank you,' said Jordan.

Mrs Ackland sat on a chair facing Jordan. She could see that Jordan felt uncomfortable.

'Phillip's dead, isn't he?' she said.

Jordan sighed. 'I'm afraid so, Mrs Ackland.'

'Please tell me what happened to him.'

Jordan took a while to find the right words. 'The Townsville Police will contact you very soon and they'll inform you of all the details.'

Mrs Ackland leant forward and put her hand on Jordan's knee. 'But I'm sure you know most of it, don't you?'

'Your son was involved with some bad company, Mrs Ackland,'

he said softly, 'and they have been arrested.'

'Was it drugs?'

Jordan nodded. 'I'm afraid so.' He stopped again, took a deep breath and swallowed before continuing. 'But I have to tell you that it wasn't from an overdose that he died … it was, ah, one of the men that supplied him that was responsible.'

Mrs Ackland put her hands to her face. 'He was murdered?'

Jordan nodded. 'Yes, but as I said, the man responsible is now in custody and will pay the full penalty.'

Tears started to flow down Mrs Ackland's cheeks.

Jordan shifted uncomfortably in his chair. 'I know it's easy to say but you have to move on, Mrs Ackland.' He stopped for another deep breath and swallowed. 'You see, my sister also died as a result of drugs so I do have an idea of the pain you feel.'

Mrs Ackland reached for a handkerchief and wiped her face. 'You too?'

'Yes, and one of those responsible for what happened to your son was also involved in the death of my sister.'

Mrs Ackland rose from her chair and went to Jordan who also stood. She put her arms around Jordan and hugged him. Silently, they held each other until Jordan stepped back.

'I'd better be going, Mrs Ackland,' he said quietly as he choked back his own tears.

Mrs Ackland managed a smile. 'Thank you for coming to see me, it's much more personal than a phone call.'

'I'm so very sorry about your son,' said Jordan.

Mrs Ackland straightened her shoulders. 'Well, as you said, at least now we know what happened and we can get on with our lives without all the wondering.' She reached up and touched Jordan on the cheek. 'Now, you take care of yourself.'

Jordan smiled. 'I'll certainly try.'

Mrs Ackland waited by the front door as Jordan walked down the pathway and out to his wagon and got in.

Jordan started the motor and turned and gave Mrs Ackland a final wave before driving away. He took a deep breath and sighed as he attempted to bring his emotions under control.

A hand gently brushed his cheek as he drove up the tree-lined street.

'You okay?' said Linda.

Jordan smiled. 'Sure, fine. Come on, let's go surprise my folks.'

'I know I'll just love your parents if they're like you!' said Linda excitedly. 'And a house in the country, oh Harris, it sounds so quaint.'

Jordan laughed. 'Yes, well, maybe I haven't quite painted the right picture.'

Linda moved across the front bench seat of the wagon and cuddled up to Jordan. 'I think I love you, Harris.'

The wagon swerved slightly.

'Sorry, does that hurt?' asked Linda.

Jordan brought the wagon to a stop under a large eucalypt. 'Oh, the pain ... the pain,' he murmured.

Interlude

Bailey stood up. 'You ready for another, Steve?'

'Oh yes, thank you, sir,' said Carmichael. He picked up his glass and quickly finished the beer before handing the empty glass to Bailey. He had been so absorbed with Bailey's story that he hadn't touched a drop during the telling.

Before Bailey could sit down after returning with refilled glasses, Carmichael was asking questions. 'So, after being dismissed from the Academy, how did he get back into the force, and how the devil did he survive the helicopter crash and what happened to the girl Linda that he had fallen for?'

Bailey smiled. 'Yeah, he sure was lucky to swim away from the crash and I thank goodness I managed to stop him from spearing Hapsfield with the paddle or his future would have taken a completely different turn.'

'And getting back into the force?'

'That was my doing. I managed to convince the powers that be that after the job he'd done in solving a murder, and discovering and putting an end to the importation of a large quantity of drugs, the reason for his original dismissal should be further investigated and overturned. Fortunately, one of the officers at his hearing who hadn't agreed with his dismissal had been promoted to a more senior position and was quick to reverse the decision and accept Harris back into the force.'

'And Linda?'

'They married and had a couple of kids.'

'Married ... kids!' exclaimed Carmichael. 'Wow, never knew that

… but where are they now?'

'Where indeed,' said Bailey. 'As you will find out if you stick in this business for any length of time, it's a job that has considerable impact on relationships and not everyone has the strength to survive.'

'I haven't heard anything about his parents,' said Carmichael.

Bailey shook his head. 'Both passed away I'm afraid. His father, as you may remember, was a bit of a goer at making a fast dollar but took one risk too many and came away completely broke. The bank fore-closed on his property so had nowhere to live. Harris got them a unit in a retirement village. Living like that proved too much for his father and he went downhill fast; had a stroke and died just six months later. His mother lasted another five years before suffering the same fate.

'Must have been tough on Harris, losing both parents so quick,' said Carmichael.

Bailey nodded. 'Yeah, just one of the rough patches he's had to deal with.'

'So, how did Harris get on back in the job?'

'Damn well, actually,' said Bailey. 'He was transferred to detective duties after five years.'

'Did he have any major crime solving during that time?' asked Carmichael.

Bailey was quiet as he thought for a minute. 'There is one that springs to mind.'

PART 2:
JUDGEMENT

Chapter 1

'Now that was a great bargain,' said Madelaine Hargraves as she pointed to the bags that her husband John was carrying.

John laughed. 'Well, if you reckon spending four hundred dollars on a pair of pants and a T-shirt is cheap, then I guess it was.'

Madelaine, tall and slim, was wearing white slacks, a pale blue silk blouse and low-heeled, comfortable white shoes. John wore jeans and a white polo neck shirt with the local yacht club's emblem on the breast pocket.

The clothes shop they had just walked out of bore the name Janelle's emblazoned in bright blue lettering across the front window, and was regarded as one of the premier clothes stores in the local area.

Aged in their early forties, the Hargraves smiled and chatted amicably as they walked the short distance along the street to where a white, late model Mercedes was parked.

John glanced at his watch. 'Time for a quick coffee down by the bay before we head home, Madelaine?'

'That'd be great, love,' she replied as she flicked her long, blonde hair away from her eyes.

John took the car keys out of his trouser pocket and activated the vehicle's automatic locking function. He opened the boot, placed the bags inside and closed it. He was about to open the front nearside door to allow Madelaine to get in when they were approached by two men in dark suits.

'Mr and Mrs Hargraves?' asked the larger of the two.

John and Madelaine turned to look at the newcomers.

'And you are?' inquired John.

'I'm Detective Albright,' said one of the men, briefly flashing an identification badge. He inclined his head towards the other man. 'And this is Detective Morrison.'

'What do you want?' asked Madelaine with concern. 'Is anything wrong?'

'At this point, I'm afraid I can't say ma'am,' replied Albright, 'but I'd appreciate it if you would be so good as to come along with us.'

'Now just a minute, Detective, what is this?' asked John. 'Do you know who I am?'

Albright nodded. 'Yes, sir, indeed I do, but it is important, sir. We wouldn't be here otherwise.'

'So, what's so damn important that you stop us in the middle of the street like this?' asked John aggressively. 'Tell me what this is all about or go away.'

Albright waited a moment before glancing at Morrison who gave a nod. 'It concerns your children, sir,' he said quietly.

Madelaine was immediately alarmed. 'The children!?'

John's manner also instantly changed. 'Tim and Amanda are at summer camp. They come home this afternoon. My God, are they alright? What's happened? Please tell me!'

Albright raised his hands as if in surrender. 'Please, folks, come with us; our car is just across the street.' He turned and walked away with Morrison following. The Hargraves rushed after them.

'Wait, oh please wait, we're coming!' said Madelaine. She turned to her husband. 'What can have happened, John?'

John had lost his bluster; his face reddened and showing concern as he approached the car of Albright and Morrison.

Morrison got in the driver's seat, while Albright had opened the rear doors and stood by them beckoning.

'Please folks, get in.' Albright placed his hand on Madelaine's head as she bent to get in. 'Please mind your head, Mrs Hargraves.'

John followed and Albright closed the door behind him, then

got into the passenger front seat as Morison started the motor and eased the car out into the traffic.

In the rear seat, Madelaine was becoming frantic. She grasped John's arm tightly as tears started to flow. 'Please officers ... my children ... what has happened?'

Morrison kept silent and continued driving. Albright turned his head slightly. 'We'll be there soon, Mrs Hargraves, but I'm afraid I'm not able to say anything until my superior talks to you.'

Albright turned his head back to face the front, while Madelaine, now sobbing uncontrollably, clung to her serious and silent husband. The car left the business district and headed into an industrial area containing abandoned warehouses.

Morrison stopped the car and got out. Albright and the Hargraves quickly followed. The area was completely deserted while in the distance could be heard the faint sound of a passing train. Albright and Morrison walked to a warehouse door and pushed it open with the Hargraves following.

Chapter 2

On entering the warehouse Albright walked on ahead into the murky interior. Morrison stood just inside the door as the Hargraves entered. John Hargraves strode after Albright while Madelaine waited to allow her eyes to adjust to the gloomy starkness of the interior after leaving the direct sunlight.

'My children, what about my children?' shouted John Hargraves to Albright who was still walking away.

Albright stopped, turned to look at John and smiled while putting on a pair of black leather gloves.

John halted abruptly, stared at Albright and frowned. 'What the hell!?'

A scuffling sound from behind prompted him to turn around. Morrison had one gloved hand around Madelaine's mouth, and in the other, held a pistol to her forehead.

John was completely perplexed at the scene. He turned back to Albright. 'Jesus Christ, what's going on here!?'

Albright motioned to a table and two chairs. 'Please sit down, Mr and Mrs Hargraves,' he said quietly and calmly.

John glanced back at Madelaine and Morrison, and reluctantly went to one of the chairs and sat down. On the table before him was a roll of grey tape and a small box. Albright picked up the tape and bound John to the chair.

'I don't understand,' said John staring at Albright. 'Why are you doing this?'

Albright tested his handiwork and looked towards Morrison. 'Okay, Sol, bring her up.'

Morrison took his hand away from Madelaine's mouth and she released a mournful sob.

'John, John, what is this? Where are the children?'

Albright pointed to the other chair. 'Please take a seat, Mrs Hargraves, and I'll explain.'

Madelaine sat in the chair and looked inquiringly at John, then at Albright and Morrison.

Albright took out a packet of cigarettes. Casually lit one and exhaled as he walked to the front of the table and smiled at John. 'Mr Hargraves, may I call you John? Please tell me the security code for your house alarm, the position of your safe and its entry code.'

John stared at Albright in silence as his jaw dropped and his eyes widened.

'Would you like me to repeat that, John?' asked Albright.

John's face flushed bright red. 'Go to hell!' he said angrily.

Morrison came forward and placed his pistol against John's head.

Madelaine yelled in terror. 'No, no, please don't.' She looked at John. 'Tell them what they want to know please, John, I beg you. Please.'

John's face stiffened as he stared at Albright. 'You must think I'm stupid,' he said through gritted teeth. 'Kill me and you'll never know.'

Albright smiled. 'Ah! I kinda figured that a hardarse like you may not want to cooperate.' He turned to Morrison. 'Sol, if you wouldn't mind.'

Morrison went to the table and opened the box from which he extracted a hypodermic syringe. Roughly, he grabbed hold of Madelaine's arm and injected her. Madelaine screamed and rubbed her arm where the needle had entered.

'You bastards!' shouted John. 'What have you given her?'

'Just something to help calm her nerves, John,' said Albright.

In less than a minute, Madelaine was sitting quietly in her chair with a slight smile on her face. She started to hum a tune with her eyes closed and appeared completely unperturbed.

John stared at his wife wide-eyed, slowly shaking his head but remaining silent. Perspiration dribbled down his forehead and drips fell off his nose.

Albright shrugged his shoulders. 'Seems John still doesn't want to talk to us, Sol; I think it's time for phase two.'

Morrison reached inside the box on the table and from it removed an electric mincer. He carried the electric cord to the back of Madelaine's chair and plugged it into a power cord that extended away to a switch on the warehouse wall. He flicked the switch and the mincer started to whine.

Albright went to Madelaine's side and whispered into her ear. 'How are you, my dear?'

'Umm ... fine ... fine ... isn't it lovely here.' She swayed gently in her chair, eyes glazed, not completely focusing.

'I have a surprise for you, Madelaine,' said Albright.

'Oh lovely ... I love surprises.' She smiled and continued swaying as if to music.

'It's a beautiful toy that will make you tingle with pleasure,' said Albright.

John seemed to suddenly understand what was about to happen. 'You wouldn't ... you couldn't ... good God man, it's inhuman!'

Albright ignored John and continued talking quietly and soothingly to Madelaine. 'The toy is on the table; see if you can find out how it works.'

'Okey dokey,' said Madelaine. She leant forward and touched the mincer. 'It's trembling just like my vibrator.' She giggled as her hands gently fondled the mincer.

John's mouth trembled as he cried out. 'Madelaine leave it alone, please, please.'

Madelaine giggled some more then slipped her right hand inside the mincer. 'Oh it tickles,' she said, and continued giggling as the mincer blades removed her fingers. She pushed forward and the mincer chewed off her hand. Blood and mulch spewed out onto the table. Morrison pulled her back into her chair where she sat grinning, and swaying as blood spurted from the stump of her forearm and unplugged the mincer.

John's face had gone ashen. His shirt soaked with sweat; he gagged and vomited onto his lap.

'The security code is 7594 … the safe is behind the painting in my study.' He paused gasping for breath. 'Its entry code is 4 left, 7 right, 2 left, 5 right … oh Christ … no more please … no more.'

He began to sob as Albright removed a pen and small notepad from his jacket pocket and wrote down the numbers. 'Thank you, John. Thank you very much.' He recited back the numbers he had written down. 'Security code is 7594, entry code 4 left, 7 right, 2 left, 5 right; is that right, John?'

'Yes. Yes,' said John. 'Now please let me loose so I can take my wife to hospital.'

'All in good time, John. Sol is going to go to your home and check out what you have just said and when he returns you'll be free to go.' He handed the notebook to Sol who left the warehouse.

John slumped forward in his chair quietly sobbing while Madelaine, feeling no pain and completely oblivious to all around, her continued swaying to the music only she could hear. The pool of blood under her chair grew ever wider as it pulsed from her mangled arm.

Albright glanced at his watch and smiled at John. 'Shouldn't be too long, John; you just relax.' He patted John on the shoulder, lit another cigarette and slowly walked around the warehouse.

Tears ran freely down John's cheeks as he watched Madelaine sway and hum, completely lost in her own world.

Half an hour passed before the warehouse door opened and Morrison re-entered.

'Alright, Sol?' asked Albright.

'About two hundred grand,' replied Morrison.

Albright smiled. 'Good! Well John, thank you very much, now all we have to do is finish up here.'

'Oh, thank God!' gasped John. 'Let me get Madelaine to the hospital,' he pleaded.

'I'm afraid, John, I can't let you do that,' said Albright shaking his head. 'You see you might be tempted to tell someone about us, and then ... well!'

He spread his hands and went to Madelaine. 'Madelaine, it's time to play again. Why don't you try putting your toes in the tickly machine?' He lifted the mincer from the table and placed it by her foot.

Madelaine leant forward smiling. 'Oh yes, can I?' she giggled. 'I love that machine.'

John frantically strained at the tape holding him to the chair. 'No ... No ... Oh Jesus ... No! I won't talk; honest. I give you my word.'

Madelaine eased off her shoes, and put her left foot into the mincer as Morrison plugged the cord back in. Pieces of meat, bone and blood oozed forth. Madelaine laughed loudly. 'It tickles!'

Her left foot was soon chewed to the ankle. Her white slacks splashed with blotches of red. She removed her left leg and placed her right foot in the mincer.

John screamed as he watched, unable to look away from the horror taking place beside him, the veins on his forehead almost bursting.

Morrison walked behind John and placed a wire over his head and around his neck. As he tightened it the screaming stopped. John shuddered violently before becoming still, eyes wide, unseeing.

Madelaine continued to sway and hum as the pool of blood under her widened further.

Morrison removed the wire from John's neck, wiped it on John's sweat-soaked shirt, put it in his coat pocket and disconnected the power from the mincer.

Albright turned to look to the blackness at the rear of the warehouse and raised his hand in acknowledgement as footsteps approached.

Albright and Morrison, together with the individual who had watched proceedings from the rear of the warehouse, exited the building, got into their vehicle and drove away.

At the rear of the group of warehouses was a disused industrial dumpster. A hand appeared over the side and then a head wearing a ragged beanie slowly appeared. The face was bearded, the hair long and unkempt. The eyes blinked in the harsh midday sunlight as they watched a car drive away from the complex.

Chapter 3

nside the police squad room, Detective Harris Jordan, now in his late thirties, wearing a sports jacket and light grey pants, poured himself a cup of coffee. He sipped it, pulled a face and emptied it into the sink. 'Jesus! Where did you get this crap, Meares?'

Meares, seated at a desk thumbing through paperwork with his jacket hung over the back of the chair, didn't particularly appreciate the remark. 'If you can do better go for it.'

He loosened his tie and sniffed while rubbing his nose with the back of his hand. 'Arsehole!' he mumbled.

Jordan stared at Meares. 'Like I said, crap; your brains must have leaked into the pot.'

A nearby officer stifled a laugh as Meares, red in the face, started to rise from his seat. A loud voice bellowed out Harris's name, and he turned to see Sergeant Winston Bailey beckoning him. Harris blew Meares a kiss and went to Bailey.

Bailey ushered Jordan into his office.

'Why don't you lay off Meares?' He closed the door of the office behind Jordan. 'I know he's a pain in the arse … but … well.'

Jordan shrugged. 'Hell, Winston, gotta do something to liven the place up; stops me from getting bored.'

Bailey shook his head and wandered to the back of his desk, picked up a scrap of paper and handed it to Jordan. 'There's something to keep you occupied. That's the address of one John Hargraves, merchant and investment banker who is considering running for mayor next election.'

Jordan frowned. 'What's his problem? Need someone to hand

out "vote for me" stickers?'

'Not quite,' replied Bailey. 'His kids came home from summer camp late this morning, went in the house and guess what? No parents and the safe's been done over.'

'Anybody talk to the kids?' asked Jordan.

Bailey nodded. 'Briefly: couple of guys from the bayside there now. Apparently, the front door was unlocked and the security turned off, so go take over.'

Jordan glanced at the address on the piece of paper he had been given. 'You sure I'll be alright in this jacket, or should I go change into my uptown gear?'

Bailey pointed to the door. 'Out! And take Yates with you.'

'Oh shit, Winston, get someone else to babysit.'

'Do it, Harris. Show what a smartarse detective can do.' He pointed again. 'Out!'

Jordan grimaced and walked out of the office without bothering to close the door behind him. 'Grumpy old goat,' he mumbled.

'I heard that!' shouted Bailey.

'Yates! With me!' said Jordan as he strode through the squad room.

A young woman, early twenties, short dark hair and wearing black slacks, stopped placing papers into a filing cabinet, grabbed a dark grey coat from the back of a nearby chair and hurried after him. Yates was the product of a broken home, but after being put up for adoption had fallen into the caring hands of Julie and Colin Yates. They had encouraged and helped her in all she had done during her formative years and as a result of that love and affection she had decided to take on their surname. Her acceptance into the police force had made Julie and Colin very proud of their adopted daughter.

As Jordan passed a scowling Meares, he gave him a wink.

Yates was trying hard to catch up to Jordan but her coat kept getting caught in her gun holster.

'Come on, Yates, haven't got all day,' said Jordan.

'I'm here, I'm here!' said Yates from close behind.

During the walk to Jordan's car at the rear of the station, Yates at last managed to get her coat on as she sat in the passenger side. 'Where to, sir?' she asked as she adjusted her seatbelt.

'Posh end of town, so watch your language,' replied Jordan as he started the car.

Soon, they were weaving their way through busy city traffic.

'Felicity, isn't it?' asked Jordan.

'Yes, sir,' replied Yates, 'but I'd prefer it if you called me Yates.'

'Whatever suits you,' said Jordan, 'and you can cut out the sir and just call me Harris. This your first outing?'

'Yes, sir ... sorry ... I mean, Harris.'

'Heard you did well on the range.'

Yates nodded. 'Yeah ... reasonable.'

'No need to be modest, Yates.'

Yates smiled. 'Well actually, top of my class.'

Jordan grinned. 'Then again you don't have to be a smartarse either.'

'Now listen,' said Yates, becoming irate.

Jordan raised a hand and smiled. 'Easy ... easy, one of these days you'll have to point that thing at a live target. Gonna be up to it?'

'It's crossed my mind,' replied Yates seriously.

'Try not to think about it too much or you'll likely freeze,' said Jordan. 'I've seen it happen. Best to let your instincts take over. If you're with me and someone is considering making a hole in me, I'd prefer it if you just blew that person away and thought about it afterwards. Okay?'

Yates shrugged. 'Okay, sir, ah sorry, Harris.'

Chapter 4

As they drove away from the city, they entered a quiet, lushly vegetated area.

'Welcome to the address of the financially advantaged,' said Jordan as they arrived at an open iron gateway supported by brick pillars. The number 57 was emblazoned upon the right-side pillar.

They entered and drove up a long driveway to an imposing two-storey brick home, outside which a police car and two unmarked cars were parked. A uniformed police officer stood at the front door. Jordan parked the car, and he and Yates walked up the steps to the front of the house.

Jordan greeted the officer at the door. 'Hi, Neill. Who's on?'

'Hi, Harris. Two of your favourites.' He grinned. 'Spurway and Roberts, they're inside with the kids.'

Jordan scowled. 'Jesus! Don and Olly!'

Neill laughed.

Yates looked at Jordan. 'Did you say Don and Olly?'

'Yeah!' said Jordan as he strode on inside the house.

The entrance was large with a spiral staircase at one side leading up to the next level. Yates took in the obvious opulence as they proceeded through into the extravagant reception area. At the far end of the room, Detectives Spurway and Roberts stood talking to the Hargraves' children Tim and Amanda, who were sitting on a couch with an elderly man standing beside them.

Spurway was short and slim with spiky hair; Roberts was heavy-set, round face and balding, with a small moustache.

Yates looked at them, trying hard to stifle a laugh, then at

Jordan who raised his eyebrows. As they approached the group, the conversation stopped. The children, sad-faced, looked at the newcomers.

'Good afternoon, Detectives Spurway and Roberts,' said Jordan. 'Bailey sent me and Yates here to take over.' He nodded towards Yates.

From the scowls that appeared on Spurway and Roberts's faces the information obviously didn't sit well.

'Thank you for staying with the children till we arrived,' continued Jordan. 'Now, if you'd be good enough to put any relevant information you have obtained on paper and forward it to my office, I'd appreciate it.' He pointed to the door. 'So, if you'll excuse us.'

Yates stood quiet, mouth open, eyes going from Jordan to Spurway and Roberts.

With anger written all over their faces, Spurway and Roberts slowly started to leave.

'Up yours, Jordan,' murmured Spurway as he passed.

Jordan ignored the remark and spoke to the elderly gentleman while offering his hand. 'I'm Detective Jordan and this is Detective Yates. Who are you, sir?

'My name is William Hargraves and I'm the children's grandfather.'

'Will it be okay to speak to the children, sir?'

'Certainly, Detective, but they have already spoken to the two detectives who just left.'

'I appreciate that, sir, but I would like you to go over it again so we'—he gestured to Yates—'can get a clear picture in our minds of what has happened, okay?'

He pulled a chair to in front of Tim, aged thirteen, and Amanda, eleven, and sat facing them. 'Now, I'm sure that you've already explained a lot to those other guys,' he said quietly, 'but can you tell me exactly what happened when you came home?'

'About midday wasn't it, Amanda?' said Tim. He glanced at

Amanda and she nodded. 'If Mum and Dad are ever out, they always leave a note, but there was nothing.' He paused and swallowed before continuing. 'Usually they are here when we come home after being away. At least Mum is. Dad too if he's not working, but today ... nothing!'

Tim shook his head, confused, and Amanda grabbed hold of his hand and held it tightly.

'And the front door was open?' asked Jordan.

'Yes, well not wide open, but it wasn't locked and the alarm had been turned off.'

'It's just not like them to go out and leave the front door unlocked and the alarm off,' interrupted Amanda. 'It's just not like them.'

Amanda started to sob, and Tim placed a comforting arm around her.

Yates looked up from her notepad, concern for the children's distress etched on her face.

'And then what?' said Jordan. 'After you came in, what did you do?'

'We shouted for Mum and Dad,' continued Tim, 'but there was no answer so we went looking for them. I went in through the kitchen and out back into the garden, and Amanda ran upstairs.'

'You saw no one?'

'No, and after the garden, I came back in and looked in the study. That's when I saw Dad's safe was open, so I rang Pop.'

'Can you show me the safe, Tim?' asked Jordan.

'Sure!'

Tim stood up from the couch, and holding Amanda's hand, headed for the study with Jordan, Yates and William Hargraves following.

On reaching the study, Tim went to the safe and was about to put his hand on the safe door when Jordan raised his voice. 'Wait, Tim, please don't touch anything.'

Tim backed away.

'Who knew the combination, Tim?'

'Just Dad, he said it was safer that way.'

'And what kind of car does your Dad drive, Tim?'

'It's a white Merc.'

'Can you remember the number?'

'Yes, it's JH 1.'

Jordan looked at Yates. 'Get forensics over and APB the Merc.'

Yates took out her mobile, waited a moment then relayed Jordan's instructions.

'Could you both stay with your grandfather while we get this sorted?' asked Jordan.

'Yes, that will be fine. I live just a short distance away,' said William Hargraves.

'Okay. Tim, you and Amanda grab a few things you might need and go to your grandfather's place while we sort this out, okay?'

Tim nodded silently and, still holding Amanda's hand, left the study.

'Go with them, Yates,' said Jordan. 'Keep an eye on them and don't let them touch too much. Just a change of clothes then get them out of here quick as you can before forensics arrive.'

Yates quickly followed the children. Jordan walked to the safe and took a handkerchief from his pocket. Using it as protection around his hand, he eased the safe door back and looked at the door surrounds. Under the door, leaning against the wall, was a painting. He bent down and studied it. Taking a plastic bag from his jacket pocket, he reached forward and removed a small piece of fluff caught in the picture frame and placed it in the bag. He stood back up and allowed his eyes to roam over the study. A high-backed leather chair sat behind an ornate desk, a computer station in one corner and neatly arranged bookshelves against the wall. His eyes returned to the safe. Inside it was a small wooden box and some papers.

'Any idea what your son kept in the safe, sir?'

'Sorry, Detective, I imagine business papers, and maybe some of Madelaine's jewellery.'

Noise from outside the study alerted them to the fact the children were re-appearing. They walked outside as Tim, Amanda, and Yates came down the stairs. Jordan nodded at Yates, who was carrying a small suitcase, and smiled at the children.

William Hargraves accepted the suitcase from Yates and ushered the children towards the front door. 'You'll keep me informed, Detective?'

Jordan nodded. 'Most definitely, sir.'

Jordan and Yates stood by the front door and watched the children and their grandfather drive away. As their car left, two police cars and a large van arrived. Two men emerged from the van carrying large bags and walked up the steps to the front door.

'Hi, fellas,' said Jordan, 'see what you can find. Looks real clean, no sign of forced entry. The safe in the study is open and again no sign of force that I can see.'

He took the small plastic bag out of his pocket and handed it to one of the men. 'Found this on the frame of the painting that covered the safe.'

The men walked past into the house, and Jordan strolled over to his car. 'Well, what do you make of it, Yates?'

Yates shrugged. 'Strange, from what I know of the Hargraves they're a respectable family. John Hargraves is a very successful banker and I understand considering standing for mayor; he has some powerful friends ready to back him.'

'And the wife?' asked Jordan.

'Helps with a lot of charity work but other than that keeps pretty much to herself. The kids go to private school, no trouble there.' She paused for a moment. 'Why not be there for the kids? Seems out of character, and what was taken from the safe?'

'Right,' said Jordan as he got in the car. 'Hargraves's bank is First City; that's as good a place as any to start.' He glanced at his wristwatch. 'Should make it just before closing.'

Chapter 5

I n the office of the director of First City Bank, Paul Norris, attired in a pinstriped suit, leant back in his leather chair and looked up at Jordan and Yates standing in front of his large wooden desk. 'Disappeared, you say?'

'Yes, sir,' replied Jordan. 'You know any reason they would leave without the kids?'

'Never!' he answered abruptly. 'They would never do that. They adore Tim and Amanda.'

'Any idea what Mr Hargraves kept in his wall safe?'

'Business papers, Madelaine's jewellery, a little cash,' said Norris with a shrug.

'How much cash?'

'Oh, not much, a hundred or so.'

'A hundred dollars?' asked Jordan.

'No, no,' replied Norris shaking his head. 'A hundred thousand.'

Jordan and Yates, who had been taking notes, both sucked in breath.

'And why is he not in today?' asked Jordan.

'He wanted to meet the children coming home from summer camp,' replied Norris.

Yates's mobile rang and she excused herself as she turned away to answer it. 'Great ... thanks.'

She replaced the mobile into her coat pocket. 'We have the Merc,' she said.

Jordan stepped forward and offered his hand to Norris. 'Thank you, sir. We'll keep in touch.'

Norris slowly sank back into his chair, and watched Jordan and Yates leave the office.

'Where is it?' asked Jordan, as they hurriedly walked out of the bank.

'Corner Thomson and Lawrence,' she replied.

Jordan pulled up behind a police car that had its blue lights flashing.

An officer stood by a white Merc. 'That it, James?' asked Jordan.

'Yeah, Harris, it's not locked.'

'You looked in?'

'No, just tried the door is all.'

After putting on a pair of surgical gloves, Jordan opened the car door, leant in, checked the glove box and pulled the boot release.

Yates looked into the boot. 'Couple of bags in here, Harris.' She peered closer to read the labels on the bags. 'Come from Janelle's.'

'Just a few shops that way,' said James, pointing up the pavement.

Jordan removed his gloves and replaced them into his jacket pocket. 'I'll leave you with it, James. The boys are on their way?'

'Should be here any minute, Harris.'

As Jordan and Yates headed towards Janelle's, two more police cars and a tow truck arrived at the scene.

On entering Janelle's, they were approached by a young woman wearing a small name tag saying "Rebecca".

'Good afternoon, sir and madam. How may I help you?' she asked with a smile.

'You the owner?' said Jordan.

'No, sir. Mrs Dominic is the owner, but I'm sure I can help you.'

'Is she in?'

Rebecca's smile vanished as Jordan displayed his ID. 'Yes she's …'

The curtains at the rear of the shop parted, and a large, middle-aged woman walked up to them. Wearing a short skirt, heavily made up, with gold trinkets hanging around her neck and wrists, she obviously was intent on not growing old gracefully.

'Detectives Jordan and Yates,' said Jordan as they both displayed their IDs.

'And how may I help you, Detectives?' asked Mrs Dominic.

'I believe the Hargraves were in here yesterday,' said Jordan.

'Yes indeed, wonderful couple,' said Mrs Dominic effusively. 'Mr Hargraves will be running for mayor you know.'

'What time did they leave?'

'Oh, about ten-thirty I would say. Is that right, Rebecca?'

Rebecca nodded in agreement. 'Yes, Mrs Dominic. Mrs Hargraves bought a pair of slacks and a top.'

'When they left did they seem okay, Rebecca?' asked Yates.

'Oh sure, fine. She was looking forward to seeing her children back from summer camp.'

'Is anything wrong?' asked Mrs Dominic with concern.

'Did you see them leave?' asked Jordan.

'No, I said goodbye then went to my office'—she pointed to the back of the shop—'while Rebecca did the paperwork.'

'Well, I processed their credit card and that was it really,' said Rebecca.

Yates had been watching another girl who had kept in the background. 'How about you, miss, did you see them leave?'

The girl was hesitant to answer.

'Speak up, Anna,' said Mrs Dominic sharply.

'I didn't actually see them leave because I was in the window adjusting the display,' said Anna, glancing from Mrs Dominic to Yates. 'But I did notice them get into a car across the road, together with two other gentlemen.'

'That's good, Anna,' said Jordan. 'Now these two men, what did they look like?'

'Oh, just men in suits,' said Anna with indifference. 'One of them held the door open so Mr and Mrs Hargraves could get in. Even held Mrs Hargraves's head so she wouldn't bump it.'

Jordan and Yates exchanged glances.

'So, they got in the car willingly?' said Yates.

'Oh yes. They did seem to be in a bit of a hurry though. Mr and Mrs Hargraves were really hurrying to keep up with them when they crossed the road.'

'The car, Anna,' said Jordan. 'What colour was it?'

'I think it was grey,' replied Anna.

'Make?'

'It was a Ford.'

'You sure of that?'

'Oh yes. My brother has one just like it.'

'I don't suppose you happen to remember its number plate,' said Yates.

'No sorry, but it did have a nasty dent over the rear wheel.'

Jordan smiled. 'You've been a great help, Anna, thanks a lot.' He handed her a card. 'If you remember anything else please give me a call.'

'Thank you also,' he said as he handed cards to Mrs Dominic and Rebecca. 'We'll be on our way.'

Jordan and Yates exited Janelle's and walked, not speaking, the short distance up the street to their car.

Jordan leant on the car door. 'So, Felicity, who do you reckon holds people's heads while they get in the back?'

Yates shook her head. 'I don't like where this is going, Harris.' She paused a moment. 'Then again, maybe a couple of guys faking it.'

'Hargraves was set to run for mayor, right?' said Jordan.

'Right,' agreed Yates.

'Know who he was up against?'

'Yeah, guy called Tony Mareno, he has a string of restaurants.'

'You got it. He's also boss of the Jets basketball team, a real up-and-comer. We'll get back to the office. I need to talk to Bailey.'

As they departed, the tow truck with the white Mercedes on board also drove away.

Chapter 6

Bailey was busy talking to the current mayor, George Owens, when Jordan and Yates walked into his office.

'Hi, Harris, how's things?' said Owens. He smiled warmly and offered his hand.

Owens was in his late sixties. A large man, but not fat, with a grey receding hairline, he was casually dressed in slacks, open-neck shirt and no tie.

'Fine thanks, Mayor,' replied Jordan accepting his hand. 'How's yourself?'

'Top of the world, Harris, and how's Linda and the kids?'

'They're all fine too thanks, Mayor.'

'Winston tells me you're looking into the disappearance of John Hargraves. What have you got?'

'Not a lot yet, still trying to piece things together,' he said, spreading his hands. 'Seems unlike them to go off without the kids and to leave the house wide open.'

'I agree, does seem odd. John is a good man. I was hoping he would win the next election when I step down. I know you'll give it your best, Harris. Please keep me informed.' He turned to Bailey and shook his hand. 'Right, better leave you lot to it.'

It was quiet in the office after Mayor Owens departed.

'Okay, Harris,' said Bailey, breaking the silence. 'Something's bugging you two or you wouldn't be in here this late in the day.' He sat down on the chair behind his desk.

Jordan took a moment before replying in a serious tone of voice. 'Not sure Winston; thought we might run it past you before going on.'

'Fair enough! Before I forget, here's a prelim on Hargraves' house.' He reached forward onto his desk for a piece of paper and handed it to Jordan. 'No sign of forced entry, no prints, the safe still had the wife's jewellery in it and a few personal papers. So, what gives?'

'The safe usually had a hundred thousand dollars in it, according to his bank's director and that's gone.'

'And?' said Bailey.

'The Hargraves were seen being helped into the back of a car across the road from where their Merc was found.'

'Being helped?' asked Bailey with an inquiring look.

Jordan nodded. 'Yeah, a very considerate bloke pushed Mrs Hargrave's head down so she wouldn't bang it getting in.'

Bailey spread his hands, 'So, you think …'

'Come on, Winston,' said Jordan curtly, 'you know what we think.'

Bailey leant forward, placed his elbows on the desk and rested his chin in his hands. 'Cops?'

'Possible.'

'So, where are they now?' said Bailey glancing from Jordan to Yates.

'Beats me, sir,' said Yates.

'Well, Harris?' asked Bailey.

'The guy running for mayor against Hargraves is Tony Mareno. I'd like to have a chat with him.'

'Why him?'

'If Hargraves is out of the race, Mareno will get in unopposed, so …' Jordan let his words trail off and shrugged.

Bailey sat back into his chair and stared at Jordan. 'Tread carefully, Harris.'

'You know me, Winston.' Jordan rolled his eyes and appeared hurt by the remark. 'I was top of the class for diplomacy and tact.'

Bailey grimaced and pointed to the door. 'Out!'

'You heard the man,' said Jordan to Yates as he walked out the office. 'Grumpy old goat!' he murmured.

'I heard that!' shouted Bailey.

Jordan and Yates walked out of the station and headed for the carpark behind the building.

'The mayor mentioned Linda and kids,' said Yates. 'Didn't know you are married.'

'Separated,' said Jordan. 'Couldn't hack the job; they're staying with Linda's mother.'

'Go to see them?'

'Occasionally,' replied Jordan as he unlocked his car door.

'And what did your Dad used to do?'

'Mind his own business,' he retorted. 'And if you've finished checking up on my family history, we'll go see Mareno. So, get in if that's alright with you, Yates, or do you need an early night?'

Yates got in the passenger side and buckled her seatbelt as Jordan started the car and drove off. 'Sorry, Harris, just making conversation,' she said apologetically.

Jordan remained quiet for the next few minutes before taking a few deep breaths. 'Sorry, I was a bit short, Yates.' He raised his left hand off the steering wheel. 'I was just thinking about Mareno. Let me do the talking, okay?'

Chapter 7

Jordan and Yates made their way through a crowded and elegantly furnished restaurant.

'How do you know he's here, Harris?'

'Oh, he'll be here. Tony and I go way back.'

'You know him?' said Yates somewhat surprised. 'Why didn't you say?'

Yates followed behind Jordan as he hurriedly made his way through the restaurant to the rear. He pushed his way through the swinging waiters' doors with Yates right behind him.

'Easy, Harris!' said Yates, who felt they were being a bit pushy.

Through the doors, they entered a hive of activity. Several chefs were busy preparing meals and waiters were constantly coming and going. In a far corner of the kitchen at a table, three men were seated, and, by the friendly camaraderie displayed, were apparently enjoying the food on the table in front of them. As Jordan and Yates approached, the men looked up and the pleasant chatter ceased.

Mareno, hair slicked back into a ponytail, stood and extended his hand. 'Hello, Harris.' He smiled and gestured at the table. 'You and your lady friend care to join us?'

The two other men, heavy-set, heads shaved, remained seated, unsmiling.

Jordan ignored Mareno's outstretched hand. 'How's the race for Mayor going, Tony?'

'Who knows?' replied Mareno with a shrug. 'The people will decide that, Harris.'

'And the competition's a bit tough?'

Mareno shrugged again. 'Politics, Harris, always tough.'

'Guess it would make it easier if Hargraves pulled out, eh, Tony?'

'And why would he do that?' said Mareno, seemingly surprised by the question.

'Oh, I don't know,' said Jordan, spreading his hands. 'Maybe, if he was talked to the right way.'

Mareno smiled. 'You offering, Harris?'

'Politics is not my thing. You know that, Tony.'

There was a brief silence as they looked at one another. Jordan inclined his head to the two men who were sitting impassively at the table watching the exchange between him and Mareno. 'Thought this was a posh joint, Tony; hope the health department doesn't find out you've been letting your dogs eat in the kitchen.'

The two men dropped their forks and started to get up.

Mareno put up his hand and the men sat back down scowling. 'You're a funny guy, Harris.'

'Can't help myself, Tony. We'll see ourselves out.'

As Jordan and Yates left the kitchen, a deadpan Mareno watched them go.

'What the hell was that all about?' asked Yates as they walked back to their car.

'Don't you find it odd, Felicity, that his only opponent goes missing just before the election?'

'Of course, but the way you spoke to him, Harris. And I asked you to call me Yates.'

'Tony Mareno is a crock of shit: always has been and always will be,' said Jordan as they arrived at the car. 'He took over the restaurant when his father died two years back and *he* was into everything: loan sharking, stand-over, prostitution, you name it. Tony has since sold off a lot of it and is trying to portray he's legit.'

'And the go for mayor?'

'Power and the opportunity to make more money, and Tony loves money.' He took a deep breath and blew out while opening the car door. 'Been a long day. We'll chase up some more in the morning.'

'Suits me!' said Yates as she climbed in the passenger side.

Chapter 8

The following morning in the squad room, Jordan and Yates were going through the forensic reports from the Hargraves' house when another officer came to the desk. 'Hey, Harris, you know that old guy Barney, who's been pulled in so many times he now gives this place as his address?'

'Sure do. What's the silly old bugger been up to now?'

'Got him downstairs. He was pulled in for trying to use a credit card to get booze.'

'And?' said Jordan without enthusiasm while continuing to go through his paperwork.

'The owner of the store took the card, rang it in and guess what? The card is in the name of Hargraves.'

Jordan and Yates almost flew out of their seats. The officer was left standing, watching them go. 'Gee, thanks!'

The interview room was entirely bare except for a small table and one chair in which was seated a particularly scruffy individual. His hair and beard were matted. The thick, grey overcoat was tattered and spotted with grime; the sleeves ragged. An unpleasant odour that emanated from him filled the room. In his hands he held a filthy beanie.

Yates stood by the door trying to hold her breath, while Jordan paced up and down in front of the table. 'So, Barney, where did you get the card?'

Barney sniffed and ran a sleeve under his nose that left a wet, silvery line. 'What card's that, Mr Jordan?'

Jordan rolled his eyes. 'The one you used to try to get booze with, Barney.'

'Sorry,' said Barney with a shake of his head, 'dunno what you're talking about.' He peeped up at Jordan from his lowered face.

Jordan stopped pacing, went to the desk and lowered his head directly in front of Barney. 'Look at me, Barney,' he said quietly. 'I know you're a helpless bastard and that you need a good feed and, by the smell of you, a good wash.'

Barney looked up as Jordan backed away with a hand over his nose.

'So, here's the deal, Barney. Tell me where you found the card and you can have two nights in a cell, all meals provided. Now then ... the card.'

'Three nights?' whispered Barney.

'You're testing my patience, Barney ... okay, three nights.'

Barney sat up straight. 'All meals?'

'Yes, all meals.'

'Found it in a dumpster near the old warehouses in Lennox Lane.'

'And what else?'

Barney shook his head. 'Nothing.'

'Just a card, you found a card and nothing else in a dumpster full of crap!?'

'I'd spent the night in there, just turned over and there it was. Honest!'

'You'd better be telling me the truth.' He stood over Barney, fists clenched and glowering as Barney cowered back in the chair.

'Gospel, Mr Jordan!'

Jordan left the room and Yates closed the door behind him.

'Strewth, he stank!' said Yates as they made their way back to the squad room where Jordan caught up with the officer who had initially told them about Barney. 'Sorry I ran off on you before, Norm, this Hargraves thing is starting to get to me.'

'How did it go?' asked Norm.

'I've gotta check out his story; hold him in there till I ring in.

I've promised him food and lodging for three days if he's kosher.'

Norm cringed. 'Jesus, Harris! He stinks worse than dog shit on a hot day!'

'Sorry, Norm,' said Jordan with a grin. He walked away and beckoned to Yates. 'Come on, Felicity. Up and at 'em!'

Yates followed Jordan out of the station with a frown on her face from the continued use of her Christian name.

Chapter 9

The area outside the derelict warehouses was deserted when Jordan and Yates arrived. A warm, gusty breeze blew dust and rubbish around. They walked over to the dumpster that Barney had mentioned and peered in. It was half full of crushed down rubbish.

Yates pulled a face at the odour. 'Well, it sure smells like Barney.'

Jordan looked around the empty space and shook his head. 'I don't buy it; no way someone would sling a card on its own in there.'

They both backed away from the dumpster.

Jordan pointed to one side. 'You check out that side, Yates, I'll go look at the other.'

Yates walked to the nearest warehouse and pulled at the door. It was locked so she moved on to the next. On the other side, Jordan was also checking doors with the same result. At last one of the doors gave way as he pushed against it. He walked around inside the empty building and looked up at the sound of pigeons in the roof. A loud yell from Yates made him turn and go outside. He looked across to the other side and saw Yates bent over, dry retching.

Jordan ran across and Yates pointed to the door behind her. 'In there.'

Jordan waited a moment after entering to allow his eyes to adjust to the gloomy interior. To one side, he made out some dim shapes and walked towards them. He grimaced as he was confronted by the sight of John and Madelaine Hargraves. He waved a hand in front of his face as the smell of death reached him. He took a handkerchief from his pocket to cover his nose and moved closer. A huge cloud of flies swarmed around the bodies.

Madelaine had a half-smile on her face. A large pool of congealed blood covered the ground beneath her. John was sat with his head tilted back, flies crawling over his open mouth and bulging eyes.

Jordan noticed an open wallet on the ground beside the body of John and bent to pick it up, disturbing the flies that billowed around him. He quickly backed away and hurried outside. On getting outside, he took a few deep breaths and looked at Yates. 'You okay?'

'Sure!' said Yates as she wiped her face with a handkerchief.

Jordan took out his mobile. 'Winston, it's Harris. We've found the Hargraves. He sure as hell won't be running for mayor this year.' He paused, listening. 'Yeah, it's pretty ugly. Get forensics down here, ASAP. The warehouses in Lennox Lane.'

He replaced the mobile in his jacket. 'Somebody removed Hargraves' wallet. Had to be that dirty old bastard Barney.'

Yates nodded after taking a few deep breaths. 'Would seem that way.'

With sirens blaring, several vehicles arrived. One small truck had "Scientific Services Bureau" emblazoned on the side.

From a station wagon with "CORONER" printed on its side stepped a short, slightly overweight, elderly man. 'What have we got?' he asked as he approached Jordan.

Jordan pointed to the warehouse door. 'Inside.'

He turned to Yates as the coroner and forensic team entered the warehouse. 'Stay here if you like, Yates.'

Yates shook her head and took a couple of deep breaths. 'No, I'll be alright.'

Together they followed the others inside. For a minute they stood still and silent as they looked at the bodies.

'Jesus Christ!' said the coroner. 'They minced her. Why the hell is she smiling?'

Jordan gestured to the hypodermic needle resting on the table.

'Reckon she was drugged, never knew what was happening. Probably bled to death. And the guy, look at his neck. He's been wired.'

Flashbulbs started popping as the forensic team went to work.

Jordan walked all around taking in the scene from every angle. He came to Yates who was stood still, staring. He tapped her on the shoulder, making her jump. 'Let's get back to the office.'

Yates turned away from the spectacle and followed him out.

Chapter 10

Back in the station interview room, Jordan was pacing up and down in front of Barney while Yates stood by the door. 'Okay, Barney, let's try it again. Where did you get the card?'

'Like I said, Mr Jordan, I found it …'

Jordan stopped pacing, stepped forward, grabbed Barney by his coat collar, lifted him out of his chair and slammed him against the wall. 'You're a filthy, smelly, lying bastard, Barney,' he yelled into his face. 'You lifted it off a dead guy!'

He shook Barney and banged the back of his head against the wall.

'Alright, alright!' wailed Barney.

Jordan pulled him away from the wall and dropped him back into the chair.

Barney rubbed the back of his head and stared at Jordan. 'I needed a drink that's all. I never touched anything else. He never had any cash so I thought I'd try the card. He sure wouldn't be needing it. Jesus, what a mess!'

'Why'd you go in there anyway?'

'Got woken up by the yelling see, then it stopped, so I peeped over the edge of the dumpster and saw these three guys get in a car and drive off.'

'So, naturally, you wrote down the car rego number eh, Barney?'

'No, no!' said Barney sounding perplexed. 'I'm no good with writing, but it was a grey colour.'

'Then what?'

'Well, I went over and had a look inside.' His eyes widened as he grimaced. 'Shit! They sure fixed them two up.'

'So, then you thought you'd better check out the dead guy's pockets eh, Barney?'

'Well, he was finished with whatever he had that's for sure.'

'You lifted his wallet, found no cash so took his card, is that what you're saying?'

Barney spread his hands and smiled. 'That's it!'

Jordan stood back from Barney and shook his head. 'You stuffed me around, Barney, so no way you get three days. You can spend the night then you're out.'

Barney's face dropped. 'But you promised!'

'And you promised me, Barney, and gave me an honest and a gospel,' snapped Jordan as he walked out of the room, closely followed by Yates.

Barney stared at the closed door, spat on the floor, pulled his coat around him and slouched down into the chair.

Upstairs in Bailey's office, Jordan and Yates conveyed to him the finding of the Hargraves.

'Better send someone around to see William Hargraves,' said Jordan. 'Wouldn't want him or the kids to find out what's happened on the TV or radio.'

'I'll get right on it,' said Bailey. 'That poor woman, and probably the husband was watching it all till they killed him.'

'I'm sure she felt nothing,' said Yates. 'She'd been drugged up, thank God.'

'That's right,' agreed Jordan. 'Reckon how it went down was they worked on the wife to make Hargraves talk, which I'm sure he did, gave them the security code and safe combination, and after that they had no use for them … so.' He spread his hands.

'But why not take the jewellery?' asked Bailey.

'These guys are smart, Winston. Try to fence the jewellery and they get fingered. Just take the cash, one hundred grand plus, not bad pickings!'

Bailey scratched his head. 'Who knew, apart from the bank's director, what's his name, Norris?'

'Yeah, Norris knew about the cash in the safe.'

'Maybe we should have another chat with Norris,' said Yates.

Bailey nodded.

'Reckon so,' added Jordan.

They were about to leave when Jordan stopped. 'Winston, that bit of fluff I bagged from the painting over Hargrave's safe, anything back on it?'

Bailey shuffled through the paperwork on his desk. 'Yeah, here it is, probably from a sports jacket, a bit of dark grey and dark red cotton.' He looked up at Jordan. 'A bit like yours.'

Jordan checked out his jacket, lifted the front and studied it. 'Well, that sure cuts down the possibilities. This is exclusive gear, probably only a million or so ever made.'

Yates grinned. 'Probably made by appointment only.'

Bailey pointed to the door. 'Out! Go see Norris.'

Chapter 11

Norris stared at Jordan and Yates, his face ashen.

'Thing is, Mr Norris,' said Jordan, 'who else knew about the cash in Hargraves' safe?'

Norris just kept staring, mouth open.

'Mr Norris!' repeated Jordan.

Norris blinked; stammered, 'B ... both dead!?'

'That's right,. Now, like I said, who else knew he had a hundred grand plus in his safe?'

Norris's eyes darted around the office. He spread his hands. 'R ... really ... I'm not sure.'

'Did you happen to just mention it to anyone ... in confidence of course?' said Yates.

Jordan glanced at Yates and raised his eyebrows. Norris straightened in his chair and looked from Yates to Jordan.

'Now, why did he have all that cash in his safe,' said Jordan, his manner more demanding, 'but never carry any on his person, Mr Norris?'

Norris started to squirm in his chair. 'Well, actually we have a small poker group. We meet once a month and we always settle in cash.'

'Where do you play and with who?' said Jordan, his voice raised higher.

'Mmm ... mmm, Judge Cartwright, Doctor Franz Heiderfall, coach Jim Tievan and Bob Furlow, the manager of the Southern Guild,' replied Norris becoming flustered. 'And we always play at Franz's place. He likes to be home in case he gets a call. He's a heart surgeon you know. He operated on ...'

Jordan interrupted, 'Okay, okay. No one else, just the six of you?'

'Yes, we thought it best not to bring in others.'

'So, when you're together there's a half mill sitting around?'

'Well, I guess so. Yes.'

'Thank you, Mr Norris,' said Jordan. 'We'll be on our way.' He turned, nodded to Yates and they walked out of the office.

Norris sat back into his chair, rubbed his hands over his face and began to tremble.

Outside the bank building, Jordan and Yates stood by their car watching the traffic.

'Any of those names mean anything to you, Yates?'

'All prominent guys; maybe one of them lost too much and wanted some back.'

'Maybe. Jim Tievan is coach of the Jets, right?'

'Yeah ... and?' said Yates.

'And the Jets have just been bought by Tony Mareno, right!?'

'Oh shit!' said Yates.

'Yeah, oh shit,' said Jordan as he glanced at his watch. 'Mareno should be coming off the course at the Glades Country Club 'bout now.'

'How ever do you know that, Harris?'

'I just happen to know his routine.' He smiled at Yates. 'Let's go brighten up his day.'

'How come you know how Mareno spends his time, Harris?' asked Yates as they walked in the front entrance of the Glades Country Club.

'He's a creature of habit: golf on Tuesday and Friday afternoons and eats at each of his six restaurants in turn.'

'Yeah, but why do you need to know that?'

Jordan smiled. 'Because, Yates, one day I intend nailing his sorry arse to the floor.'

Chapter 12

They walked through to the far end of the club lounge where Mareno was sitting at a table with three other men.

'So, the priest says … I said verger, you idiot,' said Mareno on reaching the punch line of the joke he had been telling.

The group laughed amid congratulations. Mareno noticed Jordan and Yates and smiled.

'My, my, Harris. What gives me the pleasure of your company twice in as many days?'

The three men with Mareno continued chuckling.

'Thought I'd drop in and give you some news,' said Jordan returning Mareno's smile.

'And what's that, Harris?'

'Seems like you'll go into the race for mayor unopposed.'

'Oh, I don't think so,' said Mareno with a shake of his head. 'John Hargraves is a goer for sure.'

'Yeah well, he ain't going anywhere anymore, Tony … except the morgue.'

The three other men fell silent and stared.

Mareno glared at Jordan. 'Whada you mean?'

'Somebody put a wire round his neck and choked him.' He took a breath before continuing. 'Oh, and his wife was put through a mincer … sort of.'

The three men at the table uttered exclamations of disbelief.

'A mincer … blimey!' said one.

'Not Madelaine. Oh Christ!' said another.

Mareno remained impassive and stared at Jordan who stared

back. 'Just thought I'd let you know before it got on the news. Give you time to get your sympathy speech prepared.'

He paused a moment while continuing to stare at Mareno. 'Or have you got it prepared already, Tony?'

The men at the table looked from Jordan to Mareno, their minds working furtively, not quite sure of what was said and the implications. Jordan turned and walked away with Yates following.

Mareno watched them go. One of the men said something to him; he shook his head and frowned as he continued watching Jordan's back until he left the club.

'He's not a happy boy, Harris,' said Yates as they neared their car.

'It's in his eyes, Yates. It's all down to that slimy bastard and somehow we'll have to prove it.'

'What is it between you and Mareno?' asked Yates as they got in the car.

Jordan started the engine and eased the car out onto the driveway. 'Few years back, before Linda and me split up, we were having dinner at one of Mareno's restaurants. I got called away, Linda stayed to finish her meal and Mareno tried to hit on her.'

Yates shrugged. 'So, naturally you told him to lay off or you'd break his legs.'

'Something like that.'

Yates rolled her eyes. 'Umm ... men!'

Chapter 13

Bailey watched Jordan as he paced back and forth in front of his desk.

'You sure, Harris?'

'Never surer!'

Bailey looked at Yates. 'Yates?'

'I'm with Harris, sir. The coach of the Jets, Tievan, is a player in the poker school. Mareno owns the Jets, found out about the cash, thought to kill two birds with one stone, if you'll excuse the expression.' She raised her hands. 'Sorry! Gets the hundred grand plus and removes Hargraves from the race. Sits good with me.'

'But can you prove it?'

'Ah ... now that's a different ball game,' replied Yates after a quick glance towards Jordan.

Jordan continued his pacing. 'The car that the two guys used to pick up the Hargraves was silvery grey. The girl at Janelle's reckoned it had a dent over the rear offside wheel and if they were cops ...'

'Can we find out how many silvery grey Fords our guys use and who's in them?' asked Yates.

Bailey nodded. 'I guess ... go punch the computer.'

'Right!' said Yates as she left Bailey's office.

'Harris, I know you had a run-in with Mareno,' said Bailey. 'It's not getting in the way of this, is it?'

'Course not! I certainly don't like the son of a bitch, but this ... it somehow just fits him.'

'Okay, Harris, but go easy. If you push too hard without anything solid to go on he could get you busted. So, proof, boyo, proof.'

'One hundred and fifty-seven,' said Yates as she came back into the office waving a computer printout.

'Hell!' said Jordan.

'Spread out over the entire city,' added Yates as she waved the printout again. 'Wanna get started?'

Bailey shook his head. 'It's late, Felicity, go home. You too, Harris; start fresh in the morning.'

Jordan stretched and rubbed the back of his neck. 'Yeah! See you in the morning,' he said as he walked away.

Yates studied the printout a bit more and approached Bailey at his desk.

'Maybe I could?'

'No way, not on your own. You heard me: go home.' He pointed at the door. 'Out!'

Yates backed out of Bailey's office still holding the printout.

Outside in the station carpark, she sat in her car studying the printout for a few minutes before driving off.

Chapter 14

Quietly humming to herself, Yates pulled into the carpark area of another police station. On seeing a grey Ford, she got out of her car and walked over and inspected the rear wheel arch that was slightly damaged and the paintwork scratched. She hurried back to her car and got in. Hands shaking, she picked up the computer printout, found the Ford's rego and circled it.

'Blimey, the first one!' she exclaimed.

She was about to leave when she saw a man walk to the Ford and get in. She started her car and followed. After a few kilometres the Ford stopped. The man got out and went into the nearby takeaway restaurant. Yates pulled up a few car spaces away, turned off the motor, sat back in the seat and waited. Losing patience, she glanced at her wristwatch and was about to get out to see where the man had gone, when her passenger side door opened and the man quickly slid in.

Taken by surprise, Yates jumped, then reached for her handgun but stopped when she saw that the man had a gun pointed at her.

The man smiled. 'Now then, young lady, what makes me so interesting, eh?'

Chapter 15

The following morning in Bailey's office, Bailey and Jordan were leaning over the desk studying the Medical Officer's report when Yates entered.

'Sorry I'm late,' said Yates rather sheepishly.

'Late night?' inquired Jordan without looking up.

'Yeah ... sorta.'

'You got that list of grey Fords?' asked Bailey.

'Sure!' said Yates. She reached inside her jacket pocket, took out the folded printout and handed it over.

Bailey pointed at the printout. 'Why the circle round this one?'

'I checked out a couple on my way home last night, sir.'

'And?'

Yates shrugged. 'Nothing, sir.'

Jordan glanced up at her. 'So, why the funny look on your face?'

Yates took a deep breath and blew out. 'I ah ... I ah got jumped by the driver.'

'You what!?' said Jordan loudly.

'It's okay, Harris, he was a really nice guy.'

'I told you to go home,' said Bailey seriously, 'and you chose to ignore me and scout around on your own. If that had been someone other than Eric Dark ...' He slammed his fist down onto the desk. 'Hell, Yates ... I should can you.'

'You knew?' said Yates completely surprised.

'Eric rang through this morning,' said Jordan. 'He's too good a cop to not spot a tail kiddo. Said he thought you were going to wet yourself when he got in beside you,' he added with a grin.

Yates grinned back. 'Ended up at his place and met his wife. Nice people.'

'You were lucky this time,' said Bailey. 'Learn from it.'

'Yes, sir,' said Yates.

'In any case,' said Jordan, 'if you can find a cop's car *without* a dent or scratch on it, now that would be odd.'

Jordan and Bailey both laughed while Yates pulled a face.

'These other guys in the poker school; better check them out.' Bailey picked up a piece of paper from the desk. 'What have we got? A judge, a doctor, a bank manager and the Jets' coach. Where you wanna start, Harris?'

'Top of the list, the judge. Leave the coach till last.'

'And when you get to him don't get out of line. I know the connection.'

Jordan smiled and shrugged his shoulders. Yates raised her eyebrows as Bailey pointed at the office door. 'Out!'

'Grumpy old goat,' whispered Jordan to Yates as they walked out.

'I heard that!' shouted Bailey.

Chapter 16

n the reception of the office of Judge Quentin Cartwright, Jordan and Yates approached his secretary. Her hair was tied back in a severe bun. Primly dressed and wearing just a trace of make-up, she looked sternly at them.

'And you are?'

Jordan and Yates offered their badges for inspection.

'We'd like to speak to the judge,' said Jordan.

The secretary rose out of her chair. 'Just a moment,' she said as she went to a side door, entered and closed it behind her.

Yates looked at Jordan and pushed her nose up with a finger.

The secretary reopened the door and motioned them to her. 'The judge can give you a few moments only. Don't delay him as he's due in court in ten minutes.'

Jordan and Yates walked towards her. 'Heaven forbid we should hold up justice, honey,' said Jordan.

The secretary stared coldly at them as they brushed past into the judge's room.

Judge Cartwright was a portly man in his early sixties with what was once red hair, starting to go grey. A well-trimmed grey beard enhanced his appearance.

'Make it quick!' he said as he pulled his black cloak around his shoulders.

'You've probably heard about the Hargraves, Judge, and ...' said Jordan.

'Yes, yes!' interrupted Cartwright. 'What do you want with me? Get to it, man.'

'You played poker with him on a regular basis as I understand it.'

'So?' said Cartwright as he continued to adjust his cloak.

'Took you for a bit, did he?' said Jordan.

Cartwright stopped adjusting his cloak and stared at Jordan. 'Now see here, Detective. I don't like your tone or the implication,' he said brusquely.

'No implication intended, Judge,' said Jordan apologetically. 'Just need to know more about Hargraves, is all.'

'Yes, yes, I see!' said Cartwright in a calmer manner. 'All right, as it happens, John had had a good run lately.'

'How good, Judge?'

Cartwright sniffed and pursed his lips. 'Oh, about thirty.'

'He won thirty grand of yours, sir?' asked Yates somewhat incredulously.

Cartwright nodded. 'About that, give or take.'

'And the others, did he clean them out too?' asked Jordan.

'I wouldn't say he cleaned them out exactly, but he was well in front.'

'And you were okay with him winning all the time?'

Cartwright shrugged. 'Luck changes. Over a period it evens out.' He checked his watch and walked past Jordan and Yates. 'You'll have to excuse me, but I'm late for court.'

'What a nice guy!' said Yates as Cartwright disappeared. 'And so eager to help find whoever killed his friend.'

'My goodness, Yates, how cynical! I'm getting to like you more each day,' said Jordan as they left the judge's office and entered the reception area. 'Next the doc. Need any pills?'

'Yeah, something to give men to stop them being wise arses,' said Yates.

Jordan gave the secretary a wink as he walked past. 'Thanks, darlin'. Love the outfit.'

'Oh really!' she snorted.

On arrival at the surgery of Doctor Franz Heiderfall, Jordan and Yates had immediately been shown into his office and offered seats. Heiderfall was a small, slightly built man in his late fifties and nearly bald except for a few wispy hairs over his ears.

'Thank you for giving us your time,' said Yates.

'Not at all,' said Heiderfall, adjusting his thick-lensed spectacles. 'John is ...' He stopped and took a deep breath before continuing. '*Was* a very nice fellow. How may I help?'

'You used to play poker with him,' said Jordan.

Heiderfall nodded. 'Indeed! First Saturday night of each month. More of a social evening with friends really.'

'And always at your place, Doctor?'

'That's right. I like to be near my home phone just in case something urgent arises.'

'Was Hargraves a good poker player?'

'Oh yes, very. In fact, the last few times we met I think he did particularly well.'

'How well, sir?'

Heiderfall rubbed his chin while thinking. 'I'm not exactly sure. I know I'm down about five thousand, but hopefully luck changes and next time I'll ... oh dear!' He shook his head and looked downcast.

'How about the others, sir? Any idea who's in front and who's behind?'

Heiderfall remained silent, still shaking his head, hands clasped together on his lap.

'Doctor!' said Yates.

He looked up. 'Oh yes, sorry … well, I'm not absolutely sure. I think Jim and Bob were slightly ahead. Paul was down a little, and Quentin, oh yes, he was definitely down.' He nodded to himself and thought for a moment before continuing. 'Yes, that's right, John caught him rather severely a couple of times or so. Fortunately, Quentin is not exactly short of funds and well … luck always changes.'

'Yes, luck always changes,' said Jordan. 'That's just what the judge said.'

'Well, there you are then. How are John's children?' Heiderfall asked with concern. 'It must be a terrible shock for them.'

'They're with their grandparents, sir,' said Yates.

'Oh good! They are lovely people. Met them at Madelaine and John's over dinner one evening. Yes, lovely people.'

Jordan stood up. 'Well, Doctor, we'd better be on our way. Thank you again for giving us the time.'

'Oh, not at all,' he replied. 'I wish I could help you more. I'll give the grandparents a call.'

'I'm sure they'd appreciate it, sir,' said Yates.

Jordan reached forward to shake Heiderfall's hand. 'We'll be off then.'

'Next stop, Bob Furlow,' said Jordan to Yates as they left the surgery.

Chapter 18

nside the building of the Southern Guild Bank, Jordan and Yates were ushered into the office of Bob Furlow. Aged in his mid-forties, wearing a pinstriped suit and bow tie and with his hair slicked back, he looked up at Jordan and Yates from his high-backed leather chair behind a large executive desk.

Jordan and Yates had not been offered seats, so stood looking down at him.

'Need to ask you some questions about John Hargraves,' said Jordan.

'Fire away!' said Furlow.

Furlow's "whatever" attitude didn't sit well with Jordan. He stared at Furlow for a moment and decided to get right to the point. 'You're aware of what happened to them I take it, so were you winning or losing at the poker school?'

'Actually, I was slightly up,' he replied, taken aback by Jordan's directness.

'How much?'

'I'd had a good run ... probably five or six thou, I guess.'

'And the others?'

'I think Franz was up and Jim maybe.' He paused, considering. 'John was certainly well ahead. He'd caught Quentin a few times, and Paul was down a bit, too.' He stopped and looked from Jordan to Yates. 'How are the kids?'

'They're with their grandparents.'

Furlow took a deep breath and exhaled. 'Good!'

'Any idea why anybody would want to hurt the Hargraves?'

asked Jordan.

Furlow shook his head. 'No, no, none at all. My God, Madelaine was a wonderful lady. Did a lot of social work, and John … well, he was running for mayor.' He shuddered. 'Why anyone would do that to them, I just don't know.'

'That's what we're trying to find out,' said Jordan as he turned away to leave, then stopped. 'You said the judge had been caught a few times; how much?'

Furlow thought for a moment. 'Last time, about … oh, thirty thousand.'

'Thanks,' said Jordan and turned to leave again.

'About the same as the month before,' added Furlow suddenly.

Jordan stopped once more and glanced at Yates.

'You said the judge lost big, say around thirty thousand the last two games?' asked Yates.

Furlow nodded. 'About that, yes. John was having a good run, but that's the way it goes. Luck changes you know.'

'Yeah, luck!' said Jordan. 'Keep hearing that. Thanks for your time. We'll get back to you if need be.'

Furlow's face was grave as he watched Jordan and Yates leave.

'So, the judge is down sixty, not thirty thou,' said Yates as they walked out of the building.

'Interesting, eh!' said Jordan. 'Now, last but not least, coach Tievan.'

Chapter 19

At the Jets' basketball court, coach James Tievan was putting his players through their paces. He yelled at one of the men who had just lost the ball. 'Concentrate, Todd!' To the man who stood beside him, he whispered, 'He'll have to go, Corey, the guy's just not got it anymore.'

As Jordan and Yates entered the court, Corey noticed them and gave Tievan a nudge. He looked in the direction Corey had indicated and saw Jordan raise a hand and beckon him. 'Shit! Now what? Keep the boys busy, Corey.'

He reluctantly wandered without haste over to Jordan and Yates. 'Yeah, what is it?' he asked abruptly on reaching them.

Jordan and Yates showed their badges.

'Like a quick word, someplace quiet,' said Jordan.

Tievan glanced at the badges. 'Sure, my office.' He pointed to a door at the side of the court.

Tievan opened the door and Jordan and Yates entered. Tievan slammed the door shut behind them.

He looked up and down at Yates. 'Gonna frisk me, honey?' He raised his arms and grinned.

Yates rolled her eyes. 'You played poker with John Hargraves and friends, we understand.'

Tievan's expression suddenly changed. 'Yeah, that's right. What's the beef?' he asked now, completely serious.

'Hargraves took you for a decent amount, didn't he?' asked Jordan.

Tievan grunted. 'Like hell! Who told you that shit? I usually win. Those other guys got no idea; only competition was Hargraves.'

'He was good, eh? How good?'

Tievan laughed. 'Last couple times really cleaned out the judge but good. Not that that's hard to do. Don't know why he keeps at it. Must be down a bundle.'

'How big a bundle?' asked Yates.

'Oh, I'd say about sixty to seventy grand in the last few games.'

'You sure of that?'

'Sure I'm sure. The judge keeps a record of who's taken him out. Reckons his luck will change.'

'You think it will?'

'No way! He's a born loser.' Tievan sniggered. 'Shit! Even girlie here could beat him.'

Yates rolled her eyes again. 'So, what does Mareno think of your poker playing pals?'

'No sweat! Why should it worry him? I do my job.'

'You tell him who wins and loses?' said Jordan.

Tievan glared at Jordan. 'Why should I? Like I said, I do my job and what happens outside is my business.'

Jordan returned Tievan's glare. 'Right!'

'I hear the Hargraves were messed up real good, that right?' said Tievan.

'Yeah, real good.' said Jordan.

'Hey, I'm real sorry about that. Hargraves wasn't a bad sort of guy.' He looked from Jordan to Yates. 'Still, the main competition in the poker school now having departed ... well. I guess my chances are looking up. Can't beat luck, eh!?'

'Yeah, luck,' said Jordan as he gave Tievan an icy stare.

Tievan grinned as Jordan turned away.

'Come on, Yates. Let's go find some clean air,' he retorted.

Tievan continued grinning as they walked out of the office, through the basketball court and out to their car.

'Another lovely guy,' said Yates.

'Ain't he just?' said Jordan.

'Now what?'

'Tievan is a first class prick, and you can bet he'd tell Mareno how much he won. He'd have to brag, so you can also bet Mareno knew that Hargraves was a big winner.'

'The doc?' said Yates.

'Seemed okay.'

'Furlow?'

'He appeared concerned, but could be holding back. What do you think?'

'Mmm … he seemed okay to me, Harris. What about Norris?'

'Reckon he was pretty genuine the way he acted the second time.'

'Which brings us back to the judge,' said Yates.

'Yeah, the Judge! Now why didn't he say how much he had really lost, especially as we now know he kept records?'

'Worth another chat, maybe,' said Yates.

Jordan unlocked the car doors. 'Most certainly,' he said as they got in.

Chapter 20

Back in his chambers, Judge Cartwright became angry at the reappearance and intrusion of Jordan and Yates. 'My private business is of no concern of yours, Detectives.'

Jordan didn't let up. 'Why did you say you'd lost thirty grand when in fact it was nearer seventy, Judge?'

'Like I said, none of your business. Now get out,' said Cartwright.

'Would you rather come down to the station and tell us, Judge?' said Jordan calmly. 'Makes no difference to us.' He started walking towards the door.

'All right!' said Cartwright, his face now bright red. 'It was more than I said. So what? My financial concerns are of no relevance.'

'Someone got into Hargraves's house and emptied his safe of cash,' continued Jordan. 'Now don't you reckon that if that cash had once belonged to someone else, Judge, that someone would have wanted to get it back?'

Cartwright turned white. 'Good God, man, you surely don't think ... why that's preposterous!' He sank into his chair shaking his head. 'Preposterous!' he repeated.

'So, who do you think did the deed, Judge?' asked Yates.

Cartwright's bluster was completely gone. 'I've no idea who did those terrible things to John and Madelaine. Oh God. No. No. I've no idea.' He looked up at Yates. 'You think it was me? No, no, no.'

Sweat was running down Cartwright's flabby face as Jordan turned to Yates. 'Time to go.'

As they left, Cartwright was sat mumbling to himself. 'No, no, I just couldn't.'

'Cross him off the list?' said Yates as they walked outside.

Jordan didn't seem convinced. 'Maybe. He sure wasn't capable of taking it himself, but he still could have arranged it. He has lots of contacts, both good and bad. Better go see Bailey, let him know where we're at.'

Chapter 21

Back at the station, Bailey again had the company of Mayor George Owens. Owens stopped his conversation with Bailey when he saw Jordan and Yates enter.

'Hello again, Harris, Miss Yates; thought I'd drop by and see how things are going.'

'We're making progress, Mayor,' said Jordan, noncommittally.

'Good! By the way, Harris, Tony Mareno rang me, said you'd been hassling him,' said Owens as he arose from the chair in front of Bailey's desk. He gave Jordan a bit of a sideways look. 'You know he's a candidate for mayor, don't you, Harris? Take it easy, eh!?'

Jordan nodded. 'Sure thing, Mayor.'

'Well, keep at it, Harris.' Owens turned to Bailey and shook his hand. 'Catch you later, Winston.'

As soon as Owens was out of sight, Bailey glared at Jordan. 'Jesus Christ, Harris! Fronting Mareno up like that at the golf club! What the hell was that all about? I told you to play smart.'

'He's up to his neck in it, Winston,' said Jordan sharply.

'I think Harris is right, sir,' said Yates.

'Oh shut up, Yates!' retorted Bailey. 'You're nearly as bad as he is. I thought you'd be a steadying influence on him.' He waved his hands in the air. 'But ... oh shit!'

'Winston, we haven't much to go on here, we have to rattle a few cages,' said Jordan

'Talking of rattling,' continued Bailey still just as angry as before. 'Judge Cartwright never turned up at court this afternoon. Apparently went home sick according to his secretary, just after you two left his office. What the hell did you say to him?'

Yates was about to speak but Bailey put his hand up to stop her.

'No, don't tell me. Probably better I don't know.'

Yates went to speak again until Bailey pointed to the door and shouted. 'Out!'

Jordan looked at Yates and inclined his head towards the door.

'Out!' shouted Bailey again.

'He seems a little upset,' said Yates as she and Jordan walked out of the police station.

Jordan grinned. 'Yeah, that's Winston. Pressure gets to him sometimes. What do you reckon we grab a pizza? I'm feeling a bit peckish.'

'Sounds good,' said Yates.

Chapter 22

n the Italian restaurant, Jordan finished off the last piece of pizza and wiped his mouth with a paper napkin.

'How was it, Yates?'

'Good! Fortunately, we both like olives.'

'I think we oughta compliment the chef.'

'What?' said Yates incredulously.

'You liked it didn't you?'

'Well … yes … but …'

'Well, then, we oughta compliment the chef,' said Jordan as he got up from the table.

'Harris, it was a pizza for God's sake, not lobster.'

Jordan walked off towards the rear of the restaurant with Yates following.

'Pizza, Harris. It was only a pizza,' she repeated.

Jordan pushed through a door that the waiters had been coming and going from. Yates followed, still complaining. 'Just a bloody pizza!'

She pulled up abruptly as she looked ahead into the kitchen. At a table in the corner sat Mareno with two heavy-set men.

Mareno looked up and frowned. 'Harris … again?'

'Hi!' said Jordan with a smile. 'Surprised at you, Tony. What would the health department say if they knew you keep feeding your dogs in the kitchen?'

One of the men growled, pushed his chair back and started to get up. Jordan moved forward and, just before the man got upright, backhanded him in the face. The man fell backwards onto the floor;

his legs kicked up, knocking the table over and sending plates, cutlery and food flying.

The other man pulled a gun from inside his jacket but before he could level it, Jordan grabbed his arm and twisted. There was a faint snap and the man gave a yell, dropping the gun. Jordan released his hold on the arm, punched him in the stomach and he fell to the floor holding his belly with his good arm.

The man Jordan had smacked in the face jumped to his feet and was about to launch himself at Jordan when he suddenly stopped as he felt a jab against the side of his head followed by a click.

He turned his head slowly and saw Yates holding her gun to his ear. Yates smiled and looked at Mareno. 'We just came in to compliment the chef on the pizza, Tony. Sorry about all this.' She gestured to the mess.

'Like she said, Tony, my compliments to the chef, really great pizza,' said Jordan.

Mareno sneered. 'Yeah, great!'

'Oh and by the way, luck's a funny thing, isn't it? Sometimes you win, sometimes you lose. You a poker player, Tony?'

'What the hell you on about?' said Mareno, seemingly confused.

Jordan shrugged. 'Think on it.' He nodded to Yates. 'Time to go.'

Yates lowered her gun from the man's head and slowly backed out of the kitchen behind Jordan. 'Bye!'

Mareno gave the man sitting on the floor a kick. 'Useless! The pair of you ... bloody useless!'

'Well, that was fun,' Yates said angrily as she followed Jordan along the street to their car. 'You're going to cost me my job if you keep that up. Let's compliment the chef! Shit, Harris, you knew damn well Mareno would be back there.'

Jordan smiled. 'Just lucky, Yates. Just lucky!' He spread his arms, feigning ignorance.

'Lucky, my arse!' said Yates.

'And very nice it is too.'

'Oh shove it, Harris. Take me home. I've had enough of you for one day.'

Jordan, still smiling, unlocked the car doors with the remote attached to the key ring and they both got in.

Chapter 23

The following morning, Yates was met by Jordan at the entrance to the police station squad room as she arrived.

'Morning!' said Yates gruffly, apparently still annoyed from the night before.

'Barney's dead,' said Jordan quietly.

Yates was stunned for a moment. 'Where?'

'Guess!' said Jordan as he walked off with purpose.

'Not the warehouse!'

'Got it in one.'

Jordan and Yates stood looking at the body of Barney strapped to the chair. His face was a mask of pain, his eyes wide and staring, his mouth open in a silent scream. At the point where his feet should have been was a blood smothered mincer. Both of his feet were missing; just stumps at the ankles. What used to be his feet was now a pile of mush beside the mincer.

Jordan looked away from the gruesome scene as the coroner approached. 'How'd you find him?' he asked.

'One of our guys had been off sick. Thought he'd come down and look over where the Hargraves had been found.' He shrugged. 'Curiosity I guess. He found this and, after throwing up, phoned in and then I called Bailey.'

'Same as before?'

'Looks it,' said the coroner with a shake of his head. 'This time the victim wasn't drugged though. This one felt the lot.'

Yates put her hand to her mouth. 'Jesus! The poor bastard.'

'Thanks Doc,' said Jordan.

The coroner began the woeful task of releasing the straps that held Barney to the chair and, with the help of one of the forensic unit, lowered him onto a body bag.

Jordan and Yates walked outside.

'Why Barney? It doesn't make sense, Harris.'

'Has to be a reason. He did see a car drive off. Remember?'

'So what? He couldn't ID anybody.'

'True, but he did see a car.'

Yates pointed back at the warehouse door. 'Is that what this is all about? Because he saw a car?'

'Maybe not just that. Maybe to find out if that was *all* he really did see and *who* he told.'

'Well, they'll know he took Hargrave's credit card.'

'Yeah, and they'll also know that we know that and that we know the car they drove off in was a grey Ford.'

'Right! But Barney didn't know we reckon it was a cop car with a dent over the rear wheel, and as you said, all police cars have dents.'

Jordan was about to go to their car but stopped and looked at Yates. 'Also, I said show me a cops car that hasn't a dent and that would be odd.'

'So, we look for a car that's been recently cleaned up,' said Yates with enthusiasm. 'Like maybe in the last twenty-four hours?'

'Sounds right to me,' said Jordan, echoing Yates's enthusiasm. 'We'll get back to the station and pick up the computer list Bailey took from you.'

On the way past his desk to Bailey's office, Jordan noticed an envelope resting on it. He stopped to pick it up.

'Go get the list, Yates,' he said as he turned the envelope over and absently mindedly opened it.

Yates returned from Jordan's office waving the list. 'Got it, Harris.'

Jordan was sitting at his desk staring at what appeared to be a page from a newspaper.

'What is it, Harris?' asked Yates having noticed how pale Jordan had gone.

Jordan, mouth taut, passed the page of a newspaper to Yates. An advertisement for kitchen appliances caught her eye. One of the appliances, an electric mincer was circled. Beside it was a poor drawing of two small children with an arrow pointing from the children to the mincer.

Yates swallowed. 'Jesus!'

'Reckon someone is trying to send me a message,' said Jordan in a raspy voice.

Yates swallowed again. 'Your kids!'

'That's how I see it' said Jordan from between clenched teeth. He grabbed the phone and dialled ... waited ... there was no answer.

He replaced the phone with a bang, stood up from the chair and strode away. 'Come on, Yates!'

Yates hurried after the fast-departing Jordan.

Chapter 24

With the roof light flashing and siren blaring, Jordan was driving fiercely through the traffic.

'Why this, Harris? Why threaten you?' asked Yates as she hung on to the dashboard.

'Must be getting close. Somebody is getting worried.'

'But really, we haven't got anything … *the truck!*' she yelled.

Jordan swung the steering wheel sideways and the truck, horn blaring, flashed by, just missing them.

'Possibly,' said Jordan after getting the car back onto a straight course. 'But then again, maybe we've got something but just haven't worked it out yet.'

Jordan brought the car to a halt outside a neat little house in a quiet tree-lined street. They both leapt out of the car and ran to the front door. Jordan tried the doorknob then banged on the door with his fist. Getting no answer, he raced around to the back. By the back door was a pot plant. He lifted it, picked up the key lying underneath, unlocked the door and entered. Together, they raced through the house from room to room but nothing seemed untoward.

Yates glanced out the front window as another car pulled up. 'Who's this, Harris?'

Jordan went to the front door without replying. His two children, Tracey and Stephen, jumped out the back of the car and, on seeing Jordan raced towards him, both yelling.

'Daddy, Daddy!' shouted Stephen.

'Mum, it's Dad!' shouted Tracey.

Jordan bent down and hugged them both. 'Hi guys. How's things?'

'Oh great!' said Tracey excitedly. 'You staying, Dad? I won a prize for painting.'

'Hey, that's terrific, Tracey,' said Jordan as he stood up with Tracey and Stephen both hanging from his neck.

His wife, Linda, came towards them. 'Hi, Harris,' she said with a smile, 'going to introduce me?'

'Oh yeah, sorry. Yates, this is Linda and these two scallywags are Stephen and Tracey.'

Yates raised a hand in greeting. 'Hi, Linda. Hi, kids. I'm Felicity.'

'Hi, Felicity,' said Linda with another smile before readdressing Jordan. 'Can you give Jessie a hand, Harris?' she pointed to the elderly lady lifting shopping bags from the boot of her car.

Jordan put the two children down. 'Gotta help, Nan. I'll be back in a minute.'

'Hi, Jessie,' said Jordan on reaching Linda's mother. He gave her a kiss on the cheek and reached for the shopping bags. 'Let me give you a hand.'

After dropping the shopping on the kitchen table, Tracey came to him with hands raised and Jordan picked her up. Stephen grabbed hold of his other hand.

'Can you leave that for a minute, please, Jessie?' he said as she began unpacking the shopping.

Linda's expression changed instantly. 'What's up, Harris?' she asked, concern written on her face.

'You have to go away for a while,' Jordan replied quietly.

Linda's face lost some of its colour. 'Why, Harris? What have you got us involved in now?' Both hands went to her face as she guessed the situation. 'Oh God! It's that Hargraves business, isn't it? It was on the news. Oh God, Harris, that was awful.'

Jordan was still holding Tracey as she clung to his neck, with Stephen still holding tight to his hand. Jessie stood beside Linda and placed a hand on her shoulder.

'I'm sorry, Linda. Really I am,' said Jordan. 'Look, just put a few things in a suitcase and take off up the coast for a bit. Give me a call and tell me where you've stopped, okay?'

Linda stared at Jordan for a moment then reached up and took Tracey from him. 'You and Stephen go to your rooms and pack a few things. We're going on holiday.'

'You coming, Dad?' asked Stephen.

'Sorry, son, not this time.'

Stephen's face dropped as he looked down at the floor.

'Please come, Dad,' pleaded Tracey. 'It's been so long.'

Jordan shook his head. 'I'm really very sorry guys, but not this time. I'll make it up to you. Promise!'

Tracey hugged his leg. 'Promise?'

'Sure.' said Jordan.

'Okay then.' She released his leg and grabbed hold of Stephen's hand. 'Come on Stephen, let's pack.'

'Don't pack a lot,' shouted Linda after the children, 'just a few essentials, okay?' She turned to Jordan. 'How long, Harris?'

'Not very ... I hope ... we're getting close.'

'And we have to go away because?' said Linda, hands on hips and glaring at him.

Yates intervened. 'It's the nature of the case, Linda. We can operate better knowing our families and friends are safe. Helps us keep our minds on the job.'

'Yeah, right!' said Linda continuing to glare at Jordan. 'Don't let anything happen to the kids, Harris,' she whispered.

She strode away into the rooms where the children were busy selecting holiday clothes.

Jessie came to Jordan and gave him a hug. 'We'll be fine, Harris. Don't worry.'

'Thanks, Jessie.' He leant forward and gave her a kiss. 'I'll keep in touch.'

Jessie smiled at Yates before following Linda and the kids into the back rooms.

'Nice family, Harris,' said Yates.

Jordan let out a sigh. 'Yeah!' He shook himself. 'Let's go check out that list of grey Fords.'

As they drove away from the house, Yates took a look back and saw Linda and Jessie carrying a bag each, leaving the house. Tracey and Stephen were running in front of them carrying their favourite cuddly toys.

'Wow, that was quick!'

'Yeah. Practice makes perfect,' said Jordan.

'Happened very much?'

'Too often!'

'That what split you up?'

'Sure didn't help!'

'Sorry, Harris.'

Jordan gunned the motor. 'Let's get this business sorted,' he said fiercely.

Jordan stopped the car at the parking space of a police station in the nearby Preston area and began studying the computer printout of Ford cars.

'Three greys here,' said Yates.

They walked along the line of vehicles all of which had a fair share of dents and scratches.

'We're looking for a clean one, right?'

'That's it,' agreed Jordan.

'Well, none of these fit.'

Jordan frowned. 'Right, next!'

By the time they had pulled up at a further eight stations and inspected the vehicles in car parks, night had fallen.

'How many left?' asked Jordan.

'Four at Central and that's the lot.'

Standing beside another grey Ford, also dented, Jordan banged his hand down on the roof.

'Shit! Not one clean!'

Yates let out a deep sigh. 'Not one, now what?'

Jordan scratched his head. 'The poker school, one of them just has to have something.'

Yates stretched and rolled her shoulders. 'Right. But that's tomorrow, Harris. I'm bushed.'

Jordan gave a condescending nod. 'Agreed, tomorrow it is.'

Chapter 25

At the Southern Guild Bank, Jordan and Yates were making the first call of the morning to one of the poker players, Bob Furlow.

'I really don't know what else I can tell you, Detectives. I told you who were the winners and losers, and they are all good men as far as I'm aware.' He looked from Jordan to Yates. 'What more can I say?'

'What about their private lives, Mr Furlow? Any marital problems?'

Furlow considered for a moment. 'Well, Quentin, he's not married, never has been as far as I know.'

'Prefer boys, does he?' said Jordan.

Furlow was taken aback by the question. 'Good grief, no; at least, not that I'm aware of.'

'And Doctor Heiderfall?' said Yates.

'Lost his wife to cancer a couple of years ago, his son is also in medicine. He's a GP.'

'Either of them stretched financially?'

'Hardly!' said Furlow. 'Quentin comes from a very well-to-do and respectable family, and Franz is a respected heart surgeon, certainly no money problems there.'

'What about Tievan?' said Jordan.

'Don't know a lot about Jim,' said Furlow with a shake of his head. 'He's only been in the school about five months or so. Paul brought him in, met him at the basketball. Keen supporter of the Jets is Paul. He has a box there.'

'Thank you, Mr Furlow,' said Jordan. 'We'll be on our way. Thanks for your help. We know where to find you if necessary, eh!?'

'Certainly, any time,' said Furlow. 'I hope you can get it sorted sooner rather than later.'

'We're doing our best, sir,' said Yates as she followed Jordan out of Furlow's office and closed the door behind her.

'So, Norris has a box at the Jets. Interesting, eh?' said Jordan as they exited the bank.

Yates nodded. 'Yeah, Norris … the Jets … Mareno … is that how you see it?'

'Sounds good to me,' said Jordan cheerfully. 'Let's go brighten Norris's day.'

Chapter 26

Jordan and Yates approached the reception desk at the First City Bank.

'I'd like to see Mr Norris,' said Jordan showing his ID.

The receptionist looked at the badge. 'He has someone with him at the moment, Detective. Would you please take a seat? I'm sure he'll be available very soon.'

'Take a seat, Yates,' said Jordan. He pointed to the nearby chairs. 'Read one of those mags. Find out the best way to invest your bankroll. I need to pay a visit.'

'Sure!' said Yates. 'What to do with it all is keeping me awake at night.'

Jordan walked off to the toilets while Yates took a seat and picked up a magazine.

She had briefly scanned a few pages when the door to Norris's office opened and two men walked out. Yates glanced up from her magazine and watched them walk out. She stared at the back of the men as Jordan returned.

'Harris, look!' she said excitedly.

'Where?' said Jordan.

'There, those guys leaving the bank.'

'What about them?'

'Didn't you see what they are wearing?' she said as she threw the magazine onto the table and stood up.

'Yeah ... clothes!'

Yates became frustrated. 'The jackets, Harris, the jackets, same as yours!'

Jordan appeared confused. 'They're wearing my jacket?'

Yates looked straight at Jordan and spread her hands. 'Didn't you find a few cotton threads that matched your jacket?'

Jordan looked down at his jacket then glanced at the bank's front door through which the two men had now disappeared. His face hardened as he suddenly realised the meaning of Yates's remarks. He strode to Norris's office door and barged in without knocking.

Norris was not impressed by the intrusion. 'Now see here!' he said curtly from where he stood behind his desk. His facial expression immediately changed as he noticed who it was. His mouth opened but nothing came out as Jordan came forward.

'Sit down and tell me who the two guys are who just left,' said Jordan as he stared at Norris.

Norris sat down. 'Bank customers,' he said falteringly, 'they … they were inquiring about a loan.'

Jordan leant forward and grabbed Norris by the shirt front. 'Bullshit, Norris! You've got ten seconds before I start rearranging your appearance. Now, who are they?'

Norris swallowed hard. 'They work for Fred Penski,' he mumbled.

'The bookie?'

'Yes.'

'And why were they here?' said Jordan as he tightened his grip on Norris's shirt.

'Just to fix up a small amount I had outstanding.'

'How much?'

'Five thousand.'

Jordan released his hold on Norris's shirt and he slumped back into his chair.

'So, those two goons came to collect?'

Norris nodded. 'Yes. Well, actually I owed Penski seven but they said five would do.'

'And why was that Norris? Penski's not known for his charitable work.'

'Said I was a good customer and didn't want to lose me,' said Norris.

Jordan backed away from the desk and glanced at Yates.

'Mr Norris, before we go, just one more question. When you were at the Jets' game last time and Mr Mareno came into your box, what did you talk about?'

'Oh you know,' said Norris pensively, 'how the team was going, what chance they had of making the finals.'

'Yes, I see,' said Yates nonchalantly, 'and when he asked you how your poker game was going, what did you say?'

'Oh, just that I was doing okay.'

'And you never mentioned how the other players were going?'

'Well, no, of course not.'

'You really sure about that, Mr Norris? You didn't just happen to say ... oh, I don't know ... something like Hargraves is doing well?'

Norris looked from Yates to Jordan who was staring down at him. 'Well, now that I think about it ... I ... I may have said just that Hargraves was doing okay.'

Jordan lunged forward and reached out with intent to grab him again.

'You told him Hargraves was raking it in, didn't you, Norris?'

Norris leant further back into his chair, his face ashen, with sweat breaking out on his forehead.

'You are responsible for what happened, Norris, you stupid bastard.'

Yates put a hand on Jordan's shoulder as she saw his anger. 'Leave him, Harris.'

Norris was shaking, his eyes wide. 'No. No, you can't blame me for what happened to Madelaine and John. No. No never.'

'You just sit there,' said Jordan through clenched teeth. He took out his mobile phone and dialled, while staring at Norris. 'Winston, get a car over to First City Bank and take in Norris.' He paused, listening. 'We're off to see Penski ... Yeah the bookie. I'll keep in touch.'

Jordan replaced the phone into his jacket pocket. 'When you get in front of my boss you tell him what you told us, okay, Norris?'

Norris dropped his head, trembling, his shirt now stained with sweat.

'Next stop, Penski's betting shop,' said Jordan to Yates as they left Norris's office.

Chapter 27

Jordan slowly drove up the street towards the betting shop. 'Penski's is just over there across the road,' he said as he brought the car to a halt.

'And see that, a grey Ford at the curb?' said Yates.

Jordan gave a short whistle. 'Yeah, looks real clean too.' He took out his mobile. 'Hi, Winston, we're outside Penski's and there's a grey Ford nearby.' He paused. 'Right, very possible.' He paused again. 'Yeah ... yeah!'

He threw the phone over his shoulder onto the rear seat.

'What were all the yeahs about, Harris?'

'He's sending backup, reckons we should wait.'

'And are we going to?' asked Yates, already feeling she knew the answer.

'Well, you can if you like,' said Jordan as he opened the car door and got out.

Yates got out the passenger side. 'Jesus, Harris, let's wait!'

Jordan ignored Yates's plea and strode across the road. Yates looked around gave a shrug and followed, shaking her head.

Jordan quietly opened the shop door.

'Harris, why not wait?' whispered Yates. 'Backup should be here soon.'

Jordan took no notice and slowly entered the shop. The front of the shop was empty.

Yates put a hand on Jordan's shoulder. 'Harris!'

Jordan raised a hand, his head to one side. 'Shhh!'

From a door at the rear of the shop, indistinct voices could be heard and an occasional laugh. Cautiously, Jordan moved towards it and took out his hand gun.

'Oh shit!' said Yates while also producing hers.

Jordan slowly turned the door handle, then thrust the door open and walked in.

Penski, Albright and Mayor Owens were sitting around a small table, each holding a glass in their hand. A nearly empty bottle of whiskey was on the table.

The conversation and laughter came to an abrupt halt as they faced Jordan and Yates. With a look of surprise on his face, Jordan stared at Mayor Owens.

Mayor Owens stood up and slowly placed his glass on the table. With arms outstretched he looked at Jordan. 'Harris, you don't understand!' he pleaded.

Jordan stared back at him in disbelief. 'You don't need the money and you're leaving office, so Hargraves was no threat.'

Jordan noticed that Albright had put his right hand inside his jacket and he quickly pointed his gun at him. 'You really don't want to do that. Put both your hands on the table.'

Albright obeyed.

'Nice jacket, pal,' said Jordan. 'You know, I reckon I can lay my hands on a bit of cotton to match that.'

Albright glanced down at his jacket then at the one Jordan was wearing. 'It's a very popular make,' he said with a smirk. 'I see you have one just like it.'

Jordan smiled. 'Oh I do indeed! Thing is though, mine is all here while yours has a little missing, and I got a feeling it'll match up exactly with a little something we found on a picture frame in the Hargraves' place.'

The smirk quickly disappeared from Albright's face as he looked at his jacket.

'No way.' He shook his head. 'It was Sol ...' His voice trailed off as he realised what he had said.

Mayor Owens glared at Albright. 'Shut up, you idiot.'

During the exchange Penski had remained silent, his eyes darting from one to the other. His eyes widened further when Jordan pointed his gun directly at Mayor Owens.

'What you did to the Hargraves was bad enough, Mayor, but I really take exception to you threatening my family.'

Yates, who had been standing behind Jordan suddenly shouted. 'Harris!'

'He won't be missed,' said Jordan as he used both hands to steady the gun.

'No, Harris!' repeated Yates more urgently.

'The lady said no, Harris,' said a voice.

Jordan froze as he recognised the voice. Smiles appeared on the faces of Penski, Albright and Owens. With his gun still pointed steadily at Owens, Jordan turned his head slightly to look behind him. Morrison had a gun against Yates's head and a grinning Mareno was standing beside them.

'You want to know why the Mayor, Harris? Power and recognition, that's why. With Hargraves gone that leaves me and I'll be pulling out so that means Owens here will be asked to stay on. It's that simple.'

'I bet it was your idea to treat the Hargraves that way,' said Jordan. 'You're that kind of arsehole.'

'Actually, it wasn't, Harris. The credit for that bit of ingenuity goes to Morrison here.'

Morrison grinned and pushed his gun harder against Yates's head.

Yates grimaced. 'Shoot the bastard, Harris.'

'Feisty little thing, isn't she?' said Mareno with a laugh. 'Seems we have a small problem. You shoot the Mayor and Morrison takes off the top of the lady's head. Now personally, I can get by without the Mayor.' He turned to look at Yates. 'What's your name, dear?'

'Up yours!' said Yates.

'Oh well, guess it's of no great importance,' said Mareno with a shrug. 'So, Harris, what should we do?'

A shout came from the front of the shop. 'Harris!'

Momentarily distracted, Morrison turned his head to the voice.

'Down!' shouted Jordan.

Yates dropped to the ground. Jordan swivelled around in an instant and fired. The shot hit Morrison in the forehead, and staring but not seeing, he slowly crumpled to the floor. Albright took the opportunity to reach for his gun, but as he brought it up a shot from Yates hit him in the shoulder and flung him backwards. His gun clattered to the floor.

Penski, still sitting in a chair, raised his hands. 'Don't shoot!' he yelled.

Mayor Owens slumped down into his chair looking completely distraught.

Mareno raced out a back door with Jordan hot on his heels.

O'Brien and two officers with guns drawn raced into the room. Bailey surveyed the scene in front of him. Morrison lay dead. Albright, moaning loudly, was holding his shoulder. Penski with hands still raised, continued to yell, 'Don't shoot.' And Yates was busy putting handcuffs on Mayor Owens.

'What the ...!?' said an astonished Bailey.

Yates looked up. 'I'll explain later, sir.'

'Where's Harris?'

Yates pointed to the back door. 'He's after Mareno.'

As Jordan ran out the back door of the shop he was hit in the chest by a length of wood wielded by Mareno. His gun flew from his hand and, gasping for breath, he dropped to one knee. He looked up to see Mareno swing the length of wood towards his head and quickly rolled himself to one side.

Mareno stumbled, caught off balance by the swing and miss.

Jordan leapt to his feet and flung a punch at Mareno that hit him in the mouth and knocked him to the ground.

Mareno put out a hand to help himself get up and his hand touched the gun Jordan had dropped. He grabbed it, raised it and pointed it at Jordan.

Jordan was about to attack again but on seeing the gun, stopped.

Mareno spat blood and stood up. 'Time's up, Harris.'

'Go to hell!' said Jordan.

Mareno cocked the gun and grinned. 'You first, Harris!'

Two gunshots in quick succession made Mareno jerk backwards. His grin faded to a surprised expression as he looked down at the red stain spreading across his shirt front. He looked to the side where Yates stood with a wisp of smoke coming from the gun she held pointed at him. Mareno's eyes turned upward as he fell to the ground.

Bailey came out the back door and looked down at Mareno. 'Jesus, Yates, couldn't you just have winged him?'

'Be a waste of a bullet, sir. Besides, think of the money we've saved the city in court costs.' She looked at Jordan. 'And Harris told me that if anyone ever pointed a gun at him I should take him out. That right, Harris?'

Jordan nodded while wiping dust off his jacket. 'I did indeed. Thanks, Felicity.'

Bailey shook his head, took a piece of paper out of his pocket and handed it to Jordan.

'Here. Linda rang. This is where she and the kids are. Go see them; they can come home.'

'Thanks, Winston.'

'The one inside isn't hurt too badly,' said Yates. 'Had a fake ID on him and Penski wants to make a deal.'

'And Owens?' asked Jordan.

'Been struck dumb, but with what we've got, he's a goner. Reckon we'll have to vote for a new mayor after all.' She turned to Bailey. 'What do you reckon, sir? Harris could have my vote!'

Bailey nodded in agreement. 'Sure, mine too, anything to get him out of my hair.'

Jordan looked again down at Mareno. 'Thanks again, Felicity.'

'My pleasure, Harris, now go see your family. And remember, I asked you to call me Yates.'

Jordan smiled. 'Yeah right!' He raised a hand in a brief wave as he walked away. 'See ya!'

'Yeah, go. Go!' said Bailey.

'Pushy old goat!' mumbled Jordan.

'I heard that!' shouted Bailey.

Interlude

'Another?' asked Bailey, pointing at the now empty glasses.

'Yeah, that'd be great, thanks, sir,' replied Carmichael. 'Harris was real lucky to get out of that one, eh?'

'Right ... changed a bit though ... a bit more cautious after that affair.'

'And his offsider Yates?'

'She wasn't as tough as she thought she was. The images of the Hargraves' bodies and the shooting of Mareno played on her mind so she quit the force and moved to Tasmania to get away from everything. Met a schoolteacher, got married and now living a very happy life so I understand.'

'Good for her ... Harris has never mentioned his wife Linda and his kids; what's happened to them?'

Bailey's face suddenly took on a sad expression. He shook his head, reached for his beer and took a long swallow before continuing. 'Now that was a knife in Harris's heart. Linda took off back to Queensland along with her mother right after the Mareno business; reckoned she couldn't take any more of the stress being around him. She was taking the kids to school one morning when she was hit head on by a semi-trailer; all killed instantly. They reckon the semi driver who had been driving all night fell asleep at the wheel. Bloody terrible ... bloody terrible.'

Carmichael took a deep breath. 'Blimey, that would have really got to him ... and so he's been on his own ever since?'

'Not quite ... let himself go somewhat—drinking too much, mixing with the wrong women.'

'May I ask why you are now in uniform after earlier being a detective, sir?'

'Good question, Steve. Well, after I got married and then had a couple of kids, I found that the detective work was taking up too much of my time—both day and night. As you know, being away from the family and the stress sometimes wives have to endure when detectives get in sticky situations puts a strain on relationships. I decided my marriage was too important to me to take a risk on ... look, I'll go get the drinks and continue Harris's story from when you joined him.'

PART 3:
PAYBACK

Chapter 1

Sitting slumped behind his cluttered desk, Detective Harris Jordan was far from a picture of sartorial splendour. His rumpled suit and stained tie, an indication of his non-concern with how others considered his appearance. He watched as an overweight, bleached blonde and spikey-haired youth walked out of the squad room.

Jordan had been married briefly to Elizabeth to whom he had a son Kevin. He had met Elizabeth following a drunken night out with a colleague after securing a conviction on a known break and enter individual they had been chasing for three months.

Elizabeth, or Beth as she preferred, was a dancer at a late-night strip club they had frequented. At twenty-four she had a great figure that she was only too happy to show off to the patrons, who seemed particularly keen to shove the odd five dollar note down the front of her briefs. Jordan had caught her eye, invited her back to his flat, and enjoyed a night of frenzied, drunken pleasure. The result was Kevin.

Doing the right thing, so he told himself and his colleagues, he agreed to marry Beth.

Bailey learnt of the upcoming nuptial and rang Jordan to offer his congratulations. Jordan invited Bailey around to meet Beth a few months prior to the event, and after meeting Beth, Bailey took an immediate dislike to her, not that he mentioned it to Jordan at the time. Back at his own station he did some digging into Beth's background. What he discovered didn't really surprise. She had run away from home in her early teens and survived by shoplifting and prostitution. Feeling he had to confront his friend with her history, he asked Jordan to come around to his place for dinner.

After the meal, while his wife Debbie was washing up and the kids had gone to bed, he and Jordan sat alone in the lounge room with a glass of scotch.

'Harris, I don't quite know how to say this, but I did a bit of checking into Beth's background.'

Jordan glanced sharply at him. 'You did what? Why?'

''Cause you're a friend, and I just thought something wasn't quite right about her.'

Jordan drained his glass before placing it on the side table. He stared at Bailey for a long while before speaking. 'You investigated my upcoming wife, eh. I can't remember asking you to do that, *friend*.'

Bailey finished his drink, swallowed and took a deep breath. 'Do you want to know what I found or no?'

'Sure, *friend*, let's have it.'

'Okay, but this isn't going to—'

Jordan interrupted. 'Just get on with it, *friend*.'

'She has a record for shoplifting and on the game.'

Jordan sat silently, his eyes fixedly staring at Bailey. He nodded. 'And you thought it something you should bring to my attention, eh?'

'Yes, Harris, I'm sorry, but yes I did.'

Jordan stood up. 'She's carrying my child, Winston, and I'm going to do the right thing. The past is just that, the past.'

He walked towards the front door. 'Tell Debbie thanks for the great meal. I'll see myself out. See you round, Winston.'

Bailey watched Jordan leave and slam the door behind him. Shaking his head, he went into the kitchen where Debbie was wiping the last of the dishes and gave her a cuddle.

She smiled at him. 'Did Harris just leave?'

Winston kissed her cheek. 'Yeah, he has an early start tomorrow.'

'But he didn't say goodbye.' She looked in her husband's eyes.

'There's more to it, Winston, I can tell.'

Bailey nodded. 'You could always read me. I'll help put the dishes away before we head off to bed, then I'll tell you all about it, okay?'

Jordan married Beth at the local Registry Office. The only others present were two of Beth's friends from her time in the strip club. She told Jordan her parents were dead and that she had no other family.

After the marriage, he, Beth and son Kevin lived for eighteen months in a home he bought before he moved out after coming home unexpectedly to find Beth in bed with the bloke who'd been mowing his lawns.

Once more "doing the right thing", he sold the family home and handed two-thirds of its selling price over to Beth as part of the divorce settlement. Needless to say, Beth wasted her way through her share in very quick time. As well as paying child support for Kevin, there were many occasions when Beth requested additional funds to pay for overdue bills, or for "little extras" for Kevin, such as the recent call on him to support Kevin's dream to be a rockstar.

The continued demands meant that Jordan had very little left over from his pay packet. The flat he occupied was far from extravagant, and the meagre cash left over to feed and dress himself was only too evident in his current wardrobe. Fortunately, the supplied police vehicle and petrol at least provided him a means of getting around.

While with Beth, Jordan had taken care of himself physically by regularly exercise but, following the breakup, he let himself go. Now existing on mostly takeaway and scotch, he had rapidly put on weight.

His previous interest in advancement also departed. Despite several offers from his superiors to move up the ladder he was content to just get on with the job.

Time had healed his relationship with Bailey and, now, after being at the same station for six years, he had a good knowledge of the criminal element in the district.

Unlike Jordan, Bailey had not only married and raised a family but managed to stay married despite the demanding pressures of long and late hours, and the sometimes life-threatening situations the job presented. Now, as Senior Sergeant, his time was spent more on administrative duties, and involved fewer late nights, enabling him to arrive home at more amenable hours. His three children had also left home which presented a much quieter home life. Daughter Patricia had married a solicitor and was happily settled with a daughter of her own. Eldest son Robert was also married and teaching at the local secondary school. Younger son Wesley was touring Europe with a couple of mates and hopefully staying out of trouble. Senior Sergeant Winston Bailey left his office and joined Jordan. 'Problem, Harris?'

Jordan ran a hand through his unkempt hair, grimaced and rubbed his stomach.

'My no-good ex-wife wants more money so my useless kid can have guitar lessons 'cause he's gonna be a rockstar, and my gut feels like something is trying to chew its way out.'

Bailey shook his head. He and Jordan were now both in their early fifties and looking towards retirement. 'Your gut hurts 'cause of the crap you put in it, and if you'd listened to me years ago ...'

'Well, being the nice guy I am, I did the right thing and married the bitch. After all, it was my kid.'

'Yeah ... right! Now I'm going to brighten your day up even further.'

'How's that?'

'Giving you a partner.'

Jordan thumped his desk and stared up at Bailey. 'No way, Winston, I work alone.'

Bailey shrugged and spread his hands dismissively. 'Sorry, Harris, orders, you drew the straw.'

'Geez, Winston, who?'

'Steve Carmichael.'

'Not the Mayor's son!?'

Bailey nodded. 'The one and only.'

Jordan rose from his chair and angrily stared at Bailey. He was about to give him a mouthful when he noticed a young man who was completely different in appearance to himself. Tall and fit, early twenties, clean shaven, hair short and wearing the kind of Giorgio Armani suit he could nowhere near afford.

'You owe me big for this, Winston,' he murmured.

Bailey smiled at the young man and shook his hand, then introduced him.

'Constable Steve Carmichael, this is Detective Harris Jordan.'

Carmichael, at just under two metres was slightly taller than Jordan. He put his hand forward. 'Heard a lot about you, sir. Thank you for letting me work with you.'

Jordan reluctantly accepted the hand, gave a brief nod and forced a smile, but remained silent. A few seconds passed before Bailey broke the strained silence.

'Detective Jordan has twenty-five years up. You couldn't get a better officer to show you the ropes.' He gave a sigh before handing a piece of paper to Jordan. 'Right, well, there's been an attack on a young woman, this address.'

He turned and walked back to his office, shaking his head.

Jordan studied the paper, glanced at Carmichael, jerked his head and walked off. Carmichael followed in his wake.

As it happened Carmichael's upbringing was similar to Jordan's. Carmichael's father, Bradley Carmichael, had got himself elected to the local council with the help of the builders' trade union he was in at the time, and subsequently managed to get on the right side of a local millionaire property developer. The developer happened to have a rather attractive daughter who took a shine to Bradley and, taking advantage of his luck, Bradley and Sarah tied the knot. The resultant consummation produced Steve. With money now behind him, Bradley sent Steve to the best private school and on to university. While at university, Bradley had been elected mayor and Steve was a huge disappointment to his parents when, after passing all exams with flying colours, and the possibility of a future in law, he joined the police force.

Chapter 2

The small housing estate was situated behind a light industrial area, and contained a mixture of homes. Mostly small houses with single carports, it was certainly not a "well-to-do" area, but more of a first home buyers. The odd unkempt garden and vehicle undergoing repair on the front lawn, gave the impression of not overly concerned occupants.

'Number 27, this'll be it,' said Jordan as he brought the car to halt just past the driveway.

During the drive, he had asked Carmichael about his background.

'You look fit; what do you do?'

'Played union at uni, and now turn up at the local club. Strictly weekend amateur, but it does help keep me reasonably fit.'

'What made you join up?'

'I was at uni doing a business management degree, and realised it wasn't for me. Had always had an idea about joining the police, so here I am.'

'And how did Daddy the Mayor feel about your decision?'

'Not happy at first, but when he realised it was what I really wanted, wished me luck.'

'And I have him to thank for you being placed here with me?'

'That's right, said you're one of the best.'

Jordan gave a chuckle as they got out the car. 'One of the best, eh? He sure can't think too much of the rest of the crew.'

The home at number 27 had a manicured lawn and a couple of well-maintained garden beds.

'Looks like these owners take a bit of pride in the place,' said Carmichael as he followed Jordan to the front door. As he knocked on the door, Jordan whispered to Carmichael. 'Remember what allegedly happened here, so take it easy, okay.'

The door was opened by a young, angry looking man.

Jordan quickly produced his badge. 'Good morning, Mr Martin, I'm Detective Jordan and this is—'

Before he could finish introductions Martin stood aside, ushered them in and closed the door behind them. 'This way, officers.'

They followed Martin into a small sitting room.

'This is my wife Clair and I'm Chad.'

Clair was sitting bent over on a couch. Her hands grasping her knees, hair dishevelled, her eyes red and teary.

Jordan crouched down in front of her. 'What happened, Clair?'

Carmichael, with a notepad and pencil in his hand, remained silent.

Clair just shook her head and sobbed.

'She's been raped,' said Chad furiously, 'this morning, that's what happened and I want the bastard caught and strung up.'

Jordan glanced up at an obviously uncomfortable Carmichael.

'We are very sorry for what's happened, but we will need your help, Clair, to catch the person responsible, and that means asking some difficult questions, and you'll need to see a Doctor for a medical report. But if you can give us a brief description of the man for a start.'

Clair's sobbing became uncontrollable. Chad sat beside her and hugged her, looked up at Jordan and shook his head.

'Tell you what,' said Jordan quietly. 'Take Clair for that medical, then bring her around to the station and we'll get her to look over some photos.'

Chad nodded, his face showing the signs of despair. 'Anything, just get the bastard,' he muttered through clenched teeth.

'We'll certainly do our best,' said Jordan. He raised a hand as Chad started to get up.

'That's okay, we'll see ourselves out.'

'So,' said Jordan as he and Carmichael walked towards the car, 'your first rape case?'

Carmichael swallowed, his face ashen. 'That obvious, eh?'

'And I can promise you they don't get any easier,' said Jordan.

Carmichael showed his blank notebook. 'Sorry, sir, but I didn't take any notes.'

Jordan shrugged. 'And when we're not with the public, you call me Harris, okay, Steve.'

Carmichael gave a short smile. 'Right, thanks.'

'Okay, let's go back to the station and go through the files of known arseholes,' said Jordan as he started the car. 'Might come up with a few names before Clair and Chad come in.'

Chapter 3

Jordan and Carmichael approached a group of three young men in a gymnasium who were gathered around a weightlifting apparatus. They were cheering on the man straining to bench lift.

'Push it, Johny, push it,' shouted one youth who had a particularly bad acne-scarred face.

As Jordan and Carmichael's presence is noted, the young men became silent.

'Come on, Stresyk, you can do it,' said Jordan .

Stresyk eased the bar back onto the stand and sat up. Wearing just a pair of shorts, it was apparent he did a deal of weightlifting. Tattoos covered his muscular arms, body and legs. He looked at Jordan with a broad grin on his face, and ran a hand over his shaved head. 'Well, if it isn't Detective Jordan.'

He turned to look up and down at Carmichael. 'Who's the baby, Harris?'

Carmichael started towards Stresyk, but Jordan held him back.

'Now, let's not get silly here, Johny. You need to come with us and answer a few questions is all.'

Stresyk spread his arms. ''Bout what?'

'A young lady has made a complaint, you bit of shit,' said Carmichael.

Stresyk started to laugh and the others joined in.

'You gotta be kiddin' man. I never get any complaints.' He approached Carmichael virtually chest to chest. 'And you oughta be more careful who you speak to like that, copper.'

Jordan got between them. 'Easy, Johny, or I'll have to let this officer subdue you for resisting arrest.'

Stresyk stepped back and laughed again. 'Okay, Harris, if you want to make a fool of yourselves, what the hell.'

To the jeers and cheers of the others, Jordan, Carmichael and a swaggering Stresyk walked out of the gym.

Jordan drove the car back to the police station while Stresyk sat in the back with Carmichael beside him.

'So, how things with you, Harris? Managed to prove anything lately?' said Stresyk with a snort of derision.

'Caught the odd "no-hoper", Johny, and reckon you'll be next on the list.'

Stresyk laughed. 'Oh, Harris, Harris, the ladies love me, man. No way do I get complaints. What I got they can't get enough of.'

Carmichael couldn't contain himself. He leant across and grabbed Stresyk by the throat.

'Shut your dirty mouth, you useless apology for a human being.'

Jordan saw the event in his rear view mirror. 'Cool it, Steve, he's just trying to wind you up.'

Carmichael released Stresyk and sat back.

Stresyk grinned. 'Got a live one here, Harris, better teach him to control himself before he gets himself in trouble.'

Jordan brought the car to halt outside the police station. Carmichael virtually dragged Stresyk out of the rear passenger seat, and with a firm grip on his arm, escorted him inside.

Chapter 4

n the interview room, Jordan slowly arranged paperwork on his desk while Stresyk sat in a plastic chair facing him, grinning and humming a tune.

Carmichael paced up and down behind him.

Jordan looked up from the paperwork and smiled at Stresyk. 'You've a bit of a history, Johny. Stealing a motor vehicle and driving without a licence and uninsured, break and enter, threatening a police officer etcetera, etcetera, and got away with being placed on good behaviour bonds. You've been very lucky, Johny.'

Stresyk continued grinning. 'And it was you who booked me on the motor vehicle business, eh, Harris. What is it worth it? You had all that paperwork and I walked out.'

Jordan smiled back at Stresyk. 'Well, there's always a next time, Johny.'

He picked up a sheet of paper and waved it in front of Stresyk.

'The complainant, Johny, is a young woman who lives in Glendale Street. Mean anything to you?'

Stresyk shrugged his shoulders, sniffing. 'Not a thing.'

'Thing is, Johny, she picked you out from a bunch of photos.'

'Must have seen me around and taken a liking.'

'The other thing is, she had a medical examination which discovered traces of semen that matched your DNA we hold in our data bank. Mean anything now?'

'Let me think,' said Stresyk rubbing his chin. 'So many it's hard to remember. Oh yes, think I got her. Good looking piece. Invited me in yesterday morning.'

Jordan nodded in understanding. 'Right, right, so you don't deny having sex with her?'

Stresyk spread his arms. 'Hell no! She offered, I gave, end of story.'

'You knocked on the door, and she said come in let's do it?'

'Yeah, 'bout that!'

'And why that particular house?'

'Was a hot day man; just happened to be walking by and asked for a glass of water, got invited in. What can I say man, liked what she saw, you know how it is.'

Carmichael stopped his pacing and leant over into Stresyk's face. 'You're a piece of shit, Stresyk, no respectable woman would want anything to do with the likes of you.'

Stresyk laughed in Carmichael's face, put his hands behind his head and leant back.

'Who said she's respectable, man?'

Carmichael grabbed Stresyk by the neck, pulled him out of the chair and slammed him against the wall. Jordan jumped up, and quickly pulled them apart. 'Leave it, Steve, leave it, he ain't worth it.'

He pushed Carmichael away and helped Stresyk back into the chair.

Carmichael's face was bright red. 'That bastard needs—'

Jordan interrupted. 'Constable, I said leave it. Stand away and shut up.'

Stresyk looked at Carmichael and winked.

Jordan returned to his chair and leant towards Stresyk. 'Johnstone Stresyk, you are formally charged with the rape of Clair Martin. You do not have to say anything but—'

Stresyk waved his arms 'Yeah, yeah, yeah, heard it all before, man.'

Jordan continued while getting up from the chair. 'Anything you do say will be taken down and may be used against you in a court of law. If you cannot afford a solicitor, the court will appoint one for you. Do you understand your rights?'

Stresyk shook his head 'Wasting your time, man.'

'This officer will escort you to a cell, and I'll see you next in court.' Jordan looked at Carmichael who had seemingly managed to bring himself under control.

Without a word, Carmichael grabbed Stresyk by the arm and hustled him out of the room.

Jordan grimaced, rubbed his stomach, and took a packet of tablets from his jacket pocket.

Bailey entered the room. 'Tablets, eh, Harris! Go see the doc; maybe an ulcer. Stresyk the guy?'

Jordan nodded. 'Oh, he's the guy alright, Clair Martin IDed him, and he's not denying having sex with her.'

'You're not sounding all that sure. What's the catch?'

'Stresyk says she okayed it.'

'You believe that?'

'Not for a second.'

'And Carmichael?'

'Did good. I'd asked him to play a bit of the bad guy, which he really did manage in spades. At one point I thought he was going to get properly stuck into the arrogant prick. Yeah, reckon he'll be right.'

Bailey poked him in the stomach. 'And this?'

Jordan grimaced again. 'Okay, give me a break. I'll fix a time, alright?'

Bailey was about to leave as Carmichael returned. 'Good, sooner the better. Just do the paperwork and go home. Between the two of you shouldn't take long.'

'Paperwork?' asked Carmichael when Bailey had left.

'Yeah, paperwork, now sit down and we'll get started.'

'How long's this going to take, Harris? I've got a hot date this evening.'

'The longer you keep yacking the longer it'll be, so grab a pen and quit moaning.'

Carmichael pulled a sheet of clean paper in front of him, and took a biro out of the cup of pens on Jordan's desk. He continued mumbling to himself. Jordan looked up with a slight smile. 'This ain't a nine to five shift job, Steve. Welcome to detective work.'

Chapter 5

Judge Rodney Alderton brought his gavel down on his bench with a sharp rap.

Middleton Davis, early sixties, grossly overweight, the lawyer for Stresyk, had been badgering Clair for fifteen minutes, and had at last succeeded in making her distraught and tearful.

'Mr Middleton, do you have anything relevant to ask?' said the judge.

Jordan and Carmichael, having said there piece, could now only watch the proceedings as they sat with Chad Martin beside them.

'That Middleton is a right bastard,' whispered Jordan. 'This is the way he always works. I can't stand the prick.'

Middleton referred to his notes. 'Most certainly do, Your Honour.'

He turned to face Clair standing alone in the witness box, shoulders slumped, wiping her eyes.

'Mrs Martin, you say you did not invite Mr Stresyk into your home.'

Clair replied adamantly. 'I've already told you. He asked for a glass of water, and when I opened the door to give it to him, he pushed his way in.'

'And you did not behave provocatively towards him.'

Clair shouted. 'No, no, no, of course not. He forced himself onto me.'

Morton looked down at his notes, lifted his right hand which held a piece of paper. He smiled at Clair. 'I have here the doctor's report following his inspection of your allegation, and although it confirms that intercourse took place, there is no finding of excessive bruising on any part of your body. And yet you say my client forced his way onto you.'

Clair started shaking. 'He did, he did, I begged him to leave. He said he had a knife.'

Middleton selected another piece of paper from in front of him. 'There is no report of a knife being found on my client, Mrs Martin.'

Tears streamed down Clair's cheeks. 'But he said he did, I was scared. What could I do.'

Middleton shrugged. 'Mrs Martin, I submit that you invited Mr Stresyk into your home, behaved provocatively and then had consensual sex. After all, according to a neighbour, you do often parade around your backyard in very little clothing.'

Clair's solicitor jumped out of his seat. 'Your Honour, this is—'

The spectators groaned and then shouted abuse at the solicitor.

Judge Alderton banged his gavel. 'Silence in court.'

Stresyk turned towards Jordan and winked.

It was all is too much for Clair. She screamed at her husband. 'This is ridiculous, he's making stuff up, no more, Chad, please no more.'

Chad got up and pushed his way past Jordan and Carmichael, and raced to Clair. He took her in his arms as she sobbed uncontrollably.

He pointed at the judge. 'You call this justice!?'

He glared angrily at Jordan and Carmichael.

'I'm so sorry, Chad. I told you it would be rough,' said Jordan sympathetically.

'He can't get away with this,' Chad yelled as, with his arm around Clair, he left the courtroom.

Middleton turned towards the judge. 'Cancellation, Your Honour?'

Judge Alderton glared at Middleton with undisguised dislike, shook his head, sighed and banged his gavel down. 'Case dismissed.'

A grinning Stresyk was shaken by the hand by an equally smiling-faced Middleton. Together, they turned to look at Jordan and Carmichael. Stresyk raised his hand, his middle finger extended.

Jordan turned away, grimaced and grabbed his stomach. 'Come on, Steve, I need a drink.'

Chapter 6

Carmichael handed Jordan his third large scotch as he had a sip from his glass of light beer.

'So, we just forget it and move on, is that what you're saying, Harris?'

Jordan took a long swallow. 'No choice, Steve. If you don't it'll get to you, and you won't be able to cope with whatever comes up next.'

Losing was not something that had ever sat well with Carmichael. When he played rugby union at university, as far as he was concerned coming second was never good enough. If the team was behind at halftime he would berate his teammates for their effort and demand stronger performance in the second half. On occasion, some team members would be quick to tell him to calm down and remember that it was "just a game" after all.

'But the bastard was guilty. You know it, I know it; even the bloody judge knew it.'

'Right, Steve, but if the Martins don't want to go further that's an end to it.'

'Not right, Harris, not right by a long way.'

Jordan finished his scotch. 'Tomorrow's another day, Steve, I'm off home; take the weekend off. I'll see you Monday morning.'

Carmichael watched him leave and finished his beer. 'Just not bloody right,' he mumbled as he banged the empty glass down on the bar and followed Jordan out.

Chapter 7

Monday morning Carmichael was seated at a desk studiously examining the paperwork in front of him, when Jordan turned up.

'Couldn't you sleep, Steve?'

'Just going over procedures.'

Jordan was unimpressed. 'Oh great! Procedure is the way to go.'

He pulled up a chair beside Carmichael, and dragged one of the books lying on the desk towards him. He was about to make a remark when Bailey joined them.

'Just heard; Clair Martin has suicided.'

Jordan and Carmichael looked at each other then up at Bailey. A long period of silence followed.

'Sorry, guys,' said Bailey quietly.

Carmichael flung the book he had been reading across the room. 'Shit!'

Jordan grimaced, holding his stomach. 'When? How?'

'Saturday night. Chad had gone out for a pizza, came home and found Clair in the bath; slashed her wrists.'

'Funeral been arranged, Winston?'

'Day after tomorrow ... two-thirty.'

'Bit quick!'

'Apparently something she and Chad had agreed on should the worst happen.'

'And it certainly has,' said Carmichael, shaking his head.

'Reckoned it would give the other a better chance to get on with life,' said Bailey.

Jordan grimaced again.

'Had that checked, Harris?'

'Yeah, yeah, seeing the doc ... get the results later today.'

'Let me know soon as, okay?'

Carmichael appeared confused. 'Check-up, results, what's going on, Harris?'

'He's had stomach pain for too long and been putting up with it, the silly bugger,' said Bailey as he walked away.

Carmichael got out of his chair and walked over to where the book he had thrown was resting against the wall, dusted it off and returned to the desk.

'I'll drive you over if you like, Harris.'

Jordan shook his head. 'Give over!' he said angrily. 'If I need a nursemaid I'll let you know.' He got out of the chair and kicked it to one side.

'Finish your checking up on procedures, and take the rest of the day off.'

'Hell, Harris! I was just trying to help,' said Carmichael as Jordan walked out without another word.

The unobtrusive sign above the door of the old timber home was the only indication that it was a doctor's surgery. Jordan came out and walked down the steps to the front picket fence, opened the gate and walked over to his car parked nearby.

He took the car keys from his left hand trousers pocket. On reaching the car, he brought his right hand down with a slam on the roof, and kicked the driver's door before getting in. With the tyres screeching, he drove away.

Chapter 8

The following Wednesday was cool and drizzly.

A small crowd of family and friends wearing raincoats, and with umbrellas raised, were gathered around as Clair Martin's coffin was lowered into the grave.

As the short service ended, the people dispersed, leaving Chad standing alone staring down into the grave.

Jordan and Carmichael had been standing a short distance back, but now approached Chad.

'We're so sorry for your loss, Chad,' said Jordan.

'So very sorry,' said Carmichael.

Chad turned, tears streaming down his cheeks. 'She couldn't take the humiliation; what that arsehole lawyer said about her. It's just not right they can do that. And she was pregnant too.'

Carmichael's mouth dropped open. 'Oh Jesus, Chad!'

Jordan reached out and touched Chad's shoulder. 'The law will catch up with Stresyk, Chad.'

Chad angrily brushed Jordan's hand away. 'Useless! The law is bloody useless. But that bastard will pay.'

Jordan took a step back. 'Chad, we—'

Chad interrupted angrily. 'The bastard will pay!'

Jordan glanced at Carmichael and with a slight flick of his hand signified they should leave. Without conversing, they walked the short distance through the graveyard to their car. Got in and put on the seat belts.

Carmichael broke the silence. 'Poor Chad, Clair was pregnant.'

Jordan fumbled with the car keys. Gave a groan and bent over towards the steering wheel.

'You okay, Harris?'

'Yeah, bit of reflux, the eggs I had for breakfast are fighting back.'

'How did your visit to the doc go?'

Jordan started the car and eased it out into the traffic. 'Good … just gotta be more careful what I eat.'

'What about what you drink?'

'Said I should drink more scotch, which is exactly why I'm heading for the pub.'

Carmichael shook his head. 'And you expect me to believe that.'

Jordan shrugged. 'Can't say as how I really give a shit what you believe. Now do you want to join me or shall I drop you off back at the station?'

Carmichael smiled. 'What the hell, take me to the pub, Harris.'

Chapter 9

Stresyk had enjoyed a big night out celebrating with his mates. It was after one in the morning as he stumbled along the dimly lit side street towards the old block of flats he called home. His flat was on the bottom of the two-storey walk-up. Five flats down and five up. He fumbled in his jeans pocket for the door key of the flat on the left, opened the door and entered. Not bothering to close the door behind him, he went into the bedroom and collapsed on the bed that was still unmade from the morning. Within two minutes, he was on his back, mouth open, snoring loudly.

A figure appeared at the side of the bed wearing a black plastic raincoat, black balaclava and black gloves. In his right hand, he held a short length of metal pipe. For a moment, he looked down at Stresyk before raising the metal pipe and bringing it down with force onto Stresyk's left knee.

Stresyk awoke with a howl as the figure smashed the pipe down again onto his right knee.

Chapter 10

Carmichael was pacing up and down outside the hospital emergency ward when Jordan arrived rubbing his eyes.

'So, what's so bloody important you get me here at 6 o'clock in the morning?'

Carmichael gestured towards the person lying on the bed who was practically covered from head to foot in bandages and with tubes running everywhere. Monitors behind the bed flashed numbers. A nurse stood beside the bed adjusting some of the tubes.

'Yeah ... so!?' Jordan asked.

'Stresyk,' said Carmichael.

'Stresyk?' repeated Jordan.

Carmichael nodded. 'Yeah.'

'What happened?'

'Somebody did him good,' said Carmichael as he handed Jordan a piece of paper. 'All there in the doc's report.'

The nurse noticed Jordan and Carmichael and came out of the room. 'Police?'

'Detectives Jordan and Carmichael,' said Jordan, showing his warrant card. He lifted the doctor's report. 'Not good!'

The nurse shook her head. 'That's an understatement if I ever heard one. Knees and elbows smashed to nearly pulp mean he'll be lucky to walk or hold onto anything again. Both eyeballs missing and he'll be deaf. Plus he's been castrated. Yes, I'd definitely call that not good.'

Jordan glanced at the report. 'And he's going to survive?'

'If you can call it that; thing is, someone rang triple 0 stating emergency and asked for an ambulance in a hurry.'

'The person who did it's my guess,' said Carmichael. 'Reckon whoever did it wants him to live.'

Jordan nodded in agreement. 'Seems the intention was to cause as much pain and suffering as possible and let him live with it.'

'So, who had it in for our Johny?' asked Carmichael with raised eyebrows and a knowing look.

Jordan folded the doctor's report and gave it back to Carmichael. 'I suppose the obvious is the place to start.'

Chapter 11

Chad Martin answered the door to find Jordan and Carmichael standing there. 'What now?' he mumbled.

'Sorry about this, but we need to talk to you, Chad,' said Jordan. 'May we come in?'

Chad shrugged, opened the door further and walked back into the kitchen. The shorts and stained T-shirt he had on looked like they needed laundering. Jordan and Carmichael followed closing the door behind them. The kitchen was a mess. Unwashed plates and cups were piled up in the sink, while pizza boxes and food scraps covered the bench.

Chad went to the fridge, took out a beer and took a long swig before addressing Jordan.

'Right! So, as I said, what now?'

'Have to ask where you were last night, Chad,' said Jordan.

'I was here; where the hell do you think I was?'

'Didn't go out at all?'

'Like I said, I was here. Why do you want to know?'

'Stresyk had a bit of an accident last night.'

'Nothing too minor I hope,' said Chad, taking another swig of beer.

'Actually, he got beat up pretty bad, Chad,' said Carmichael.

Chad laughed and took another beer from the fridge. 'Well, here's to whoever did it. I thank you for coming to cheer me up, not that it will bring Clair back. Still, I remember you did say it would catch up with him, Detective.'

'We said the law would catch up with him, Chad,' said Carmichael, 'and this was not the law.'

Chad was unperturbed and laughed again. 'Yeah, well, who's complaining?'

'Nothing you can tell us, Chad?' asked Jordan.

Chad went quiet as the smile on his face disappeared. 'Apart from "hoo-bloody-ray" and someone deserves a medal, no!'

Jordan took a deep breath and exhaled slowly. 'We are obliged to investigate, Chad.'

'Right, well go to it, Detective.' Chad finished his beer and dropped the empty bottle in the sink among the unwashed plates and bowls. 'Anything else?'

Jordan shook his head. 'Not at this time, but we may need to talk to you again.'

'Whatever!' said Chad.

There were a few moments of uncomfortable silence before Jordan spoke. 'Right, well, thank you, Chad. We'll see ourselves out.'

Jordan and Carmichael made it back to their car and turned to look at the house.

'What do you reckon, Harris?'

'He did seem surprised, and, although he stands out as the most likely, I'm not convinced.'

'Me neither, and forensics haven't turned up anything yet.'

'Clair wasn't the only woman Stresyk attacked. We'll go over the other failed complaints against him, see what we can turn up. There'll be others with no particular love for our Johny.'

After stopping at the nearby McDonalds for what Jordan described as a healthy lunch of hamburgers, chips and coke, they arrived back at the station in early afternoon. With their suit jackets hanging over the back of their chairs, they were busily going through old files when Bailey came out of his office and called Jordan over.

'Need to talk to you, Harris,' he said and walked back inside his office.

Jordan got up, looked at Carmichael and raised his eyebrows in an "I don't know" manner, and went to Bailey's office, closing the door behind him.

Carmichael looked up from going through the files. They appeared to be having a heated argument. Arms were being waved around, fingers being pointed. As the door was closed, Carmichael was unable to hear anything. After a few minutes, the two men stopped talking. Jordan extended his hand towards Bailey who waited momentarily before nodding and accepting it.

Jordan walked back out of the office to Carmichael. 'So! What have you got?'

Carmichael pointed down at the file on the table. 'Couple of names.' He gave a quick glance towards the office where Bailey stood looking at them. 'You and Bailey, Harris?'

Jordan waved his hand. 'Nothing! Just a slight difference of opinion is all.' He indicated the paperwork on the table. 'Okay, if you got the addresses for the names we'll go check 'em out.'

Carmichael picked up his notes. The phone rang and Jordan answered.

'Detective Jordan.' He rolled his eyes as he listened. 'Oh for Chrissake, Beth! Look, I'll send you some extra next week, now I gotta go, I'm busy!'

He slammed the phone down and saw Carmichael staring at him. 'Don't ever get involved, kid, they'll bleed you bloody dry. Come on, let's get out of here.'

With Carmichael in his wake, Jordan strode off.

From his office, Bailey watched them leave.

Despite interviewing the two possibles that Carmichael had uncovered from the list of past offenders, the rest of the day proved completely uneventful. Each had ironclad alibis for the night of Stresyk's attack. After stopping off back at the station to advise Bailey of the lack of progress, Jordan and Carmichael called it a day and headed home.

Chapter 12

Ambulance crews, police and forensics had gathered outside a rundown house near an industrial area when Carmichael arrived. Jordan was standing at the back of an ambulance as a stretcher bearing a heavily bandaged body was carried out of the house. He greeted Carmichael with a nod towards the stretcher. 'Victim is one Barry Monkton. Previously found guilty of the abduction and rape of a fourteen-year-old. Sentenced to six years but released yesterday after serving only eighteen months for good behaviour.'

Carmichael appeared stunned. 'Let out after only eighteen months of a six year sentence. For what he did he should have been put away for life.'

'Couldn't agree more,' said Jordan.

Carmichael took a deep breath. 'Was he—'

'Yeah!'

'Someone is on a crusade.'

'Could be.' Jordan indicated to the forensic team. 'What's the betting they won't find anything?'

Carmichael shook his head in agreement. 'So, who do we talk to first, Harris?'

'As much as I find it hard to believe, I suppose it's back to Chad Martin.'

'Do we bring him in?'

'Let's see what he has to say first.'

As they left, they were approached by an attractive young woman impeccably dressed in blue slacks, white blouse and wearing high heels. She gestured towards the ambulance. 'Same as Stresyk, Harris?'

Jordan had to stop to prevent walking into her. 'No comment, Jill.'

'Come on, Harris, another rapist getting what he deserves! Somebody doing your job?'

She turned to Carmichael and smiled. 'Who's your new friend, Harris?'

'Still no comment,' said Jordan as he brushed past her.

She gave Carmichael, who was close behind Jordan, a smile and a small wave.

Carmichael caught up to Jordan. 'And she is?'

'Jill Maynard, local reporter, good at her job.'

'Quite a looker!'

'Forget it, Steve, she'll eat you alive!'

Carmichael laughed. 'Could be worse ways to go.'

'I see you've been allowed to bring Dad's runabout today,' said Jordan, indicating the classy BMW sports car parked near his tired-looking Ford police vehicle. 'Reckon you can keep up with me on the way to Chad Martin's place?'

'I'll do my best, Harris, but it doesn't really like not getting out of second gear.'

'Ha, bloody ha, try not to get lost.'

It was late morning by the time they arrived at Chad Martin's. They stood waiting patiently after knocking. It was several minutes before Chad opened the door.

Just wearing pyjama shorts, hair tousled and rubbing his eyes, he appeared to have just got out of bed. He squinted at Jordan. 'What's your problem now?'

'Have to ask where you were last night, Chad.'

Chad's face brightened as he studied the serious faces of Jordan and Carmichael.

'Don't tell me another piece of shit has got what's due.'

'Just tell us where you were, Chad,' said Jordan. 'Can we come in?'

Chad shook his head. 'No way, and I got nothing more to say, so piss off!'

With that, he slammed the door shut.

'That went well,' said Carmichael.

'And you expected what?' asked Jordan as he turned and walked back to the cars. 'At present all we got is a gut feeling, absolutely nothing to say for certain he's the guy.'

'It's gotta be him, Harris. He's obviously been up most of the night just like last time we spoke to him about Stresyk, and he's certainly got good reason for doing it. I reckon we should pull him in and tackle him hard.'

Jordan was silent for a moment as he considered Carmichael's words. He looked up and down the street. 'Okay, Steve, you ask next door if they have seen or heard anything out of the ordinary last night in the area. Don't be specific in mentioning Chad, be non-committal about names. After asking them what they may have seen, then ask where they were, and say, "Oh by the way, did you see what your neighbours were doing?" Something along those lines.'

'Okay, Harris. We might learn something.'

Jordan nodded. 'Yeah maybe, I'll start across the road,' he said as he walked off.

A couple of hours later they returned to the cars.

'Well!' said Jordan.

'Nothing! No one remembers seeing Chad come, or go, and no one wants to get involved in anything. Most of 'em can't seem to remember what they were doing themselves for the last couple of days.'

Jordan looked up and down the street. 'Everyone around here knows what happened to Clair. One elderly woman said Stresyk should rot in hell and if Chad did it he should get a medal.'

'I thought you didn't want us to mention Chad.'

'Didn't have to. People ain't completely stupid.'

'So, now what?'

'Couple of beers and start again tomorrow.'

Jordan got in his car and drove off. Carmichael looked up and down the street again, then back towards Chad's house.

'Just gotta be him,' he mumbled as he got in the BMW and put on the seatbelt. He glanced at Chad's house again, shaking his head as he drove away.

Chapter 13

n the police squad room, Jordan and Carmichael with a few other officers had turned on the TV to watch an afternoon talk show.

Chad Martin and another couple, Ian and Karen Trescoth were being interviewed by the show's host Vivienne Evans.

The station phone rang and Carmichael picked it up. 'Officer Carmichael.'

As he listened, he looked furtively around before speaking quietly. 'Sure, why not ... seven-thirty ... fine ... see you then.'

He replaced the phone, leant back in his chair and looked back up at the TV.

Vivienne Evans held up the morning paper so the audience could see the headlines. 'Victims applaud attack on rapists.' Quiet murmurs came from the audience. She replaced the paper on the table beside her before turning to face Karen Trescoth.

'So, like Chad, Karen, the man who brought despair to your home is now also in hospital.'

'Yes! And not a day goes by that my mind doesn't go over again and again what that animal did to me,' she stated angrily. 'And although I know he has been brutally treated, I just can't find it in myself to be anything but happy about it.'

The audience clapped and shouted words of support for Karen.

'We're with you!'

'He got what he deserves!'

When the applause eased, Chad raised his hand and the audience quietened. 'I know exactly how Karen feels, Viv. Every day the pain is with you, every day.'

Chad paused as tears ran down his cheeks. He took a couple of deep breaths before continuing. 'You have to realise that these … animals, are the lowest of the low. I would like to thank whoever is bringing justice when the law seems unable to.'

The studio audience erupted with more cheers of support and applause.

In the station, Bailey strode to the TV and turned it off. 'If you blokes haven't got anything to do, come see me.'

He threw the morning paper onto the table in front of Jordan. 'You getting anywhere with this?'

'Gotta be the work of the same guy,' said Jordan, 'but so far no forensics and no real prospect.'

'I'd bet on Chad Martin,' said Carmichael. 'He's one seriously pissed off guy. I reckon we should bring him in and lean on him.'

'Harris?' said Bailey.

Jordan shook his head. 'There's no hard evidence to connect him to either assault, Winston.'

'We need this sorted, Harris, and soon!' said Bailey as he walked back to his office.

'It's gotta be Chad,' said Carmichael. 'We should bring him in.'

'And charge him with what? Being happy the bloke who raped his pregnant wife has been beaten up and is in hospital? We need more than that, Steve.'

Carmichael was about to add something further but Jordan cut him off. 'Go back over the files again of the other rape victims; see if we've missed something.'

'It's him, Harris, I can feel it,' said Carmichael.

Jordan grimaced and grabbed his stomach, took a packet of tablets from his pocket and carefully extracted one from the aluminium foil. He made it to the water container in the corner of the room and washed it down before heading for the door past Carmichael.

'I'm going for a drink. You go through the files, "Sherlock".'

Chapter 14

Carmichael entered the cocktail bar at right on seven-thirty. At the bar, Jill Maynard was obviously keeping her three male companions amused by the laughter surrounding them. The high heels, low-cut, tight-fitting red dress she was wearing certainly held their attention.

She glanced at the large mirror which ran the length of the wall behind the bar, excused herself from her companions and walked towards Carmichael.

'Hi, Steve … drink?'

'Thanks … scotch on the rocks.' Carmichael stood back a pace and looked Maynard up and down. 'Very swish … going someplace?'

Maynard turned and returned to the bar where she caught the bartender's eye, ordered the scotch and brought it back to Carmichael. 'Cheers.'

Carmichael took a drink while peering over the top of the glass. 'Thanks, Jill. So, to what do I owe the pleasure?'

'My, we are cynical, aren't we?'

Carmichael finished his drink and pointed to the men Jill had been with at the bar.

'Come on, Jill, those guys are your scene. I might be green, but hopefully not altogether stupid.'

More patrons entered the bar and the noise level increased. Maynard smiled at Carmichael. 'Let's go somewhere quieter.' She took his glass and placed it on a nearby table as she pointed towards the exit.

Carmichael walked around the apartment before going to the

lounge window and out onto the balcony. Maynard poured drinks from a well-stocked cabinet and joined Carmichael.

'Great view,' said Carmichael. 'You must be well paid.'

'I do all right,' she said as she handed him a glass.

'Thanks ... so!?'

She took a long drink before replying. 'The reason I do okay is because I'm a good reporter.'

'So Harris Jordan told me.'

Maynard raised her glass. 'Well, thank you, Harris.'

'You known him long?'

Maynard nodded. 'About ten years.'

Carmichael gave her a sideways look. 'So, why would he say you would eat me alive.'

Maynard coughed on her drink. 'He said that?'

'Sure did.'

Maynard was aware that Carmichael had been studying her, and smiled. 'Maybe because when I want something I go after it.'

'Such as?'

'Such as information; after all, a reporter is only as good as what is reported.'

Carmichael shrugged. 'Unfortunately, Jill, I have nothing to tell you.'

'I didn't ask,' retorted Maynard.

'Oh!' said Carmichael quietly.

They stood looking at each other for a moment

'Like I said, Steve, if I want something I go after it.' She reached up and gently touched Carmichael's cheek.

Chapter 15

Carmichael stared up at the ceiling with his hands behind his head while taking several deep breaths. Beads of sweat cover his naked body.

'Not bad!' said Maynard from beside him.

Carmichael grinned. 'I'd say, Harris was half right.'

Maynard laughed and leant over Carmichael. 'So, Steve, who are you looking at for the attacks?'

Carmichael put up a hand. 'What!'

'Come on, Steve, you must have somebody in mind.'

'Look, Jill, there's no—'

Maynard raised herself and sat astride him. 'No one?'

'Jeez, Jill!'

Maynard started to sway. 'No one?'

Carmichael took a deep breath and exhaled slowly. 'Well, I think Chad Martin, but Harris is not so sure.'

'Forensics,' whispered Maynard.

'Nothing, scenes were clear.'

'You'll let me know?'

'Sure ... sure!'

'Then I guess we better shut up and get down to business,' said Maynard as she pushed down.

Chapter 16

The following afternoon, outside the County Court, Vincent Henna walked down the steps.

A large group of journalists and photographers approached. Among them was Jill Maynard who managed to get up close to Henna.

'Mr Henna, you have just been discharged from an alleged accusation of rape. As I understand, it was due to a mistake by the victim's council. Are you concerned for yourself considering previous attacks on rapists?'

Henna grinned at Maynard, gave her the finger and pushed his way past.

At 9 am the next morning, outside a dingy block of flats, uniformed police had set up a seclusion barrier. Carmichael was talking to one of the officers when a dishevelled and bleary-eyed Jordan arrived.

'Strewth, Harris, you look bloody awful.'

'Just get on with it will ya!' snapped Jordan.

Carmichael shook his head and referred to his notebook. 'Vincent Henna, aged forty-three; walked free from court yesterday when the judge threw the case out because of a prosecution legal blunder. He had a history of molestation, and was up for rape. According to the DI on the case, he was as guilty as sin, and should have been locked up and the key thrown away.'

Jordan sighed and ran a hand through his hair. 'And you suggest?'

'Bring in Chad Martin.'

Jordan threw his hands in the air. 'Okay. Do it.'

As they walked to their cars, another vehicle arrived. Jill Maynard got out and walked towards them. 'Hi, Harris!'

Jordan was surprised to see her. 'What the ... how did you?'

'Hi, Steve,' said Maynard while giving him a smile.

Carmichael returned the smile and raised his hand slightly.

Jordan looked from one to the other and realisation hit him. 'Oh shit!' He strode away shaking his head as Carmichael and Maynard exchanged grins.

Maynard took a piece of paper out of her bag and handed it to Carmichael. 'This arrived at our office in the early mail.'

'Wow!' said Carmichael after reading it.

'We'll be running it in the late edition, Steve.'

'I've gotta get this to Harris. Can you not run it till tomorrow, Jill? It'll give us a chance to chase something up.'

'Okay, Steve, I'll hold off till tomorrow, but keep me informed. Okay?'

'Thanks, Jill, I will,' said Carmichael as he hurried to his car.

Chapter 17

n the police interview room, Chad Martin was sitting calmly at a desk. On the other side sat Jordan while Carmichael paced impatiently up and down behind him. On the desk was the paper which ran the story of Stresyk's attack.

Jordan looked from the paper at Chad. 'It's not that we don't understand how you feel, Chad, after what happened to Clair, but ...'

Chad leant forward and stared at Jordan. 'How bloody dare you. You have no idea how I feel. And yes, I think what was done to Stresyk and that other animal was great. Should give whoever did it a medal.'

Carmichael picked up the newspaper. 'Oh, we have an idea of how you feel, Chad'—he picked up a small piece of paper and waved it in front of Chad—'especially since you sent this bit of poetry to the paper.'

'What poetry?' said Chad.

Carmichael glanced at Jordan who nodded before he started reading.

'As he has crippled, so will he be crippled.
As he has caused suffering, so will he suffer.
His knees and elbows were shattered so that his freedom of movement was removed.
He was blinded so he can no longer see the beauty he wishes to defile.
His tongue was removed so he can no longer lie.
His testicles were removed so his vile seed can never reproduce.
Similar justice will greet all rapists.'

Carmichael finished reading and slammed the piece of paper down onto the table in front of Chad who reached forward and picked it up. After reading it, he placed it gently onto the desk, looked up at Jordan and Carmichael, and smiled.

'Justice at last,' he said quietly.

Jordan made no reply as he calmly looked at Chad. Carmichael picked up the paper and threw it at Chad.

'Easy, Steve, easy!' said Jordan.

Carmichael was unable to contain himself and slammed his fist onto the table. 'It's you, Chad, we know it's you.' He pointed at the paper. 'This is how you think, it's what you've wanted ever since Clair died. You said Stresyk would pay ... It's you, it's you, admit it ... it's you.'

Chad stared at Carmichael, his face contorted with anger and hatred. 'Yes, it's what I wanted.' He stood up and shouted, 'Stresyk and the others got what they deserved. They can't hear, can't speak, can't move, it's perfect. All they have left is their minds to drive them, hopefully, crazy.'

Jordan also stood shaking his head. 'Chad, you ...'

Carmichael interrupted Jordan and yelled at Chad. 'So, it was you ... admit it, Chad. It was you.'

Chad glared at Carmichael, his face red. 'Alright, alright ... why not; anyone would be proud to deal out justice at last to those bastards.'

Jordan stared at Chad who was shaking with anger. Carmichael, with perspiration streaming down his face, loosened his tie. He took a few deep breaths to bring himself back under control, then addressed Chad again. 'Chad Martin, I am arresting you for the attacks on Johnstone Stresyk, Vincent Henna and Barry Monkton. You do not have to say anything, but anything you do say will be taken down and may be used in evidence against you. If you cannot afford an attorney, the court will appoint one for you. Do you understand these rights?'

Chad shrugged. 'Fully!'

Jordan had remained quiet, staring at Chad.

Carmichael, however, was obviously pleased with what had eventuated. 'I'll take him down, Harris, get him booked in.'

Jordan shook his head. 'I'm not sure this is right, Steve.'

Carmichael was unable to understand Jordan's reluctance. 'Jeez, Harris, he's admitted to it.' He grabbed Chad by the arm and led him out of the room.

Bailey, who had been watching the proceedings from his office, came out and stood beside Jordan and picked up the piece of paper with the poetry on. 'Is he the guy, Harris?'

Jordan shrugged. 'So he says!'

'And you couldn't find the typewriter this was written on.'

'Searched Chad's house from top to bottom, but no sign of it.'

'Pity, there's a couple of letters which show some sort of damage to the typeface, which would have sealed it. The papers are calling whoever did it "The Avenger" for Chrissake,' said Bailey. 'What is this, a bloody comic strip? The local TV's interviewed a couple of women's groups who reckon the doer is a hero.'

Jordan remained silent

Bailey threw the paper back down onto the table. 'Get it sorted.' He put a hand on Jordan's shoulder. 'You okay?'

Jordan nodded. 'Sure!'

Bailey waited a moment, then turned and walked back to his office. Jordan's face contorted in pain as another spasm hit his midriff. He took a small bottle out of his inside jacket pocket, extracted a tablet and swallowed.

Chapter 18

The courtroom was mostly packed with women. There was total silence as the jurors returned from their deliberations. They had been gone for a little over a half hour. Chad Martin was sitting quietly in the dock. The judge waited for the jurors to regain their positions before speaking.

'Ladies and gentlemen of the jury; you have reached a verdict?'

The foreman stood. 'We have, Your Honour.'

'Very well.' The judge appeared surprised at the speed of their decision. 'On the charge of occasioning grievous bodily harm to one Johnstone Stresyk, how find you?'

'Not guilty, Your Honour.'

Gasps came from the courtroom.

'On the charge of occasioning grievous bodily harm to one Vincent Henna, how find you?'

'Not guilty, Your Honour.'

More gasps came from the courtroom followed by complete silence as the judge continued to read from the charge sheet. 'And on the charge of occasioning grievous bodily harm to one Barry Monkton, how find you?'

'Not guilty, Your Honour.'

The judge raised his gavel and brought it down with a bang onto his desk.

'Case dismissed. Mr Martin, you are free to go.'

The courtroom erupted into applause and loud cheering. A smiling Chad stepped out of the dock and was immediately mobbed. He looked towards Jordan and Carmichael and shrugged.

Carmichael shook his head. 'Bloody ridiculous!'

'The people have spoken,' said Jordan. 'Get over it.'

As Chad exited the courthouse, the steps down to the street were packed with supporters. Reporters from print, radio and television jostled to get close while firing questions.

'How do you feel, Chad?'

'Are you surprised at the verdict?'

'So, if it's not you, who do you think is The Avenger?'

That evening during a prime time current affairs television programme, front persons Frank Batriano and Paula Scones were commenting on the day's events.

'One of the apparent legal surprises today is the non-guilty finding against Chad Martin for the malicious assault on three men,' said Batriano.

'Actually, Frank, I for one am not at all surprised,' said Scones. 'The men on whom the assaults occurred were convicted rapists, and the feeling I get from the people is that they got what they deserved.'

'As I understand it, Paula,' said Batriano as he looked into the camera, 'Martin confessed to the assaults when interviewed by the police.' He paused a moment, then turned to look seriously at Scones. 'Surely, Paula, we cannot condone the acts perpetrated here!?'

Scones raised her eyebrows. 'The confession you allude to, Frank, was obtained under duress and therefore inadmissible. And after all, Martin lost his wife and unborn child as a result of rape, and sees what happened to the rapists as justice.'

Batriano shook his head. 'Even so—'

Scones interrupted. 'The justice department has said that since the second assault, the incidence of rape and other attacks on women have dropped dramatically.'

Batriano tried to speak. 'Perhaps, but—'

Scones continued talking over the top of him, her voice raised. 'Not only that, but judges have to hand down stronger sentences to convicted assailants so that ten years means ten years, and no time off for so-called good behaviour, or because they've just found God!'

Batriano sat back in his chair. 'Are you saying that our justice system is wrong?'

Scones stared at Batriano in disbelief. 'Is the Pope Catholic? Where have you been, Frank? How can it possibly be justice when a woman who has been raped is subjected to the type of humiliation that happens in our courtrooms. And then, if the assailant is found guilty, he is either given a slap on the wrist because his mummy used to spank him when he misbehaved as a child, or let off because the police forgot to say please when they arrested him, or because he's discovered religion ... Jesus, Frank!'

Scones threw her hands into the air. 'Three cheers to The Avenger!'

Batriano stared at Scones, eyes wide and mouth agape before managing to regain his composure. He managed a brief smile at the camera. 'Okay, we'll take a break and be back after these important messages.'

As soon as he realised he was off air, his smile vanished. 'Paula that—'

'Oh stick it, Frank!' exclaimed Scones as she thrust her chair back and stormed off the set.

Chapter 19

The following morning, Bailey was pacing up and down in his office before Jordan and Carmichael, waving another piece of paper. 'Jimmy Collis has just walked and he was up for aggravated rape. The case was a no-bloody-brainer, but another stuff-up by the legal eagles and he's back on the street, but this Avenger crap needs putting to rest. I'm giving you Horvis and Langstrim to help out, Harris. Work it, shift about keeping an eye on Chad Martin; he should be easier to watch than Collis.'

After a week of alternate day and nighttime shifts parked in their car a hundred yards up the road from the Martins' house, Jordan and Carmichael were both experiencing a deal of difficulty staying awake on their fourth night.

'A week, Harris! We've been at this for a week and nothing,' said a frustrated Carmichael. 'Martin's not a fool; he's not going to do anything silly. He's made his point and got away with it. This is a waste of time.'

Jordan yawned and stretched. 'It's the job, Steve. I'm sure Daddy the Mayor is proud of you sitting here keeping the streets safe.'

Carmichael slapped the dashboard. 'I joined the police because I wanted to make a difference, do something useful, Harris, and I don't see how sitting here is doing that.'

'And screwing Jill Maynard was doing useful police work, was it?' said Jordan.

The retort took Carmichael by surprise. 'Harris, that's—'

'If Bailey finds out you've passed on info. You'll be screwed too, Steve. And I don't think Daddy the Mayor would be particularly overjoyed either.'

Carmichael became serious. 'I've told her nothing she couldn't have picked up by herself, Harris.'

'Was she good?' asked Jordan with a slight grin.

Carmichael grinned back. 'Bloody incredible!'

'Daylight in a couple of hours,' said Jordan as he checked his watch. He grimaced and leant forward against the steering wheel.

'You still got indigestion, Harris?'

Jordan nodded. 'Yeah!' He reached in his pocket for his bottle of tablets.

'Have you changed your diet?' asked Carmichael with concern.

'Oh sure, lots of fruit and veggies and drinking lots of water,' said Jordan as he swallowed a tablet.

Carmichael rolled his eyes, shook his head and settled back down into the seat.

Chapter 20

Carmichael came running from his apartment block towards a waiting car, carrying his jacket and holster. The passenger door was opened as he reached it. Jordan gunned the motor and took off at speed. Carmichael managed to put on his shoulder holster and jacket, then took out the roof light, leant out the window and attached it to the car's roof.

'It's 2 am!' he said after checking his watch. 'What's happened?'

'The guys at Chad's place got suspicious when the bedroom light never went out,' replied Jordan. 'Went to check it and he's missing. They're on their way to Jimmy Collis's.'

'He'll be there, Harris, I bet ya.'

'Maybe!' replied Jordan.

It took only ten minutes for Carmichael and Jordan to arrive at the block of flats where Collis lived. Another car was parked nearby.

'That's Horvis's car,' said Jordan. He pointed towards the flats where Horvis and Langstrim stood outside Collis's flat with guns drawn. 'Up there, second floor!'

Horvis saw them and indicated for them to go around to the back. Jordan and Carmichael climbed the back steps to the second floor and waited outside Collis's back door.

'Hear anything, Harris?' asked Carmichael.

'Nothing!' replied Jordan. 'This could be a cock-up.'

Suddenly, there was a yell from the front. 'Police, open up!'

There was a crashing sound as the front door was smashed in.

'Oh shit!' said Jordan as he slammed himself against the back door, forcing it open. With gun drawn, he raced inside with Carmichael close behind. They came to a stop as they reached Horvis and Langstrim who were standing with guns pointed at Chad Martin. Chad, with a knife in his hand, was leaning over the unmoving, naked figure of Collis. Collis's knees, arms and face were bloody. A length of pipe was lying on the bed beside him.

'Drop the knife and step back,' said Horvis.

Chad looked at the four men. 'This piece of shit had it coming.' He sneered and waved the knife. 'I am The Avenger!' he shouted.

'Jesus, he's totally lost it,' Carmichael whispered.

Calmly and slowly, Jordan started towards Chad. 'This isn't right, Chad.' He put his hand out. 'Just give me the knife, eh!'

Chad laughed. 'Soon as I finish!' With eyes staring wildly he reached down, grabbed Collis's scrotum and raised the knife.

'Chad, no!!' shouted Jordan as the guns of Horvis and Langstrim fired simultaneously.

Chad fell backwards, staring at the red stain on the front of his shirt.

'Shit!' exclaimed Carmichael.

'He was going to cut him, Harris,' said Langstrim almost apologetically.

Jordan went to Chad, who lay gasping on the floor, and knelt beside him. 'Stupid, Chad … plain stupid.'

Chad grimaced. 'Had to do it, it was expected, for Clair.' He coughed as blood erupted from his mouth, then he went still.

Jordan stood up and turned on Horvis and Langstrim. 'Did you have to kill him for Chrissake?' he shouted angrily.

Carmichael quickly moved to stand between them. 'Harris, he was about to cut the guy's balls off.'

Horvis and Langstrim stared silently at Jordan as he gave a groan and grabbed at his stomach. He reached inside his coat pocket and took out his small bottle of tablets and took one. 'Call for an ambulance and forensics,' he said as he looked over at Collis on the bed. 'Tell them to move it.'

Carmichael took out his mobile and walked outside, leaving the others looking down at the bodies.

Chapter 21

The funeral of Chad Martin was televised and covered by Frank Batriano and Paula Scones.

'As you can see from our roving cameras,' said Scones, 'the streets are lined with thousands of onlookers who watch in complete silence as the vehicle carrying the coffin of Chad Martin passes.'

'These are scenes that must baffle our law enforcement agency,' retorted Batriano. 'After all, this is the funeral of a man who was shot while committing a most heinous crime, and who was obviously guilty of at least three previous malicious assaults.'

'Perhaps, Frank,' said Scones, 'you should remember against whom these alleged assaults were committed.'

'Notwithstanding the background of the persons against whom—' began Batriano in a most condescending manner before Scones interrupted him.

'Notwithstanding the background? Those scum were rapists, Frank!' stated Scones as she started to lose her cool. 'What they got was no more than they deserved, and the people of this city are paying their respects to someone who had the guts to do that which our legal system could not.'

Batriano tried again. 'I think you are missing the point, Paula. This man—'

Scones interrupted with eyes blazing. 'The point is, Frank, that you are a complete arsehole. Maybe if your wife or daughter had been the victim of rape you just might be able to understand why the crowds are out there.'

Batriano obviously didn't know when best to shut up. 'Paula, legally this man—'

Scones smiled at Batriano. 'Oh, sorry, Frank, how could you possibly imagine that? Try instead to think of how you would feel if your partner, what's his name? Oh yes, Julian, isn't it, was raped.'

Batriano's chin dropped as he looked at Scones, completely lost for words. Scones managed to regain her composure and continued.

'As you can see, many among the vast crowd are weeping openly as the solitary vehicle passes.'

Alone in his flat, Jordan had watched the funeral of Chad Martin. A near empty bottle of scotch whiskey stood on the table beside him. He grimaced, bent forward and held his stomach as another wave of intense pain hit him. He reached for the bottle, raised it to his lips and swallowed the little that was left. His eyes settled on the gun that lay on the table beside him. He picked it up, placed it against his temple and pulled the trigger.

Chapter 22

Three days later, a number of officers, all in dress uniform, were gathered in the squad room in readiness for the funeral of Jordan in the early afternoon. Carmichael was talking with Bailey in his office.

'He had cancer?' asked Carmichael.

'Yeah!' replied Bailey.

'And you knew?'

'Yeah.'

'The stomach pains,' continued Carmichael. 'He said it was indigestion.'

Bailey nodded. 'Didn't want anybody to know.'

'And he said he intended to—'

Bailey interrupted. 'Shit no!'

'But you're not surprised?' said Carmichael.'

'Guess not,' replied Bailey with a shrug.

They both glanced out the office window as Beth and Kevin walked into the station. Beth was wearing a tight black dress, and Kevin was in his black leather jeans and jacket. Beth stopped to talk to one of the officers who pointed to a passageway that they then continued walking to.

'Paperwork?' inquired Carmichael.

'For sure,' said Bailey. 'That'll be about Harris's super. Not one for patience is Beth, when the possibility of getting her hands on a dollar appears.'

In the administrative office down the passageway, Beth and Kevin were sat facing a desk behind which a man was thumbing through a pile of papers.

'Ah yes, here it is.' He looked up and smiled at Beth. 'Detective Harris Jordan, yes?'

'Yes, that's right,' replied Beth, hardly able to hide her excitement, 'and how much!?'

'Detective Jordan instructed that upon his death his superannuation'—the man glanced up from the paperwork to smile again at Beth before continuing—'holiday pay due, and any salary owing should be immediately forwarded to …' He paused as he turned the page over.

Beth leant forward expectantly. 'And that is?'

The man looked up at Beth. 'The Saint Mary's Church, to be used in the assistance of rape victims.'

Beth was incredulous. 'The what!?'

'The Saint Ma—'

Beth jumped up from her seat, her face red and distorted. 'This ain't right!' she yelled furiously. 'I'm his wife and this is his kid, it's gotta be ours!'

'Actually, madam, you are his ex-wife,' said the man quietly. 'Some time ago as I understand and therefore—'

Beth interrupted. 'This is all crap, that money is mine. The bastard can't do this to me.' She pointed a red-nailed finger. 'I'll fuckin' sue you!'

'Of course, you have that right,' replied the man calmly, 'but rest assured, you will lose, and your court costs would be considerable.'

'The son of a bitch!' screamed Beth. 'I hope the bastard rots in hell!' She stormed out of the office with Kevin in her wake.

'I don't understand, Mum!' said Kevin as he almost ran to keep up with Beth. 'You said we would be okay when Dad died.'

'Oh for Chrissake, he wasn't your Dad.'

Kevin was lost. 'Then who is?'

'How the hell would I know?' said Beth.

'But what about my guitar lessons?' asked Kevin.

'You'll have to get a job, you lazy little shit!' said Beth as she continued muttering obscenities about Jordan.

With Kevin trailing behind her, she fumbled to light a cigarette. Bailey met her at the station door.

'Hi, Beth, how did—' asked Bailey.

Beth elbowed her way past. 'And fuck you too!'

Bailey watched Beth and Kevin depart with a wide smile creasing his face. 'Good one Harris,' he murmured to himself.

Chapter 23

The crowd of officers who had attended Harris Jordan's funeral slowly departed the graveside. Bailey and Carmichael remained. Carmichael was the first to break the silence between them. 'Didn't see his ex or son.'

'No! No great surprise there,' said Bailey. He reached inside his coat pocket and took out an envelope.

'You might like to read that,' he said, offering it to Carmichael. 'Received it this morning. It's from Harris.'

Carmichael opened the envelope, extracted the paper inside, and began to read.

'So, it wasn't Chad Martin,' he said in disbelief.

Bailey shook his head. 'So it seems.'

'That explains why Harris was never keen on bringing him in, and why he was so angry when he was shot.' He handed the paper back to Bailey. 'And you had no idea that it was Harris?'

'Not a clue! I guess knowing he had only a short time left he decided, as he wrote in this'—he waved the piece of paper—'to balance the ledger.'

'So, why did Martin have a go at Collis?' asked Carmichael. 'Doesn't make sense.'

'Well, the press had built him up to such an extent, after all he was The Avenger, remember. Reckon he just tried to live up to his own publicity.'

'So, what now?' asked Carmichael indicating towards Harris's note.

Bailey thought for a moment. 'Harris was a good cop, and Chad

Martin is gone and considered a sort of hero.' He looked down into the grave. 'Be a pity to mess up the memories of both of them.'

'Best the truth lies buried for everyone's sake.' He looked at Carmichael. 'Agreed?'

Carmichael nodded. 'Agreed.'

Bailey screwed up the paper and envelope and threw them into the grave. They stood silently for another few moments.

'Come on,' said Bailey, 'let's go for a drink.'

The inside of the bar room was crowded with police in dress uniform. Bailey walked behind the bar, rang the bell and asked for silence.

'Here's to Harris Jordan. We started out together some twenty-five years ago. He was a great cop and a great friend.' He raised his glass. 'To Harris!'

Throughout the bar room, glasses were raised and the words 'To Harris!' rang out. Carmichael was seated facing the bar, glass in his hand, watching a newscast on the TV behind the bar.

'We now go live to Central Court,' said the newscaster.

A crowd of photographers, and reporters were gathered, including Jill Maynard, as Middleton Davis escorted Curtis Bradshaw down the steps. Cameras flashed and microphones pressed towards the pair.

'Another successful defence, Mr Davis?' asked a reporter.

'Thank you, thank you,' Davis replied smugly.

Jill Maynard managed to thrust her way in front of him. 'It sure helps when the rape victim doesn't want to continue, Mr Davis.'

Davis smirked, enjoying the moment in the limelight. 'The law demands that I do everything I can to defend my client.'

'Even when your client is a disgusting piece of shit like Bradshaw,' said Maynard.

The rest of the reporters went silent as Davis glared at Maynard. 'The court has found that my client had no case to answer.'

He tried to push past Maynard who blocked his way. 'No case

to answer! Crap! The girl was bashed senseless; his DNA was all over her, and this is the third time this arsehole has been up on rape charges.'

'And there have been no convictions, madam.' He pushed past Maynard with Bradshaw at his side.

'Hey you, Bradshaw, scumbag!' shouted Maynard as he passed her. 'Wouldn't it be great if you got what the others got!'

Bradshaw stopped and turned towards Maynard, blew her a kiss and grinned before following Davis away.

Chapter 24

Back in the bar, Carmichael and Bailey had watched the proceedings on the TV.

'It never ends,' said Bailey sadly.

A grim-faced Carmichael lifted his glass and downed the contents. 'Want another?' he gruffly asked Bailey.

'No, thanks, I'm done; going home to my wife.'

Carmichael watched him leave then slammed his glass down onto the bar. 'Same again, thanks.'

The refilled glass returned and he swallowed it down in one. He looked around, taking in the sound of raised voices and laughter, and walked out.

Snoring loudly, lying on his back, an empty beer bottle in his limp left hand, Curtis Bradshaw was sleeping soundly. Since his acquittal, it had been one long pub crawl with a couple of friends. Eventually, unable to pour any more down his throat, he had somehow managed to stagger home to his rental flat.

A figure dressed in black, wearing a black balaclava appeared at the bedside. A rubber-gloved hand raised a short length of steel pipe and brought it down with extreme force on Bradshaw's right knee which reduced his kneecap to a mass of splintered bone.

Bradshaw awoke with a howl of pain as the pipe descended again onto his knee causing even further damage. His eyes widened with fear and disbelief when he saw the figure raise the pipe again.

'No! No! Can't be; you're dead!'

His eyes widened further as the pipe began to descend again. 'Jesus, noooo!'

The pipe connected with Bradshaw's left knee with a crunch and bone splinters flew aside. Unable to even scream, due to the extreme pain, Bradshaw's mouth trembled uncontrollably as the figure raised a knife and leant forward. The figure put the knife down on the bed beside Bradshaw and placed a hand either side of his head. He pressed his thumbs into the eye sockets and removed the eyeballs. He then pulled down Bradshaw's pants, grasped his scrotum and picked up the knife. Luckily for Bradshaw, he passed out before the knife was used.

At a nearby ambulance station, the telephone receptionist replaced the telephone and shouted to a paramedic. 'Bob! Better take this one.' She handed the paramedic a piece of paper she had written an address on. 'A man needs urgent attention; sounds real bad.'

A couple of streets away a man was standing inside a red telephone booth. The rain that was falling made it impossible to determine anything but the shape of the caller. On the ground nearby was a holdall with a short length of steel protruding. The man replaced the handset, backed out of the booth and adjusted his hat. He pulled up the collar of his overcoat as the wind blew rain into him. He picked up the holdall, shrugged and looked up at the streetlight.

'That one's for you, Harris,' murmured the man as he walked away.

Interlude

Harris Jordan's suicide brought Inspector Winston Bailey's time in the police force to an end.

A week after the funeral, he made the decision to retire and handed in his notice.

Immediately after doing so, he called Steve Carmichael into his office. With a downcast face, he asked Carmichael to sit on the chair in front of his desk.

'Jordan and I joined up at the same time, Steve, and I reckon now he's gone it's time for me to do the same. It's just not the same without him around.'

Carmichael raised his hands as if in surrender and nodded his head. 'I can appreciate how you are feeling, sir, and I have made a major decision as well. I also want to make a move. Not leave the force, but a change of workplace. My sister lives up on the Gold Coast so I'm going to apply for a transfer up there.'

Bailey managed a smile. 'It's a damn sight better weather up there, Steve.' He stood up and offered his hand. 'You're a good copper, Steve, and I know you'll have a great future in the Force, I wish you all the very best.'

Carmichael accepted the offered hand and they stood for a while smiling at each other.

Bailey released his hand and gave a cough. 'Take good care of yourself, Steve, and if you need any report on your background I'll be more than happy to help.'

'Thank you, sir, that could be necessary.'

Bailey shook his head. 'No worries, take care of yourself, Steve.'

Carmichael raised his hands. 'I'll keep in touch.'

Carmichael

PART 1:
WHY?

Chapter 1

It was a warm, moonlit summer night. She was having difficulty opening her eyes. Her mind was also having trouble comprehending where she was. She raised her hands, brushed her long, blonde hair away from her face, rubbed her eyes and shook her head.

She looked around at her surrounds. She was sitting with her back against the trunk of a large tree. A few metres in front of her was a stretch of still water. More trees and bushland to either side. There were no houses to be seen.

'Where am I?' she murmured. She looked down at the black slacks and multi-coloured T-shirt she was wearing.

'Why would I come here dressed like this, where have I been?' she mumbled.

As her head began to clear, she dimly remembered a crowded dance floor with loud music playing.

She had been at the nightclub as a means of getting back at her boyfriend of two years, who, she had discovered only the day before, had been cheating on her. Although badly hurt, she had determined not to let the knowledge completely ruin her life ... hence the night out.

She pushed her hands onto the ground beside her, and was about to stand up when a person moved around from behind the tree she was sitting against and stood in front of her with his arms raised above his head.

She looked up, unable to make sense of what was taking place.

'Who are you and how did I get here?' she asked.

They were to be the last words to ever pass her lips.

Chapter 2

Steve Carmichael was playing golf on his day off. He was stood on the third green looking down at his golf ball and concentrating on how best to strike his two metre putt to score a one under par birdie.

'Slightly to the left, Steve,' suggested Stuart, one of his playing partners.

'I reckon it's to the right,' added Vic, his other playing partner.

Carmichael raised a single finger towards the pair and adjusted his feet in preparation. He was about to swing his putter when a mobile phone sounded. He dropped the putter, took the mobile phone out of his back pocket, raised it to his left ear and spoke.

'Inspector Carmichael.'

Stuart and Vic remained silent. The smiles that had filled their faces moments before now gone.

Carmichael nodded as he listened to his mobile. Then a few seconds later. 'Be there in about thirty minutes.'

He replaced the mobile into his back pocket and turned to his fellow players. 'Sorry, guys, gotta go!'

'No worries,' Stuart said, 'leave your gear, we'll take care of it.'

'Thanks,' said Carmichael, and at a fast pace, walked off back towards the club house.

Stuart and Vic stood silent for a few minutes watching their friend walk away. Vic picked up the putter Carmichael had dropped and replaced it into his golf bag.

'What do you reckon?' said Vic.

'Think I'll give it away,' replied Stuart with a shake of his head.

'Every time he leaves like that it's not the best.'

He and Vic stood silent until Carmichael disappeared from view. Without further talk, they gathered their golf bags and slowly made their way back to the club house.

They had been friends of Carmichael for many years and had learnt to understand that it may be some time before they were to meet up again.

It was eight years previously that Stuart Mansfield, Victor Aynesley and Steven Carmichael had first met.

Carmichael, accompanied by three other police, were at an old weatherboard rental house intending to arrest a man suspected of several cases of arson. After knocking on the front door, stating who they were and requesting entry, Carmichael looked down and noticed fluid streaming under the door and the smell of petrol. Carmichael and the other police immediately stepped back as a friendly voice from inside invited them in.

'Come on in, there's a warm welcome awaiting you arseholes.'

A peal of laughter followed as the three officers retreated further back.

Carmichael took out his mobile. Rang his office and requested the sending of the fire department.

Within twenty minutes, two fire engines and eight firies were at the scene.

A police negotiator also arrived.

It took sixteen hours for the negotiator to convince the wanted man to open his front door and walk out where he was handcuffed by Carmichael and taken away in a police car.

Inside the front door of the home, the area had been drenched with petrol. A full container was also there. Should this have been set alight, anyone nearby would have been consumed in flames and suffered terrible burns and possible death. Following the departure of the police, the firies were left with the responsibility of cleaning up.

During the sixteen hour waiting period, Carmichael had time

to spend chatting with the firies. Among them was Mansfield and Aynesley. Since that time, the three, and their wives and children, had become firm friends, often meeting up for BBQs and, on some occasions, the three men managed a relaxing morning away from their serious work lives on the golf course.

Since moving to the Gold Coast ten years previous, Carmichael had become a much respected officer, and now, at the age of thirty-six, he was Detective Inspector.

He had met his wife Barbara at the Palm Beach surf club during a fundraising event for the local lifesaving group. She was very supportive of him, and fully understood when he was late home some nights because of the demands of his job. Their two children, Keith and Sally, had also learnt to understand why Dad was sometimes too busy at work to come along with them and Mum for a fun time at the beach.

Chapter 3

Carmichael parked his car as close to the police tape as possible. There were several other police vehicles nearby and an ambulance. He had gone home and changed out of his golfing gear of baggy shorts, runners and T-shirt, and was now more formally attired in long, grey pants, black shoes, white shirt and tie.

A constable met him. 'This one's not nice, sir.' He pointed behind him. 'Your offsider is down by the water, and that young bloke sitting in the back of my car came across this when walking his dog. I asked him if he'd seen anybody, but apparently saw nothing. Said it's always quiet here and that's why he brings the dog for a walk.'

'Thanks, mate,' said Carmichael as he walked to the water's edge where a young woman was standing dressed in slacks and light jacket. Carmichael reached out and put a hand on her shoulder. 'Hi, Jenny, that bad, eh!?'

Jennifer Macintyre nodded and took a few deep breaths. She had joined up with Carmichael only a month previous after being promoted to Detective Sergeant.

At 180 centimetres tall, she was only a few centimetres shorter than Carmichael. In her spare time, she enjoyed playing netball and going to the gym. Her height and fitness ensured she was a good player. She had joined the police force at the age of twenty-three, and similarly to Carmichael, her positive outlook towards her job was appreciated. Hence her promotion to Detective Constable and her recent promotion to Sergeant.

'I've seen bodies before, sir, but nothing quite like this.'

'Okay, Jenny, you stay here and I'll go take a look.' He turned and approached the park bench where a man was leaning over the body.

'Morning, Mark, what have we got?' he asked.

Pathologist Doctor Mark Baker stood back and pointed.

'Oh shit!!' exclaimed Carmichael.

'Never seen anything like this before,' said Baker with a shake of his head.

Jennifer managed to make it back to the body and the three of them stood silently staring at it for a while. The body was obviously that of a young woman. Congealed blood everywhere.

Her body was still sitting upright on the park bench, but her head had been completely sliced in half down to her shoulders. Accordingly, the left side of her head rested on her left shoulder, and the right side on her right shoulder.

Carmichael broke the silence. 'What do you reckon, Mark?'

'Sword, cane cutters, machete, had to be extreme force ... axe maybe,' replied Baker.

'Any ID, and how long ago?' asked Carmichael.

'Nothing yet ... midnight ... early morning,' said Baker.

'But who could possibly want to do such a thing?' said Jennifer.

'That's where we come in,' said Carmichael. He turned to Baker. 'Autopsy?'

'Come see me about five,' he replied.

Carmichael walked towards three police officers nearby. 'Guys, will you check around the place. Look for tyre marks, discarded bits of anything lying around, you know the drill.'

He stood still, staring around and listening. 'Can't see any buildings. Bit of traffic noise in the distance. Whoever did this picked a pretty secluded spot so probably knows the area. Come on, Sergeant, time to go to work. You came in your car didn't you?'

'Yes I did,' she replied.

Carmichael held out his hand. 'Give me the keys, Jenny.'

Jenny handed over the keys.

'You're coming with me,' said Carmichael. He walked over to one of the officers. 'These are the keys to Sergeant Macintyre's car; drive it back to the station when you've finished here please, Joe.'

'No worries,' was the reply.

As Carmichael and Macintyre neared his vehicle, another car arrived. Two men got out and approached and stood in their way. One with a camera and the other pushing a microphone towards them.

'Oh the bloody reporters!' murmured Carmichael.

'What's the name of the victim?' asked the man with the microphone.

'Sorry, guys, nothing to report at present ... please keep well back and do not take any film of the scene. I will be more than happy to give you information later this afternoon ... thank you.'

He brushed past them to his car and got in. Macintyre quickly getting into the passenger side.

'So, you will be talking to them this arvo?' asked Jenny as they sped away.

'Not if I can help it,' replied Carmichael.

'That bench is just about hidden from view in there among the trees,' said Jenny. 'Do you think that means it's likely that someone from this area might be who we are looking for?'

'Yes I do,' replied Carmichael. 'So, we'll start off calling on the locals see what answers we get ... trouble is, the locals around here are still a good distance off. I never saw any buildings nearby when we were near the body.'

'Me neither.' Jenny pointed to her right. 'There's a house, shall we start there?'

'Good as any,' said Carmichael as he turned into the driveway.

Chapter 4

t was right on 5 o'clock when Carmichael and Macintyre entered the pathologist's rooms. Doctor Baker was sat at a bench writing on a sheet of paper.

'What have you got for us, Mark?' inquired Carmichael.

Baker looked up. 'From the state of the body, I reckon it happened nearer to 1 o'clock in the morning.'

'And what was used?'

'Because of the bone the blade went through, I believe it to be most likely an axe. Also, there was only a small nick on the seat behind the head and if a sword had been used, because of the length of blade, it would probably have struck the timber cross member.'

'And?' said Carmichael, feeling there was more to come.

'There is a showing of Rohypnol in her system.'

'That's a date rape drug,' said Jenny.

Carmichael nodded. 'So, she was likely at at some nightclub the night before.'

He looked down at the sheet-covered body lying on a table nearby. 'Have you managed to put her head back together, Mark?'

Baker stepped forward and pulled the sheet back to reveal a re-shaped head.

Carmichael and Jenny both showed surprise on their faces. 'Oh my goodness, you've done a great job,' said Cartwright.

'She was a good looking young woman,' said Jenny quietly.

'Can I have a photo of her?' asked Carmichael.

Baker reached behind himself, picked up a piece of paper and handed it to Carmichael. 'Such as this?' he stated with a smile on his face.

'Oh, Mark, you are awesome,' replied Carmichael.

'Did you find anything out asking the locals this afternoon?' added Baker.

Carmichael shook his head. 'Nothing of any use. Just told that people were seldom seen in the area. A couple said they had fished there without luck.'

Baker reached behind himself again, picked up a small plastic bag with a receipt inside it and held it out to Carmichael.

'Where did you get this?' he asked.

'One of the police at the scene, Joe I think his name is, dropped it in about a half hour ago, said he knew you would be here soon.'

Carmichael handed the receipt to Jennifer. 'It's for a bag of dog food.'

She studied the receipt. 'It was probably dropped by the lad who found the body. He had a dog with him.'

Carmichael nodded his head. 'Yes, that's what I reckon, Jenny.'

Jennifer handed the receipt back to Carmichael. 'I've been thinking about how the woman was dressed and where she might have been that evening. Could she have been at a party or maybe even a dance?'

'Yeah, good thought, Jenny ... the nightclub is very popular with the young-uns.' He looked at his watch. 'Let's go check it out before it starts filling up again.'

'Maybe one of the staff will recognise the photo,' said Baker.

Carmichael glanced at the photo. 'You did a bloody good job getting her face back together, Mark, let's hope we can get lucky.'

Chapter 5

t was just before 7 o'clock when Carmichael and Macintyre walked up the steps to the door of the nightclub.

A well-built man welcomed them with a smile. 'Nice to be early, eh, guys?'

Carmichael proffered his police badge and returned the smile. 'Here to chat to your people, pal.'

The man's smile faded as he stood aside and pushed the door open.

'Thanks,' said Macintyre as they walked past him and into the nightclub.

Another man met them as they approached the bar. Carmichael again showed his police badge and introduced himself. 'I'm Inspector Carmichael and this is Sergeant Macintyre. We'd like to talk to you about a young woman who might have been here last night. And your name is?'

'Alex Spencer,' the man replied.

Carmichael took the photo out of his inside jacket pocket and held it towards the man. 'Do you remember her, Alex?'

The man stared at the photo shaking his head. 'Sorry, Inspector, no I can't, the place was packed last night and I was flat out helping behind the bar and stuff.'

'Will you get the rest of your staff out here so I can also ask them?' said Carmichael as no other staff were to be seen.

Spencer turned and walked behind the bar and through a back door. A few seconds later, five men and two women came through the door. They stood side by side in front of Carmichael and Macintyre.

'I'd like you all to have a good look at this photo and tell me if you recognise her,' he asked.

He slowly walked from one to the other, holding the photo only a short distance from each person's face. There was no recognition. He returned to the first person in the line. 'Can you please have another look? It's very important that we get to know who she is.'

But the reaction was the same as before.

Carmichael replaced the photo into his jacket pocket and nodded at the group. 'Thanks for that, guys.'

The staff turned away and went back through the door behind the bar.

'Sorry we couldn't be of help,' said Spencer. 'Friday and Saturday nights are a madhouse in here. Last night we had the men from the axe man championships in here and they sure kept the bar busy, and they're big buggers too, so we had to keep our eyes on them.'

Carmichael and Macintyre both took a step towards him.

'Axe men?' said Carmichael and Macintyre as one.

Spencer's face lit up in surprise at the reaction. 'Yeah, there was a dozen or so of them here.'

'Championships?' asked Carmichael.

'Yeah, being held in the Convention Centre.'

'Is it on every day?'

'Yeah, all next week too.'

'Where do they all stay?' asked Macintyre.

'I think they're in several motels along the coast.'

Carmichael held out his hand towards Spencer. 'Thanks for that information, Alex.'

Spencer accepted the offered hand. 'No worries ... hope it's of help.'

Carmichael and Macintyre walked off towards the entry. 'You never know,' said Carmichael with a wave. 'Thanks again.'

'Axe men, would you believe?' said Carmichael as he and Macintyre headed back to their car.

'I guess we're heading to the Convention Centre to find out where they are all staying,' said Macintyre.

'You're guessing right, Jenny … could be the break we're looking for.'

It was only a short drive from the nightclub to the Convention Centre. Carmichael parked near the front door.

As they went to walk in the main entrance, a security guard stood in front of them. 'Sorry, sir, but you can't leave your car there; there is a parking area around the back.'

Carmichael again showed his identification card. 'Probably be a quick visit, just have to ask the reception a few questions, that be okay? I'm Inspector Carmichael and this is Sergeant Macintyre.'

The guard glanced at the card and stood aside, waving them both in.

Carmichael and Macintyre walked up to the reception area. Carmichael again showed his identification to the female receptionist. 'Evening, miss, will you please tell me where the men involved in the axe competition are?'

'They are not here at the moment,' she replied.

'So, where are they?' asked Carmichael.

'They are probably all out for dinner somewhere, or back in their motel rooms.'

'Will you tell me what motels they are staying at please, as I need to talk to them.'

The receptionist reached under the reception table and began lifting up bundles of paper. 'I can certainly do that, but there are a number of different motels they are staying at, you might be better off coming back at around midday tomorrow as they will all be here for the competition that starts at one pm.'

'That could save a lot of running around,' said Macintyre.

Carmichael nodded in agreement. 'Yes, I think you're right,

Jenny. It is getting a bit late after all and, as the receptionist said, they could be all out on the town somewhere.'

He turned to the receptionist. 'Yes ... your suggestion makes sense. However, if you do have a list of the motels they are staying at handy, I would appreciate a copy.'

The receptionist looked through the papers she had lifted up. 'Ah ... here's the list.' She turned around to a long table behind her on which rested a computer and copier. In a matter of seconds, she turned back to face them and handed over a copy of the list of motels.

Macintyre accepted the list. 'Thank you for this, we'll be here to see you again tomorrow.'

Carmichael and Macintyre gave a brief goodbye wave, exited the building and walked towards their car.

'No need to get up early tomorrow, Jenny,' said Carmichael. 'Have a lie-in and we'll meet up in the station about eleven before we head back here.'

Chapter 6

t was just before midday when Carmichael and Macintyre walked into the Convention Centre. The same receptionist as they had talked to the day before was at the desk. She looked up and greeted them.

'Good morning, Inspector.' She pointed to a passageway. 'The men you want to see are all down there in the first door on your left.'

'Thank you,' replied Carmichael, and walked to the passageway with Macintyre.

As they came to the door, they could hear voices from inside. He knocked on the door before entering.

When they entered, the talking immediately stopped. Macintyre touched Carmichael on the arm and then pointed to the right side of the room.

A number of axes were leaning against the wall. One of the men came towards them.

He offered his hand. 'G'day, my name's Les Hartford. I'm the bloke in charge of this lot. I understand you want to talk to them. Can I ask what it's all about?'

Carmichael shook Hartford's offered hand. 'I'm Detective Inspector Carmichael and this is Sergeant Macintyre. Thank you for all being here like this.'

Carmichael looked towards the group of men. 'I understand some of you were at the nightclub two nights ago and we would appreciate your looking at the photo of a young woman to see if you recognise her.'

He reached inside his jacket pocket, took out the photo that the pathologist had made and held it up towards the men. Macintyre also held up a photo.

Before leaving the police station earlier, he had made a copy of the photo provided by the pathologist.

'If those of you who were at the nightclub would please step forward and take a look.'

Eight of the men came forward to Carmichael.

'My sergeant has a similar photo, so if the rest of you would also take a look, that would be great.'

Of the eight men with Carmichael the first five all shook their heads. 'Sorry, can't remember seeing her,' was the common statement.

The sixth man stared a moment longer than the others. He looked up at Carmichael. 'Yeah, I reckon she was there, good-looking woman. Had on black slacks and a coloured T-shirt, I think.'

One of the others came back for another look. 'Yeah, you're right. You had a bit of a chat to her didn't you, Carl?'

Carl nodded. 'Yeah, I did, only for a minute or two though, then she took off.'

'That's great, guys. About what time was it she left, and did you get her name, Carl?' asked Carmichael.

Carl shook his head. 'No, sorry, didn't have a chance.'

A shout from Macintyre made Carmichael turn towards her. 'Over here, sir.'

Carmichael quickly thanked Carl for his information and went to Macintyre.

She indicated the man in front of her. 'Garry reckons he saw her at the Currumbin RSL around ten-thirty Friday night.'

Garry pointed at the photo. 'I'm sure it was her, good-looking girl, she was talking to a young guy and having a drink or two.'

'Can you describe the person she was with, Garry?'

Garry closed his eyes and put a hand to his forehead. 'To be honest, I looked more at the girl than the bloke ... ah ... I think I got him, mid-twenties, slim, jeans, blue shirt … yeah, that was him.'

'Did they leave together?'

'Sorry, I can't help you there, I didn't see her leave.'

'You've been a great help, Garry.'

Carmichael looked over all the men. 'Thanks a lot, guys,'

'Why are you looking for her?' asked one of the men.

'Regrettably, she was murdered a couple of nights ago.'

'Oh shit!' was a joint reaction from the men.

'Might it have been the bloke she was talking to?' asked Garry.

'Not sure, but it gives us something to look at.'

'We hope what we've said will help you get the bastard who did it.'

'Time will tell,' said Carmichael. He pointed to the axes leaning against the wall. 'They look pretty special tools.'

'They are indeed,' replied Garry. 'They are Hults Bruk Atran felling axes and were all hand-forged in their foundry from Swedish steel. They've been operating since 1697. They have a 4.25 inch cutting edge and 32 inch handles.'

Carmichael was impressed. 'Wow, nice tools indeed.'

He raised his hands in appreciation. 'Thanks again for your information gentlemen,' he said as he and Macintyre turned away and left the room.

'Currumbin RSL?' inquired Macintyre as they walked to their vehicle.

Carmichael nodded and grinned. 'Of course, and you knew it before you asked.'

'I did indeed,' agreed Macintyre, 'especially since the body was found up the valley.'

Chapter 7

After parking the vehicle in the ample parking area near the entrance to the Currumbin RSL situated on the Currumbin Creek, Carmichael and Macintyre entered the building.

Once more, Carmichael did the duty of introducing himself and Macintyre to the lady on reception, then produced the photo. The badge on the receptionist's blouse indicated her name was Rachel.

'Did you see this lady in here last Friday night, Rachel?'

The receptionist smiled and quickly said, 'Oh that looks like Lisa.'

'Are you sure?' asked Carmichael.

'Oh yes, she's been in a few times with her boyfriend Darren.'

'Was she on her own on Friday, Rachel?'

'She came in on her own, her boyfriend was already here.' Rachel's smile turned to a frown. 'Why are you asking, Inspector, is Lisa okay?'

Carmichael ignored the question. 'Do you have her address, Rachel?'

'She became a member a few months ago so I'm sure we do.'

'Would you give it to me, please?'

It took only a minute for Rachel to locate the address, print it and hand it across to Carmichael.

'Thanks for that, Rachel. We'll go on and have a chat to some of the staff, okay?'

Rachel watched Carmichael and Macintyre walk away into the club room, her face reflecting the concern she was feeling for Lisa.

Carmichael approached the centre bar.

Macintyre went to the food service area and showed her police ID and the photo to the two ladies on duty. 'This young lady was here last Friday night, probably sometime after 9 o'clock, did either of you see her?'

They both looked at the photo and shook their heads. 'Sorry, no, I'd clocked off before then,' said one.

'I was here till late, but I can't remember seeing her,' said the other with a shake of her head. She glanced at the photo again. 'Wait a minute though, that looks a bit like Lisa, so yes I did see her if that's who it is.'

'Was she with anyone?' asked Macintyre.

'Not with someone she wanted to be,' she replied with a smile.

'And why was that?'

'The guy she used to be with was here.'

'And?'

'She had given him the boot for cheating on her.'

'And?'

'After a few words he cleared off and she stayed on and had a few drinks.'

'Did you see her leave?'

'No, I didn't, she was still here when I clocked off at ten.'

'Thanks for that,' said Macintyre as she turned and walked away.

The ladies at the food service turned to each other. 'What was that all about?' they both said.

Macintyre found Carmichael at the bar talking to the man behind. 'I've got something, sir.'

'Right,' said Carmichael. 'Just a minute.' He looked back at the bartender. 'Thanks for that, Steve.'

'No worries, I hope it helps,' replied the bartender.

'I've got something as well,' said Carmichael. 'Let's go back to the car and we can talk about it.'

Back in the car, Carmichael took a deep breath before saying, 'You first, Jenny.'

'Okay ... well, apparently Lisa had a bit of a row with her boyfriend who she had found out had cheated on her and made him leave their place.'

Carmichael nodded. 'Yes, I got the same info from the bartender. He also said that one of the axe guys had a short chat to her but she gave him the cold shoulder. But there was another guy who she had a bit of time drinking with outside overlooking the creek.'

'Does he know the guy?' asked Macintyre.

'Said he didn't recognise him.'

'Did he see them leave?'

'No he didn't.'

'So, we don't know if they left together or individually.'

'Any CCTV?'

'No.'

They sat quietly for a moment or two, their minds turning.

Macintyre broke the silence. 'So, I guess we'd better go to Lisa's address, then track down the boyfriend.'

'That's the plan,' said Carmichael as he started up the car. He took out the piece of paper with Lisa's address on and read it out. 'Unit 4, Swinbourne Drive, Palm Beach.'

Chapter 8

Macintyre pointed to her right. 'That's the block of flats over there on the other side.'

Carmichael did a U-turn and pulled up outside the two-storey block of flats. 'And that's number 4, bottom right.'

They both exited the car, walked to the door and knocked. There was no response.

'Well, that's no surprise,' said Macintyre.

'You try number 3 and I'll go to 5,' said Carmichael.

Macintyre knocked on number 3 and the door was quickly opened by an elderly lady. Macintyre displayed her police badge. 'Good afternoon, ma'am. I'm Jennifer Macintyre, do you know the young woman who lives next door?'

The lady smiled and nodded. 'Yes, indeed I do, lovely girl, that's Lisa Edwards.'

Macintyre returned the smile. 'And what's your name, please?'

'I'm Valerie ... why are the police asking about Lisa?'

'Could you tell me when you last saw Lisa please, Valerie?' said Macintyre.

Valerie put a hand to her face and closed her eyes. 'Oh, let me see now ... I think it was a couple of days ago.'

'Did you talk to her, Valerie?'

'Just a little, she was not feeling the best because of her boyfriend Darren playing up.'

'Do you know where Darren has moved to since leaving here?'

'I'd guess back to his parents' place up in Burleigh.'

Carmichael, having no success after knocking on the door of

flat number 5, was now standing beside Macintyre.

Macintyre introduced him to Valerie. 'This is Inspector Carmichael, Valerie.'

'Oh my goodness,' said Valerie with concern, 'now you have me really worried ... is Lisa okay?'

'I'm afraid it's not good news, Valerie,' said Carmichael. 'We believe Lisa was murdered and we need to find out all we can about who she has been with a few days ago.'

Valerie gasped and put her hands to her face again. 'Oh no ... not Lisa,' she murmured, 'she is a lovely girl.'

'You mentioned Darren's parents in Burleigh, Valerie,' said Macintyre. 'Do you know their address?'

Valerie was shaking. 'No, I'm sorry.'

'Do you know his surname?' asked Carmichael.

'Yes, Nicholls ... it's Nicholls,' replied Valerie.

'That's good, thank you, Valerie.' Macintyre realised how upset Valerie was. 'Are you going to be alright Valerie? Would you like us to contact anyone to come stay with you?'

Valerie shook her head. 'My husband will be back shortly; he only went out to get some tablets from the chemist.'

'As long as you are sure you'll be okay ... we'll have to be on our way, Valerie, thank you very much for your help.'

Valerie turned around and closed her door.

'That poor lady is very upset; I hope she'll be okay,' said Macintyre as they walked back to their car.

Carmichael had his mobile out. 'I'll check addresses for Nicholls in Burleigh ... got one,' he exclaimed, '29 Barton Street.'

The home looked recently renovated and the front garden well attended with a large garden bed full of exotic plants and flowers. The double garage doors were open, displaying a Volvo and Hyundai.

As they approached the front door, a man came out the garage door. 'Looking for someone?' he asked.

Carmichael produced his ID. 'Yes we are, sir, Darren Nicholls, is he home?'

'Yes, he is ... what do you want with him?'

'Just need to ask him a few questions, sir. You are his father, I presume?'

'That's right, and like I said, what do you want with him?'

'Like I said, Mr Nicholls, just need to ask him a few questions. May we come in?'

Mr Nicholls looked Carmichael and Macintyre over for a moment or two, his face serious, before saying, 'Oh, alright, this way.'

He re-entered the garage and lead them through a back door into the living area.

'Darren,' he shouted, 'police want to talk to you.'

Darren came inside from out the back, carrying a magazine. 'What's up?'

Carmichael approached him. 'You have a girlfriend named Lisa, I understand. That right, Darren?'

Darren laughed. 'I did till a few days ago ... why do you ask?'

'When did you last see her?' asked Carmichael.

'Last Friday night ... she told me to piss off.'

'And why was that?'

Darren glanced at his father. 'Sorry, Dad, she found out I'd been with another girl.'

His father reached forward and punched him in the shoulder. 'You what? ... You cheated on her? ... You'd been together for two years ... she's a lovely person.'

Darren shrugged. 'Yes, I know, Dad, but I met this other girl and ... well it just ... you know, happened.'

Macintyre interrupted. 'So, where did you go when you left her, Darren?'

'Came straight home.'

'Is that right, Mr Nicholls?'

Nicholls nodded. 'Yes, he got here about ten ... look, officers, what's this all about?'

Carmichael ignored the question. 'And he stayed here?' he asked.

'Yes, I went to bed after a minute or two,' said Darren.

Carmichael realised that Darren could not have been responsible for Lisa's murder.

'I'm sorry to have to tell you, but Lisa was found dead on Saturday morning.'

Both Darren and his father gasped.

'Oh shit!' said Darren. 'Did she crash her Hyundai?'

'Afraid not, she was murdered.'

Darren's legs began to give way and his father reached out to hold him. 'Oh no, that's bloody awful.' He put his arms around his father. 'Why would anyone do that, Dad?'

Nicholls shook his head. 'Now I understand why you're here, officers. Have you any idea who is responsible?'

'We are following a number of leads, Mr Nicholls, and we had to see your son as he was at the club on Friday night.'

'Darren, I have to ask if you noticed anyone approach Lisa when you left her.'

Darren shook his head. 'No, I didn't, she walked out the front towards the creek and I went to my car and came home.'

'Okay, thanks for your help, we'll see ourselves out.'

Carmichael and Macintyre turned away and went back out the same way they had entered through the garage.

Darren and his father stood together silently, watching them go.

'So, now what?' said Macintyre when they were seated back in the car. 'Darren's cleared, where do we go from here?'

Carmichael frowned and scratched his head. 'I reckon we're back to square one ... the young lad who found her.'

'Darren mentioned a car crash ... where's her car?'

'Good thought, Jenny, that had passed me.'

'Tomorrow?' said Macintyre.

Carmichael nodded. 'Yeah, been a long day ... meet up in the office in the morning.'

Chapter 9

Macintyre looked up at Carmichael as he walked into the police station office. 'Morning, sir.'

Carmichael looked at his watch. 'It's only 8:30, what are you doing here so early?'

'Had things on my mind, sir.'

'Yeah … me too.'

Macintyre held up the plastic bag containing the receipt found at the scene of the murder. 'It's for Natures Goodness dog food from the Petbarn at Burleigh.'

'The young lad who found the body had a dog with him, didn't he?'

'Yes, he did, shall we call around there first? Joe took down his name and address when he was sitting in his car.'

'Oh and another thing,' said Macintyre. 'There's a car been sitting in the parking area at the RSL that has not moved for days.'

'That would have to be Lisa's surely, if it's a Hyundai.'

'Yes, it is a Hyundai.'

'Then it must be Lisa's.'

'Our folk are there now checking for fingerprints and anything else that might be useful,' said Macintyre.

Carmichael began pacing the office. 'I reckon we could be getting somewhere, Jenny. Come on, let's go see the young lad.'

From the Palm Beach Police Station to the home of Cameron Atkins just off Currumbin Creek Road was only a short drive. The home was set back a 100 metres from the road on a large block of land that was well- fenced. There were a number of cattle grazing nearby.

As they approached the home after parking the car, a dog could be heard barking. Carmichael was about to knock on the front door when it was opened by a woman.

'Knew there was somebody here due to the dog barking,' she said.

Carmichael produced his ID. 'Good morning, are you Mrs Atkins?'

'Yes I am,' she replied. 'Are you here about that poor girl that Cameron found?'

'Yes, we are Mrs Atkins, is Cameron in?'

'Yes he is, but he's just about to leave for school. Please come in.'

Mrs Atkins walked ahead of Carmichael and Macintyre as they entered the home. 'The police are here to see you, Cameron,' she shouted.

Cameron, wearing school uniform and carrying a small satchel, came out of a side room and walked up to them. A small dog was by his side.

Macintyre leant down and touched the dog, 'Nice fella, Cameron. A beagle, isn't it?'

Cameron smiled. 'Yeah, it follows me everywhere.'

Carmichael held out the plastic bag with the receipt inside. 'Did you buy this food for it?'

Cameron looked at the receipt. 'No, sir, not me. That's pretty expensive stuff.'

'Okay, thanks for that, Cameron. Now, since you regularly take the dog for a walk down there by the lake, do you see anyone else with a dog?'

Cameron nodded. 'There are several people who go there, but the one I see most often is Arnold with a big Alsatian.'

'Do you know where he lives, Cameron?' asked Macintyre.

'I think he's in the old farmhouse up the road on the left.'

Cameron pointed at the receipt in Carmichael's hand. 'That receipt has a date on it, and since it's expensive stuff the Petbarn may be able to tell you who bought it that day.'

Both Carmichael and Macintyre couldn't help but smile and chuckle at Cameron's remark.

'My goodness!' said Carmichael. 'That is an excellent thought. You may have to join the police force when you leave school.'

Mrs Atkins also chuckled. 'It is something that's been mentioned.'

'I thank you both for your time,' said Carmichael. 'We had better be on our way now or you'll be late for school ... would you like a lift?'

'That would be great,' replied Cameron excitedly.

'Okay, then let's go,' said Carmichael.'

Cameron gave his mother a quick kiss, patted the dog, and said, 'Stay, Bobby.'

The dog sat and whimpered as the three of them left the house and closed the door behind them.

Chapter 10

After delivering Cameron to his school, Carmichael and Macintyre soon arrived at the Petbarn in Burleigh.

They approached the manager, once again displayed their IDs, and showed him the receipt for dog food.

'Do you, or any of your staff, remember selling the product Natures Goodness last Friday?' asked Carmichael.

The manager shook his head. 'I certainly didn't as I was in the office doing paperwork all day, but Ellen was on the floor most of the day, we can ask her.'

He took Carmichael and Macintyre to a display of pet accessories where a lady was stocking the shelves. 'Ellen, these are police officers. Do you remember selling any bags of Natures Goodness last Friday?'

Ellen thought for a moment then nodded. 'Yes, I think I did.'

'Do you recall the buyers?' asked Carmichael.

'Sure ... it was Arnold, he's a regular, always gets the same.'

'Does he pay cash or credit card?'

'Always credit card,' said Ellen.

'So, would you happen to have his address on file?' asked Macintyre.

'Probably, I can look it up if you like.'

'That would be great, Ellen.'

Ellen walked to a desk near the entrance where a computer and cash register were situated. She operated the computer. 'Yes, here it is, his address is 24 Wellcome Road, Currumbin.'

Macintyre wrote the address down in her notebook.

Carmichael shook the manager's hand, and thanked him and Ellen for the information before leaving the store.

'Is this going to be him?' said Macintyre as they got back in their car.

Carmichael smiled. 'Let's go check him out, eh?'

Carmichael brought the car to a halt at the gated entrance to 24 Wellcome Road. A home could be seen about two hundred metres up the driveway.

Macintyre got out and pulled the gate aside to enable Carmichael to drive in. Macintyre closed the gate and re-entered the car.

'Big old Queenslander,' said Carmichael as they approached the home.

'Looks like a big shed around the back,' said Macintyre.

Carmichael parked the car at the wooden stairway that led up to the verandah. As they walked up the stairway, a woman came out of the front door. 'Yes!?' she said sharply.

Carmichael produced his police badge. 'I'm Inspector Carmichael and this is Sergeant Macintyre. We are investigating the death of a young lady nearby and we are calling on everyone in this area to see if anyone noticed any strangers recently.'

The woman put her hand to her face. 'Oh yes, that was terrible.' She shook her head. 'I'm sorry, I haven't seen anyone I don't know around here.'

'Thank you for that, Mrs?' asked Macintyre.

'Oh, I'm Glenda Bradford, please call me Glenda.'

'Would your husband, or perhaps children, have seen anyone?' asked Carmichael.

'There's just me and my son here I'm afraid ... My husband passed away a few years ago. My son Arnold is back in the shed chopping firewood if you'd like to ask him.'

'Thank you, Glenda, yes, we'll wander up and see him if that's alright?'

'Yes, that's fine.' She pointed to the large shed. 'His dog is there with him, but you don't have to worry about him, he's very friendly.'

Carmichael and Macintyre thanked Glenda again then made their way back towards the shed.

'And a friendly dog,' said Macintyre.

'Wonder if Arnold is friendly?' said Carmichael.

As they neared the shed, the sound of wood being chopped reached them. They stopped and glanced at each other.

'Better be careful what we say, Jenny. I don't trust anyone holding an axe.'

They stopped at the front of the shed. A young man, holding an axe standing in front of a pile of chopped timber, looked up at them.

'Hi, you must be Arnold. Your mother said we could come and have a chat to you, if that's alright?'

Arnold walked to the front of the shed where Carmichael and Macintyre were standing. He carried his axe with him.

'Thanks for this, Arnold,' Carmichael held out his police badge. 'I'm Inspector Carmichael and this is Sergeant Macintyre. It's about the young girl that was killed a few days back; we are asking the locals if they've seen any strangers around lately.'

Arnold was quiet for a moment; his face serious. Then with a slight grin on his face, he swung his axe back and forth. 'No, not me, I don't go out much.'

'Did you happen to go to the axe men show, Arnold?' asked Macintyre.

'Oh yes, I went to that.'

Carmichael pointed at his axe. 'Looks like you could teach them a thing or two, Arnold.'

'Yeah, reckon I could.' He continued swinging his axe.

'Do you go to the Currumbin RSL at all, Arnold?'

Arnold's grin faded. 'Sometimes, why?'

'Wondered if you might have seen any of the axe crowd there.'

'Oh yes ... think I did.'

'What night was that, Arnold?' asked Macintyre.

Arnold shrugged. 'Mmm ... last week sometime, I think.'

A bark came from the back of the shed and a large dog walked to Arnold and sat down.

'He looks a well-fed fella,' said Carmichael. 'What do you feed him?'

'Only give him Natures Goodness; keeps him fit and healthy.'

Carmichael glanced at Macintyre before looking back at Arnold. 'Okay, well thanks, Arnold, we'll be heading off now.' He turned away and looked again at Macintyre. 'Come on, Sergeant.'

Together, they returned to their car.

'The inside of the shed would be worth looking around, and the ute inside there, and the dog eats Natures Goodness,' said Macintyre.

Carmichael nodded in agreement. 'Yes, the whole place is worth checking out, but I'd like to get authority first. We'll drive away and then make a phone call.'

On reaching a place well down the road and out of sight of 24 Wellcome Road, Carmichael stopped and reached for his mobile.

'Hi, boss, I reckon we are onto something, but I'd like official authorisation before we go inside a property. It's 24 Wellcome Road, Currumbin. The owner is a Mrs Glenda Bradford.'

He waited a moment as the address was repeated back to him.

'So, if you can arrange that and get the authorisation brought along ASAP with a few extra guys in case we need them, that'd be great.'

He moved the mobile away from his ear and grinned at Macintyre. 'Yes, boss, I appreciate it's urgent, but I wouldn't like any evidence to be destroyed.' He paused a moment. 'Thanks, boss.'

He put the mobile down. 'He's not happy, but help should be here in forty minutes. There's a small shop down the road, fancy an ice cream while we wait?'

Macintyre laughed. 'Sounds good to me!'

Chapter 11

It was only thirty-five minutes later that two police cars came to a stop beside Carmichael and Macintyre as they just finished their ice creams. A warrant to enter the Wellcome Road premises was produced.

The three vehicles drove to number 24, up the driveway and stopped outside the home.

Mrs Bradford came out the front door, her expression serious. 'What now? I thought I'd told you I haven't seen anyone.'

Carmichael went to her. 'Yes, you did, Mrs Bradford and we appreciate it, but we have to speak to Arnold again and look through the shed. Is he still up there chopping timber?'

Mrs Bradford was confused. 'Yes, he is, but why do you want to do that?'

Carmichael turned away towards the four police officers from the other cars. 'Please be careful, guys, he has an axe that he's very handy with.'

As they approached the shed, Arnold came to the front. On seeing the police, he quickly turned and ran back inside.

'Two of you around the back,' shouted Carmichael. He, Macintyre and the other two police followed Arnold inside.

They came to an abrupt halt as Arnold stood before them waving an axe in each hand. He grinned. 'Anything I can help you with, gentlemen?'

Carmichael took a step towards him and raised his hands. 'We need to have another chat, Arnold, so please put the axes down.'

Arnold began swinging the axes and started walking towards

him. 'Better still, why don't you all fuck off?'

The two police behind Carmichael drew their firearms. One shouted, 'Stop right there!'

Carmichael took a few paces backwards, his hands still raised. 'Please stop, Arnold, think of your mum.'

Arnold stopped, breathing heavily. Slowly, he lowered the axes.

'Drop them on the ground and step back please,' said Carmichael.

He moved forward and reached out to the axes. He was just about to grab hold of them when Arnold let out a yell. With his face a mask of anger and aggression, he swung the axes towards Carmichael.

One of the axes sliced across Carmichael's right arm before two shots rang out. Arnold fell backwards, dropping his axes. Macintyre rushed to Carmichael who was holding his right forearm with blood seeping out.

Macintyre removed a handkerchief from her handbag and wrapped it tightly around his upper arm. 'You need to get to a doc and quick,' she said.

Carmichael nodded. 'I think you're right, Jenny.' He turned to the police officers. 'Will one of you guys hurry me down to the hospital?'

As he and an officer walked away, he looked back at Macintyre. 'Jenny, it's your job to carry on till I get stitched. I should be back in an hour or so.'

Macintyre nodded. 'No worries, see you soon.'

She took out her mobile and rang the office. 'Hi, sir, got a problem here. Our suspect went a bit ballistic; swung an axe at Carmichael and sliced his arm that'll need stitching. Can you call Tugun Hospital and let them know he's on his way? Oh and we need an ambulance as the suspect has been shot.'

She nodded as she listened to the reply. 'Yes, sir, I will.'

Mrs Bradford came running up to the shed. 'I heard shooting, what's happened?' she exclaimed.

Macintyre stood in front of her preventing her from moving on.

Then she saw Arnold lying on the ground; his shirt front red.

One of the police was kneeling beside him. He looked up at Macintyre and shrugged his shoulders with an unsure expression on his face.

Mrs Bradford screamed and fell to her knees. 'No, no! ... what have you done to my son?'

Macintyre knelt beside her and placed her hand on her shoulder. 'I'm very sorry, Mrs Bradford, he left the officers no choice.'

Mrs Bradford broke into uncontrollable sobbing.

Macintyre's mobile rang, she listened. 'Yes, sir.'

She spoke quietly to Mrs Bradford. 'An ambulance is on the way with paramedics and I know they'll do all they can for Arnold.'

She addressed the other police officers. 'Keep out of the shed, guys, don't touch the axes or go near the ute, it'll have to be dusted for prints, crime scene guys are on the way.'

A few minutes later, sirens could be heard. An ambulance, followed by three police cars, came up the driveway. The ambulance was directed to the front of the garage. Paramedics quickly went to Arnold. 'He's still with us, but we need to get to hospital ASAP,' said one of the paramedics.

With police assistance, Arnold was lifted on a stretcher and placed in the ambulance.

Macintyre stood beside a trembling Mrs Bradford as the ambulance sped away. 'If you would like to go to the hospital, one of the police vehicles will take you, Mrs Bradford.'

She nodded. 'Yes please,' she murmured.

Macintyre waved over one of the officers. 'Take Mrs Bradford to the hospital please, Jake.'

'Of course,' he replied. 'Do you want to take anything with you, ma'am?' he asked.

She shook her head.

'Okay ... that's my car just over there.' He took hold of her arm and helped her the short distance.

Macintyre walked back to where a white-coated and masked officer was taking photographs of the inside of the shed. Another similarly attired officer was dusting the ute for fingerprints.

A police car with lights and sirens blaring raced up the drive. As soon as it came to a halt, Carmichael got out and rushed to Macintyre.

'How's it going?' he asked.

Macintyre looked at his arm with a sling holding it. 'It's going fine, boss. How about you? You were quick.'

'Oh, I'm fine,' replied Carmichael.

'How many stitches?' asked Macintyre.

'Twenty-three!'

Macintyre grimaced. 'Good job you weren't a bit nearer him or it might have been your head that collected it.'

The police and crime scene officers began packing up. One of the officers approached them.

'All done?' asked Carmichael.

The officer nodded. 'Yeah ... area all photographed, and we managed to lift several prints from inside the ute. One set was small and I'm guessing it will be the girl's. Should have results later today.'

'Thanks, guys,' said Carmichael.

Carmichael and Macintyre watched the officers drive away as they walked to their car.

Carmichael was about to open the driver's side door, then stopped, a grimace on his face. 'Reckon you'd better drive, Jenny.'

Macintyre had just opened the passenger side door. She left it open and walked around to the driver's side and got in. She adjusted her seatbelt, started the car and looked across. 'Starting to feel it, eh?'

Carmichael nodded and forced a grin. 'Yes, reckon the

anaesthetic is starting to wear off. As soon as we've finished our reports, you can drive me home if that's okay?'

'No worries! All seems clear-cut'—she glanced across at his arm—'if you'll pardon the expression.'

Carmichael gave a chuckle. 'Oh good one, Jenny.'

'One question we don't seem to have the answer to,' said Macintyre.

'And that is?'

'Why ... why ever did he choose to do it?'

Carmichael shook his head. 'That's something we're never going to know, Jenny.'

At 6 o'clock that afternoon the report on the fingerprints confirmed that some belonged to the murdered girl Lisa Edwards.

A trace of the date rape drug was also found in the car's glovebox.

With that piece of information there was no doubt that Arnold Bradford was the person responsible.

Half an hour later, Carmichael and Macintyre had finished their report. It was duly signed and handed to the Chief Inspector.

Macintyre drove Carmichael home as he had requested.

She then drove herself home to her unit, poured herself a glass of wine and slumped down onto her couch.

Chapter 12

The evidence pointing to Arnold Bradford re the death of Lisa Edwards, and his subsequent death, made it unnecessary for a trial.

A follow up by an internal police review into the shooting of Bradford stated that the officer who fired the shots that resulted in his death did so to prevent Bradford possibly killing Carmichael, and accordingly no further action regarding the incident would take place.

Both Carmichael and Macintyre were commended for their efforts in solving the murder of Lisa Edwards.

They continue to work together.

Mrs Bradford sold her property on Wellcome Road and moved into a retirement village.

Back on the golf course four weeks later with his friends Stuart and Vic, Carmichael was lining up his drive on the first tee when his mobile rang.

'Sorry, guys!' he remarked as he dropped his driver onto the ground, put the phone to his ear and took a few paces away.

Stuart and Vic glanced at each other.

'Here we go again,' said Stuart.

After a minute or two, Carmichael replaced his mobile into his shorts pocket, and with a serious expression walked back to Stuart and Vic. He shook his head. 'I have to pick up a couple litres of milk on the way home,'

He picked his driver back up and laughed.

The expressions on Stuart and Vic's faces changed from serious to grins.

'Had us going there, you bugger!' said Stuart.

Carmichael went to them both and shook their hands. 'Thanks for being here, guys, means a lot to get my mind off stuff.'

'That's what friends are for,' said Vic. He pointed at the ball sitting on a tee. 'Now, for goodness sake, go hit the bloody thing.'

PART 2:
OH SHIT!

Chapter 1

Carmichael's life changed dramatically only six months after the axe murder.

A letter from Inspector Bailey's wife that arrived at his Burleigh office was the first torment. She advised that Bailey had passed away from an unexpected heart attack, and that he had left instructions for the enclosed sealed envelope to be forwarded to Carmichael.

Inside the sealed envelope was a folded small piece of paper with only three words written on it:

I DID IT.

Carmichael grabbed a chair and sat down. His breathing quickened as he came to terms with the meaning of the three words. Bailey, he figured, was admitting to the attack on a rapist following the suicide of Harris Jordan. And now the question he asked himself, was Bailey also responsible for all the previous attacks that he had presumed to be the work of Harris Jordan and should he report it?

His mind was racing. He left the office and headed for the nearest hotel. He needed a drink. He hadn't drunk alcohol for many years; since before his marriage in fact. The drink relaxed him and he made the decision to keep the information to himself as he reckoned as both Jordan and Bailey were gone, so there was no point.

Only a week later, a kingpin drug supplier had mentioned in court when undergoing sentencing, that he had paid Carmichael five thousand dollars to get him off the charge.

He was immediately placed on permanent leave while the alleged bribery allegation was investigated.

Despite vehemently denying any association with the man, and explaining his exemplary record to superiors, some officers tended to believe the allegation and treated him as guilty.

It took six months for the investigation to be finalised in Carmichael's favour, but by then the damage had been done to his character.

It was at that time that he decided to cut ties with the police force and move on.

During the six month investigation, his marriage to Barbara crumbled. She had been having trouble coping with his irregular hours of duty beforehand, and seldom being home when she needed him, for herself and for the children, Keith and Sally. During the time of his investigation, he had started drinking heavily and slipped into periods of depression.

He moved out of the family home, and, for the following three months, continued his bouts of heavy drinking. It was a visit from his golfing friends and their severe admonishment that made him turn things around. He started going to the gym regularly and soon brought his weight back from an excessive one hundred and ten kilos, to his current weight of ninety-five kilos.

Looking and feeling more respectable, he contacted Barbara to try and patch up the marriage. Barbara was not interested, however, and wanted a divorce. She would keep the children, but he would be allowed to visit them at any time provided that he didn't go off the rails again.

Now he needed a job, and after studying the vacancies section in the local newspaper, the ad for head of security at the casino caught his eye. With his policing background, he was accepted for the job and asked to start immediately.

Although the position entailed a great deal of late-night work, he found he was able to take time away during the day to catch up with the children. He had explained to the casino general manager when offered the position that he would want to attend sporting events or suchlike his children were involved in. The general manager, being a family man, fully understood and okayed his wish.

Since starting at the casino, there had been no shortage of suitors. At thirty-eight, unattached, good looking and fit, and surrounded by attractive female employees, he was, after all, quite a catch. No real relationship developed however, his mind always drawn back to Barbara and the two kids.

Chapter 2

The man watched from his position on the king size bed as the incredibly beautiful woman unzipped the back of the red dress that clung to her like a second skin. The dress fell to the floor, and the man gasped as his eyes examined the 170 cm of glorious femininity displayed before him. As he was wearing only his underpants, his appreciation of the figure before him was more than apparent.

'My God, Velda, you are even more magnificent than I had imagined,' said the man.

Velda smiled. 'And you, Harold, appear to be much more of a man than I had imagined.'

Harold Ashgrove—aged fifty-five, grey hair receding, overweight with a substantial amount of the weight gathered around his middle—was not in fact a particularly attractive man, and why this beautiful young woman had taken a shine to him he still hadn't quite figured out, but he had no intention of asking and possibly destroying what he had visions of being a night to remember. She spoke with what Harold thought to be a middle European accent, maybe Polish, not that at this point in time Harold could really give a damn.

Velda stood at the side of the bed in her brief bra and even briefer panties. She ran her tongue over her lips. 'Oh, Harold, I think you deserve something really special.'

She picked up her handbag from the bedside table, opened it, and took out four pink, silken ribbons. She placed one knee on the bed and leant forward, allowing Harold a better view of her breasts.

Harold moaned in anticipation. She tied a ribbon to each of his ankles and then to the end of the bed. She sat astride him, held his arms and pushed them to the top of the bed. She tied one end of a silken ribbon to his left wrist and the other to the bedpost. Then she tied his right wrist to the right bedpost.

She leant forward and kissed him on the lips. 'Can you move, Harold?' she asked.

Harold gave his arms a tug, and a wriggle of his spreadeagled body. 'No I can't.'

'In that case all is as it should be,' said Velda with a smile.

'Please feel free to do with me whatever you please,' said Harold as he closed his eyes and gave a shiver of anticipation.

Velda reached into her handbag again, took out a roll of tape, tore off a strip and quickly placed it over Harold's mouth. Harold opened his eyes with a start and a grunt at the feel of the tape. He was a little unsure of this turn of events.

Velda continued to smile at Harold as she removed herself from over him and stood beside the bed. She walked around to the other side of the bed and picked up Harold's jacket from where he had hung it over a chair. She extracted the wad of bills from the inside pocket. Harold began to struggle on the bed in an attempt to free himself, but the ribbons around his wrists were knotted and tied securely. With the tape over his mouth all he could utter was a quiet mumble of disbelief. The eight thousand dollars was the cash he had won on the roulette wheel in the casino earlier in the evening,

Velda placed the cash in her handbag, redressed and picked up her shoes. She looked down at Harold as he stared wide-eyed at her and shaking his head. 'Oh dear, Harold, it looks as if you have lost all interest in me.' She waved her handbag. 'But thank you for this.' She blew him a kiss as she left the bedroom and closed the door behind her.

Harold had been having an unbelievable run of good luck at the roulette table when the young woman sat at the chair beside him.

She gave him a brief smile before turning her attention to the wheel and the numbers on the table.

For the next three spins, she placed a five dollar chip on number seven that unfortunately failed to win. Harold, on the other hand, had managed to double his investment by betting on overs or unders to come up.

He decided to offer advice to the woman. 'Excuse me, miss, I don't want to tell you your business, but if you changed your betting style you might increase the odds in your favour.'

'But isn't seven a lucky number?' the woman asked.

'Unfortunately, that's not necessarily the case,' said Harold.

Over the next hour, Harold and the young woman discussed the chances of winning on certain numbers, and of how he had been managing to win. Harold also learnt the young woman's name ... Velda.

Velda was at last up by sixty dollars, but then decided to try her luck again on number seven. She gave a smile and a shrug as the croupier removed her chips. 'I'm obviously not meant to win, Harold,' she said dismissively.

Harold returned her smile. 'How about I buy you a drink, Velda? I know you haven't won, but I have had quite a successful evening.'

'Well, thank you, Harold, that would be very nice of you,' replied Velda.

'First, I'll go cash in my chips,' said Harold as he stood up from his chair.

Velda accompanied Harold to the exchange booth where his total chips amounted to eight thousand dollars. 'Even better than I'd thought,' said Harold as he placed the pile of dollar bills into the inside pocket of his jacket.

After more than just a few drinks at the bar, Harold was feeling very relaxed. The bar became more crowded and noisy with late night revellers. Harold and Velda had to lean closer to make themselves heard. 'Tell you what, Velda,' said Harold in a slightly slurry voice, 'how about I buy a bottle of bubbly and we take it up to my room where it's a lot quieter.'

'Oh, Harold!' said Velda. 'That sounds a bit naughty.'

Harold sat back and raised his hands with a look of anguish. 'Oh I'm sorry. I didn't mean … I mean!'

Velda placed a hand on Harold's arm. 'Harold, I think you are a really nice person, and that sounds a lovely idea.'

Up in Harold's room Velda made sure that it was Harold who consumed the, by far, largest quantity of the bottle of champagne, and when one thing started to lead to another, Harold didn't take a lot of convincing to remove his clothes.

Chapter 3

Ex-cop Steven Carmichael had spent most of the morning checking up on the security cameras that were dotted all around the casino. This was a regular part of his job and an important aspect of the casino's security. At midday, he was about to grab a bite to eat from the café when his mobile rang. The screen indicated a call from the general manager.

'What's up, Arthur?' He began walking hurriedly towards the lifts. 'What room number? Name?'

Carmichael exited the lift on the sixth floor and turned to his left. Two cleaning ladies, Liz and Carole, were standing outside of room 614.

'Hi, Liz, you ladies got a bit of a surprise I understand,' he said with a grin.

'You won't believe it,' said Liz while stifling a laugh.

'We thought it was empty, after all, it is after twelve; never seen anything like it,' said Carole with a giggle.

'Okay, now it's my turn, so you two ladies go on about your work and I'll try to sort it out.'

'Can't we come in with you?' asked Liz with a smile.

'Go on, clear off you two,' said Carmichael. 'Reckon you've had enough excitement for one day.'

Carmichael opened the door, walked in and closed it behind him. He walked across the lounge area floor to the bedroom and looked in to see Harold lying on the bed struggling against the pink ribbons confining his arms and legs. Carmichael walked away into the kitchen and returned with a knife.

Harold went completely still and looked up with wide eyes as Carmichael leant over him with the knife raised and cut the ribbons.

Harold quickly sat up and ripped the tape from his mouth. 'I've been robbed … I've been fuckin' robbed.'

Carmichael tried to assist Harold to remove the knotted ribbon from his wrists, but Harold pushed him away. 'The bitch stole all my winnings.'

Harold continued to shout and swear as he dressed. 'I'll sue this fuckin' place.'

Carmichael spoke quietly. 'My name is Steve Carmichael, Mr Ashgrove, and I am head of security here. Of course, that is your prerogative, sir, and I will make every effort to retrieve your winnings. So, if you would be good enough to tell me exactly what happened, how much you have lost and how it was taken.'

'Well, it was eight thousand dollars the bitch took.'

'And how exactly did she take it, sir?'

'Isn't that obvious?' said Harold, raising his arms with the ribbons still attached.

'I can see this is difficult for you, sir. If you could please accompany me to the general manager's office, I can take a full statement from you, then you can go home and we will contact you in due course following a complete investigation. We do have your address, don't we, sir?'

Harold looked at Carmichael for a moment before answering. 'My address … you would contact me at my home?'

'Of course, sir, we don't expect you to stay here while we investigate; it may take some time to track down the person you say is responsible before we can take her to court … and who was that person, sir?'

'She was … ah, she was … look if you take her to court, would I have to testify?'

'Indeed, sir, your testimony would be vital.'

Harold gave a long, drawn-out sigh and went for a slow walk around the room. He shrugged his shoulders and shook his hands. 'Look ... slight problem, pal ... you see I don't think my wife would be too happy ... if you get my meaning.'

'So, you would prefer us to do what, sir?' asked Carmichael.

'Perhaps we'd better just ... ah ... forget it.'

Carmichael nodded his head. 'It's entirely your decision, sir.'

Ashgrove waved his hands and shook his head. 'Yeah right, my decision ... shit!'

'Tell you what, Mr Ashgrove, I'll make arrangements for whatever you have paid for accommodation, food and drink to be refunded to you, and for a docket to be issued to allow you free accommodation for three nights on your next visit, would that be okay?'

'Yeah, I guess so,' said Harold without great enthusiasm as he continued dressing himself.

'Do you have a suitcase, sir?' asked Carmichael as Harold pulled on his socks and shoes.

'Yeah, not much to go in it though ... there's a few things in the bathroom.'

Carmichael retrieved his belongings from the bathroom and placed them beside Harold's small suitcase that he had placed on the bed. 'When you're ready, we'll go to my office and you can help me list out all your expenses, sir.'

'I'm ready now,' said Harold angrily. He picked up his suitcase and followed Carmichael to the outside door.

Carmichael opened the door and stood aside and indicated to his right as Harold exited. 'This way to the lift, sir.'

The sound of supressed giggling made them look down the passageway where the two cleaners were standing. Carmichael gave them an icy stare as he ushered Harold into the lift.

In his office Carmichael made an itemised list of Harold's expenses. 'Would that just about cover everything, sir?' he asked as he showed him the list.

Harold gave the list a brief glance. 'Yeah, I guess.'

'I'll have to get the general manager to sign off on it, sir, then we can issue a cheque,' said Carmichael as he took out his mobile. 'Hi, Arthur, can you come to my office please?'

Carmichael put the mobile down and looked at Harold. 'Can you give me a description of the young woman, Mr Ashgrove?'

Harold shrugged. 'Twenty-six … seven … brunette … bit shorter than me.'

'Australian?'

'Slight accent … maybe Polish … said I deserved something special; well, she was right there.'

'Anything else you can add?'

Harold gave a grunt. 'Yeah, the bitch had a great body.'

'Ah, here's the general manager,' said Carmichael as Arthur Musgrove entered the office.

'Hello, Mr Ashgrove, I'm truly sorry for what's happened and we will fully compensate you your expenses.'

Carmichael handed him the list he had made. Musgrove gave the list a cursory glance. 'Yes, I'm sure that will be fine. If you would please stop at our check-in desk as you leave a cheque will be waiting there for you.' He looked at Carmichael. 'You will accompany Mr Ashgrove, Steve?'

Carmichael nodded.

'Thank you, Mr Ashgrove,' continued Musgrove, 'and once again, my apologies for what's happened, and we look forward to seeing you again in the future.' He nodded again to Carmichael and left the office.

'Not so bloody sure I'll be coming back though, pal,' mumbled Ashgrove grumpily as he watched Musgrove depart. He picked up his suitcase and looked at Carmichael. 'Come on, let's get that cheque then I can get the hell out of here.'

After escorting Ashgrove to the front desk, and ensuring he

received the cheque, Carmichael watched him leave the casino then made his way to the general manager's office.

'All fixed, Steve?'

'Yeah, he's not a happy camper though; he's pissed off that the woman took eight grand from him.'

'But at least he's not taking it any further, eh?'

'Yeah, doesn't want his wife to find out.'

'In that case we got off cheap, good work, Steve.'

'I'd still like to find the woman, Arthur. Has there been anything similar happen?'

'Not to my knowledge, but it's the kind of thing not many blokes would want to come public about.'

'That's true … Look, I'll see if I can find anything on the recordings from the last couple of days on the security cameras.'

'Good luck with that, keep me posted on anything you find.'

Chapter 4

Over the next few days, in between all other events, Carmichael only managed to review a few hours of security footage.

It seemed that everything untoward that could happen did happen. Eight o'clock in the evening, he was called to the upmarket restaurant when a party of four had complained about their meals, refused to pay and pushed one of the waitresses to the floor. The restaurant was noted for its cuisine and fine dining.

When Carmichael arrived at the scene two chefs and two security men were attempting to calm down one of the male diners who was obviously drunk and hurling abuse at the chefs.

Carmichael asked the chefs and security men to leave and he stood alone in front of the group. He raised his hands in submission as the drunk advanced towards him. 'Please, folks, will you let me pay for your meal?'

The drunk stopped, looked at Carmichael, then at his companions, then back at Carmichael. 'Now you're talking,' he slurred out with a lopsided grin.

'Thank you, sir. Now, if you would be good enough to accompany me.' Carmichael began to walk out of the restaurant and the group followed. He looked at the other security men as he passed them and signalled for them to follow. Outside the restaurant, Carmichael stopped and signalled to another security guard to approach him.

Carmichael turned and faced the group as they caught up to him. 'Thank you for leaving the restaurant, and now I would appreciate it if you would leave the casino.'

The drunk laughed. 'You're joking, pal, we're gonna celebrate.' He looked at the others. 'Eh guys!?'

Carmichael smiled and took a step towards the drunk. At thirty-eight years old, just under two metres tall, and ninety-five kilos, he was extremely fit from sessions in the casino's gymnasium. He seemed to tower over the man. 'Not tonight, people ... Now, are you going nice and quietly, or would you prefer us to assist you?'

The drunk was about to speak again when a hand fell on his shoulder from one of the females. 'Craig, please stop it ... you'll get hurt.'

The drunk looked around at the now four security men and realisation seemed to come to him of what may possibly happen if he pushed further. He stepped back and looked up at Carmichael. 'Oh alright!'

'Wise decision, sir,' said Carmichael. He pointed at the security men. 'These gentlemen will escort you outside.'

Carmichael watched as the three security men and the four diners made their way to the casino entrance and left the building. His mobile rang. 'Yes, Glen.'

'Got an elderly lady helping herself to other people's tokens at the pokies in area fifteen.'

'Keep an eye on her, Glen, I'll be there soon as.' Carmichael hurried to the pokies area where he found Glen with an elderly couple.

'Reckon it's all sorted, Steve. This is Mr and Mrs Chandler. Mrs Chandler couldn't remember which machine she had been playing after going to the toilet, and unfortunately thought it was one that another lady was playing.'

'My wife gets a little forgetful,' explained Mr Chandler. 'I'm very sorry if we have caused any trouble.'

'Yes, I'm very sorry,' said Mrs Chandler, 'I thought that other person was stealing my tokens.' She pointed to another elderly lady standing nearby.

'I'll have a talk to her,' said Carmichael as he went to the other lady.

'Is everything alright Mrs …?'

The lady smiled. 'Weston … yes of course it is; she just made a mistake, that's all. I think she has a touch of dementia, poor dear.'

'Thank you, Mrs Weston, would you please wait a moment while I have another talk to the couple?'

Carmichael returned to the couple. 'Well, Mr and Mrs Chandler, the other lady, Mrs Weston, doesn't wish to take it further, so you can go on and enjoy your evening.'

'Oh that's wonderful, thank you so much,' said Mr Chandler. 'I think I'll see if she would like to join us for a drink.'

'That sounds a good plan,' said Carmichael. 'Why don't I organise it?' He beckoned the other lady over. 'Mr and Mrs Chandler would like you to join them for a drink.'

'That would be lovely,' said Mrs Weston with a smile.

Carmichael took out his wallet and extracted a fifty dollar note that he handed to Mr Chandler. 'And the drinks will be on me.'

He returned the smiles and waved a hand as Mr and Mrs Chandler, and Mrs Weston walked away to the bar area.

'Well, that was an easy one,' said Glen.

'Yeah, if that's as bad as it gets tonight I'll be one very happy man.'

'Give it time, Steve, the night is still young,' said Glen with a laugh.

Carmichael's mobile rang and he looked at Glen. 'You and your big mouth.'

Glen laughed again as Carmichael walked off with the mobile to his ear. 'No kidding! … Where are you? … on my way!'

It was a quick walk to the blackjack table and security guard Dave standing nearby. He inclined his head to the table and the woman wearing a red dress. 'Could she be the one, Steve?'

Carmichael walked around the table, viewing the woman from

all sides, and back to Dave. 'Not sure, do you have a name?'

'No I don't, but she certainly seems very friendly with the bloke beside her, could be leading him on. What do you reckon?'

Just then, the man beside her threw his cards on the table and pushed his chair back. Carmichael deliberately allowed the man to bump the chair into him. 'Ouch!' he exclaimed.

The man turned and looked apologetically at Carmichael. 'Oh I am sorry, didn't realise you were right behind me.'

'No worries!' said Carmichael with a smile. 'Reckon I'll live. Did you have any luck with the cards?'

The man laughed. 'No way ... I reckon they're fixed. My daughter came away well in front though, didn't you, love?'

'If you consider three dollars to be way in front, yes I did, Dad.'

'Let's hope you both have better luck next time. Enjoy your evening,' said Carmichael as they walked away arm in arm.

He turned to Vic. 'Reckon they're okay, but it was worth checking out. If the woman wants to pull the same stunt again she'll probably dress differently. I once had a guy wear four different get-ups when robbing post offices. We'd been thinking four different blokes till we nabbed him on his last effort.'

'Think she'll be back?'

'Wouldn't surprise me.'

Chapter 5

t was two days later, just before midday, when Carmichael was asked to make haste to the seventh floor. On stepping out of the lift, he found the cleaners Carole and Liz with huge smiles on their faces.

'Got us another one, Steve,' said Carole.

'Just like the other one,' added Liz.

'What room?' asked Carmichael.

'Just down on the left, seven-one-five,' said Liz.

'Thanks, ladies, now please don't stand here laughing this time when I bring him out, okay?'

'Won't be easy,' said Carole, trying hard to suppress a giggle.

'Go on, clear off,' said Carmichael with a grin as he walked down the passageway.

Inside the unit, he found Larry Spicer in the same predicament as Ashgrove with a tape over his mouth, and tied spreadeagled on the bed.

After removing the tape, Spicer's reaction was altogether different from Ashgrove ... he began to laugh. 'When I tell my mates about this they're going to go right off.'

Carmichael started to untie Spicer's wrists.

'Wait a minute,' said Spicer. 'There's a camera in my suitcase; will you take a photo first, mate?'

Carmichael did as Spicer requested.

Spicer continued to laugh as he was cut free. 'I tell you ... what's your name, pal?'

'It's Steve Carmichael, Mr Spicer.'

'Call me Larry, Steve … This is the most exciting thing that's happened to me in a long time … jeez, she was a good looking woman,' said Spicer as he started to get dressed.

'Can you describe her for me, Larry?'

'Sure … 'bout my height, thirtyish, long, black hair.'

'Where did she come from do you reckon?'

'Thailand, Philippines, something like that.'

'How much have you lost?'

'Good question!' Spicer reached for his wallet from the bedside table. 'Three thousand, give or take.'

'If you would come to my office, I'll make a note of all that's happened so that when we catch this woman we can get her into court, and then with your testimony we—'

'Wait on, wait on!' said Spicer. 'No need for all that.'

'Don't you want to see her prosecuted?' asked Carmichael.

'Hell no! I certainly have no wish to stand up in court and tell all and sundry what a bloody fool I've been. Anyway, it's only three grand and I've got some great pictures and a great story to tell my mates.'

'Well, if you're sure that's what you want, Larry.'

'Yeah! … Just put it down to experience.'

'Is there anything else you can think of about her that might help us stop it happening to anyone else?'

Spicer thought for a moment. 'Not really, I was pretty pissed at the time. She did say I deserved something special and she sure delivered on that score.' He grinned at Carmichael. 'Great body, Steve, great body.'

'We can't give you back the money you've lost, Larry, but will you let us refund your room cost and a bit extra for whatever you've spent on food and drink?'

'That would be terrific, thanks a lot. I'm staying one more night so you never know, I might win it all back and more besides.'

'I wish you a ton of luck, Larry, and there'll be a cheque waiting for you at reception when you leave. And please be careful who you chat up tonight, okay?'

'I most certainly will,' said Spicer with a laugh.

'All the best to you,' said Carmichael as he walked to the door.

In the general manager's office, Carmichael explained to Arthur Musgrove the meeting with Larry Spicer. 'Exactly the same as with the previous bloke Ashgrove, but Spicer has taken it completely differently.'

'And you reckon it's the same woman?'

'Yeah for sure; dressed up different and different accent, but I'm sure it's the same woman.'

'So, how are we going to catch her?'

'I'll go through the security camera recordings again. Pretty certain she'll be on there somewhere, and compare the pictures with those from the last one. I'll get all our staff to take a look and tell them to contact me if they notice a woman, whatever she looks like, seeming to be making a play for a bloke.'

'Okay, Steve, let's hope she moves on after making two successful hits.'

'Maybe, but I got a feeling she'll be thinking it's all too easy and have another crack.'

'By the way, if it's all reasonably quiet here next Sunday, how'd you like to come around to my place for a BBQ lunch?'

'Sounds great, thanks, Arthur. Yeah, I'll be there.'

Chapter 6

Carmichael managed to find footage of Larry Spicer with what appeared to be a woman of Asian appearance, and over the next few days all security staff, and staff from the gaming areas, were shown the recording as well as the recording of the woman in the red dress who took down Ashgrove.

Carmichael's time was taken up with all the ongoing familiar problems. There were drunks wanting to fight security staff or falling down stairs and considering suing the casino, a drunken woman claiming a security man had molested her, a couple of cars stolen from the garage, a car smashing into another in the garage and the owner wanting to sue the casino for poor lighting, a couple claiming their clothes had been stolen by the room cleaners, and a man claiming a bar attendant had short-changed him.

In all instances, Carmichael had managed to settle the problems with a few soft words or offer to repay, and in one particularly unfortunate incident when a man had drawn a knife after being asked to leave following an argument with a croupier he had accused of underpaying him, a fast couple of punches had soon overcome the matter.

His mind was still on the woman who liked to tie her victims up however, and every good looking young woman he saw made him take another look.

A week later, his expectation came true, but this time with a difference. At just before midnight, he was summoned to the general manager's office. He entered the office to find Musgrove sitting at his desk, with another man on a chair in front of him.

'Steve, this is Adam Havers, apparently he has been—'

'There's no fuckin' apparently, pal, I've been robbed, that's what's happened.'

'Mr Havers, I'm Steve Carmichael, head of security. Can you tell me exactly what's happened, please?'

'Not much fuckin' security, pal.'

'What happened, Mr Havers?' asked Carmichael.

'The bitch tasered me and stole my money, that's what happened,' shouted Havers as he stood up from his chair and jammed a finger into Carmichael's chest.

Carmichael stood still and fixed Havers with a steady stare. 'Like I said, Mr Havers, what exactly happened?'

Havers stepped back. He was shorter than Carmichael, and although angry, he realised that Carmichael was not a man to be taking on. His shoulders dropped and he slumped back down into the chair. 'Oh shit!'

No one spoke as Havers sat forlornly shaking his head.

'Mr Havers,' said Carmichael.

'I ... I thought I was onto a good thing ... jeez.'

'What happened when you took her to your room, Mr Havers?'

'We had a couple of drinks from the room fridge, and then she made a suggestion and I just couldn't wait ... you know?'

'Yes I think so ... and then?'

'Well, she undressed down to her undies and bra ... and then she tasered me.'

'What made her do that, Mr Havers?'

'Got out some pink ribbons ... said she was going to tie me up ... said I deserved something special.'

'So, she tied you up?'

'No, I didn't let her. I grabbed her and pushed her onto the bed.' He paused.

'And?'

'She rolled away off the bed, took what I thought was a mobile phone out of her bag, and zapped me. I was buggered, fell down twitching, knew what had happened but couldn't do anything about it. Then I must have passed out. When I came round she was gone and so was my cash.'

'Can you describe the woman?' asked Carmichael.

'Around forty, brown curly hair ... ah ... dark slacks, bluish blouse.'

'And you'll be happy to describe what's happened in court when we find the woman?'

'Court! No thanks. I don't want to go to court.'

'But we can't get your money back for you if we don't prosecute her, Mr Havers.'

'You find her, you do her over, then send me my money, okay!'

Musgrove interrupted. 'How about we refund you the cost of your stay with us, plus another thousand and when we catch the woman, we keep your name out of it?'

'But the bitch took more than that!' said Havers angrily.

'Then you will need to appear in court,' said Musgrove. 'Your decision.'

Havers gave a loud sigh and shook his head in resignation. 'Alright, you pay for my stay plus a thousand.'

Musgrove pulled open a desk drawer and extracted a cheque book. 'I'll make it out for cash ... that okay?'

'Yeah ... thanks.'

Musgrove made out the cheque, stood up and handed it across to Havers. 'I understand you're booked out today, so may I wish you a safe journey home.'

Havers accepted the cheque, then turned and left the office without another word.

'Another satisfied customer,' said Carmichael.

'We have to get this woman before she really hurts somebody, Steve.'

'Yeah, I'll go over the security footage again, but let's hope that her having to use the taser will make her think again about continuing.'

'We live in hope; at least so far we've managed to keep it all under wraps ... and don't forget Sunday.'

'I won't,' said Carmichael.

The BBQ turned out to be just what the doctor ordered for Carmichael and Musgrove. For a few brief hours, they were able to take their minds off work and its associated problems. And to top it off, Musgrove's cousin Jessica just happened to be there.

With the meat cooked, Musgrove, his wife Kylie, son Benjamin, daughter Coral, Carmichael and the cousin Jessica sat around the outside garden table to eat, somehow Carmichael ended up sitting beside Jessica.

The conversation flowed easily, and it seemed all too soon when Carmichael looked at his watch and realised it was 4 o'clock. He stood up from the table. 'Sorry, folks, but I really do have to go. Thanks for everything, Kylie it was a great BBQ.'

'Do you really have to leave, Steve?' asked Kylie.

'I really do I'm afraid, my son is playing football this arvo and I said I'd be there for the second half.'

'I understand,' said Kylie.

Carmichael leant forward and kissed her on the cheek. 'Thanks again, Kylie, bye kids, see you tomorrow, Arthur.' He offered his hand to Jessica. 'And it was very nice meeting you, Jessica.'

'Same here,' said Jessica with a smile. 'Maybe we'll meet again.'

'Yeah ... I'd like that,' said Carmichael, returning her smile.

They all remained quiet for a moment as Carmichael and Jessica continued holding hands and smiling.

Carmichael gave a cough and stepped back. 'Right then, I'd better be off.' He walked around the side of the house to his car parked out the front, got in and gave a wave to the assembled family as he drove away.

Jessica grabbed hold of Musgrove's arm. 'He didn't know I was going to be here, did he, Arthur?'

'Well … ah … no!'

'Are you trying to fix us up?'

'Oh, Jessica … would I do that?'

'You're a stirrer Arthur Musgrove.'

'Was he really that bad, Jess?'

'Umm … we'll see.'

Laughing together, they all returned to the back garden.

Chapter 7

I t was the middle of the following week when more trouble came to the casino. A man was assaulted in the under building car parking area and robbed. Due to injuries sustained, he was taken by ambulance to hospital. He had been discovered by another patron on leaving the casino at 10 pm, lying on the ground and bleeding from a head wound.

Security had been informed and Carmichael contacted the police. Apparently, the man had been about to get into his car when he had been hit by a taser, fallen writhing to the ground, hit his head on the car door and on the concrete floor of the carpark. The police had talked to security staff who had patrolled the area during the evening, but nothing had surfaced to lead to the perpetrator.

Carmichael was in Musgrove's office describing the event to him. 'Hit with a taser, just like the last bloke we had in the unit.'

'Same woman do you reckon?'

'Sure makes you wonder, doesn't it?'

'Shit! ... Do we have any security footage?'

'I'm about to go over it now, if I can find anything I'll give it to the cops.'

Carmichael spent the rest of the night going over security footage. Red-eyed and weary, he came into Musgrove's office in the morning. 'Nothing, Arthur, can't find a bloody thing around the area the bloke was attacked.'

Musgrove groaned. 'Nothing?'

Carmichael shook his head. 'We'll have to have security camera coverage increased.'

'Agreed … Organise it today, Steve.'

'Will do!' said Carmichael. He left Musgrove's office and took out his mobile.

Within the hour men were installing additional cameras in all the casino parking areas. Carmichael did his best to ensure that coverage was complete by watching the screens in the main security room.

'How's it going?' asked Musgrove who had just walked in the room late in the afternoon.

Carmichael looked away from the screens and rubbed his eyes. 'Looks okay, but time will tell, Arthur.'

'You look buggered, Steve, go home.'

'Think I'd better, I could do with a sleep that's for sure.'

'Yeah, you're certainly not much good looking like you do now.'

Carmichael rubbed his eyes again. 'Right, see you tomorrow.' He stretched and left the office.

He was about to walk out of the front of the casino when he felt a tap on the shoulder. He turned and smiled at Arthur Musgrove's cousin. 'Hi, Jessica, how are you?'

Jessica returned his smile. 'I'm fine, thanks. I was just calling in to see Arthur … but you look worn out, Steve, what's up?'

'I was awake all last night going over the security footage, and spent all day overseeing the installation of more cameras.'

'No wonder you look tired, the sooner you get home and get some rest the better. Arthur told me about what's been happening, did you manage to come up with anything new on the security tapes?'

Carmichael shook his head. 'Nothing I'm afraid, but at least now we are better covered should anyone try the same.'

With Jessica standing in front of him, Carmichael suddenly felt his tiredness disappearing. 'Look … I reckon it would better if I stayed up a bit longer, then I might get to sleep the night through … So, how about joining me for a coffee?'

'You sure, Steve?' asked Jessica with concern.

'Definitely!' said Carmichael.

'Okay then!' said Jessica with a smile.

Carmichael placed a hand gently on Jessica's arm. 'Good ... coffee shop's this way.'

Carmichael and Jessica sat together in the coffee shop. Conversation seemed to come easy. Carmichael hadn't felt so at ease with a woman in a long time. He enjoyed the way Jessica had eyes only for him, and was not distracted by the goings on around them. Time passed quickly.

Jessica glanced at her wrist watch. 'Oh my goodness, look at the time, we've been here for nearly two hours ... You should be getting home and having a good night's sleep.'

Carmichael was amazed. 'Two hours! ... Has it really been that long?'

Jessica laughed. 'Yes, it has.'

'Doesn't time fly when you're enjoying yourself?' said Carmichael jokingly.

Jessica nodded and gave a brief smile. 'Yes, it does.'

Carmichael looked into the brown eyes smiling at him. 'I'd very much like to see you again, Jessica.'

Jessica reached out her hand and rested it on Carmichael's hand. 'Yes please, Steve.'

For a moment neither spoke.

Carmichael gave a self-conscious cough. 'Can I have your number?'

Jessica took out a pen from her small handbag and wrote on one of the coasters on the table. 'Anytime!' she said as she handed the coaster to Carmichael.

Carmichael accepted the coaster and stood up while placing it in his jacket pocket. 'I think it is time for me to be heading home now.'

Jessica pushed her chair back and stood. 'Right!'

'Yeah … well … see you then.' He reached out as if to shake her hand, then withdrew it.

Jessica could sense his dilemma. She came close.

Carmichael leant down and placed a gentle kiss on her cheek then stood back. 'I'll call.'

'Make sure you do,' said Jessica as Carmichael walked away.

On arrival at the small unit he now called home, Carmichael sat still for a moment. His mind in turmoil. Was he falling in love? Could this beautiful young, intelligent woman, with big brown eyes and shiny, black page-boy hair possibly be interested in him?

Chapter 8

The following morning, a refreshed Carmichael arrived at the casino and headed direct to the security room. 'Anything happen overnight, Ed, any more taser attacks?' he asked the man sitting in front of the screens.

'Nothing, Steve. All quiet,' Ed replied with a shake of his head.

'Thank goodness for that; with any luck it'll stay that way.'

'Wouldn't be much fun being hit by a taser,' said Ed.

'That's for sure. Trouble is, the bloody things are too easy to come by, just gotta get onto the internet and there's a stack of them available.'

'Should be outlawed except for police use,' said Ed.

'That would make sense, but these days you can get hold of anything and everything via the net.'

Carmichael was about to leave when his mobile rang. 'Hi, Steve Carmichael here,' he said.

'Hi, Steve, Sergeant Simon Rickard here, I saw you over the taser business you had.'

'Oh yeah, I remember you, Simon.'

'Thought you might like to know there's been another robbery with a taser used.'

'Where this time?

'Small shopping centre—a bloke had withdrawn a bit of cash from an ATM and was hit as he was about to get into his car.'

'Same perp as ours you reckon?'

'Well, it was a taser used, unfortunately, no CCTV available.'

'And no witnesses?'

'Right.'

'Whoever it is has got away with it twice now, and I've got a feeling will keep on till you catch her.'

'What makes you say *her*, Steve?'

'We had a woman use one on one of our customers a short time back.'

'If you mean on the man in your carpark, I didn't think you had any security footage, so why say her?'

Carmichael silently cursed himself for his slip. The woman he was referring to was the one that robbed the customers in the rooms, and those events had been kept "indoors" and not referred to the police. Now he had no option but to explain what had occurred.

'We had an incident a short time back with a guest,' he said, and gave Sergeant Rickard the full story.

'Might have been helpful if we'd known all that.'

'I'm sorry, Simon,' Carmichael said apologetically. 'We were hoping to keep it all under wraps; didn't want our customers to feel there was a possibility of any of them getting similar treatment.'

'So, you reckon the same woman may have robbed in the carpark?'

'Just seems to fit.'

'Right ... I'll have our blokes concentrate more on that possibility.'

'Sorry again for not informing you, Simon. I'll definitely keep you posted if we have further troubles.'

'Do that ... and I'll keep you in the picture with anything we turn up.'

'Thanks, Simon.'

'Okay, bye for now.'

Carmichael took a deep breath and blew out his cheeks after Sergeant Rickard rang off. Now the police knew of the three in-house robberies, there was the distinct possibility of it all becoming common knowledge after Sergeant Rickard told his superiors and workmates. After all, he had once been a cop, and he was very aware of how interesting events found their way into the newspapers via a casual remark to a reporter, or even more likely given to a reporter for a bit of cash imbursement.

He made his way to the general manager Arthur Musgrove's office. 'Got a slight problem,' he said.

'Oh shit!' was Musgrove's initial response as he banged his fist down onto his desk.

'Had no option but to tell him,' said Carmichael.

'Pity though ... Would have been good if we could have kept it in house, although we can't guarantee one of our staff wouldn't seize an opportunity to make a few extra dollars, one way or another I suppose it's going to get out.'

'Do you think we should go public before it gets out some other way?'

Musgrove sat back in his chair and rubbed his eyes. 'Might be some sense in that, Steve. I'll get in touch with the CEO and get his opinion.'

'Don't want to appear pushy, but I know how stories can escape from police stations, so might be a good idea to do it soon as. Better for the chiefs to hear it from you than read about it in the daily rag.'

'Very true!' Musgrove picked up his phone and dialled. It was immediately answered. 'Sir, I have something important come up and need your urgent advice.' He listened to the brief reply before saying, 'Yes, sir.'

Musgrove replaced his phone and pushed his chair back. 'He'll see me right away,' he said as he stood, adjusted his tie and reached out for his suit jacket that hung over the back of his chair.

'Better tell Sergeant Rickard that it could be made public. I don't reckon he'd be too happy to learn about it second hand.'

'Yeah, I'll leave that to you, Steve.'

'Good luck,' said Carmichael as Musgrove hurriedly left his office.

Carmichael immediately placed a call to Sergeant Rickard who, although not over impressed at having events made public, fully understood how it was better for the casino to come forward and explain the robberies, than for the newspapers to publish the story attributed to having been advised by a so-called *reliable source.*

Chapter 9

The full story appeared in the next day's leading newspaper together with a photograph of the casino, and of the CEO and his expressed opinion that the person responsible would soon be apprehended thanks to the diligence of the local police.

It was midmorning when Carmichael received a call from Sergeant Rickard. 'Another taser attack outside the same small shopping centre as the last one, Steve.'

'Same perp, Simon?'

'No doubt about it.'

'I'm guessing it won't happen again at the same place.'

'Probably not ... For the next few evenings we're going to have guys positioned at several other likely places just in case we can get lucky.'

'How about if a few of my security guys cover places you aren't at?'

'Great idea, Steve, I'll call you back later and make arrangements.'

Carmichael advised Musgrove of his discussion with Sergeant Rickard.

'Sounds a good idea, Steve, the sooner we can get this business cleaned up the better.'

'The CEO did a good job with the newspaper, Arthur, and it would be even better if our guys can catch the person,' said Camichael with grin.

'Would it ever,' agreed Musgrove. 'How many guys can we spare for a couple of evenings?'

'Maybe we don't need to be short staffed, Arthur. How about

we offer a few a bit of overtime plus a bonus if they catch anyone?'

'Great idea ... set it up, I'll okay whatever you come up with.'

'I'll give Sergeant Rickard a call soon as I know how many of our men will be into it.'

It only took an hour for Carmichael to round up men who were willing to do the job. He rang Sergeant Rickard to advise him and was given the addresses he wanted covered.

'Tell your men to call me immediately if they catch anyone please, Steve, and I'll have our officers come and make the arrest.'

'Will do, Simon, let's hope we can get this sorted soon as.'

For the next three nights, nothing happened, and Carmichael was starting to think that the recent newspaper article had frightened the attacker off.

It was just past midnight on the fourth night that he received the call he'd been hoping for.

'I've got her!' said an excited Ed from his position in the carpark of the local RSL.

'Great, Ed, have you called Sergeant Rickard?'

'Yes, and I've also called an ambulance. She'd tasered a bloke before I could get to her.'

'How is he, Ed?'

'I reckon he'll be fine; he's with a couple of the RSL guys now.'

'Does she look like our woman?'

'Could be ... she seems similar build and height.'

'Okay, I'm on my way, see you shortly.'

Carmichael arrived at the RSL and pulled up beside Ed's car. He noticed a woman in the back seat. 'Well done, Ed, has she had much to say?'

'Only "fuck off you arsehole" when I grabbed her,' said Ed with a grin.

A police car pulled up alongside. Rickard and another officer came to them.

'Good work, guys,' said Rickard. 'We'll take over now, thanks.'

He turned to the other officer. 'Put her in our car, Blair.'

'The guy she tasered is in the RSL, Simon,' said Carmichael.

'I'll go have a chat to him, see if he'll give us a statement,' said Rickard.

He turned to Ed. 'And if you would come into our office and make a report in the morning that would be appreciated.'

'No worries,' Ed replied.

'You'll keep us informed on what you get from her, won't you, Simon?' asked Carmichael.

'Sure will, and thanks again,' said Rickard as he walked towards the RSL.

Carmichael slapped Ed on the back. 'Bit extra coming your way.'

'I certainly won't say no to that,' said Ed with a broad smile.'

'After you've given your report to the police in the morning take the rest of the day off,' said Carmichael.

'Thanks, Steve, meantime I'll head home to bed and tell the missus.'

'Yeah, bed sounds great … see you, Ed.'

Sergeant Rickard called Carmichael shortly after his arrival at the casino in the morning.

'The young woman has been charged with assault with an offensive weapon causing bodily harm outside the RSL, and has put her hand up to that, but she is refusing to admit to anything else.'

'Do you reckon she did the attacks here, Simon?'

'It's a pretty safe bet she did the taser attack in your carpark.'

'How about the guys that were took down in our units?'

'Went through that but got nothing. Trouble is, we have no one willing to testify as far as I understand it.'

'Yeah, that's right, they all want to keep it secret, don't want to be made fools of for allowing themselves to be taken that way, and don't want their wives to know about it.'

Rickard laughed. 'Can understand that, Steve.'

'What'll she get?'

'Definitely a term inside, but for how long I can't say, depends on the judge.'

'I'll be in touch if we get any further troubles, Simon, but hopefully we won't. Look me up if you ever come into the casino and I'll buy you a drink.'

'Will do, Steve, bye for now,' said Rickard.

Carmichael called in on Arthur Musgrove's office and brought him up to date with the events of the previous night, and of Sergeant Rickard's thoughts on the matter.

'With any luck this'll be the end of it, Steve. Oh, and one other thing, Jessica's coming in for a bit of lunch around one, care to join us?'

'Thanks, Arthur, yes I would,' replied Carmichael, trying to stop a wide smile from appearing.

Musgrove waved a finger at him. ''Course, if there's anything more important you have to be doing!'

'Oh, I reckon I can spare an hour or so, wouldn't want to appear rude, Arthur.'

Musgrove laughed. 'Yeah right, you ain't fooling me, pal!'

Carmichael looked seriously at Musgrove. 'Sorry … not sure what you're on about,' he said as he turned and walked out.

Chapter 10

Over the next few weeks the relationship between Carmichael and Jessica became stronger with every meeting. Carmichael found himself thinking of her at odd times during his time at work and in particular when he was alone. He decided it was time for her to meet his kids and organised the meeting at McDonalds on a Saturday lunchtime.

At first, Keith and Sally were standoffish towards Jessica, but Jessica's friendly nature and interest in their schooling and after-school activities soon won them over.

'I have a football match on tomorrow morning,' said Keith to Jessica. 'Dad will be coming, would you like to come and see me play as well?'

'Yeah, that would be great,' said Jessica with enthusiasm.

'And I'm playing netball in the afternoon,' said Sally, 'if you can make it.'

'Sure ... sure,' said Jessica, 'I would love to.'

'Right, then that's tomorrow sorted,' said Carmichael. 'But now I reckon it's time to take you guys home.'

After dropping the children off at Barbara's home, Carmichael drove his car a short distance then pulled up.

'Why are you stopping?' asked Jessica.

Carmichael leant towards her and kissed her on the cheek. 'That's why! You were wonderful with the kids, Jess.'

'Oh, they are great, I really enjoyed meeting them.' She leant towards him. 'But I have to tell you that was a pretty pathetic kiss.'

Carmichael reached out and pulled her to him. 'I think I'm

falling in love with you, Jess.' He kissed her, slow and gentle.

Jessica sat back and placed a hand on his face. 'I think you'd better take me back to your place, Steve.' She sniffed. 'Oh damn, I hope I'm not getting a cold.' She reached into her handbag, took out a handkerchief, and blew her nose.

The drive back to his unit seemed to Carmichael to take an eternity. Every set of traffic lights somehow managed to be against him. At long last they reached his building. He parked the car in the building basement carpark. Holding hands, they walked up the stairs to his first floor unit. With fumbling hands, Carmichael unlocked the door and stood aside to allow Jessica to enter. On closing the door behind him, Jessica put her arms around him. Carmichael felt as if his mind was losing control. Somehow, he guided her to the bedroom.

Later, Carmichael was lying breathless, holding Jessica curled up against him. His mind went over what had just happened between them. Neither spoke for some time.

Jessica broke the silence. 'That was wonderful,' she whispered. 'And I love you too, Steve.'

Carmichael turned to face her. 'I never thought I would ever feel this way again, Jess ... Thank you so much for coming into my life.'

'Oh, believe me, it's my pleasure.' Jessica moved over him and gave him a short kiss. She ran her fingers through his hair. 'I think you deserve something special,' she said while giving him a sexy grin.

She looked away and reached out towards her handbag which she had placed on the bedside table.

Carmichael returned the grin. Suddenly, a memory came to him. He had heard the phrase '*I think you deserve something really special*' before. Images flashed through his brain of two men tied to the bed by ribbons.

No ... this couldn't be ... His grin froze as he watched Jessica reach into her handbag.

Jessica looked back at Carmichael as she withdrew her hand. Carmichael saw that she was holding her handkerchief and he gave a deep sigh of relief. *What the hell have I been thinking?*

Jessica gave her nose a quick blow. 'Sorry about that.' She threw the handkerchief back at the handbag and leant back against Carmichael. 'Now, where were we?' she asked as she moved slowly against him.

Completely lost in each other, neither noticed the handbag slip off the bedside table, fall to the floor and the small piece of something pink that poked out.

Jackson

Book 3: Retired Not Out

Chapter 1

After 30 years in the police force, Detective Inspector Portland Jackson was enjoying the goodbye party of soft drinks, crisps and speeches provided by his colleagues. A number of gifts were handed to him, including a very nice gold watch which had apparently been purchased by his immediate superiors following a whip-round. In fact, it was something his sergeant had discovered in the lost luggage drawer that had been lying there unclaimed for the last ten years.

The truth was they were all more than glad to be seeing the back of him. His peers could not understand how a man with such obvious unsuitability for the job managed to make Detective Inspector. Jackson was a bumbler, who, despite the considerable high opinion of himself, had never solved, or been involved in any major investigation during his entire career. The reason he had attained the exalted position of Detective Inspector was because, during his time in the Force, the officer in charge of whichever station he had been at realised that the best way to get rid of him was to recommend a promotion.

To the cheers of his colleagues, and glasses raised in wishing him well in his retirement, Detective Inspector Portland Jackson left the station. Once he had departed and driven off, bottles of scotch and upmarket beer began to appear, along with plates of hot pies, sausage rolls and cooked prawns.

'Christ almighty!' exclaimed Sergeant Palmer. 'I thought he was never going to leave.' He wrenched the twist top off a bottle of XXXX. 'Here's to actually getting things done. Get stuck in, boys!'

The celebratory party continued well into the night while ex-Detective Portland Jackson spent a quiet evening at home with his wife discussing their future.

Portland Jackson was not a particularly big man, standing at one hundred and seventy-five centimetres and weighing in at sixty-seven kilos. In order to enhance his appearance, he had grown a moustache to copy that of his television hero Hercule Poirot. Unfortunately, all it did was make his colleagues laugh behind his back.

His name was another setback. His father had decided on the Christian name of Portland. At the time of the child's birth, father was employed by a local building company, and part of his job entailed ordering building materials. A product he ordered a great deal of was Portland cement, and the name Portland, father decided, would be more than fitting for his newborn.

However, when introducing himself as Detective Inspector Portland Jackson people at first assumed his surname was Portland, and Jackson his Christian name, and that he was just trying to be friendly by mentioning his Christian name second. At high school he received a good deal of ribbing regarding his name, often being asked if he would start to set if he was out in the rain.

He had known Nell since secondary school. She was a quiet young girl with few friends, as had Portland, and the two of them were accordingly drawn to each other. The friendship developed after leaving school and they were married in their early twenties. Nell gave up her job at the local chemist shortly before the birth of their first child, a boy they called Walter. The second child, a girl they named Melissa followed two years later. Following in his father's footsteps, Portland had until then been employed by the same building company but took and managed to pass the entry exam for the police force.

During the later years, it been decided between Portland and his wife Nell, that following his retirement they would like to spend as much time as possible before old age, and possible infirmity overtook them, travelling around the country. In fact, they had already purchased a six metre Winnebago motor home that stood loaded up and awaiting departure in their carport.

It was only a week later that they were waved goodbye by family and friends as they set of on their big trip around Australia.

Leaving the city, its hustle and bustle, bright lights and traffic snarls, behind them they headed up the coast. It was a very relaxed couple who pulled in at a small caravan park on the sea front. The park manager, introduced himself as Desmond, booked them in, and after the usual friendly banter, discovered the fact that Jackson had just retired from the police force.

'And this is your first stop then?' asked Desmond.

'Indeed it is,' replied Portland.

'And this looks a most wonderful spot here on the beach front,' added Nell.

'Well thank you,' said the manager. 'How long would you like to stay?'

Nell looked at Portland. 'We're not in any particular hurry, are we, love, and this does look very nice. How about we stay for a week before moving on?'

'Good idea,' agreed Portland.

'In that case, I'll put you on site 29 that is absolute beachfront,' said the manager and handed them a park map, and a couple of pamphlets showing local places of interest.

Soon, they were set up on their site, sitting quietly in the shade of a tree beside the motorhome and enjoying a cup of tea. Now out of police uniform, Portland had on shorts and T-shirt. Nell, having become somewhat cuddly, was wearing a flowing caftan.

'What a lovely place, and so peaceful,' said Nell relaxing back into her chair. 'I could get to like this.'

A frail, elderly, grey-haired lady came walking by and introduced herself. 'Good afternoon to you both, my name is Lynn, Lynn Trout,

I see you've got yourselves nicely settled in already.'

'Indeed we have,' replied Nell. 'I'm Nell and this is my husband Portland, I guess you are staying here as well.'

'Been here for a year: nice place and nice people,' said Lynn happily. 'I'm in a small caravan about five sites along. Perhaps we can have a drink together one evening.'

'That would be wonderful,' replied Nell.

'Lovely,' said Lynn. 'I'd better be off. Have to get tea ready for my son, bye for now.'

'Wasn't that nice,' said Nell as Lynn walked away. 'I think we'll have a very pleasant week.'

The next day, Portland and Nell spent the time walking along the beachfront and talking to others in the park. At late afternoon, they were again sitting under their tree enjoying an afternoon glass of red wine, when Lynn Trout came towards them at what appeared some considerable haste.

'Oh dear, oh dear,' she exclaimed breathlessly. 'I really need to talk to you, Portland.'

'Well, certainly,' replied Portland. He stood up and gestured to his chair. 'You look like you need to sit down, Lynn, please have my chair.'

'Thank you, thank you. Something terrible has happened.'

'Please explain,' said Nell.

'My pet has been poisoned,' stated Lynn.

'That is awful!' said Portland with concern.

'Yes, it really is,' continued Lynn. 'And, seeing as how I've just found out you are a detective, I was hoping you could help me find out who did it.'

Nell was quick to speak. 'I'm afraid Portland has retired and left all police work behind him, Lynn.' She looked at Portland with a slight glare. 'Isn't that so, dear?'

Portland's eyes lit up. He never noticed Nell's shake of her head.

He was instantly intrigued; an allegation of poisoning just could not be ignored.

Lynn Trout's pet was a canary. Nell tried her best to prevent Portland from becoming involved, but a possible crime of poisoning, even if only a canary, was something he could not let pass.

The occupants of the caravans on either side of Lynn soon became prime suspects in the dastardly act on such a poor defenceless bird, when Portland learnt of their hate of the bird that apparently sang from morning till night. Lynn's son also was put on the possible list after Portland heard him complain of the amount of money spent on canary food.

Having no luck in pinning the crime on any particular individual after subjecting the suspects to some severe questioning, Portland finally convinced Lynn to take the deceased bird to a local veterinarian for an autopsy.

The finding—death by misadventure brought about by a rather large pine nut that the canary had managed to swallow but unfortunately had been too large to pass out its anal passage thereby causing bloat. That had accounted for its blown-up appearance when discovered on the floor of the cage with its feet in the air, and the subsequent assumption of poisoning.

Needless to say, those whom Portland had virtually accused of committing the dastardly deed were far from amused, and the atmosphere in the caravan park turned more than a little dark towards Portland. Nell was feeling particularly uncomfortable and convinced Portland it was time to leave.

The Jacksons drove out of the caravan park accompanied by jeers from Mrs Trout's neighbours and her son, while Lynn timidly waved goodbye.

As the motorhome departed Nell gently placed a hand on Portland's arm.

'When will you ever learn, dear?'

Chapter 2

After a couple of weeks travel further north enjoying the coastal scenery, whenever they pulled into a caravan park Nell would always say to Portland, 'Now remember you are retired, dear.'

Since the episode with the canary, fortunately no great incident had occurred to involve investigation by Portland, much to Nell's relief.

The present park they were staying at was situated on a river estuary with easy access to the bay. The Jacksons had been readily accepted by the other residents, and Portland had even been taken fishing with a couple of keen anglers.

This afternoon they were attending a get-together for afternoon tea and drinks during happy hour when the park manager interrupted the session to exclaim to Portland that another resident, Mrs Blayney, had just reported the sighting of a dead body in the shrubbery behind the toilet block.

Unable to contain himself, and despite the fervent entreaties of Nell to leave it to the local constabulary, Portland rushed off with the manager and Mrs Blayney to investigate.

On arrival at the toilet block, the mysterious body had disappeared. Mrs Blayney insisted that, despite her advanced years she was not completely gaga yet, and that there had indeed been a body.

The local police were contacted, but as they could not unearth a body they quickly suspended their investigation and left the caravan park.

Portland Jackson, however, was not so easily convinced that

the old lady was so sadly mistaken and determined to continue seeking the truth.

As he began his questioning of the park staff and residents, he found that a visitor to one of the residents was seen to arrive on that fateful day but had not been seen since. This was possibly the break that Portland had been hoping for.

He further discovered that the neighbour of the person who received a visitor that day, had his bicycle disappear, and that a fisherman found his dinghy washed up further along the beach than where he had left it, with its outboard motor missing.

The obvious scenario came easily to Portland. The body had been slung over the bicycle and taken down to the water's edge. The bicycle and body then put into the dinghy, taken out to deep water and dumped overboard.

Now that Portland had determined what had happened, all he had to do was prove it, and what better way to flush the perpetrator out into the open, than to hold a meeting of all the park residents in the community hall where his interrogation skills would surely uncover the truth.

The community hall was full of park residents when Portland called the meeting to order.

Also in attendance was the local Police Inspector that Portland had invited along to observe, and arrest the villain when Portland revealed him.

Portland grilled many of the residents, accusing them of being the perpetrators. That produced anger and animosity between those who had been neighbours and friends for some considerable time.

Fortunately, it didn't take too long for the facts to become known.

The bicycle owner revealed that he had lent it to another park resident who had unfortunately fallen off and damaged it to such an extent that it was now in at a repair shop.

The dinghy had apparently been left on the beach below the

high tide mark and subsequently drifted away when the tide came in. A well-meaning person had removed the outboard motor just on nightfall as a precaution against being stolen and was keeping it safe until the owner returned from a couple of days away.

The body Mrs Blayney had seen was in fact an inflatable sex aid that the owner had been averse to admitting to for fear of reprisals from his wife who apparently "failed to understand his needs". While removing the offending "lady" from his car, he had dropped "her" on seeing Mrs Blayney approach and hid "her" in the bushes. He then retrieved "her" after she ran off.

The meeting erupted with shouts and jeers, and the invited Police Inspector left, shaking his head in dismay.

A very red-faced Portland was laughed out of the hall, while poor Nell shrank down into her chair trying to hide.

The following morning the caravan park quickly emptied as residents departed. Once friendly neighbours' amiable rapport forever upset by Portland's investigation and questioning technique.

As Portland and Nell departed the now practically empty caravan park in their motorhome, the park manager's shouts of derision accompanied them.

Back on the open road once more, Nell gently placed a hand on Portland's arm.

'When will you ever learn, dear?'

Turner

BOOK 4: BAD TO WORSE

Chapter 1

He put down the glass of beer onto the bar and checked the time on his watch ... two minutes to nine. He glanced up at the clock on the wall behind the bar and confirmed the time. He picked the glass back up and swallowed the small amount in the bottom, eased himself off the bar stool, adjusted his suit jacket and tie, and gave a brief wave to the bartender.

'Be back in a couple ... save my spot.'

He exited the hotel's side entrance and walked around the back to the carpark that was poorly lit by a single dull light pole. A Harley Davidson motorcycle was parked in the shadow of a large tree. He approached the bike and the leather-clad man standing beside it. Neither spoke.

The leather-clad man reached inside his jacket and took out an envelope. The back of his hands were covered in tattoos, as was his neck and most of his face. He handed over the envelope, before getting back onto the bike, starting it up, and driving away.

He weighed the envelope in his left hand then opened it. He thumbed the side of the thick wad of dollar bills with a smile, closed the envelope, placed it in his inside jacket pocket, and returned to the hotel.

'I'll have a scotch thanks, Pete,' he said to the bartender as he resumed his position on the bar stool.

Pete nodded. 'Ice?'

'Yes thanks, Pete, make it a double, and have one yourself.'

Pete placed the two glasses of scotch on the bar. 'Here's to you, Greg!' he said as he took an enjoyable swallow.

Detective Greg Turner of the Organised Crime Squad raised his glass. 'And to you, mate!'

'Managing to put a few crooks away?' asked Pete.

'Oh you know … doin' me best, Pete!'

Pete drained his glass and licked his lips. 'Reckon you oughta look into why Sky Chariot didn't even get a place in the two-thirty last Saturday. Bloody thing was clear favourite and finished fourth to Anderson's other horse which started at twenty to one. Can't tell me there wasn't a fix in that.'

Turner inclined his head. 'Apparently, Sky Chariot came up a bit sore, so nothing wrong with the effort it put in, and Anderson had mentioned before the race that his other horse, Night Shift, had a rough chance of a place.'

'Sore my arse!' said Pete. 'Not the first time he's had two in the same race and the no-hoper's got up.'

Turner shook his head, finished his drink and slid off his stool. 'Sorry, mate, can't find anything on him.' He continued shaking his head as he left the bar and made his way to his Toyota Camry parked around the back. A broad grin lit up his face as he eased behind the steering wheel. 'Twenty to one … you beauty!'

He took out his mobile phone and entered a number. It was answered quickly. 'All good, Monty!' he said. He waited a moment before adding, 'No worries!' He placed the mobile on the passenger seat beside him, started the car and headed out of the carpark singing to himself.

Turner's success with the horses wasn't his only bit of profit for the day. The envelope from the bikie was payment for information supplied to the gang's boss regarding a probable raid on a house suspected of being a drug laboratory. The raid had taken place two days previously with not a trace of drugs being found.

The information regarding the address had come from what had been considered a reliable source. The resultant "clean house" was not only a surprise, but as the officer in charge of the raid had stated it was 'a complete and utter cock-up'.

Chapter 2

Turner had entered the police force just after his twentieth birthday. His education had been through the public school system. Although not showing great promise as a student, he had performed reasonably well at mathematics and English ... in other words he could add up and write a sentence or two.

He was also very fit from playing rugby league at school, and joined the town league club when he left. One of the coaches at the town club was the local copper, and he suggested to Turner that he might find a career in the police service. At the time Turner was unemployed, so the idea of a full-time job with a regular pay packet seemed a good idea.

Now aged thirty-two, Turner had been in the police force for twelve years, and had been with the Organised Crime Squad for eighteen months. In order to join the squad, applicants must have a minimum of four years operational service as a general duties police officer, and complete a field investigation course at the Police Academy where they then receive an advanced diploma of public safety qualification. Turner had passed with flying colours and was now in the specialist unit involved in investigating the racing industry, money laundering, trafficking illicit substances and services from east Asia, and high-level organised crime. And with this position came the opportunity to obtain even greater financial benefit.

He had come from a poor family. His father drove a waste truck for the council, and his mother managed to earn a few extra welcome dollars as a cleaner at the local pub. Every extra cent his mother managed to bring in was necessary to feed herself and her son, as his father spent nearly all he earnt on booze, cigarettes and gambling.

His father died from lung cancer and sclerosis of the liver when Greg was seventeen. Greg had left school immediately and taken any job he could find to help his mother. She had been overjoyed when he had told her of his intention to join the police force, and Greg had handed over nearly all of his pay packet to her until her untimely death by a heart attack when Greg was twenty-five.

Until that time, the Turner family had been living in a housing commission home. Now on his own, Turner moved out and rented a small flat.

It was at that stage that Turner's life took a turn. He had been paired with another copper called Brian Larkin, and it was Larkin who first introduced him to the opportunities that, being a police officer, at times were presented. Larkin took Turner to a coffee shop one morning and ordered coffee and cake for himself and Turner. Turner got up to pay when they had finished and Larkin stopped him from walking to the counter.

'On the house, Greg,' said Larkin as he guided him outside. 'Caught the owner half-pissed driving down a one-way street three months back.'

'So, why the free coffee?' said Turner.

'He begged to be let off ... promised me free coffee for life ... bloody good deal, don't you reckon?' Larkin slapped Turner on the shoulder. 'Gotta take advantage when you can, pal.'

Turner and Larkin stayed paired for another two years, and Turner became adept at accepting small sums for overlooking driving indiscretions and forgetting having seen a small bag of suspicious white powder, or drug paraphernalia.

The step into the big time came late one afternoon after he had dropped Larkin off at his home, and he was on his way back to the station. The vehicle two cars in front of him went through a red light. With his lights flashing, Turner came up behind the vehicle until it came to a halt. He approached the driver's door and signalled for him to wind down the window.

'Went through a red light back at the last crossing, sir, any reason for that?'

The driver shook his head and waved his open hands. 'I'm terribly sorry, officer ... you see I've just had a bit of a row with my wife.'

Turner smiled. 'Yes, of course you have ... and being a bit upset you just weren't quite concentrating, eh?'

'Exactly!' the driver replied.

'Now, how many times do you reckon I've heard that, sir? Now, you just sit here quietly while I write out a ticket.'

He started to walk back to his patrol car when the driver shouted, 'Officer, officer, can I speak to you a minute?'

Turner stopped. 'Yeah, what is it?'

'Would this help?'

Turner saw that the driver had four fifty-dollar notes spread out. He looked from the bills up at the driver. 'You're kidding, mate!'

The driver added another two fifties. 'How about that?'

'Have you any idea what you can get for trying to bribe a police officer?' Turner said in as serious a voice as he could muster.

Another two fifties appeared.

Turner swallowed and glanced up and down the road before reaching out. The fifties were placed in his hand, which Turner quickly folded and placed in his pocket. He nodded at the driver and tilted his head sideways. 'Get!'

He returned to his patrol car and got in as the other car sped away. Turner counted the bills ... four hundred dollars. This was a whole new dimension from free coffee and cake, and the odd fiver from a druggie. He decided to keep the incident to himself ... no need to mention anything to his partner, Larkin.

Two weeks later, Turner had just finished grocery shopping and was placing the bags in the back seat of his Holden Commodore, when a black Volvo pulled up beside him.

'Officer Turner?'

Turner turned abruptly towards the voice. He saw a dark-suited, middle-aged man looking at him from the open passenger side window,

'It is Officer Turner, isn't it?' the man repeated.

'Who wants to know?' asked Turner as he mentally tried to fathom out what was going on.

The man reached across and opened the passenger's door and offered his hand. 'My name is Pax Granger … I'm a solicitor.'

'Right … so?' said Turner, still at a loss to understand.

'I have been asked to approach you with an idea that could prove financially profitable for you.'

'Yeah … And how's that?'

Granger slid back across his seat and beckoned Turner. 'Please, Officer, get in and I'll explain.'

Turner waited a moment, then thought, *What the hell.* He slid into the seat but kept his door open. *Just in case.*

'Okay … so what's this all about, Granger?'

Granger smiled. 'You allowed a person who drove through a red light a couple of weeks ago to drive away without a ticket.'

'I have no idea what you are talking about,' said Turner as sternly as he could muster.

Granger continued to smile. 'And he gave you four hundred dollars.'

'Bullshit!'

Granger reached into the rear seat and picked up an iPad. He pushed a few buttons and turned the screen towards Turner. 'This was taken from a windscreen camera on a car that stopped some one hundred metres behind you.'

Turner's jaw dropped as he watched the incident replay on the iPad.

'Now, I have no wish to present this to your superiors, Greg ... is it all right if I call you, Greg?' asked Granger.

Turner silently nodded.

'All I ask is that you supply me with a little information occasionally. That information could benefit my employer, and of course greatly benefit you also.'

Turner managed to clear his throat. 'And your employer is?'

'All in good time ... all in good time, Greg. I presume you have a mobile, so, if you would be so good as to tell me the number, I'll be in touch when necessary.'

Turner recited his mobile number and Granger wrote it down on a small notepad. 'Thank you, Greg, you may go now.'

Turner got out of the Volvo. The door closed behind him and the car drove away. He stood there and watched the Volvo disappear before getting into his own car. He sat staring out the windscreen going over what had just taken place.

Chapter 3

It was some two weeks later at 10 o'clock at night as he was about to turn in that his mobile rang. It was Pax Granger.

'Good evening, Greg, I have a bit of information for you.'

'You have information for *me*?' said Turner somewhat surprised. After all, it had been his belief that any flow of information would be from him and not to him.

'There'll be a green Toyota Camry pulling up outside number 148 Leighton Street tomorrow afternoon between two-thirty and three-thirty … I suggest you take a look.'

The call ended abruptly. Turner stared for a while at the mobile before replacing it on his bedside table and getting into bed. He spent an almost sleepless night with the call from Granger going over and over in his head.

The next day in early afternoon, in the patrol car with Larkin, Turner suggested that they take a drive around the suburb that he knew Leighton Street was in.

'Haven't been that way for a while … what do you reckon?'

'Suits me!' replied Larkin.

Just before 3 o'clock, Turner saw a green Toyota Camry some distance ahead. He was about to say something when it turned right without indicating.

'Did you see that, Greg?' said Larkin. 'That car just turned without signalling.'

With that, he accelerated and sped after it.

Turner glanced at the street sign as they turned in. It was Leighton. The car came to number 148 and entered the driveway.

Larkin brought the police car to a stop across the driveway. 'Let's go see what this bloke has to say for himself.'

Turner and Larkin walked up the driveway towards the Camry as the driver got out. 'Any reason you failed to indicate when you turned right back there?' Larkin asked.

'Sorry, officer ... I'll be more careful in the future,' the young man replied.

Turner glanced at Larkin. 'I'll take a look inside.' He leant in the driver's side door and felt under the seat ... nothing; then into the rear and felt around ... nothing. He came to the driver and put out his hand. 'Keys!'

The driver took a step back and shrugged his shoulders. 'Nothing in there but the spare wheel, officer.'

Turner put out his hand again. 'Keys!' he said sternly.

'Come on, guys, I told you, just the spare wheel ... give me a break, eh?' He reached inside his back pocket and took out his wallet. He extracted a couple of fifties and held them out.

'What do you reckon?'

Larkin turned to Turner, smiled and raised his eyebrows.

Turner didn't return the look and Larkin's smile vanished as Turner grabbed the driver by the shirt front. 'I said keys, arsehole!'

The driver handed over the keys as the blood drained from his face and he started to shake. 'Look, I'm just delivering the car for a friend.'

Turner took the keys, went to the rear of the car and opened the boot. 'Brian, better come take a look.'

Larkin reached forward, held the driver by the arm and together they walked to the rear of the car.

The boot was half full of suspicious looking plastic bags.

'Jesus!' said Larkin.

'I'll call it in,' said Turner as he walked to the police car.

Later that afternoon Turner and Larkin were back at the station filling in their reports on the events of the day.

'To think that if I hadn't noticed him fail to use his indicator we would have missed it,' said Larkin.

'Something about him made me want to check him out,' said Turner.

'Bloody good call, Greg … I was close to taking his cash,' whispered Larkin as he leant in closer to Turner. 'The driver made a full statement when he was told of how long he would go down for … gave up quite an organisation that the drug squad had been chasing for some time.'

'Even so, he'll cop some time, and it won't be easy for him when the rest of the gang realise who ratted on them,' added Turner.

Pax Granger rang Turner at 10 o'clock that evening. 'I understand you made quite a collar today, Greg.'

'Yeah! Four kilos of cocaine and ten kilos of weed.'

'Glad to be able to help you, Greg, shouldn't do your chances of promotion any harm down the track.'

'This is just a wild guess, Granger, but it wouldn't have been the opposition by any chance, would it?'

Granger gave a slight laugh. 'I'll be in touch.' Then he rang off.

Chapter 4

Turner decided he should try to find out all he could about Pax Granger every bit of time he wasn't working he spent in that pursuit. After locating Granger's office, he parked his car a hundred metres or so away and watched all coming and goings. If Granger drove anywhere Turner followed at a reasonable distance.

The break came one Saturday afternoon when he followed Granger to a race meeting. Granger made a bet with one of the on-course bookies and then went to the rails to watch the race. A heavily built man came and stood beside him. They talked for a while before going their separate ways.

Turner decided to follow the other man, who left the racecourse, got in a dark blue Ford station wagon and drove off. Turner followed at a safe distance until it pulled into a light industrial area. Slowly, he made his way forward and saw that the wagon had stopped beside a number of motorbikes outside a building displaying a sign saying BIKE REPAIRS.

He was about to drive off when two bikes pulled up in front of him, and another two bikes behind; he was boxed in. The driver of the Ford station wagon walked towards him, stopped beside his car window and knocked.

Shit, now what! Turner thought as he wound down the window.

'Would you come with me, please?' the man said as he opened the car door and stepped back.

Realising he didn't have any choice, Turner got out and followed the man to the BIKE REPAIRS building.

On entering the building through a heavy metal door, he was

confronted by eight leather-clad, tattooed men sat silently around a large table. To the side was a large refrigerator from which another man was extracting several bottles of beer. This man was aged in his mid-thirties, dressed in jeans and blue singlet, but with no visible tattoos.

'Care for a coldie, Greg?' said the man.

'Thanks,' Turner replied as he felt the steady stare of the other men.

The man placed the beers on the table and pointed to a vacant chair. 'Take a seat.'

Turner sat and a beer was pushed in front of him. 'So, what's this all about then?' he asked, trying to be as casual and calm as possible.

The man who had brought the beers took a drink from his bottle and pulled up another chair beside Turner. 'Well, Greg, since you have been following Granger around for the last couple of weeks I thought it best we have this meeting to clear a few things up. My name is Monty Thorington and this is my business.' He waved an arm around.

Turner looked around the virtually empty room and nodded his head. 'Right … bike repairs, eh, Mr Thorington?'

Thorington smiled. 'Oh, I do have the odd other interest … and you may call me Monty.'

'One of your other interests wouldn't happen to have anything to do with pharmaceuticals?' said Turner. 'And I wouldn't have been partly responsible for shutting down an opposition by any chance, Billy?'

'Well, Greg, that was a great bit of police work, eh!'

'So, what exactly are your other interests, Monty?'

Thorington took another drink from his beer and glanced around at the other men at the table before continuing. His smile vanished and his eyes stared darkly at Turner as he leant towards him. 'Before we talk further, Greg, I need to know if you are interested in making more money, or in talking to your superiors, which I have to add would undoubtedly result in you experiencing severe trauma.'

Thorington sat back in his chair.

'Well, Monty,' said Turner, after looking around again at the other men who remained staring silently, 'since you already have me by the short and curlies thanks to that little movie, I don't have a lot of choice, and I certainly would prefer to make a bit of cash to the alternative.'

Thorington put his hand forward. 'Good choice, we'll shake on it.'

Turner accepted the hand and the other men also put their hands forward, stating their name as they did.

'We'll keep our relationship distant,' said Thorington, 'and not get you involved unless absolutely necessary, that way we will more easily avoid being known to each other.'

'Agreed!' said Turner. 'Will Granger be an intermediary?'

'At times ... we'll see how we go.'

'Right!'

Thorington pulled a drawer out from the table, extracted an envelope and handed it to Turner. 'Welcome aboard!'

Turner accepted the envelope and felt its heavy weight. 'Blimey, Monty!'

'Just the start of what, hopefully, will be a profitable arrangement for both of us ... Care for another beer?'

Turner stood. 'No thanks, better be going ... don't want to be pulled up for drink driving.'

They all shared a laugh and Turner headed out the door and on to his car. He glanced back at the industrial complex as he drove off, shaking his head in partial disbelief of what had taken place.

Chapter 5

Over the next few years, Turner was contacted on several occasions by Pax Granger. Most times it was drug-related to either shut down opposition, or to ensure no patrols were in the area when Thorington's men were bringing stuff in, but also to close down brothels which were operating not under his control.

Not only did Turner profit admirably, but Thorington's sphere of operation also increased dramatically. The bike repair shop in the industrial complex remained Thorington's headquarters. He had acquired the buildings on either side but kept them closed as a means of deterring unwanted traffic. Closed circuit cameras had also been placed to keep check on visitors.

Although the vast number of men involved in Thorington's "business" were owners of Harley Davidson motorbikes, the decision had been made not to adopt a gang name such as The Rebels or Hells Angels. To do so, they suspected, would only draw more attention to themselves, although the name Thor's Arms, relating to the Norse mythology God of Thunder, had been suggested, particularly due to its relevance to Thorington's name.

Now, after promotion into the Organised Crime Squad, Turner had become of greater use to Thorington and his ever-increasing illegitimate enterprises.

Of particular interest to Thorington was the squad's ongoing investigation into fraud in the racing industry. Turner had managed to convince the squad that a well-known trainer named Anderson was okay and that his odd horse that didn't run as expected was nothing untoward, as all horses, he managed to convince the squad, sometimes had an off day.

As it happened, Thorington had Anderson in his pocket due to an indiscretion he had made one night after too many drinks. He had visited a brothel that was owned by Thorington, and the visit had been caught on one of the many cameras that were carefully hidden in all the rooms.

Thorington now had the trainer by the genitalia, as the last thing Anderson wanted was for his family to be made aware of his naughty night out. It was that connection that enabled a betting plunge on the outsider Night Shift to secure a healthy profit for Turner and for Thorington.

Turner received an unexpected phone call from Thorington late one evening. 'Hi, Monty, this is a surprise, what's up?'

'Major problem, Greg, one of my boys is in a bit of trouble. He was riding down James Street and got pulled over by your radar traps.'

'Doesn't sound like a big deal. Tell him to pay the fine and get on with it,' said Turner.

'Bit more to it, Greg, he gave a bit of lip and was then searched. The silly bastard was carrying a pistol that was used in a bank heist six months back.'

'Shit! ... Is he still being held or been bailed?'

'Bailed ... I've just come off the phone to him. He bought the gun a couple of weeks ago from some guy down south. Trouble is, he's got a bit of a record for going tooled up, so getting out of what they decide to throw at him won't be easy.'

'So, why tell me?'

'Any chance you could get hold of the gun?'

'Asking a lot, Monty ... it'll be in lock up and I certainly don't want to be caught removing it. When's he due for appearance?'

'Two weeks.'

'That's quick ... who's he coming before?'

'Magistrate by the name of Stanmore.'

'I know the guy ... he can be tough ... I'll do some checking and you do the same ... might be able to turn something up on him.'

'Okay ... we'll keep in touch.'

In the office the next morning, while having coffee with fellow detectives, Connell and Preston, Turner casually asked who they considered the most severe and the most soft in sentencing of the magistrates and judges they knew.

'That Charlton is hard as nails, he'd give everyone life if he could,' said Connell.

'And Vernick is soft as shit, gives a slap on the wrist and tells 'em to promise to be good in the future,' said Preston.

'I hear that bloke Stanmore can be tough,' said Turner.

'Yeah, that's right ... likes his holidays in Thailand I've heard,' said Preston with a grin and a roll of his eyes.

'You're joking?' said Connell. 'And he hasn't been pulled up?'

'Nope! ... Got connections apparently.'

Turner put down his cup and stood away. 'Gotta use the loo ... catch you boys later.'

On entering the toilet, he ensured that he was alone before using his mobile. 'Monty, I may have something ... Stanmore goes regularly to Thailand.'

'I'm on it,' said Thorington and rang off.

Thorington rang Turner back that evening. 'Good one, Greg ... my contact in Bangkok told me that Stanmore is well-known in the lady-boy bars in Nana Plaza.'

'Reckon you should get Pax Granger to pay him a visit,' said Turner. 'Don't get heavy with him on the first visit, just that he's received information from an unknown source and he had better be careful in the future ... that way Granger will appear to be doing him a favour ... then follow up a few days later and tell him to be soft on your boy or film that has come to hand may be made public.'

'Like the way you think, Greg ... catch you later.'

Turner took a few deep breaths after Thorington rang off. He felt sure that whatever happened concerning Stanmore couldn't reflect on him, and with luck he could be in for another big payday if, all being well, Thorington's boy got off light.

It eventuated that Stanmore gave Thorington's boy a virtual slap on the wrist by issuing a good behaviour bond and a five hundred dollar fine for abusing the police officer who initially pulled him in. The prosecuting police solicitor was astounded by the leniency but was left with no alternative but to accept the decision.

Turner's mobile rang shortly after. 'All's well that ends well,' said Thorington. 'Will you be in your favourite pub again this evening?'

'Most likely.'

'Nine o'clock ... the carpark ... little bonus.'

'Thanks, Monty!'

Chapter 6

Not having a permanent female relationship, Turner overcame his sexual frustration by regular visits to brothels which he knew were controlled by Thorington. The episode with Stanmore had resulted in a ten thousand dollar bonus as Thorington now had Stanmore firmly under his control.

He now had bank accounts with three different banks with his total savings amounting to a little over four hundred thousand dollars. His relationship with Thorington had proved to be extremely fruitful.

To celebrate hitting the four hundred mark, he had a few more drinks than usual and decided he needed a bit of female company.

'Ah … good evening, Mister Smith!' exclaimed the young Asian lady as he stumbled into the brothel. 'You like see Susie again?'

'That'd be great,' spluttered Turner who was more than slightly pissed.

The receptionist pressed a button on her desk, and a few seconds later an extremely attractive young Japanese girl came through a side door. 'Please, please,' she said to Turner as she put out her hand, 'I so happy to see you again, please come with me.'

In less than half an hour, Turner was back at reception taking cash out of his inside jacket to pay for what had been a most uneventful interlude due to the over-abundance of alcohol he had consumed affecting his lovemaking ability.

The large roll of notes that Turner took out to pay for his virtual non-event made the receptionist's eyes widen, and as soon as

Turner walked out she picked up the phone and chattered excitedly to the person on the other end.

Turner walked unsteadily away from the brothel and down the road to where he hoped to find a taxi to take him home. As he passed a darkened alley, two figures reached out, grabbed him and dragged him back into the narrow lane. In his drunken condition, he was no match for the assailants and he was soon knocked semi-conscious to the ground. His pockets were emptied and his wad of notes found and taken. Giving a final kick to the side of his head, the assailants departed.

Turner came around several minutes later, and with difficulty stood up and exited the laneway. One of his jacket sleeves was hanging by a thread and his pants pockets torn open.

Blood ran from his nose and a cut below his left eye. As he came to his senses, he realised that his wad of dollars was missing along with his wallet that contained his police identification.

Unfortunately, he realised he was going to have to report the event that would mean rebuke from above, but worse still, he was sure to cop a ribbing from a lot of his fellows.

Luckily, he managed to find a taxi with a driver that knew him and dropped him at his flat.

'I'll get the fare to you in the next day or so,' he promised the driver.

He flopped onto his bed and once more passed out. He awoke at daybreak, stripped off the clothes he had slept in, went into the bathroom and inspected the damage. His nose was swollen, a black left eye and his torso was covered in blue bruises. In his bathroom cabinet he found a packet of Panadol and downed two with a mouthful of water as he stood under the shower. As he allowed the stream of cool water to run over him, the previous nights' events went through his mind. *Was it a random attack or had somebody tipped his attackers off about the cash he was carrying?*

After drying off and putting on clean clothes he picked up his mobile. 'Monty ...'

'Do you know what time it is?' said Thorington after recognising the caller.

'Yeah, I know it's bloody early, sorry about that but I could do with some help.'

'What's up?'

Turner quickly explained what had happened.

'Leave it with me,' said Thorington before ringing off.

Deciding he might as well face the music and get it over with, Turner went into the police station and into the office occupied by the Organised Crime Squad.

'Jesus, Greg ... who did you fall out with?' asked Connell.

By the time Turner had given an account of what happened, most of the listeners were trying hard to contain themselves from laughter. It was exactly what he had expected.

'So, when you going back for a refund?' asked Preston, which managed to tip the others over the edge.

The laughter subsided immediately when the squad's boss, Fullmore, entered the room. 'Like to fill me in on the joke?' he said with a smile.

Turner approached him. 'Need to have a chat, Boss,' he said quietly, 'your office.'

Together, they left the squad room and entered an adjoining small office. Turner closed the door behind him as the boss took a seat behind his desk and looked up at him. After once again explaining what had occurred, the reaction from his boss was completely different than that from his co-officers.

'You bloody idiot, Turner ... getting beat up is one thing, but losing your ID is a real pain in the arse.'

'Yeah ... sorry, Boss.'

'Any idea at all on who attacked you?'

'Maybe ... got somebody chasing it up ...'

Fullmore raised a hand, stopping Turner from continuing.

'Don't tell me, I don't want to know … just get it sorted, and quick … now get out.'

Turner left Fullmore's office once more, closing the door behind him. He pulled a face and shrugged his shoulders as he passed the other officers on his way out. He took a few deep breaths as he left the station and headed towards his car. He had just opened the car door when his mobile rang.

'Your pub's carpark in half an hour.'

Turner recognised the voice of Thorington, got in his car and sped off. He arrived at the pub's carpark in twenty minutes and parked in his usual spot under a gumtree.

Ten minutes later, a single motorbike pulled up beside him. The leather-clad rider reached inside his jacket, took out an envelope and handed it through Turner's open window. 'Reckon that's what you lost,' he said in a voice muffled by the helmet he was wearing.

'Thanks, pal!' said Turner as he accepted the envelope.

'Thanks for helping me with the gun problem,' replied the rider as he revved the bike and rode away.

Turner watched the rider disappear and realised he had to be the one given the lean sentence by Magistrate Stanmore. He opened the envelope and found his wad of cash and his wallet that, on opening, had his ID card still inside.

A gasp of relief escaped him. He picked up his mobile, rang the squad room and asked for Fullmore. 'Got my ID back, Boss.'

'Good … I don't want to know how.' Fullmore rang off before Turner could say more.

That evening, Turner decided to do a little digging of his own. He drove to the brothel. The receptionist was not the same as the previous night.

'Good evening, sir, you like company?' she said with a smile.

'No, not tonight, thank you … I was hoping to have a chat to the girl that was here last night.'

'Oh, she not here anymore.'

'And why's that?' asked Turner.

The girl shook her head. 'She had a nasty accident and won't be coming back,' she said sadly.

Turner didn't need to ask further. She had obviously been questioned by Thorington's men. He walked out of the brothel and used his mobile as he got to his car.

'Monty, thanks!'

'No worries ... don't go around half-pissed next time, okay!'

'Right!'

Once again, the call ended abruptly. He went back to his flat, took a beer out of the refrigerator and turned on the TV. An item mentioning the finding of two, as yet unidentified Asians beaten almost beyond recognition grabbed his attention. One of them was not expected to survive. It wasn't hard to put two and two together to place a bet on them being the two guys that had robbed him.

Turner raised his beer in salute at the TV. 'Up yours, you bastards!'

Chapter 7

The following morning in the squad room, Fullmore had gathered the entire group.

'Guys, this is Toby Curtice from the Southside nick, and he's going to join us for a particular investigation.'

Curtice was just under two metres tall, solidly built, clean shaven, aged mid-forties and wearing suit and tie. He looked clean cut and had a certain air of confidence. He looked around the group of officers and greeted them with a smile.

'Morning all ... as the boss mentioned, this is to be a particular investigation, and it's into the racing industry. It's concerning the trainer Pat Anderson.'

There was an immediate group moan at the name Anderson.

'Been there, done that on Anderson,' said Connell.

'He's clean,' said another.

'You sure we need to spend the time and money going over the same stuff again on Anderson?' asked Turner. This was the trainer that Thorington had in his pocket, and that he had helped shut down the investigation on some time before.

'Got some new info and a stable lad on the inside who's working with us,' added Curtice.

Turner felt a slight turn in the stomach. Thorington would not be happy finding out one of Anderson's employees was passing information to the police. If Anderson did get done for fixing, you could bet your life that he'd give up Thorington's involvement if offered a chance of making things easier for himself. It wasn't looking good.

'Greg, you were very much involved last time, so I'd like you to partner up with Curtice in this,' said Fullmore.

Curtice walked over to Turner and offered his hand with a smile. 'Hi ... how you going?'

Turner took his hand. It was a firm grip. 'Good, thanks.'

'I'll leave you with it,' said Fullmore as he went into his office.

'Okay, Boss,' said Turner.

'So ... Toby ... what's your history?' asked Turner as he sat in a chair and pointed to another.

'Joined up when I was eighteen ... did the usual time in uniform, then managed to get into detective training school and here I am.'

'Sounds just like me, Toby. So, what do you know about Col Anderson?'

'Not much ... heard of him, of course, but that's it ... Read up on the file on Anderson from last time.'

'And how did you get hold of the stable lad?'

'He got pulled up drunk driving couple of weeks back ... started bragging to the PCs how he'd made a packet on one of the horses he looks after and indicating he had inside knowledge. One of the PCs gave me a call before they charged him. I went to see him where they were holding him in the booze bus and told him I might be able to get him out of losing his driving licence if he told me what he knew about the horse business.'

'Is he going to contact you if he has anything?'

'Yeah ... I gave him my mobile and I have his.'

'Have you had anything to do with the industry before?'

Curtice shook his head. 'Nope.'

'Do you bet?'

'Nope!'

Turner grinned. 'Well, Toby, maybe we'll start by going to the track and seeing what happens. Local races are on tomorrow.' He reached into the desk drawer, took out the day's paper and passed it over. 'Go to the racing page and see if you can pick a winner or two.'

Curtice took the paper and turned to the racing page. 'Got a pin, Greg? I reckon that's as good a way as any of picking a winner.'

'Put a mark beside a horse in each race and we'll see how you go.'

'What about you?' said Curtice.

'Give me the paper when you're done and I'll mark what I reckon has a chance, okay?'

Turner knew that Anderson had two runners in the fourth race, and he had already been told that the least ranked horse was primed to win.

Curtice finished marking his selection and passed the paper to Turner. 'All done … let's see yours.'

Turner took the paper and quickly went down the listed races and placed a mark beside his selections. He made sure that the horse he picked in the fourth was not one of the two trained by Anderson. He tore the racing page out of the paper, folded it and handed it across to Curtice. 'You look after that, Toby … I need to use the loo.'

He stood up and went down the passageway to the toilets. He entered a cubicle, took out his mobile and waited a moment making sure no one else entered before punching in a number. 'Monty … yeah, it's me,' he whispered. 'For Chrissake, shut up and listen, you gotta tell Anderson to do it right tomorrow 'cause there's a problem … Look, I gotta go, I'll call you back later.' He rang off just as he heard someone enter the toilets. He flushed and walked out of the cubicle to the wash basin.

Curtice was standing at the urinal. 'Feeling better?'

'Yes, thanks, can't beat a good clear out,' said Turner.

Curtice finished and adjusted his pants before standing beside Turner at the wash basins.

'My stomach don't feel too good,' said Turner. 'Reckon I'll take off home and hope it clears by tomorrow.'

'Good idea, don't give it to me or I might pass it on to the wife and kids.'

'What you got?'

'Boy eight and girl five.'

'Perfect pair.'

'Yeah, that'll do us, the wife has said enough.'

'Married long?'

'Ten years.'

Turner grabbed at his stomach. 'That's it … I'm off … see you here tomorrow.' Hurriedly, he left the toilet and made his way outside to his car.

Once inside, he took out his mobile.

'Hi, Monty, sorry about before … had some chance of being overheard.'

'So, what's the problem, Greg?'

'There's another look at Anderson about to start and I reckon it would be wise to tell him to make sure his horses in the fourth tomorrow run on merit.'

'Shit! I've already laid out a bunch.'

'Seems the new guy who's joined us has a stable lad giving him info.'

'You got his name?'

'Not yet … we're going to the track tomorrow and hopefully I'll find out then.'

'When you do, let me know and I'll sort it.'

'Don't try to cancel your bets, Monty, or word might get back.'

'I won't, but it's sure going to cost me.'

'I'll be in touch,' said Turner and rang off.

Chapter 8

Turner met Curtice at the entrance to the race track a half hour before the first race was due.

'How's your insides feeling today?' asked Curtice.

'Bloody sight better, thanks, Toby,' replied Turner with half a smile and a rub of his stomach. 'Can't say as how I had lots for breakfast though.'

Curtice took out the racing page they had both marked the day before. 'My wife, Desley, looked over the horses and she has marked the ones she fancies.'

Turner managed a grin. 'She'll probably do better than either of us. Come on, we better get in or we'll miss the first.'

As they entered the gate, Curtice handed the paper to Turner. 'Race four, the trainer Anderson has two horses running.'

'Yeah, I know ... one is favourite and the other a bit of an outsider ... not considered much of a chance.'

'Be interesting to see how they go,' said Curtice.

Turner nodded. 'That's right, if the long odds one gets up your info could be spot on ... Anyway, let's go see a bookie and place a bet on the first.'

After the first three races, the only winner they had forecast between them was one Curtice's wife had picked.

'That's three races and I'm fifteen dollars down ... don't reckon I'll make this my full-time job,' said Turner.

'Same here,' said Curtice, 'but Desley is eight dollars fifty up thanks to the winner in the last. Race four next, the result could be interesting.'

In race four, the favourite finished first by a length and Anderson's other long odds horse came in second last.

'Well, nothing particularly iffie there,' said Turner with an inner feeling of relief. Obviously, Thorington had got in touch with Anderson to ensure the horses ran as anticipated by the punters.

Curtice frowned. 'Yeah! ... After what young Erroll said I'm a bit surprised the long-odds one didn't at least get a place.'

'Did you pick it?' asked Turner.

'Matter of fact, I did.'

'So, that's another fiver down, eh?' said Turner. 'What did Desley pick?'

'The one that finished dead last I'm afraid.'

'Well, there's another three races to get our money back, or I'll have to make do with beans on toast for tea tonight.'

By the end of the day they were all out of pocket.

'First and last time I'll be betting on the horses,' said Curtice without humour. 'Bloody mug's game.'

'You got that right, Toby,' said Turner. 'Might be a good idea to have a quiet chat with your informant and make sure he wasn't just slinging a line to get off the drink driving charge.'

'Yeah I will, first chance.'

Together, they walked out of the racecourse and to their parked cars.

'I'll catch up with you in the squad room in the morning, Toby, and tell Desley that at least she picked one winner.' Curtice smiled as he got in his car. 'See you, Greg.'

Turner took out his mobile as he opened his car door. 'Monty, the new guy dropped the name Erroll.'

'That all you got?' asked Thorington.

'Well, we know he's a stable lad, so that ought to narrow it down.'

'Fair enough, I'll check it out.'

'Don't get heavy with the lad, Monty, or that'll look suspicious, okay?'

'Give me credit for a bit of sense, Greg,' replied Thorington angrily before ringing off.

Turner threw the mobile onto the passenger seat as he got behind the wheel and took a few deep breaths. *Sense … yeah … like what happened to the girl in the brothel and the two Asian guys.*

Chapter 9

Turner was already in the squad room in the morning when Curtice walked in.

'Morning, Toby, what did Desley say when you told her she was the only one that picked a winner?'

'Like I said yesterday, she reckons it's a mug's game and I've been officially banned from ever laying another bet.'

Turner laughed. 'Sounds wise to me.'

Curtice joined in the laughter. 'Do people really think they can beat the bookies, Greg?'

'Indeed they do, but if you can show me a poor bookie I'll be very surprised.

'Got hold of the lad who gave me the info ... meeting him in the pub a short distance from the stables at ten-thirty ... want to come along?' asked Curtice.

'Yeah, I'd like to hear what he has to say for himself.'

'That's for sure ... if he's been having me on I'll make sure he's done for the drink driving and have his digs done over on the hope there's a stash hidden.'

'Tell you what, Toby, I know a good little café ... What say we go for a coffee and cake first?'

'Sounds good.'

'Okay ... I'll drive.'

Turner took Curtice to the café that he had been having free coffee at ever since being introduced to it by Larkin. 'My shout!' he said as they got up to leave. 'I'll see you outside, Toby.'

Being cautious just in case Curtice was watching, he went to the counter and paid, much to the surprise of the café owner and the waitress who had been handing out free coffee to him for years.

As they drove past Anderson's property on the way to the pub where the stable lad had agreed to meet Curtice, a black Volvo car drove out of the gates. Turner recognised it as the car belonging to Pax Granger, the solicitor that Thorington used. Granger glanced at Turner then quickly looked away as he saw there was a passenger.

Turner continued on to the pub and parked in the parking area behind. He and Curtice made their way into the public bar and ordered a beer each. Being early, there was only one other customer who was slumped against the bar with a half-empty glass in front of him.

The bartender approached them. 'What you having?'

'My shout, you got the coffees,' said Curtice.

'Just a light, thanks,' said Turner.

'Make that two lights, thanks,' said Curtice as he checked his watch.

'It's just after ten-thirty, better give him a bit of time to make it here,' said Turner, thinking that it would be bloody amazing if the lad actually turned up. After seeing Granger leave the stables, he felt sure that Anderson would have advised the lad how unhealthy it would be for him if he didn't keep his mouth shut.

At 11 o'clock, Curtice had lost his patience. 'The bastard's stood me up.'

'What do you want to do?' asked Turner.

Curtice took out his mobile. 'I'll ring him.'

There was no answer.

'Now what?' said Turner.

'We'll go into Anderson's property and look for him.'

Turner shook his head. 'You sure that's a good idea, Toby? You don't want Anderson getting wind of anything.'

'I'll just say I'm looking for him regarding the drink driving charge ... that should be okay.'

'Your call, Toby,' said Turner, somewhat concerned over what Anderson might say.

Turner drove through the property entrance and up the long driveway. The areas on either side were enclosed by timber fences. Brood mares and their foals wandered through the well-maintained paddocks. A number of horses with riders were being exercised around a track behind a number of out buildings and stables.

They stopped outside a rambling country house.

As they got out of the car, a man came out of the front door. 'Can I help you, gentlemen?' he inquired.

Curtice took out his wallet and displayed his police badge. 'And who are you, sir?'

'Name's Pat Anderson.'

'We would like to talk to Erroll please, Mr Anderson,' said Curtice.

'Oh, the stable lad Erroll,' Anderson answered. 'What's the silly bugger done now to warrant you guys turning up?'

'It's in regard to a possible drink driving charge,' said Turner.

'Well, he's not here at present,' said Anderson. 'Took off home about an hour ago, reckoned he was feeling crook.'

'Right … thanks for that, Mr Anderson, we'll see if we can catch him there.' Curtice gave Turner a quick glance and a roll of his eyes as he turned away and started back to the car.

When Curtice had his back to him, Turner looked straight at Anderson and was delivered a brief smile and a wink.

Turner quickly about faced and followed Curtice. It was apparent that when Pax Granger was there earlier on, he must have not only made Anderson aware of the possibility the police would be in to see him concerning Erroll, but had also told him that Turner was on his side.

Curtice referred to his notebook as Turner drove back down the driveway. 'His home address is flat 3, 48 Gordon Street … do you know it?'

Turner nodded. 'Yeah ... two streets up on the left ... bit of a rough area.'

'If he left the stables as long ago as Anderson said, he had plenty of time to make it to the pub,' said Curtice.

'That's true!' agreed Turner, while trying to think why he hadn't turned up.

He brought the car to a stop outside a rundown block of flats. 'This is it, Toby.'

The fence along the street front was partially fallen down, and what may have once been a garden bed inside the fence was an overgrown mass of weeds.

Curtice got out and made his way along the gravel path to the door with the number 3 scrawled in white paint and knocked. There was no answer.

As Curtice knocked again, Turner went to the front window and peered in. The inside was a mess. Empty beer bottles on the floor as well as takeaway containers. Obviously, Erroll wasn't the tidiest individual. 'He's not here, Toby,' he said as he walked to the front door.

'Seems not ... I'll try his mobile again,' said Curtice.

After a couple of minutes, Curtice returned the mobile to his jacket pocket.

'Still no contact?' asked Turner.

'Something not right, Greg,' said Curtice shaking his head. 'I've got a nasty feeling about this ... not turning up ... no phone ... going off sick.'

If Thorington has anything to do with it, I'm betting the lad's very *bloody sick*, thought Turner. 'Try him again tonight, Toby, hopefully you'll get hold of him then with a good explanation.'

'I most certainly will, and his explanation had better be a good one,' said Curtice as they walked back to their car.

During the drive back to the police station both men were silent. Turner drove into the police carpark and pulled up. He could tell that Curtice had been deep in thought. 'Got any more ideas, Toby?' he asked as Curtice opened the car door.

'Gonna make a few phone calls ... see what I can dig up on Anderson.'

'Right! Reckon I'll go talk to a couple of my snitches.'

'Okay ... and if I come up with anything I'll call you.'

'Me too ... otherwise see you back in the office tomorrow.'

Curtice walked away into the building and Turner drove back out of the carpark. After a short distance, he pulled up and took out his mobile and rang Thorington.

'Monty! ... What's happened to the stable lad?'

'Any problems?' asked Thorington.

'Problem is the lad's gone missing.'

'Why is that a problem?'

'Because we needed to talk to him and just have him say he was pulling the cops' dicks, Monty. That would have ended the whole thing, but now it looks like he was warned off.'

'No lad ... no fuckin' problem,' said Thorington with annoyance.

'On the contrary, Monty ... the guy with me at the stables thinks there's something fishy going on and is digging around.'

'You can rest assured nobody will talk.'

'Don't be so sure, Monty. When someone's arse is on the line you'd be surprised just how quick their memories return.'

'None of my boys will talk, and neither will anyone else when they're given an option.'

'So, what have you done with the lad?' asked Turner.

'I told you ... he's gone!'

'Jesus, Monty! ... Who's next? Granger?'

Thorington went quiet.

'Monty, you still there?'

'Yeah ... why say Granger?'

'He was leaving the stables as we drove past this morning. I saw him, so my offsider probably did too.'

'Granger is solid so quit worrying.'

'I'm not worried, Monty. I'm just telling you like it is and suggesting you play it cool is all.'

'Okay, Greg … point taken … keep me up to speed with what's happening, eh?'

'Will do.'

Turner rang off and sighed. Obviously, the stable lad was somewhere he wouldn't be found. That probably meant he was dead and buried. Who would be next? He felt sure that Thorington would have no compunction in getting rid of anyone who posed him a problem. The person who knew more about Thorington's activities than anyone else was Granger, so he was someone Thorington would be keeping a close eye, and ear, on. Then of course there was himself. He was going to have to be extra careful from here on.

Chapter 10

Turner walked into the squad room in the morning to be confronted by Fullmore. 'Bad news, Greg ... that trainer, Anderson, has been taken to hospital. Apparently got kicked in the head by one of his horses early this morning.'

'How is he?' said Turner as Curtice came running into the room.

'Just found out about Anderson ... any news on his condition?' asked Curtice.

Fullmore shook his head. 'Not looking good so the medics have implied. May be the end of your investigation,' he said as he went into his office.

'Could be,' said Turner.

Curtice gave Turner an inquiring look. 'What do you reckon, Greg ... stable lad goes missing and now Anderson gets a kick in the head ... bit strange, eh?'

'Certainly puts an end into chasing him for fixing if he doesn't make it,' said Turner seriously.

Fullmore came out of his office and approached them. 'Just had a call, Anderson didn't make it. Sorry, Toby, but that's the investigation done for, you better head on back to your nick.'

He reached out to shake his hand. 'Might have you back here another time.'

'Yes, thank you, sir.'

Fullmore returned to his office, leaving Curtice and Turner in the squad room.

Curtice stood shaking his head. 'Something smells, Greg— Anderson dead and the stable lad missing, what do you reckon?'

'I don't know, Toby; our previous look at Anderson came up empty so maybe he was clean, and the stable lad could have shot through 'cause he lied to start with.'

Curtice nodded and pulled a face. 'Umm, maybe … then again maybe not.'

'Look, if anything turns up in the future that could tie them into something I promise I'll give you a call, meantime you gotta clear off and I better check up with the other guys and see what they're into.' He smiled and offered his hand. 'Thanks, Toby.'

Curtice took his hand and grinned back. 'Yeah, no good dwelling on it, see you round, Greg.'

Turner gave Curtice a brief wave as he left the squad room. His smile disappeared. *Accidently kicked in the head by a horse, yeah right … Bloody Thorington was putting him in the shit.*

A shout from the doorway made Turner look around. Curtice was beckoning him over. He walked across. 'What's up?'

'I just remembered the car that was leaving the stables yesterday, black Volvo it was, the bloke gave us an odd look as we passed … you remember?'

'Oh yeah, I remember the car, but didn't get a look at anyone in it, I was watching the road.'

'Fair enough … reckon it's worth a look at though … if anything shows up I'll be in touch … see ya!'

Curtice departed again. Turner's mind was racing. Sure as eggs it wouldn't take Curtice long with his contacts to find out the Volvo belonged to Granger, and Granger knew everything. The shit was getting deeper.

He went outside to the carpark … took out his mobile. 'Monty, got another problem.'

'What now for Chrissake?'

'The other cop who went to see Anderson with me, name of Toby Curtice, he saw Granger's Volvo leave the stables yesterday and is going to check it out.'

'Nothing to worry about, Greg, Granger will see the guy away empty handed ... guaranteed!'

'I sure hope you're right, Monty.'

'I couldn't be surer, Greg; go have a drink and take it easy eh!'

Turner stood staring at the mobile for a while after Thorington rang off. It was time, he decided, to get some protection organised.

That evening, he spent several hours on his computer recording his association with Thorington; from his initial meeting at the bike repair shop to all that had happened since.

At least now he reckoned he had a bargaining tool if Thorington ever turned against him.

Three days later, Curtice rang Turner. 'I traced who that Volvo belonged to, Greg, and went to see the guy.'

'And?' said Turner with trepidation.

'Apparently just called in to say hi while passing.'

'So, what do you reckon now?'

'Seemed okay to me ... he is ... I mean, was, Anderson's solicitor and had no knowledge of him having any involvement in fixing.'

'Do you reckon he was telling you the truth, Toby?'

'Yeah I do ... his sister was there at the time and she thought the idea ridiculous. She knows the family and said how upset they all are at the accident.'

'Do we need to look anymore, Toby?'

'No, I don't think so, nothing to chase.'

'Okay, Toby ... so long for now then.'

'Bye again, Greg.'

Turner took a few deep breaths and sighed with relief ... case closed ... hoo-bloody-ray.

A couple of days later, Curtice rang Turner again. 'You're not going to believe this, Greg.'

'Believe what?' said Turner, more than a little surprised at another call from Curtice.

'Pax Granger drove his Volvo into a tree last night; it caught fire and he was incinerated.'

'Bloody hell!' said Turner.

'Yeah, not good news; I'm going to call round to his sister and pay my respects. Least I can do after my last visit.'

'Good idea, and pass on my regards as well please, Toby.'

'Will do … see ya!'

Turner stared silently at his mobile. *Bloody Thorington*. The shit was now well over his head. *Maybe time to get out … I've got a good stash … move away.*

Chapter 11

After a sleepless night, Turner walked into the police squad room and went straight to Fullmore's office.

'Need to talk to you, boss,' he said as he closed the door behind him.

Fullmore looked up from the paperwork on his desk that he had been studying. 'Go ahead.'

Turner shuffled his feet uncomfortably. 'I've decided to quit … this is my statement of resignation.' He handed the letter across the desk.

Fullmore sat back in his chair, stared at Turner as he accepted the letter. 'Right … and what's brought this on?'

Turner shrugged. 'The stuff-up with the ID was one thing, but there's other things I'd rather not talk about … let's just say I'm not sure this is what I want to do anymore.'

'Your decision, Greg,' said Fullmore. 'We'll be sorry to lose you, but if that's how you feel, okay.'

'Yes it is, Boss.'

'Better give me your ID then.'

Turner extracted his ID from his wallet and passed it over.

'How long you served?' asked Fullmore.

'Coming up to thirteen years.'

'Well, you'll have a bit of pension accrued.'

'Yeah … that'll be a help.'

Fullmore extended his hand. 'Take care of yourself then, Greg, and good luck for the future.'

Turner accepted the offered hand. 'Thanks, boss.' He left the office, walked out of the squad room and out of the police station as a civilian.

Chapter 12

The small cottage was merely a stone's throw from the river and a hundred metres or so from its nearest neighbour. On the front verandah, wearing just a pair of shorts, Turner was enjoying a cold beer in the late afternoon.

After quitting the police force he had wasted no time in leaving the city. That same day he packed his few possessions into a couple of suitcases and drove away from his rented flat after ringing the real estate agent to tell him of his intention.

Not wanting to be contacted, he smashed his mobile and threw it in a roadside garbage bin.

The underhanded money that he had stashed away paid for the cottage with plenty left over, and the police pension he was entitled to, along with the few dollars he made helping out in the local village pub, was all he needed.

Life was pretty good. He had not contacted anyone to say where he was; particularly not Thorington, who he was sure would be pretty much pissed off at his leaving without telling him, and he had no wish to see, or hear from him or any other person from the past.

He finished his beer and went inside to grab another from the refrigerator.

A knock caused him to put the beer down. *Guess I'm wanted at the pub*, he thought as he went to the front door and opened it.

'Hi, Greg!' said Curtice cheerfully, 'How's things?'

Turner stood in shock for a moment. 'Toby! ... Good, thanks.'

Curtice indicated to a young woman beside him. 'This is Marian, alright if we come in?'

'Sure!' said Turner as Curtice and the woman had already started walking in anyway.

'Not a bad place you've got here,' said Curtice as he walked through and looked out at the front verandah towards the river. 'Do any fishing?'

Turner closed the front door behind them and followed Curtice and the woman to the front window. The last thing he wanted was to see anyone from the past. And who the hell was the woman anyway? 'Why are you here, Toby, and who's your friend?'

Curtice turned away from the window. 'I do apologise, Greg,' he said with a smile, 'this is Marian Granger … poor Pax's young sister.'

Turner's face dropped as he looked at Marian. 'Oh, Miss Granger, I'm so sorry, I didn't know. I trust Toby conveyed my condolences as I asked him.'

'Yes, he did … I hadn't known till a few days ago just how well you and Pax knew each other,' she replied without a trace of a smile on her face.

Turner was taken aback. What made her think that he knew Pax at all … let alone well? He looked at her quizzically, and she returned the look with a stony stare.

'Reckon I can help you there, Greg,' said Curtice. He reached inside the small suitcase he had carried inside, extracted a small notebook and waved it in front of Turner.

'Seems Pax kept a record of all the, can I say *odd*, dealings he had with those of a questionable character.'

Turner looked from a smiling Curtice to a grim-faced Marian, and back at Curtice. He remained silent.

'I found it a week ago when I was cleaning up Pax's place,' said Marian. 'After reading through it I realised I had to give it to the police, and since Toby had been so nice to me after Pax died, that's who I called.'

'And a very wise decision it was too, Marian, as we wouldn't have liked it to get into the wrong hands.' He looked straight at

Turner and grinned. 'Such as a certain police officer who rates quite a few mentions.'

Turner swallowed and felt his heart start to race. The notebook would probably also contain details of his relationship with Thorington. It wasn't looking good.

'So, here we are, Greg, and I thought it only fair that I brought Marian here to see you before I took it any further.'

'You killed Pax and made it look like an accident to shut him up, didn't you?' shouted Marian angrily. She pointed to the notebook in Curtice's hand. 'Well, it hasn't worked has it? ... I hope you hang!'

'No, Marian. No!' said Turner, shaking his head vigorously. 'Yes, I knew Pax, but no way did I kill him ... no way!'

'He's right, Marian, Greg didn't kill Pax,' said Curtice.

'That's right, it would probably have been one of Thorington's men,' said Turner feeling a bit of relief at Curtice's statement.

'I'm pretty sure I know who did though,' added Curtice quietly.

Both Turner and Marian turned to look at Curtice as he once again reached into his small suitcase. Their eyes opened wide in disbelief at the gun he now held.

He pointed the gun at Marian. 'It was me!'

Fitted with a silencer, the gun made barely a sound when he pulled the trigger. The bullet hit Marian above the right eye and she dropped to the ground. A pool of blood slowly spread around her head.

Curtice turned quickly and pointed the gun at Turner.

Turner's mind was racing. 'And the stable lad ... I guess that was you too.'

Curtice shrugged. 'What can I say? ... needs must.'

'And Anderson?'

'Ah ... that was indeed just an accident ... can't beat luck, eh!'

Turner's shoulders sagged as the full understanding of past events came to mind. A feeling of stillness and peace came over him.

'Somehow, I doubt that notebook will go any further will it, Toby?'

'Sometimes things have a way of coming together nicely, Greg,' said Curtice with a grim smile. 'And I see you have been amusing yourself on that laptop computer on the table.'

Turner glanced at the computer in which he had been detailing his involvement in unsavoury activities, and with whom. 'I like some of the games on it.'

'Of course you do, Greg.' He stared at Turner. 'Wouldn't just happen to be recording certain events, eh?'

The silenced gun fired again and Turner fell backwards with a bullet in his chest. He lay on the floor, twitching ... Curtice stood over him and fired once more into his head. Turner lay still.

Curtice placed the gun, the notebook and the computer into the small suitcase. He took a mobile from his jacket pocket and punched in a number.

He nodded as he listened to the person accepting the call.

'All sorted, Monty,' said Curtice.

Frampton

BOOK 5: RESULTS

Chapter 1

Penelope moaned, passed a hand over her face and rubbed her eyes. With difficulty, she sat up and looked around. She moaned again and clutched at her chest. She looked down at the ugly red and painful burn marks that covered her naked breasts.

What the hell? she thought.

Without success, she tried to remember the previous evening. She could recall dancing in a nightclub ... but then what?

She saw her clothes on the floor beside the bed and reached down for them. Her head started spinning and her stomach heaved as she bent over. She sat back up and vomited over herself and the bed.

At the side of the room was a door to a bathroom. She unsteadily made her way in and sat on the toilet. Urinating was uncomfortable; she felt tender and bruised. Did she have sex last night, and if so with who? She turned on the shower and stood under as the warm water cascaded down. Her mind was in turmoil ... *Where am I, what's happened, how did I get these burns?*

She stood under the shower for what seemed an eternity before stepping out and drying herself on a towel she found lying over a rack. As she managed to take some control of herself, she picked up her clothes from the floor and dressed. On the floor against the wall, she saw her shoulder bag. She picked it up and fumbled inside. Her purse was still there but no cash, and her mobile was missing.

She opened the bedroom door and looked out. Two cars were parked to the left and one to the right. This was a motel. A woman was pushing a cart with cleaning equipment and linen towards her. 'Morning, miss, I'll do yours after,' she said as she went past.

Penelope just nodded; she was finding it difficult to speak.

She walked along the front of the motel onto the pavement and looked up and down the street.

Recognition came to her; this was the main street into town, but what the hell was she doing here? She walked back to the Comfort Motel reception.

The receptionist looked up with a smile. 'Hello, miss, and how are you feeling this morning?'

Penelope shook her head. 'Not too good actually.'

'You were certainly under the weather when your friend helped you in last night.'

'My friend?' asked Penelope.

'Yes, I don't think you would have made it to your room without her assistance.'

Penelope tried hard to remember last night and her friend, but no details would come to her.

'Unfortunately, I haven't any cash to pay you, but could I please use your phone to ring someone to come and get me?'

'Certainly,' said the receptionist as she handed her mobile across the desk.

With a 'thank you very much', Penelope accepted the phone. She had to think really hard before the number she wanted to call came to her.

'Hi … Shelly … yes, it's me … did you drop me off at the Comfort Motel last night? … You didn't?'

This was even more confusing. If her close friend Shelly didn't bring her here, then who was the so-called friend who did?

'Shelly, I seem to be in a bit of trouble, I haven't any cash for a taxi so could you please come and pick me up? … Yes, the Comfort Motel, I'll explain when you get here … Thanks, Shelly, see you soon.'

She handed the mobile back to the receptionist. 'My friend from last night, can you tell me her name?'

The receptionist looked down at her diary. 'Yes … it was Penelope Gardener.'

'But that's my name,' said Penelope as she opened her purse, found her driving licence and showed it. 'So, what was hers?'

The receptionist shook her head. 'I'm sorry, but that is what she showed me.'

'So, did she look just like me, you know like the photo on the licence?'

'I'm sorry, I didn't really study the photo,' said the receptionist with a shrug of indifference.

'What did she look like then, as I would like to know who it was that looked after me?' said Penelope earnestly.

The receptionist put her hand to her chin and thought for a moment. 'She was a little taller than you and had long black hair.'

There was a beep from a small blue car that pulled up outside. Penelope gave the receptionist a not-too-friendly look and walked out to her friend Shelly. She eased herself carefully into the passenger seat.

Shelly looked at her and saw the anguish and pain on her face. 'Penny, are you alright?'

Penelope burst into tears. 'I think I've been raped.'

Shelly's jaw dropped. 'Oh, Jesus!'

'Can you please pay the motel and then take me home,' Penelope managed to say as she was overcome with deep sobbing.

Shelly drove with as much speed as legally possible back to the unit they shared. Penelope was still sobbing as Shelly took her to the couch. 'I'll make a cuppa,' she said as Penelope sank into the cushions.

When Shelly returned with the tea, Penelope had managed to stop crying. 'Whenever you're ready,' said Shelly as she handed a cup over, and sat down beside her.

It was several minutes before Penelope spoke. 'It's so weird, Shelly … I just can't seem to remember what happened.'

'Not anything?'

'No ... and there's this.' Penelope opened the front of her dress, revealing the burns on her breasts.

Shelly gasped. 'Oh my God, Penny!'

'Yeah ... and I know I had sex 'cause I'm ... you know, a bit tender, so it must have been rough, and my mobile is gone and all my cash.'

'So, are you going to the police?'

'You reckon I should?'

'What if it happens to someone else, Penny?'

Penelope put her head in her hands. 'First off, I need another shower, and a change of clothes then I'll think about it'

Chapter 2

nspector Bret Hounslow walked out of his office and shouted, 'Frampton!'

Detective Stephanie Frampton looked up from her desk to see the inspector beckoning her. She raised her hand in acknowledgement, closed the file she had been reading, stood up after pushing her chair back and walked towards him past other desks at which fellow officers were sitting. Dressed in dark grey pants and jacket, 160 cm, slim, jet black hair to her shoulders, at twenty-eight she was a very attractive young policewoman.

As she passed them, she was greeted with whispered remarks.

'Now you're for it.'

'He wants your body, Steph.'

'Try to be nice, Steph.'

'Being transferred back to uniform, Steph?'

She ignored all the remarks but still gave them the finger behind her back as she walked into the office and closed the door behind her.

'What's up, Boss?' she asked, as she stood before the desk that Hounslow had seated behind.

'Pretty serious I'm afraid,' said Hounslow seriously with an icy stare.

Frampton took a quick intake of breath. *What the hell have I done now?* she thought.

Hounslow stood up and, with a smile, extended his hand across the desk. 'Seems like you've passed the sergeant's exam. Congratulations Detective Sergeant Stephanie Frampton.'

'Wow … thank you, sir,' said Frampton with a sigh of relief. 'You really had me going there.'

Hounslow sat back down behind his desk. 'Not sure what will be happening with you, but for the time being you'll be staying here. There is a possibility you could be transferred elsewhere but for now you'll have to put up with us.'

'Staying here is fine with me, Boss,' she indicated behind her, 'they're not too bad a bunch out there.'

'Might be a bit of jealousy over your promotion ahead of some of them, so take care.'

'Yes, sir.'

'Okay … I'll adjust some of the rosters starting next week, so off you go, and good luck.'

'Thanks again, boss,' said Frampton as she turned and left the office.

As she approached the other officers, they stood and clapped.

'Well done, Steph!'

'Don't get too bossy, will ya!?'

She could feel her face redden as she made her way back to her desk. 'Thanks, guys, I'll try to be gentle with you.'

The officers came to her to shake her hand. However, she did feel that a couple of smiles appeared forced.

At the end of the shift, they called in at the local hotel for a few drinks to celebrate. Not being a big drinker, Frampton had just a couple of wines before saying her goodbyes and heading back to her unit that was in what might be called a more upmarket part of town.

The unit had been bought for her by her parents who had not been particularly happy over her decision to become a police officer, and had said that, although she would be dealing with the lower classes, she could at least live in a respectable neighbourhood.

Stephanie had stated her wish to be a policewoman at the age of fourteen. At the time, she was very near the top of her class at the private school she attended. Her parents—Ronald, a respected orthopaedic surgeon, and Jacqueline, a highly regarded figure in consumer rights—had naturally assumed this to be a ridiculous teenage fantasy, as they were absolutely assured she would follow in their footsteps either into medicine or law.

The family—Ronald, Jacqueline, Stephanie and her younger brother Matthew—lived in an exclusive gated community that was occupied by other well-to-do families. Her Aunt Carolyn and her two children had moved into the adjoining house following the unfortunate accidental death of her uncle.

Stephanie was an outgoing, friendly young girl, and made many good friends at the private school she attended.

On finishing high school, the next step was of course to attend university to fulfil her parents' dream. Neither her parents, nor her friends found it easy to come to terms with her determined desire to forego university and join the police force.

Despite all the negativity presented to her, at the age of nineteen after allowing a year to pass at her parents' request to enable her to more easily see the error she would make if not proceeding with a career more worthy of her status, Stephanie enlisted in the police force.

She threw herself wholeheartedly into the introductory course, passed all examinations with flying colours, and was subsequently placed at an inner city station where her enthusiasm, and work ethic, were recognised and appreciated by her peers and superiors alike.

After a nominal period, she applied to become a detective, and once again achieved the position with ease.

Her parents had at last come to accept her decision to join the police, particularly now she had started to climb the ladder. They had no doubt that the position of Police Commissioner would soon be well in her grasp.

Because of her success, her younger brother Matthew had also stated an interest in policing. However, just because Stephanie was doing okay, Mum and Dad certainly didn't see that as a valid argument for another member of the family to take the same course.

Since becoming a detective, Stephanie had decided to take a deeper look at what had been reported as a tragic accident that claimed her uncle's life. Somehow the idea of him falling from a worksite didn't quite fit with how she remembered him as a fit and careful person. After all, he had been involved in erecting tall buildings for years, and some of the people who had worked with him described him as extremely safety conscious. To date, the only thing that had arisen was a slight conflict with the Builders Workers Union. Her involvement in current cases made it impossible to devote any great length of time in following the matter up.

Chapter 3

Frampton was going over a recent crime report on drug-related offences when her desk phone rang. She picked it up. 'Frampton.' She had still not quite come to terms with saying Sergeant Frampton.

It was the front desk. 'Got a couple of young ladies here who would like to speak to a female officer, Sergeant Steph.'

'Be right out,' she replied with a smile. The man on the front desk was Bill Copeland who had twenty-five years up, and was always friendly, especially to Stephanie. Up until a few years ago, Bill had been on regular duty among the public. Following a bout of depression after having to shoot a teenage lad who had already knifed two elderly shoppers and was threatening to knife another, he had been given desk duties.

'How can I help you?' asked Frampton when she approached the two young women standing by the front office desk.

They glanced at Bill Copeland who gave them a smile.

'Could we possibly have a talk to you in private?' asked one of the women.

Frampton had noticed their glance at Copeland. 'Certainly, please come with me.' She led them to a door a few metres past reception, opened it, and gestured for the women to enter.

The small room contained nothing but a desk and four chairs. Frampton could tell from the look on their faces that they were having difficulty dealing with the situation. Instead of sitting behind the desk, she arranged three chairs into a more intimate arrangement in front of it.

'Please take a seat.'

The women sat down. 'In your own time, tell me the problem.'

'I was raped!' one of the women blurted out.

The other women put an arm around her shoulder and nodded. 'A week ago in the Comfort Motel.'

Frampton stood up. 'Just a moment please.' She went around the desk, opened a drawer, took out a writing pad and pen and returned to her seat.

'I am so very sorry to hear that ... may I have your names, please?'

'I'm Shelly Carter, and this is my friend Penelope Gardener who was attacked.'

'And when exactly did this happen, Penny? Is it alright if I call you Penny?'

Penelope nodded.

'Last Friday night,' said Shelly.

'And can you tell me why has it taken you nearly a week to report it?'

'I just thought I would, you know, just get over it, but I can't,' said Penelope as tears started to run down her cheeks.

'You're very brave for coming in,' said Frampton, fully understanding how difficult it must be to relate to someone what had occurred, 'and we need to catch the person responsible before it happens to someone else.'

'Yes, we talked it over and that's why we're here.'

'I appreciate it won't be easy, but I need you to tell me exactly what happened and who it was that attacked you.'

'That's one of the problems,' said Penelope. 'You see, I just can't remember everything.'

'Then just do your best and we'll take it from there,' said Frampton.

After relating all she could remember, Penelope opened the front of her dress and displayed the red and black scab marks on her breasts.

Frampton stared with dismay. 'Oh my God, Penny, that must be painful!'

'It's not as bad as at first, thank goodness!'

Frampton stood up. 'Leave this with me, Penny. I can assure you I'll treat this with the utmost seriousness. I have your address, and I'll be in touch when I have something to report.'

After showing Penelope and Shelly out of the station, Frampton went to Inspector Hounslow. 'Boss, I have a rape that seems bloody nasty.'

'Recent?'

'Week ago.'

'Where?'

'Happened in a motel room.'

'Well, all chance of any forensics will be long gone by now … which motel?'

'Comfort.'

'Yeah, I know it, not the best in town, that's for sure.'

'I got a feeling the victim was drugged.'

'Date rape?'

'Not exactly, she can't remember most of what happened, but there was another woman involved.'

'Go back over last month's sex crime reports, see if you can find anything similar, and go out to the motel, won't hurt to have a word with them.'

'Right, boss, reckon I'll go to the motel now while it's all fresh in my mind.'

'Okay … take one of the guys with you.'

Stephanie left Hounslow's office and approached one of the other detectives. 'Sid, will you come with me, please?'

'No worries,' replied Sid Marsden, 'glad to get out for a while … what's up?'

'Got a probable rape to look into.'

A voice came from a nearby desk. 'Not another one complaining of getting what she asked for?'

Stephanie turned towards the voice. 'You're an arsehole, Digby.' She walked out with Marsden close behind.

'She got you taped, boyo!' said Marsden to Digby as he went past.

Marsden was considered short for a policeman at 175 cm. But he was stocky and strong, as some offenders who had considered themselves to be something of hard men had found out to their cost. He was also an easy-going man with a likeable personality.

Digby, on the other hand, was 180 cm tall and slim of build. He wasn't one to back away from intimidation but would happily allow another to step into a fray in his stead. Accordingly, other officers didn't have a great deal of time for him.

Digby's attitude towards Frampton had been small-minded ever since she was upped to Sergeant. The relationship between them hadn't been particularly friendly from day one when she joined the squad. He had stated his belief that women detectives were not really up to the job, and when Frampton had stated her intention of going for Sergeant, he was quick to denounce the idea as unattainable.

When she did become Sergeant, it riled Digby even further as he had failed the promotion test some three months previous, and had to wait a further nine months before he could reapply. The only reason she had made it, he claimed, was because of her family "upper crust" background.

Now that Frampton was his superior, he was finding it even more difficult to be civil as he considered himself superior to all women.

Frampton and Marsden's visit to the motel provided no information of greater benefit than already supplied by Penelope and Shelly. The room had been occupied on four separate occasions since and, due to the cleaning process following each departure, all trace of a week prior was extinguished.

'So, it's back to the paperwork I guess, Sid,' said Frampton as they drove away from the motel.

'Can't wait!' replied Marsden with a roll of his eyes.

'Who you gonna vote for?' asked Frampton.

'Who ... what?' asked Marsden.

'The next election ... haven't you seen the placards plastered all over town?'

'Not really interested to be honest.'

'Come on, Sid ... Dyer or Maddox ... What are you labour or liberal?'

'Like I said, not interested. All politicians are only in it for the money if you ask me.'

'You sound a bit of a cynic, Sid.'

'Comes with the territory in this job, Steph.'

Chapter 4

Frampton and Marsden spent the next couple of days going over current and old files looking for anything that might correlate with Penelope's attack.

Midmorning on the third day, Inspector Hounslow opened his office door and went to Frampton at her desk. 'Had a call, Steph … girl found dead in a room at City Lights Motel, and she has burn marks on her chest.'

Frampton dropped the file she had been going through onto her desk. 'You mean similar to the girl at Comfort Motel?'

'Could be … better go look.'

'I'm on it, boss.' She grabbed her jacket from the back of her chair and called to Marsden, 'Sid, let's go, might have another one.'

On arrival at the City Lights Motel, several police cars had beaten them to it. "No go" tape was being set up and forensics were busy going through the room.

Frampton recognised a couple of the PCs. 'What you got, guys?'

'Hi, Steph … sorry, Sergeant,' said one with a friendly grin.

'And hello to you too, Elliot,' replied Frampton, returning the smile.

'Young girl, early twenties, naked on the bed, has what looks like burns on her breasts … nasty!'

'Who found her?' asked Marsden.

'Cleaner … it was past checkout time so knocked first, then when no reply, opened the door and went in … she's sitting in reception pretty shook up, as you can imagine.'

'How long before we can go in the room?'

'Forensics should be nearly done … just a minute, Steph.' The PC shouted into the doorway. 'Can a couple of Ds come in, Bob?'

'Gloves and boot covers on back seat,' came the reply from inside.

Suitably attired, Frampton and Marsden entered the motel room to be greeted by the forensic examiner. 'Hello, Steph, congratulations by the way,' said Bob Pemberton.

'Thanks, Bob, what can you tell me?' asked Frampton as she looked at the naked body on the bed.

'Name's Margaret Elder. Driving licence in that handbag.' He indicated the bag on the table by the bed. 'I'll need to do a more thorough examination back at the morgue before I'm sure, but I would say raped and asphyxiated.'

Marsden leant over the body. 'These burn marks, could they be from cigarettes?'

The examiner nodded. 'That's what I reckon.'

'Any butts been found?'

'Not that I'm aware of.'

'I had a young girl come into the station several days ago with similar burns, believed she'd been raped but couldn't remember much,' said Frampton.

'Drugged probably,' said Marsden.

'That would be gamma hydroxybutyrate, commonly known as GHB,' said Pemberton. 'I'll be able to confirm after I take a blood sample.'

'Thanks, Bob, soon as would be great,' said Frampton.

'Of course it would,' said Pemberton with a smile, 'as if I would make you wait, Steph.'

Frampton returned the smile. 'By the way, Bob, you remember my Uncle Andrew who fell off the high rise? You did the post mortem, didn't you?'

Pemberton nodded his head and sighed. 'Yes, you know I did, Steph … what's on your mind?'

'Oh, I just happened to be talking to a bloke who knew him

pretty well, and he said that for a safety conscious guy like Uncle Andrew, it was odd that he would make the mistake of going so close to the edge of a building that high, and I was wondering if you found anything unusual.'

'Accidents do happen, Steph, and I couldn't find anything untoward.'

'Okay, thanks, Bob ... just thought I'd ask.'

Frampton walked outside with Marsden close behind. 'Cigarette burns, eh! Good pick up, Sid.' She went to the PCs outside. 'Elliot, the girl may have been burnt with cigarettes, can you check around outside and nearby, and collect any butts you find? ... Might get some DNA.'

'Will do,' replied Elliot.

'So, what's the thing about your uncle, Steph?' asked Marsden as they made their way to the motel's reception.

'He fell off a high rise some ten years ago, and I reckon it smells a bit fishy.'

'Wow, ten years back will be hard to check up on.'

'Yeah I know; I'm scratching around in my spare time is all.'

'Well, if you want some help just yell.'

'Will do, thanks, Sid.'

Frampton and Marsden arrived at reception and talked to the cleaner and the receptionist.

The cleaner gave them no information of value as she had merely opened the motel room door, seen the body, screamed and rushed away.

The receptionist's story however confirmed the booking in of the girl to be the same as the previous one at the Comfort Motel.

'Not much doubt about it,' said Marsden as he and Frampton returned to their car, 'same MO.'

'Yes, but why kill the girl? That wasn't necessary if she'd been drugged as she wouldn't remember anything, just like Penny.'

'Well, at least we have the girl's name and address from

reception, so I guess ...'

Frampton sighed. 'Geez, I hate this, but it has to be done.'

They drove immediately to the girl's address from the driving licence and knocked at the door of the small weatherboard house. The front garden was neat and the lawn well-mown. A woman in her early fifties answered the door. 'Yes, can I help you?'

Frampton showed her police ID. 'Mrs Elder, I am Detective Frampton and this is Detective Marsden, may we please come in?'

Mrs Elder's hands went instantly to her face. 'Oh my God, what's happened?'

It was fifteen minutes later when Frampton and Marsden left Mrs Elder and returned to their car. They sat staring silently at the windscreen for several more minutes before Marsden spoke. 'So, the girl, I mean Margaret, was an asthmatic.'

Frampton nodded. 'That poor woman, her only child, and the husband died two years ago ... shit! ... Life can be bloody unfair.'

'Done many of these, Steph?'

'A few when I was in traffic ... sure doesn't get easier.' She started the car and eased away from the kerb.

'I don't reckon Margaret was deliberately killed, Sid. Since she was asthmatic she probably needed medication that the perps knew nothing about.'

'After knowing what was done to her, I find it hard to think of it as an accidental death, Steph. It's definitely a manslaughter charge.'

'Yeah, I hope the pathologist can give us some more answers.'

Chapter 5

The following morning, Frampton received a call from the pathologist. 'Blood test showed sample of GHB. It was probably slipped into her drink when she'd been distracted.'

'And that would have made her lose her memory?'

'Oh yes, GHB contains sedative and anaesthetic properties that leaves you with amnesia, impaired movement and speech, and of course it's impossible to taste in drinks.'

'According to the mother, her daughter was also asthmatic.'

'That also fits, Steph, her lungs were in a bad shape.'

'The GHB definitely ties in with the first victim's account,' said Frampton.

'Hope you get the person responsible before it happens again, Steph.'

'So do I, Bob.'

Frampton put down the phone as Marsden came to her desk. 'Definitely GHB, Sid.'

'And I just had a call from the lab, gotta hit on one of the cigarette butts collected from the ground outside the motel room,' said Marsden.

Frampton's face lit up. 'That's great, tell me!' she said with enthusiasm.

'Female by the name of Shirley Walker, and here's the really interesting part, her DNA was on record due to being done for soliciting and shoplifting a couple of years back.'

'Photo?'

'On my laptop.'

'Address?'

'Berkdale Street.'

Frampton hurried across to Marsden's desk. 'Print the photo, Sid, then we'll shoot out to the motels … you drive.'

The receptionists at Comfort and City Lights Motels both confirmed Shirley Walker as the woman that checked the girls in.

'Got an idea before we go check out Walker's address, Sid,' said Frampton.

'And that is?'

'Call into a few more motels and show the photo, see if they can remember Walker checking in with another woman who was under the weather.'

It didn't take long before recognition occurred, and going back through booking in details the names of a likely two more victims surfaced.

'Always the same; but the man, if there is one involved, is never seen,' said Frampton as they walked to their car.

'I'd lay odds on there being a bloke involved,' said Marsden, 'but he's being bloody careful to stay out of sight.'

'We now have the names of two more possibles, Angela Scott and Rebecca Ivans, and thanks to the last motels being more diligent with their check-in procedures, we have addresses too, so we'll go check them out and maybe learn something new,' said Frampton.

Chapter 6

Their first call was to Rebecca Ivans, but she made it clear in no uncertain terms that she had no interest whatsoever in taking the matter further.

'It's over and done and that's it!' was her reaction when she slammed her door shut in Frampton's face.

'So, on to the next one eh, Steph?' said Marsden.

Marsden knocked on the front door. It was opened by an elderly, grey-haired lady.

'Good afternoon, madam, I'm Detective Marsden.' He showed his ID and smiled. 'Can you tell me if Angela Scott lives here?'

The elderly lady squinted at the ID. 'Policeman?'

'That's right,' replied Marsden. He indicated towards Frampton. 'And this is Sergeant Frampton.'

'We'd just like to ask her a couple of questions if she's in,' said Frampton.

'You'd better come in then,' said the lady.

Frampton and Marsden followed the elderly lady into the house. The inside was not expensively furnished, but it was neat and clean.

'Would you be Angela's grandmother, Mrs Scott?' asked Frampton.

'Yes I am. Angela is staying with me for a holiday, but she hasn't been too well to get out and do much for a couple of weeks. I think she has a bit of that nasty flu that's going around.'

'I'm sorry to hear that,' said Frampton.

'I'll go and get her, she's having a lie down at the moment.'

Marsden whispered to Frampton as Mrs Scott departed. 'Flu

or something else?'

Frampton raised her eyebrows and nodded.

Mrs Scott returned with Angela close behind her. 'Here she is, Detectives, but she isn't feeling too well so please don't keep her too long.'

'We won't, Mrs Scott,' said Frampton as she looked at Angela and offered her hand with a smile. 'Hi, Angela, my name is Stephanie and this is Sid; as your grandmother's probably told you, we are detectives and we'd like to ask you a couple of questions about your stay at the Welcome Rest Motel.'

Angela's face dropped. 'I ... I ... I'm not sure if—'

Frampton interrupted her on seeing her anguish. 'Just a minute, Angela.' She turned to Mrs Scott. 'Do you think we could have a cup of tea Mrs Scott? Sid here will give you a hand ... won't you, Sid?'

Marsden instantly understood. 'Sure will! ... Come on, Gran, let's go put the kettle on, eh?' He put a friendly arm on Mrs Scott's shoulder and escorted her out of the front room and towards the kitchen.

Frampton smiled at Angela and pointed at the sofa. 'Shall we sit down, Angela?'

Angela slumped onto the sofa. 'I ... I can't talk about it,' she said in a whisper, her eyes moistening.

'I think we know what happened there, Angela, so I'm not going to press you about it.' She took the photograph that Marsden had taken off his computer from her jacket pocket and showed it to Angela. 'Do you know this woman?'

Angela shook her head. 'No, I don't think so ... why?'

'You didn't see her any time before you went to the motel?'

'All I can remember beforehand is having a milkshake because it was a hot afternoon and I'd been walking around the park.'

'And where was that?

'The little café just inside the park.'

'And you were on your own?'

'Yes ... there were others in the café, of course.'

'Can you remember anyone in particular?'

Angela thought for a moment. 'Well, there was a woman at the table beside me who dropped her handbag and I bent down and picked it up for her.'

'Dropped her handbag, eh, Angela?'

'Yes, she thanked me and ...' Angela stopped, reached across and grabbed the photograph from Frampton. She looked at Frampton. 'This is her, this is her, did she have something to do with what happened to me?' she asked anxiously.

Frampton nodded. 'Could be, Angela.'

'Oh my God!' She opened the front of her dress. 'This is what *she* did?' she asked.

Frampton saw the burn scars on Angela's breasts. 'And not just to you, Angela, there have been others.'

Angela's demeanour changed. 'The bitch!' she exclaimed angrily. 'And what about the bloke, there had to have been a bloke, have you got him?'

'We're working on it, Angela; we will get him, and when we do, will you be willing to tell your story to the judge?'

'Bet your life on it,' said Angela with absolute conviction.

Marsden and Mrs Scott came back into the room with a tray that Marsden was carrying.

'Oh thank you, Mrs Scott,' said Frampton as she stood up from the sofa. 'But unfortunately it's late and we really must be going.'

Angela also stood up and took the tray from Marsden. 'It's okay, Gran, I've had a good talk to Stephanie.'

Mrs Scott smiled. 'Thank you, Detective. I see Angela appears to have picked up, perhaps the flu is clearing up.' She gave Frampton a knowing look.

Frampton returned her smile. 'I certainly hope so, Mrs Scott.' She turned to Marsden. 'Come on, Sid, work to do.'

Mrs Scott and Angela stood by the front door and waved as

Frampton and Marsden drove away.

'Twenty-seven Berkdale Street, flat 4?' asked Marsden as he drove away from the Scotts' house.

'Too right, Sid. We definitely got enough to pull her in.'

'That's for sure! Shirley Walker is the woman involved, all we have to do is get her to tell us the man.'

Marsden brought the car to a halt outside the two-storey walk-up block of flats in Berkdale Street. There was rubbish strewn along the concrete pathway leading off the pavement to the doors.

'Very lugubrious!' said Marsden in disgust.

'Now, now, Sid.'

'How difficult is it just to put your rubbish in a bin?' said Marsden.

'One shouldn't judge,' said Frampton with a grimace as she stepped over a cardboard box containing a few empty beer bottles and food scraps and knocked on the door of number 4.

The door was opened by a middle-aged woman with a cigarette in one hand and a half-empty bottle of beer in the other, clad in jeans and a none to clean grey singlet. She looked at Frampton and Marsden. 'Oh jeez, cops.' She took a drag of her cigarette and blew smoke into Frampton's face. 'You can smell 'em.'

Marsden stepped forward and showed his ID. 'Shirley Walker, we'd like you to accompany us to the local police station to assist us in our inquiries.'

Walker laughed, stubbed out her cigarette on the door jam and flicked the butt at Marsden. 'Piss off!' she said as she stepped back and went to close the door.

Frampton reached forward, grabbed hold of Walker's left arm and twisted it behind her back. 'I'm arresting you with regard to the murder of Margaret Elder at the City Lights Motel.'

Walker dropped her beer bottle and struggled without success to break the hold Frampton had on her. 'You gotta be fuckin' jokin'!'

Marsden took a small plastic bag from his jacket pocket, bent down and picked up the butt that Walker had flicked at him. 'Very far from a joke, Walker, and thank you very much for this,' he said with a smile as he waved the bag in front of her.

Frampton pulled Walker away from the flat. Marsden closed the door and followed her back to the car. He opened the rear door and Frampton pushed Walker in.

'I'll drive, Sid ... you can sit in the back with Walker and make sure she behaves.'

Chapter 7

n the interview room, Frampton sat at the desk with Walker in front. Marsden leant against the wall behind Frampton. Frampton pushed a button on the recorder on the desk.

'I am Detective Sergeant Frampton, together with Detective Steven Marsden, and we are interviewing Shirley Walker. Miss Walker, we are here to ask your involvement in the rape and abuse of Penelope Gardiner and Angela Scott, and the murder of Margaret Elder. Would you please state your name for the record.'

'You know my name, idiot!'

'For the record please, miss.'

'Oh strewth, I'm Shirley Walker and this is all a fit up.'

'And what is it that you consider a fit up, Miss Walker?'

'This crap ... pullin' me in here.'

Frampton looked down at her notebook. 'Do you deny being at the Welcome Rest Motel on the night of the ninth?'

'Never been there.'

'Do you deny being at the City Lights Motel on the night of the twenty-third?'

'Never heard of the place.'

'Do you also deny being at the Comfort Motel on the night of the fourteenth?'

Walker put a hand to her chin, then scratched and shook her head. 'Can't place it.'

Frampton sat back in her chair and sighed. 'Is that so, Miss Walker? ... So, please tell me why the receptionists from each motel have a clear recollection of you being there.'

Walker shrugged her shoulders. 'Well, they've obviously mistaken me for somebody else, 'aven't they?'

Frampton pushed a piece of paper across the table. 'Do you remember when we first came in the officer on the front desk asked you to enter your name and the date into his diary so he had a record of comings and goings?'

'Yeah, so what?'

Frampton pushed another piece of paper across. 'This is a copy of the "in" register from City Lights.'

Walker looked at the paper. 'Yeah … so what … that's not my name.'

'It certainly isn't,' said Frampton as she pushed two more pieces of paper across.

'And my name isn't on them either … I said this was a fit up.'

'However, Miss Walker, our writing expert has confirmed that, although the three names are different, they are all signed by the same person and the handwriting is identical to that on the front desk's register you've just signed.'

Walker studied the papers. 'It's a trick, you got nothin'.'

Marsden stepped to the desk and placed the plastic bag with the cigarette butt in it in front of Walker. 'C'mon, Shirley, you're not that dumb, surely? We have three people who saw you at those motels, and on top of that'—he stabbed a finger at the plastic bag—'this butt that you threw at me I can guarantee will supply the same DNA as the butt we collected at the room of the City Lights Motel.'

Frampton and Marsden remained silent as Walker looked from the papers with her handwriting to the plastic bag. She bit her lower lip. 'I didn't murder her, for Christ's sake!' she blurted out.

'Didn't murder who, Shirley?' asked Frampton quietly.

'That one at City Lights,' replied Walker with a shake of her head.

'What happened, Shirley?'

'Silly bitch stopped breathing.'

'So, you did what?'

'We cleared off.'

'We?' said Frampton.

Walker put her hand to her mouth.

'We know the girls were raped, Shirley, so who was the man?'

Walker remained silent.

'Do you want to be responsible for all that happened and be charged accordingly, or perhaps make things easier for yourself by giving us a name?'

Walker looked up at the ceiling and sighed. 'Shit! … Alright, alright, it was Mick Ansell.'

'And where can we find him, Shirley?' asked Frampton.

'He's working on the new high rise opposite the station.'

'And his home address is?'

'Where you picked me up, we live together; should be home by five.'

'What does he drive, Shirley?'

'Brown ute.'

'Thank you, Shirley; now just one more question. Why did you burn the girls' breasts with your cigarette?'

'Wanted to see if they were really, you know, out to it,' she replied with a wave of a hand as if it was a natural thing to do.

'But why then keep on doing it?' asked Marsden.

Walker shrugged her shoulders. 'I dunno … it wasn't hurtin' 'em, was it?'

Marsden stood back and shook his head at the callous disregard Walker felt for what she had inflicted.

Frampton turned off the recorder. 'I'll get this interview typed up, Miss Walker, and then you can read through it and sign it.' She stood up and turned to Marsden. 'Take her to the cells, will you, Sid; I'll go see the boss about picking up Ansell.'

Chapter 8

The decision was made to arrest Ansell at the flat rather than at his place of work due to the logistics of the high-rise site. At the high-rise it would require a considerable force to contain the site and possible exits, whereas a small contingent of officers would only be needed at the flat.

Frampton, with Marsden in the front passenger seat and two officers in the back, parked their car a hundred metres up the street where they could keep an eye on the front of the flats. A vehicle containing four other officers was parked out of sight a further street away.

Marsden picked up the two-way as a brown utility stopped outside the flats. He watched as the driver got out and walked to flat number 4, took out a key, unlocked the front door and went in, closing the door behind him. 'Go, go, go!' he said as Frampton started the car and sped to the flats.

Frampton and Marsden stood close behind the two officers as one knocked on the door. 'Police officers, Mr Ansell,' he shouted, 'please open the door.'

After a moment with no reply, the officer was about to force his way in, when a shout came from the back of the flats. 'Round here, Sarge!'

A few seconds later, a handcuffed Ansell was escorted to the front of the flats.

'You can do the honours if you like, Sid,' said Frampton.

'I would indeed, Sarg ... Michael Ansell, you are being arrested for the rape of Penelope Gardiner and Angela Scott, and the rape and murder of Margaret Elder. You are not obliged to say anything, but anything you do say will be taken down and may be used in evidence against you.'

Ansell grinned. 'Bullshit, this is bullshit!'

'Take him to the station please, guys,' said Frampton to the officers holding him, 'I'll see you back there.'

In the same room that Shirley Walker had been interviewed, it was now Ansell that sat facing Frampton. As Ansell was a large man, it was considered prudent to maintain the cuffs on him.

'Mr Ansell, I have to advise you that this interview is being recorded.'

Frampton went over, as she had with Walker, the details of what had occurred to the three women, and Ansell in each instance denied any knowledge.

Ansell looked at Frampton, yawned and grinned. 'Have you finished? 'Cause I've had a hard day at work and want to go home and have a shower and beer.'

'Would it help your memory if I told you that we have a woman in custody who has stated that she was complicit with you in these rapes?'

Ansell's grin disappeared. 'Whoever it is, she's a liar!'

'Now, that's not a nice thing to call your girlfriend,' said Marsden.

Ansell stared at Marsden and back at Frampton but said nothing.

'Oh, and by the way,' said Marsden, 'the DNA from the sperm found inside the girls will confirm without doubt the person responsible.'

Ansell threw his head back and laughed. 'Well, now I know you got fuck all 'cause I wore a condom each time.'

Marsden looked at Frampton and smiled. 'He wore a condom, Sarg.'

They both looked at Ansell and continued to smile. Ansell's grin slowly faded from his face as realisation of what he had just said hit him.

'Mr Ansell, is there anything you would like to tell us, in particular concerning the death of Margaret Elder, before we finish this interview?' said Frampton.

Ansell's shoulders drooped and he remained silent.

Frampton waited a couple of minutes before speaking. 'Mr Ansell?'

'She just stopped breathing,' he said quietly with a shake of his head. 'I was ... you know ... and she just stopped breathing.'

'She just stopped breathing, and then you did what?' asked Marsden.

'We pissed off ... nothing else we could do.'

'You rape, abuse and burn Margaret, and when she stops breathing you shoot through. Maybe if you'd called an ambulance she could have been revived, you useless piece of shit!' said Marsden angrily.

Frampton raised a hand at Marsden as Ansell slumped further down into his chair.

'This interview will be typed up and you will be required to read and sign it, do you understand, Mr Ansell?'

Ansell nodded.

'Take him, Sid.'

Ansell looked up. 'Wait a minute, I didn't murder the girl, she just stopped breathing.'

'Take him away, Sid,' repeated Frampton with a wave of her hand as she stood up.

'No, wait a minute, what if I can give you a real murderer, will that help me?'

Marsden dragged at Ansell's shoulder. 'Come on ... you arseholes will try anything.'

'No, look, that developer bloke who they reckon fell off a building ten years ago, I know who pushed him.'

'Hold it, Sid!' said Frampton. Marsden stopped and looked at Frampton whose face had suddenly paled.

'Are you referring to Andrew Mills?' asked Frampton quietly.

'Yeah, that's the one,' said Ansell.

'I'll have a word with my superior and see what he has to say … take him away, Sid.'

Frampton sat back down heavily onto her chair as Marsden took Ansell from the room.

Marsden returned to the interview room ten minutes later to find Frampton still sitting in her chair staring blankly at the wall. She didn't react to his presence. 'Steph, was Andrew Mills the person I think he was?' he asked.

Frampton took a moment to respond. 'Andrew Mills was my uncle.'

Chapter 9

abor member of Parliament Roger Dyer was busy answering questions from the accompanying media pack as he walked around the shopping centre. He had a reputation for belittling his opponents in the political arena, and for demanding better conditions for those in the building industry. At thirty-eight years of age, just under two metres tall, a full head of hair with a hint of grey, he also had a reputation as a bit of a ladies' man.

Among those asking questions was a female reporter from the local weekly newspaper. 'Could you tell me if you will be supporting the opposition's suggestion to bring in workers from overseas, Mr Dyer?'

Dyer stopped in his tracks and stared at the reporter. 'You must be joking! It's jobs for Aussies full stop! You obviously don't know me very well to ask such an inane question as that.'

'Perhaps I should get to know you better, Mr Dyer,' she said.

'Perhaps you should,' replied Dyer.

The reporter handed Dyer a card and turned away. Dyer watched the sway of the reporter's rear as she walked off, then placed Laura Taylor's card in his pocket.

It was three days later, in the early evening, when Laura answered the knock at the door to her eighth-floor high rise apartment. She smiled at the man standing there. 'Mr Dyer, won't you please come in?'

Dyer returned the smile and walked into the unit and looked around. 'Hmm, nice place you have here; must be good money in the newspaper business.'

'Not really,' replied Laura, 'my parents help me out.'

Dyer proffered a bottle of wine he had brought with him. 'Hope you like this stuff. Are you a red or white woman, Laura?'

Laura collected two glasses from the kitchen. 'Oh, I have no preference, Mr Dyer.'

Dyer accepted the glasses, 'Please, call me Roger.' He poured the wine and offered one of the glasses to Laura. 'After all, I am here so you can get to know me better.' He smiled and deposited the bottle on the kitchen bench.

Laura took a sip of the wine and ran her tongue over her lips. 'So true, Roger.' She sat down on the couch and patted the position beside her.

Roger sat down. 'So, what would you like to know, Laura?'

'Well … how did you get into politics for a start?'

'Natural progression, Laura. I was involved in the union movement from the time I started work until about ten years ago when a few colleagues suggested I try out for the Labor party.'

'And here you are now with the possibility of a position in the cabinet.'

'Oh, that's just wild speculation,' said Dyer with a wave of his hand. 'But what about you, what's your background?'

'Nothing dramatic I'm afraid: went to uni, did an arts course, got a job at the paper running errands to start with, then got a chance to be a reporter and here I am now.'

Dyer reached out and took Laura's glass. 'Time for a refill.'

He walked to the kitchen, poured more wine and returned to Laura. He raised his glass. 'Here's to you, Laura.'

Laura was about to drink then stopped. 'Oh dear, sorry, but I need to … you know.' She stood up and went past the kitchen and into the bathroom.

'Phew, that's better,' she said with a grin as she returned and sat back down on the couch. She raised her half-empty glass. 'And this stuff has one hell of a kick, Roger.'

Dyer returned the grin. 'Oh, Laura, you don't know the half of it.'

Laura sighed and shook her head. 'God, I feel weird.'

Dyer took out his mobile and punched in a number. 'Yeah … come on up.'

'Now, miss reporter, what was it in particular you wanted to ask about?'

Laura made a mumbling sound, dropped her glass and collapsed back into the couch.

There was a knock at the door. 'Come in!' said Dyer.

A man entered and closed the door behind him. He walked up to the couch and looked down at Laura. 'Good stuff that GHB, eh?' he said.

'Bloody oath!' replied Dyer. He took a small bottle out of his pocket and showed it to the man. 'This stuff you gave me really does the job, thanks a lot, I owe you.'

'No worries, pal,' said Marsden, 'when I found out what Frampton intended doing I reckoned having you on my side will do me more good than being on hers.'

'You can bet on that,' said Dyer.

'Yeah, the past is just that, the past,' said Marsden.

'Yeah … her uncle was a bloody fool.'

'Andrew Mills, wasn't it?'

'Yeah, that's him. If the silly bugger had coughed up the twenty grand we'd asked for he'd still be here.'

'Is that all you'd asked for?'

'Yeah … that was to avoid union trouble on the site, but no … he had his principles so he said.'

'And he fell?'

Dyer laughed. 'Yeah fell, mind you, I did give him a punch in the face when he refused to pay up.' He laughed again. 'Shit, he was a mess when he hit the ground, served the silly bugger right.'

Marsden pointed at Frampton. 'What'll we do with her?'

'Well, she was going to try and screw me, so I reckon I'll screw her.' He took off his jacket and unbuckled his trousers. 'You want a piece after me?'

Marsden shook his head and looked at the woman on the couch. 'I reckon that might just about do it, what do you reckon, Sarg?'

Frampton sat up. 'Sure do, Sid.'

Dyer looked perplexed at Frampton and then back at Marsden. 'You said that ... and she!'

Marsden took out a pair of handcuffs, turned Dyer around, pulled his arms back and cuffed him. 'All yours, Steph.'

Frampton stood up, reached behind the couch and held up a recorder. She put her face close to Dyer. 'Roger Dyer, I am arresting you in regard to the murder of Andrew Mills, you don't have to say anything, but anything you do say will be taken down and may be used in evidence against you.'

Back in the station Frampton and Marsden finished booking in Dyer and were confronted by Inspector Hounslow. 'Great results you two, now all you have to do is the paperwork.'

'Thanks, boss, can hardly wait,' said Marsden.

'Yeah, always a thrill!' said Frampton.

'Well, you better get on with it,' said Hounslow with a grin.

As Frampton and Marsden returned to their desks, Digby walked past. He had heard of Frampton coming on to Dyer in order to trick him into revealing his actions. 'Suppose you'd have gone all the way to get a result ... typical!' he said with a snort of derision.

Marsden started towards Digby, his face showing his anger. 'Digby, you're a—'

Frampton pushed in front of Marsden, and placed a hand on his chest. 'Let it go, Sid, he's not worth it.'

It was late evening by the time Frampton finished her paperwork. Exhausted from the long day, she was about to get into her car in the station carpark when Digby walked up to her. 'Great job!' he said with a sneer.

Frampton took a step towards him and kneed him with as much power as she could muster between his legs.

Digby let out a deep groan and fell to the ground clutching his genitals.

'Next time you speak to me, you arsehole, don't forget to add "Sergeant".' She opened her car door and got in.

Before driving off, she wound down her side window and looked at Digby writhing on the ground in a pool of vomit. 'Yes, it was a great job, Digby, and thank you for the perfect end to a great day.'

Nolan

BOOK 6: JUSTIFICATION

Chapter 1

t was one o'clock in the morning.

In the semi-darkness, under a small footbridge, a homeless man lay sleeping. A grubby blanket was wrapped around him.

A kick against the man's leg woke him.

'Do you like banana?' the kicker asked.

The homeless man looked up, but in the semi-darkness was unable to make out the person before him. 'Sure,' he mumbled. He extended his right arm to receive the banana and the blanket fell to his side.

'I'll peel it for you,' the kicker said. A gloved hand passed a piece of banana.

'Thanks,' said the homeless man before placing it in his mouth.

'Taste okay?' the kicker asked.

The man nodded as he chewed and swallowed.

The kicker glanced to both sides. They were alone.

'I'll adjust your blanket for you,' said the kicker. As he reached down and lifted the grubby blanket, his right arm thrust forward.

The homeless man's eyes widened. Blood and half-chewed banana spilled from his mouth. Without a sound, he slumped to one side.

The kicker withdrew his arm then reached for the man's left hand. He cut off the tip of the small finger with the knife he held. He wiped the knife on the blanket before wrapping it back over the body.

With a small stick, he drew a fish in the nearby dirt.

He stood silently staring down at the man for a moment before quietly walking away.

Chapter 2

'How about we all go to the park?' asked Jeff Nolan, casually dressed in shorts and T-shirt, who was enjoying a day at home with his wife Katherine and children Samuel, aged seven, and Lucy, aged four.

'Yeah,' shouted Samuel and Lucy together while jumping about in joy.

'Okay you two,' said Katherine, 'put your runners on and we'll be off.'

Laughing and clapping their hands, the children raced to their bedrooms.

Katherine turned to Jeff and gave him a hug and a kiss. 'So good to have time together, isn't it, my love?'

Jeff was quick to return the kiss and held Katherine close. 'Sure is,' he replied. 'I'll go get a ball and the frisbee and we'll be off.'

Jeff had taken two steps when his mobile that was lying on the kitchen table rang. His shoulders slumped as he turned and looked back at Katherine before picking it up. 'What's up?' he asked.

He listened to the reply before saying, 'Where?'

Katherine's face displayed her disappointment. This wasn't the first time Jeff had received a call that had initiated the succinct reply of "where?".

Detective Inspector Jeff Nolan came back to Katherine and hugged her again. 'Sorry, love,' he whispered in her ear. 'Sounds like a bad one.'

Katherine forced a smile and pushed him away. 'They all are, Jeff. Off you go. I'll take the kids to the park.'

Samuel and Lucy raced back after putting on their trainers.

'We're ready?' said Samuel enthusiastically.

Nolan leant down and gave them both a cuddle. 'Sorry, guys, I have to go to work, but Mum will still take you to the park.'

'Oh, Dad,' whimpered Samuel, 'I want you to come too.'

'So do I,' said Lucy as tears began to flow down her cheeks.

Nolan sorrowfully looked at Katherine before, with effort, putting a big smile on his face. 'Come on, you two, you'll have a great time with Mum and you can tell me all about it when I get back, okay?'

Katherine wiped Lucy's face then bounced the large ball she was holding. 'Dad's right, we'll have a great time and maybe even get an ice cream, so come on, let's jump in the car and we'll be off.'

She went to the pantry, took a set of car keys from the hook attached inside the door and walked to the front door with the children just behind her. As they walked out, Samuel turned and gave Nolan a frosty look. Nolan shook his head and mouthed, *sorry*.

He went into the bedroom, took off his shorts and T-shirt and changed into suit and tie. Collected another set of keys from inside the pantry, and, after locking the front door behind him, headed to the white Ford parked in the driveway and drove off.

Jeff Nolan, aged thirty-two, just on 180 cm tall and weighing in at ninety kilos, had been promoted to inspector at the early age of twenty-nine. His promotion had been rapid after joining the police force at the age of eighteen. His father had been a police sergeant, but unluckily lost his life when mowed down by a teenager in a stolen car when Jeff was only thirteen. It was an event that made Jeff determined to join the police force and follow in his father's footsteps in an effort to put a stop to all forms of criminality.

After joining the force as a constable, he studied hard and passed the sergeant's exams at age twenty-two. At twenty-four, he was transferred to the detective division and made inspector after another five years.

Chapter 3

The area surrounding the footbridge had already been taped off by uniformed police when Nolan arrived at nine-thirty. The bridge, in a small park of about two hectares, had once been a means of walking over a large pond that contained carp and water lilies. Over the years, the pond had fallen into neglect. The carp had died and most of the water filled with weeds. The local council pumped out what water remained in the pond, filled it with soil and then mowed the grass that grew. The bridge now existed as merely a play area for young children.

Nolan approached the three men standing around the body under the bridge. 'What have we got, guys?' he asked.

Sergeant Stan Webber replied, 'Male, by the look of him, homeless and living rough, aged about forty, stab wound through the chest and into the heart. I'm guessing death would have been instantaneous. That right, Doc?'

Doctor Wayne Griffiths, the local pathologist, nodded his head. 'Can't see anything different at the moment, Jeff, but when we get him back to the morgue I'll be able to give him a more thorough going over.'

'How long ago, Wayne?' asked Nolan.

'Rough guess at the moment, around eight hours. Come see me mid-afternoon and I might be able to confirm my guess.'

'Thanks, Wayne.'

The pathologist lifted the man's right arm and pointed at the hand. 'This might interest you, Jeff.'

Both Nolan and Webber leant forward. 'Oh shit, shit, shit!'

exclaimed Nolan. 'The killer has taken a trophy. You know what that means, this is just the start.'

Wayne placed the arm back down and nodded. 'Reckon you could be right, Jeff.'

Nolan took a few deep breaths in an effort to compose himself. He looked around the area. 'Seen anything odd around the place, Stan?'

Webber pointed to an area of dirt close to the body. 'Looks like the shape of a fish has been scratched in the dirt on the other side of the body.'

Nolan walked around. 'Mmm ...' he knelt down and looked closer. 'There's a shoe print near it ... get photos and a plaster mould of the shoe print, it might give us an idea of the foot size of the wearer. Who found him, Stan?'

'Young fella out walking his dog. He rushed home and told his folks and they rang us.' He referred to his notebook. 'Name of Driscoll, they live close by, number 37 Montpelier Close.'

Nolan turned to the uniformed police. 'Guys, will you walk around the area for about fifty metres or so and see if you can find anything odd lying on the ground?'

He turned away from the scene. 'Come on, Stan, we'll go talk to the young fella and knock on a few doors nearby.'

Sergeant Stan Webber, aged twenty-six but looking much younger, had been Nolan's offsider for three years. Whereas Nolan was tall and well-built, Webber was merely one hundred and fifty-five centimetres tall and slim in appearance. He spent a lot of his spare time in the local gymnasium and was proficient in all forms of martial arts. On several occasions, large male criminals had learnt to their cost that size wasn't everything.

Chapter 4

The Driscoll residence was across the road from the park in the suburb of Chumleigh. Mrs Driscoll answered the knock on her front door and invited Nolan and Webber inside after they had displayed their police identification.

'It was your son who found the man, wasn't it, Mrs Driscoll?' asked Nolan.

'Yes, he was out walking the dog,' she replied.

'Could we have a few words with him, please?'

'He's a bit upset, Inspector,'

'We understand, Mrs Driscoll, and we promise to not upset him further.'

'Okay, he's in his bedroom. I'll go get him.'

She returned with the boy. 'These are the two policemen I told you about, Brad, and they'd like to ask you a few questions about this morning.'

Nolan offered his hand. 'I'm Inspector Nolan and this is Sergeant Webber, but you can call us Jeff and Stan, Brad.'

Brad accepted Nolan's hand and they had a brief shake.

'How old are you, Brad?' asked Nolan.

'Eleven,' he replied.

'And you take the dog for a walk every morning, do you?'

Brad nodded. 'Most mornings, but not if it's raining.'

'So, this morning, what exactly happened, Brad?'

'He was running along in front of me then he stopped and barked.'

'And you went in under the bridge to see what he was barking at, that right?'

Brad nodded and looked up at his mother. 'The man wasn't moving and had blood on him, Mum.'

Mrs Driscoll put an arm around Brad and held him close.

'Did you see anyone else?' asked Nolan.

'No, I told Sniffer to come away, and we ran home and told Mum.'

'That's when I rang you,' said Mrs Driscoll. 'Do you need to ask Brad anything else?'

Nolan shook his head. 'No, I don't think so.'

He looked at Brad and gave him a smile. 'Thank you, Brad, you've been terrific.' He turned towards Mrs Driscoll. 'And thank you, Mrs Driscoll. Your quick phone call will help us get on top of things.'

'This is a quiet neighbourhood, Inspector. The only people we tend to see are the ones who live here.'

'Sometimes a runner comes past,' said Brad.

'Runner, Brad?' said Nolan.

'Yes, probably keeping fit for football or something.'

'Do you remember when one went by last?'

Brad looked at his Mum. 'A few days ago, wasn't it, Mum?'

'Yes it was. Looked a very fit young man,' said Mrs Driscoll.

'Do either of you remember what he was wearing?' asked Webber.

Mrs Driscoll shook her head. 'Not really. Shorts and a T-shirt I suppose.' She looked at her son. 'Do you remember, Brad?'

Brad scratched his head. 'I think his shirt was white with something blue written on the back.'

Nolan turned to Webber who had been scribbling in his notebook. Webber nodded.

'Well, thanks again, Mrs Driscoll, and you, Brad. We'll be off now.'

Nolan and Webber both gave a wave as they walked back to their vehicle.

'What do you reckon, Stan?' asked Nolan.

Webber shrugged. 'There's all sorts of sport played around here so I'm not surprised at a young guy running to keep fit. But then again, who knows. Somebody checking the place out, do you reckon?'

Nolan spread his arms. 'As you say, who knows. We'll go back to the station, write up notes on what we've seen and heard.' He punched at the air. 'It's this cutting off the finger that has me most concerned. We better get to the morgue first and see if Wayne has come up with anything new.'

'Afternoon gentlemen,' remarked the pathologist as Webber and Nolan entered the morgue. 'Not a lot to report, I'm afraid. Definitely a stab to the chest did the job. Knife blade of approximately fifteen centimetres long and one centimetre wide. Entered the chest between the third and fourth rib directly into the centre of the heart.'

'No other wounds?' asked Nolan.

'Apart from the piece taken off the end of the little finger, no.'

'And nothing in his pockets?' asked Webber.

Wayne shook his head. 'Sorry, guys, not much help, I'm afraid.'

'Can you take a photo of his face please, Wayne? And we'll call in on all the welfare places tomorrow to see if he's recognised, try to get a name.'

'Already done, Jeff.' He reached to the table beside him, picked up a couple of photos and handed them to Jeff.'

Nolan smiled. 'Thanks, Wayne. You're ahead of us as usual.'

Chapter 5

Nolan took off his shoes before entering his home, not wanting to wake the children or Katherine. All was quiet. He went to Samuel and Lucy's rooms and peeped in. They were fast asleep. As he entered his bedroom, he found Katherine sitting up in bed reading.

'Long day, Jeff?' she asked.

He went to the bed, leant forward and gave her a kiss. 'I'll have a quick shower,' he replied as he headed for the en-suite bathroom.

A few minutes later, he returned and got into bed beside Katherine.

Katherine placed the book she had been reading on the bedside table and cuddled up to him.

'Yeah ... long day, Kath, and I reckon there's going to be more.'

'Want to talk about it?'

Nolan proceeded to give Katherine a brief run-down on the day's events, including the taking of the finger.

'I think you're right about the killer being a trophy taker.'

'Yes ... that's what's been going over in my mind.'

Katherine kissed him on the neck and ran a hand over his thigh. 'Maybe I can help you take it all off your mind for a little while, my love.'

Nolan gave a low moan as Katherine moved over him. 'Now, why didn't I think of that,' he said with a smile. 'But remember, I have to get up early tomorrow to get to work, so please be gentle with me.'

Jeff and Katherine had been together for ten years. They had met when Katherine was employed as a nurse in the local hospital and

Jeff had just been made a sergeant. Jeff had come to the hospital to speak to a severely injured shopkeeper who had been attacked by two thieves attempting to steal from his store.

Katherine happened to be the nurse on duty at the time, and Jeff had taken an instant liking to her. The following day he returned to the hospital and seeing Katherine again asked for a date. Romance blossomed and they were married two years later.

When Samuel was born Katherine stopped working until he began pre-school and then returned to nursing on a part-time basis. She always made sure she was finished at a reasonable time of the day in order to collect Samuel. The birth of Lucy also stopped her nursing for a few years. Now, with both children at full-time schooling, she was able to return part-time to the job she loved.

Chapter 6

The following morning at 9 am, Nolan and Webber set off from their station to call on various charities to see if any of the workers could recognise the murdered homeless man from the photo they presented.

'Oh yes, I've seen him,' said Marjorie, one of the helpers. 'He's been in a few times when we have put on meals. Quiet fellow, but always appreciative of what he's given.'

'You wouldn't know his name by any chance?' asked Nolan.

'No, sorry,' replied Marjorie with a shake of her head. 'Hang on a minute though, I'll nip out to the kitchen and see if any of the others know him. Can I take the photo?'

'By all means,' said Nolan as he handed over the photo.

In less than a minute, Marjorie returned with another lady beside her. 'This is Sylvia and she thinks she knows him,' she said.

Sylvia nodded her head. 'Yes, I've spoken to him a few times. Said he was called Graham.'

'Anything else, Sylvia?' asked Nolan. 'Surname, or where he came from, for instance?'

Sylvia shook her head. 'Don't know his surname I'm afraid. Not many of them tell us that, but I can remember asking where he came from, and he laughed and said the posh end of town. Yes, that's what he said, the posh end of town.'

Nolan reached out and took back the photo. 'Thanks a lot, Sylvia. That could be a great help.'

Marjorie and Sylvia stood silently looking at Nolan and Webber.

'Ah,' said Nolan with a smile. 'You are wondering why we want to know about him.'

'Naturally,' said Marjorie.

'It's bad news I'm afraid. He was found murdered in the park yesterday, and we would like to be able to find and notify his family, if he has any.'

Marjorie and Sylvia both took in a breath and placed a hand to their faces.

'Oh, that's terrible,' said Sylvia. 'Like I mentioned, he seemed a nice fellow.'

Webber, who had been standing back and taking notes, took a step forward. 'I don't suppose you've heard of any of the others who come here having trouble such as anyone calling them names or even beating them up?'

Marjorie and Sylvia looked at each other for a moment.

'I'm afraid that sort of thing happens quite a lot,' said Marjorie.

Sylvia nodded her head. 'Yes, it's mainly the teenagers who do it. They tend to think it's funny somehow. Very sad really, but what can you do when some of the parents don't seem to care what their kids get up to.'

A few moments silence followed as they all considered Sylvia's remarks.

Nolan broke the silence. 'Well, thanks again, ladies, we'll be off now and do our best to get it all sorted.'

'Good luck,' said Marjorie and Sylvia with a wave as Nolan and Webber departed.

'The posh end of town,' said Webber as they got in their car. 'Where do you reckon?'

'How about that new area around the beachfront? Most of those houses are around the million dollar plus mark and it's a gated community.'

'Good a place as any to start,' replied Nolan as he started the car.

Chapter 7

Nolan brought the car to a stop at the entrance to Fairshore Villas.

A man was using an edge trimmer to tidy the grass against the ten metres of brick wall that abutted the entry. A fence of cream Colorbond continued the enclosure of the estate.

The man noticed the car, turned off his trimmer and came to the car as Nolan wound down his side window. 'Can I help you, sir?' he politely asked.

Nolan presented his police identification. 'We're Detective Inspector Jeff Nolan and Sergeant Stan Webber. And you are?'

'Bruce Ferguson,' he replied.

'Had this job long, Bruce?'

The man nodded. 'Ever since it first opened three years back. I do most of the general maintenance.'

Nolan held up the photo of the face of the dead man. 'We're trying to locate the family of this man; do you know him?'

Edwards stared at the photo for a moment. He scratched his cheek. 'I'm not a hundred per cent sure, but it could be Mrs Saunders's ex-husband. If it is, he looks pretty rough compared to what he used to be.'

'And his Christian name?' asked Nolan.

Edwards scratched his face again. 'Germain, or something like that.'

'Maybe Graham?' said Nolan.

Edwards face brightened. 'Yeah, that's it. Graham.'

Nolan pointed at the code box on the pole beside the gateway.

'What's the code please, Bruce, and the number of Mrs Saunders's villa?'

Edwards recited the entrance code and gave Nolan directions on the best way to find villa 87.

The villas were all freestanding, painted white and very similar in appearance. Each were two-stors with double garages and a small garden bed in the front.

From the look on his face, Webber was not impressed. 'These things all look the same,' he said. 'There's no real character about the place. Why anyone would want to spend a million or more to live here is beyond me.'

'Guess it's for the safety of being fenced in, in order to keep the non-descripts out, and maybe because you're among similar so-called financially well-off and possibly socially upmarket neighbours,' said Nolan. 'When you win the lotto you'll be in here like a shot.'

'No way, mate. I'll be off to a small seaside village up north,' replied Webber with a laugh. 'And from what I know about you, you'd do the same ... and there it is, number 87.'

Mrs Saunders came to the door a few moments after Nolan had pressed the doorbell. She looked at Nolan and Webber through the wire-screened outer door. 'Yes, who are you and what do you want?' she said abruptly.

Nolan showed his police identification. 'I'm Detective Inspector Jeff Nolan and this is Sergeant Stan Webber. May we come in please, Mrs Saunders?'

Mrs Saunders gave a wave of her hand. 'And why should I let you into my home?' she added dismissively.

'It concerns your husband Graham, Mrs Saunders. I think it better if we talked inside.'

'He's not my husband, we are divorced,' she stated firmly.

Nolan proffered the photo. 'Can you then confirm that this person is Graham Saunders?'

'Yes, that's him ... miserable sod.'

'I have to tell you that he is dead, Mrs Saunders.'

Mrs Saunders grinned. 'Is he really? Well, what do you know. The drunken bastard has gone where he deserves at last, to hell.'

'Actually, he was murdered, Mrs Saunders. Are you aware of any enemies he might have?'

Mrs Saunders gave a chuckle. 'Apart from me and my son Gerald, and the accountant's office that sacked him, who knows ... murdered, eh?' She chuckled again and closed the door with a slam.

Webber looked up at Nolan. 'What a lovely lady,' he remarked with a smile as they walked back to the car.

Nolan shook his head. 'No wonder the poor bugger took up drinking. How about we ask the neighbours what they thought of him?'

They were walking towards the neighbour's door when it opened and a man looked out. 'Saw you go next door. Police, aren't you? Anything I can help you with?'

Nolan nodded and produced his ID. 'Detectives Nolan and Webber. We're trying to find info on Graham Saunders.'

'You better come in,' said the man. 'Name's Perry Craigburn.' He directed them to a lounge area and asked them to sit. 'So, what's the poor bugger been up to?'

'I'm afraid he's dead, Perry, murdered, actually,' said Nolan.

'Oh shit!' exclaimed Perry.

'We thought he was married to Mrs Saunders next door, but she advised they were divorced.'

'Yeah, well, that wasn't much of a surprise. She's not what you might call the easiest person to get on with, and his getting on the drink was what ended it.'

'Anyone you know of didn't get on with him apart from his wife?'

'He used to give his son a rough time. Smack him around a bit if he didn't do exactly as he was told, especially when he played up with the kid across the road.'

'Do you know why he had to leave the accountant's office?' asked Webber.

'As far as I know he was turning up to work half-pissed and falling out with clients. I used to get on with him okay before he began overdoing the drink, then he started keeping to himself.'

'When we found him he was more of a down and out,' said Nolan. 'But his wife's place is worth a dollar or two, so what happened to what might have been his share in the divorce?'

Perry shook his head. 'Can't help you there. I believe the accountants he used to work for, Jenkins and Ferris in Fairbank Street, may have helped.'

Webber added the information into his notebook.

Nolan stood up and offered his hand to Perry. 'Thanks, Perry, you have been a good help.'

'No worries,' Perry replied. 'I hope you catch the arsehole responsible.'

Back in the car, Nolan checked his watch. 'Lunchtime. What do you reckon we grab a Maccas and coffee before calling on the accountants?'

'Sounds good to me,' replied Stan.

Chapter 8

After displaying their IDs to the receptionist, she made a quick phone call then escorted Nolan and Webber into the office of one of the accountant business's owners, Warwick Ferris. He came out from behind a large desk he had been sitting at and extended his hand.

'How can I help you, gentleman?' he asked. 'Always happy to help the police if possible.'

'We'd appreciate a bit of background on one of your ex-employees Graham Saunders,' said Nolan after they had shaken hands.

Ferris pointed to the two chairs in front of the desk. 'Please take a seat.' He walked around the desk and sat back down. 'What would you like to know?' he asked.

'Firstly, we understand you asked him to leave because of his drinking problem, is that correct?' asked Nolan.

Ferris nodded. 'I'm afraid so. He was behaving badly to not just myself and the staff, but also to clients. He had been a really terrific employee until alcohol took over his life. Used to give his son a hard time too. It was a shame to watch his deterioration.'

'And you also helped in his divorce?' said Webber.

'Yes, that's right, only somewhat though. The wife's solicitor made sure she got the best of it.' Ferris raised his hands and looked from Webber to Nolan. 'Look, officers, before we go any further, please inform me the main reason you're here.'

'Saunders was found murdered yesterday morning,' said Nolan.

Ferris sat back in his chair. He closed his eyes for a moment, took a deep breath and exhaled. 'Murdered, you say?'

Nolan waited a moment for Ferris to settle before stating firmly, 'And naturally, we need to know of the people he knew and why a man, who we assume must have earnt a reasonable salary, died as a homeless vagrant when his ex-wife lives in a million dollar home in Fairshore Villas.'

'A vagrant, homeless?' Ferris seemed at a loss.

'That's right, he was surviving on hand-outs from charities.'

'I suppose that's no real surprise. In his divorce he signed over all his property to his wife. His initial property value came from his parents, but his wife made him sell that in order to go more upmarket at the villas. But he still had money in his bank account that he meant to go to his son when he reached twenty. Nice fellow, the son. Graham brought him here sometimes. Used to do things with him every weekend. Then again, the wife may have got her hands on that too.'

'You sure of that?' said Webber.

'Well, yes ... but of course he may have just used that all up since ... or as I said, transferred more to his wife.' He paused and scratched his head. 'I presume you've met his wife?'

'Yes we have.'

'Then you will be aware she is a forceful individual. If she had asked for more, Graham would have passed it over, anything for peace I would say. Oh, poor Graham ... murdered ... he sure didn't deserve to end that way.'

'No one does, Mr Ferris.' Nolan stood up and proffered his hand. 'Thanks for the information.'

Ferris shook Nolan's hand. 'But I didn't know he was homeless. I thought he was still living in the flat.'

'Do you have the address, Mr Ferris?' asked Webber.

Ferris pulled out a drawer from his desk and took out a small book. 'Ah yes, here it is, flat 2, 19 Dawlands Street, Chumleigh.'

'Thank you, Mr Ferris. We'd better be off.'

'I hope you catch the individual responsible,' said Ferris earnestly as Nolan and Webber left his office.

'So, what have we learnt today, Stan?' asked Nolan when they reached their car.

Stan referred to his notebook. 'That he gave everything to the wife who hated his guts. That he used to smack his kid around, and maybe even the neighbour's kid across the road. That he was a pretty good bloke before the drink got to him, and that he survived on charity. That someone stuck a knife in his chest after feeding him a banana, then cut off the end of his little finger and drew a fish in the dirt.'

Nolan slammed his hands onto the steering wheel before starting the car and driving off.

'Yeah, that's the size of it, Stan. So, what, if anything, are we missing?'

'So far, nothing's jumping out at me, Jeff. Except that we now know he had a flat in Chumleigh which is the suburb where he was found.'

'Well, that is something new. Better get back to the station, write up what we have got, call it a day and check out the flat tomorrow.'

Chapter 9

The flat at Dawlands Street, Chumleigh couldn't have been more different in appearance than Fairshore Villas. Number 19 was a block of three-up and three-down timber sheeting and very much in need of renovation. The timber stairs leading to the upper storey looked ready to collapse. There was no garden to speak of in the front as it was used as parking space for cars.

Nolan and Webber approached flat 2 on the downstairs left. The window facing the street had grey tape covering several cracks in the glass.

'Nice place,' remarked Webber with a roll of his eyes.

Nolan knocked at the front door and took a step back. There was no answer.

'I'll try next door,' said Webber.

The door was opened by an elderly man wearing jeans and a black T-shirt. He looked at Webber then to the side at Nolan as he came towards him. 'So, what can I do for you guys?' he asked.

Nolan and Webber were about to show their IDs.

The man raised his hands. 'No need for that, I know what you are.'

Nolan smiled. 'That obvious, eh, and you are?'

The man nodded. 'I'm Pax, so who you looking for?'

'Next door, thought a guy called Graham Saunders lived there, Pax.'

'Used to. Haven't seen him for about three weeks. Guess he's moved out.'

'What do know you about him?' asked Nolan.

'Not a bad bloke as far as I could tell. Liked a drink, but who doesn't?'

'Did he have any visitors?'

'His son used to turn up fairly regularly. Nice kid, always used to bring him a feed of some sort, burger or such like, and a bottle of milk. He was here ten days ago with a mate. I told him his dad had gone.'

'Did he ask where he'd gone?'

'Yeah, but I couldn't help him with that. He gave me the burger and milk, like I said, nice kid.'

'Did he ever fall out with anybody about the place?' asked Webber.

Pax shook his head. 'Not so far as I know ... kept pretty much to himself. He did mention once after the kid left that he was proud of him. Apparently at uni studying medicine. Look, if I happen to see Graham around the place I'll tell him you were looking for him.'

'Thanks, Pax, but that won't be necessary as Graham is dead.'

Pax's downtrodden face reflected his sadness. 'Oh, the poor bugger. What happened, drunk and walked in front of a truck or something?'

'Something like that,' said Nolan. 'Thanks for your help, Pax.'

Nolan and Webber walked back to their car while Pax, shaking his head, watched them go. Webber looked down at his notebook as they drove away. 'Regular visits from the son, eh, Jeff?'

'Yeah, and with a mate who I guess is the one who lives across the road from his place in Fairshore Villas.'

'If the son is studying medicine, he's probably staying in one of the uni's dorms, Stan.'

'Worth a visit you reckon?'

'For sure. After all we ain't got anything else to chase up, have we?'

Webber checked his watch. 'And unis usually have a good café.'

'Another good reason for going there, eh?'

Chapter 10

Nolan and Webber joined the crowd of students in the university cafeteria taking a midday break. After choosing a couple of egg sandwiches and a bottle of lemonade each, they managed to find an unoccupied table. Four young women at a nearby table kept glancing their way.

'So what are you guys studying?' asked one of them with a smile.

Webber returned the smile. 'What do you reckon?' he asked.

'Hard to say,' she replied. 'Maybe the anti-aging process.'

'Actually, we've already been through all that. My friend and I have just turned one hundred and five.'

The girl grinned. 'Well, it seems to be working really well for both of you. Perhaps you should consider writing a thesis,'

'So, what are you studying?' Webber asked.

'Forensics,' she replied.

Nolan pushed back his chair and stood up. 'Better be moving on, Stan.'

As Webber rose from his chair, he was pushed in the back. A tall, well-built young man in shorts and T-shirt put a hand on his shoulder. 'What do you think you're doing, arsehole? That's my woman you're talking to.'

The girl Webber had been talking to raised her hands. 'Ernie, there's nothing to get uptight about, we were just talking,' she remarked earnestly.

The smiles on the other three girls vanished and the chatter from the surrounding tables stopped as Ernie gave Webber another push. 'Yeah, well, I don't happen to like the look of the little prick.'

Webber stood and went to walk past Ernie. 'Sorry, man,' he said quietly.

Ernie laughed. 'A little prick and a wuss.' He raised his hand to give Webber another shove.

Webber grabbed the hand, twisted it and slammed Ernie's face down onto the table.

Nolan shook his head. 'They never learn. Come on, Stan, back to work.'

Webber released Ernie and was about to join Nolan when he stopped. He took a business card from an inside pocket and offered it to the girl he had been talking to. 'If you ever need help, give me a call.'

She accepted the card and glanced at it before looking back at Webber with a smile. 'Thanks.'

As Nolan and Webber left the café, they received a burst of applause.

Ernie sat down with a dribble of blood running from his nose while the girls rose from their chairs and left him on his own.

Chapter 11

After visiting the administration centre and learning the dormitory of Gerald Saunders, Webber knocked on the door of number fifty-three.

A young man in jeans and T-shirt answered the door. 'Yeah, guys, what's up?'

'Are you Gerald Saunders?'

The young man shook his head. 'No, mate, Gerry's gone home to see his mother.'

Nolan showed his ID. 'And you are?'

'I'm his mate Rick. I live across the road from Gerry at Fairshore Villas. Shit, man, what's happened now?'

'Can we come in?'

Rick stood back. 'Sure, sure, come in.'

Nolan and Webber entered the small flat. Two single beds were in one small room with a bathroom to the side. The living space was also cramped. Against one wall, a bench with a sink, and small refrigerator under. Against another wall, a table and two chairs with a TV on the wall above. A well-worn couch faced the TV.

'Nice place,' remarked Nolan.

'You reckon?' exclaimed Rick.

'What are you both studying?'

'We hope to be doctors.'

'Hard work, I guess?' said Webber.

'Bloody right it is ... Look, you haven't said why you want to talk to Gerry.'

Nolan went into the bedroom and opened the drawers of the

two bedside tables. 'Not a big change of clothes, Rick.'

'Don't need it,' Rick replied. 'We take everything home for our mothers to take care of.'

Nolan pulled a white T-shirt out of a drawer. 'This yours, Rick?'

'Yeah, why?'

Nolan held the T-shirt up. He glanced at Webber as he turned it around showing the blue lettering on the back reading "fast tracking". 'Go out running with it on, do you?'

'Yeah, I like to keep reasonably fit.'

'Ever go running around Chumleigh Park way?'

'Sometimes, yeah.'

'And Gerald has one of these shirts?'

'Yeah, he does.'

Nolan indicated under the beds. 'Care to take a look in here, Stan?'

Webber looked under the beds. Two fishing rods plus gear was under the right one. He glanced at Nolan then turned to Rick. 'Which is your bed, Rick?'

'The one on the left ... why?'

Nolan threw the T-shirt onto the bed and left the bedroom. 'Well, thanks for everything, Rick, we'll be on our way now.'

Rick stood at the door with a puzzled look on his face as he watched Nolan and Webber walk to their car.

'You can drive, Stan,' said Nolan. 'I'm thinking you know where to.'

'Reckon our original idea of all this was a bit off-beam, Jeff?' asked Stan.

Nolan nodded and gave a big sigh. 'Seems that way.'

Gerald Saunders glanced at the police IDs being proffered to him, opened the fly screen door and stood back. 'You better come in,' he said.

As Nolan and Webber entered, Mrs Saunders came out of a back room. 'Not you again?' she said loudly. 'Why did you let them in Gerald, they have no right to—'

Gerald raised his hand. 'It's okay, Mum, they just want a chat with me.' He indicated towards the sitting room area. 'Please take a seat.'

Nolan shook his head. 'No thanks, Gerald, this shouldn't take long.' He pointed at Gerald's feet. 'Nice runners.'

Mrs Saunders butted in. 'Yes, they are, and quite expensive, I bought them special for Gerald.'

'I wonder if they'll match the imprint we have,' said Webber.

'Imprint?' asked Mrs Saunders. 'What imprint?'

Nolan ignored her. 'Your Dad used to take you out with him at weekends, eh, Gerald?'

'Yeah, he was great like that. Sometimes down the beach for a swim or a walk.'

'And sometimes fishing?' added Webber.

Gerald smiled. 'Yeah, he loved fishing.'

'And that's why you drew the fish?' said Webber.

Mrs Saunders stamped her foot, a confused look on her face. 'Fish, imprint?' she exclaimed. 'What's this all about?'

Gerald looked from Webber to Nolan. 'You know,' he said quietly.

'But why the finger?' asked Nolan.

Gerald took a gold chain from around his neck. A small locket hung on it. He handed it to Nolan.

'Oh, that's nice,' said Mrs Saunders with a big smile. 'I gave that to Gerald for his eleventh birthday.'

Nolan pressed the catch on the side and the locket opened.

Mrs Saunders leant forward to get a better look. 'It has a small photo of me inside and of course Gerald wears it all the time.'

Her eyes widened and a hand went to her face when she saw what was inside the locket. 'What is that, and where is my photograph?' she shouted at Gerald.

'It's part of Dad. His small fingernail,' said Gerald emphatically.

'Dad ... Dad ... whatever did that no-good drunken idiot ever do for us?' she exclaimed angrily.

Gerald went to his mother and stared into her face. 'He cared for me and loved me, that's what he did. All you ever cared about was yourself.' He thrust a pointed finger at her. 'You drove him to be what he was.'

Mrs Saunders's face turned ashen at the outburst. She took a few steps back.

Gerald turned back to face Nolan. 'Dad was a physical and mental wreck. He didn't know where he was or what he was doing most of the time.'

'So, you decided to put him out of his misery?' said Nolan.

Gerald nodded as tears began to run down his cheeks.

They all stood in silence for a few moments.

Webber put a hand on Gerald's shoulder. 'You have to come with us now,' he said quietly.

Mrs Saunders watched Webber, Nolan and Gerald walk to the car. She turned and slammed the door shut as they drove away.

Chapter 13

As Samuel and Lucy chased each other around in the back garden, Nolan stood at the barbecue cooking sausages while Katherine placed plates, knives, forks and tomato sauce on the table on the patio.

It was a week since Gerald Saunders's arrest for the murder of his father. Nolan and Webber had finished their paperwork, and the matter was now in the hands of the prosecution and defence lawyers.

'Hope you don't overcook the snags,' came a shout from behind Nolan.

Nolan turned to see Webber and a young woman approaching. 'Well, hello there,' he said with a grin. 'We met in the uni café, didn't we?' He offered his hand. 'Nice to see you again under more pleasant circumstances.'

She returned the grin. 'Yes indeed, my name's Pauline.'

Nolan turned to Webber and slapped him on the shoulder. 'And as for you!'

Webber shrugged. 'When someone asks you for help what can you do?'

Nolan laughed. 'Yeah, help … you're very welcome, Pauline, hope you like sausages.'

Thirty minutes later, they were all sat around the table enjoying a cornetto ice cream each.

Katherine stood up and walked back towards the house. 'I'll go make us a cup of tea,' she said.

A couple of minutes later she returned. She held out her hand to Nolan. 'It's for you, Jeff.'

Nolan took the mobile phone and leant back in his chair. 'G'day whoever. What can I do for you?' he said cheerfully.

After a moment, the smile left his face as he stood and turned away from everyone. He listened intently.

The happy atmosphere changed abruptly when they all heard Nolan say 'where?'

www.ingramcontent.com/pod-product-compliance
Lightning Source LLC
Chambersburg PA
CBHW061611210726
48287CB00001B/85